Of Love

Of Love & Duty

Nelson, the Hamiltons, the Prince & Miss Knight

A novel

by

S R Whitehead

© S R Whitehead, 2018

Published by Ashmount Press
www.srwhitehead.com

All rights reserved. No part of this book may be reproduced, adapted, stored in a retrieval system or transmitted by any means, electronic, mechanical, photocopying, or otherwise without the prior written permission of the author.

The rights of S R Whitehead to be identified as the author of this work have been asserted in accordance with the Copyright, Designs and Patents Act 1988.

A CIP catalogue record for this book is available from the British Library.

ISBN 978-0-9552835-4-3 (mobi)
ISBN 978-0-9552835-5-0 (ePub)
ISBN 978-0-9552835-6-7 (Paperback)

Book layout by Clare Brayshaw

Cover design by Emma Charleston

Cover detail from JMW Turner watercolour D16101 licenced by Tate Images

Prepared by:

York Publishing Services Ltd
64 Hallfield Road
Layerthorpe
York YO31 7ZQ

Tel: 01904 431213

Website: www.yps-publishing.co.uk

For Sim & Tim

Two good men

AUTHOR'S NOTE

Although this novel dramatizes real events, the love affair between Cornelia and Francesco is a fiction – a fiction created to crystalize the conflicts that all those involved had to face.

CHAPTER ONE

"Mother, we are not going to Florence with that man."

"Will you keep your voice down? He is just beyond that door."

"Let him hear us. We have pussyfooted with him for so long, he actually thinks we are going."

"And we must!" Mother gushed. "He is the last man we know with a coach. All the rest have fled."

"And whose fault is that?" I glared fiercely at her and she turned aside, looking out over the boards of our once-lovely apartment. "Who was it," I pressed her, "that told everyone, *Oh, no, we don't need to flee, we knew General Berthier's mother at Versailles in '76?*"

"Well, we did know his mother at Versailles in '76. He was brought up a gentleman and he did promise that when he entered Rome, he would respect our persons and property."

"But Mother," I despaired, "Versailles was twenty years ago. There has been the Revolution. Alexandre Berthier is not a gentleman now, he is a Jacobin general and his promises dust. He will sack Rome just as Bonaparte sacked Milan."

Mother sank down onto a packing-case. I hated having to confront her – she was seventy-three and used to her own way – but, in this, she was horribly wrong and time was running out. I decided on a last try for Naples.

"We can go south. Angrisani's is still operating. We can get a diligence to Naples tonight."

"We cannot go to *Naples*." She spat out the name. "You know that perfectly well."

"But why? Because you embarrassed yourself with the queen all those years ago?"

"There was a lot more to it than that. You forget. We had to leave the country."

"No, I do not forget. You embarrassed yourself and *chose* to leave the country." Mother shifted and mumbled and ground her few teeth. "So," I put it to her, "rather than go back to Naples, you would sacrifice me to that limp Lothario, Adolphus Funnell."

"You speak my name?" The man in question, still fingering his breeches' buttons, swung open the door.

"Adolphus! Dear boy!" Mother sprang to her feet. "Cornelia was just marvelling at the great sacrifice you are making for our safety. She is quite moved." Mother shot me a look, "Aren't you dear?" and Adolphus proffered his piss-pot.

"What to do with it. Can't find a servant."

"They have all left," I told him, "like everyone else." Mother stepped up.

"Don't you worry about the piss-pot. I shall see to that while you and Cornelia make your plans." And, with a parting glare at me, she took his piss-pot and left, pulling the door closed behind her.

Adolphus, looking the very image of a pantomime parson in his black silk suit and powdered wig, attempted a jowly smile.

"Miss Knight," he cooed, "or, may I presume, Cornelia?"

I had moved away to the window at the far end of the room but Adolphus stepped forward.

"I would sacrifice much for you, you know; this is only the least I would do for your safety." He stepped forward again. He would have to be checked.

"You have taken a house in Florence, Mother tells me." He paused.

"I have taken a villa *near* to Florence, fifteen miles distant." His pink sausage fingers were flexing at his sides. "Oh, Cornelia, it is so beautiful. You, with your acute sensibilities, will fall in love with it. A domestic temple after Palladio, built for a steward to the Medici, its walled garden is a paradise …"

He sounded on about his rented villa while I contemplated the nightmare of confinement with him in a walled garden fifteen miles from a town. Mother had misled me: she had definitely said *in* Florence.

"Mr Funnell," I drew myself up to look down on him, "it will be very kind of you to convey Lady Knight and myself to Florence where I am sure we can make our own arrangements."

I set off round him, heading for the door, but he side-stepped, grabbing my arm and placing a hand on my hair.

"Ah, those tumbling dark curls," he sighed, "matchless in all Rome, as I am sure you know."

"Mr Funnell!" I glared down at him and, slowly, he withdrew his hand and let go my arm. I pulled open the door and Mother was behind it.

"Mr Funnell will take us to Florence," I told her. "His carriage will be here at six and I have told him we shall be ready." Then I went off to the kitchen, leaving Mother to see out her guest.

The second week of February. It was dark by six o'clock, and cold. Mother and I stood at the window looking down into the Corso; she in the black velvet cloak that the Contessa di Santa Croce had passed down to her and I in the old soldier's coat we had bought in Vienne for another hasty flight. The coat was hideous and I loathed it but, I told myself, if I were to spend four days confined with Adolphus Funnell 'hideous' might be the better look. Nothing was moving in the Corso and, with so many houses closed, few torches burned – it was another abandoned street just waiting for the French. I looked down at Mother and her face was wrung with worry. I shouldn't have let it come to this: the last minute of the eleventh hour. All our English and French émigré friends had been leaving at their leisure for the past three weeks and we had received many offers of help but 'no' Mother had known Berthier's mother so we would be safe. That was the line she had peddled anyway but I think I knew better. The truth was that, after our twenty-four years of travelling the Continent, Mother had found a cosy nest at a charity rent and she had hoped to end her days there but it was not to be.

"What time is it?"

"It must be nearly six. I don't think he's late yet."

"Have you got all our papers and our money?"

"Yes, Mother. I have all our papers and our money."

"We must ask Adolphus ..." There was a bang. "What was that?" We heard shouting, then another bang, coming from the Piazza Venezia. Mother and I put our noses to the window but the angle was too acute to see and, anyway, it was dark. We heard glass smash now and more shouting, then a man went racing past followed by another holding a child by the hand – all running as hard as they could. I opened the window and put out my head. I could see torches, about thirty of them, bobbing and swaying in men's hands, and they were moving up the Corso. I pulled back into the room.

"Torches."

"What do you mean, *torches*?" Mother put her head out of the window and I opened the next to look too. The torches were darting over the street and up to the fronts of houses. We heard more glass smash and the splitting of timber and the shouting, we now heard, was in French. It was a marauding party – there could be no doubt about it – a soldierly mob and, as our eyes grew accustomed to their torchlight, we began to make out their shapes. Some were shouting up at windows, others were breaking down doors. Small groups were running into houses and bringing things out, piling them onto wagons while, from inside, owners shouted and screamed and all the time the mob moved towards us. I saw Mr Bertoni come out. He and his family occupied a ground floor apartment only a hundred yards from ours and he was shouting and gesticulating at two of the soldiers. I was fairly sure that Mr Bertoni did not speak French and after only a few seconds one of the soldiers raised his bayonet and struck Mr Bertoni on the head with the pommel. Mr Bertoni went down like a sack. I touched Mother's waist and we both drew back into the room.

"It's Jacobin looters," Mother said, her eyes wide and fearful. "Did you see Mr Bertoni?"

I went round the room and snuffed out the candles.

"I did Mother. Close the windows."

"Do you think he's alright? Do you think we should …"

I went back to the windows and shut them myself. Mother's fingers were in her mouth. "Do you think they'll come here?"

"Why would they not?" I snapped, angry and frightened. "It doesn't seem to matter whether apartments are occupied or not."

"But we have nothing worth taking."

"Do the Bertonis? And, anyway, how do you suppose the Jacobins will discover that?"

Then, from the street, we heard the unmistakable rumble and jangle of a carriage and four. We moved back to the windows. It was Adolphus's yellow coach, no mistaking it, and it had pulled up among the French soldiers just short of our door. The coachman and footmen were already on the ground and running away and when the carriage door opened, Adolphus stepped out. He was wearing a full-length fur coat and hat and brandishing a cane.

"No trouble here I hope, Sergeant?" we heard him say in French. He seemed not to have noticed that his servants had fled. Mother quietly reopened a window.

"English?" asked the sergeant.

"And nothing wrong with that, I believe," replied Adolphus, "lawfully about my business." A soldier was holding his lead horses and a second was climbing onto the box.

"On your way!" the sergeant shouted at Adolphus, who now looked about him.

"Where is my coachman?" he demanded, and the sergeant – a short, thick-set man with a stubble head – pushed him in the chest.

"I said, on your way!" He pushed him again. "Walk! You don't get the coach." The men with the horses were now turning the coach round and Adolphus panicked.

"I say!" he protested. "You tell your men to leave my equipage alone. I don't think you quite understand who I am."

The sergeant snatched Adolphus's silver-topped cane and examined it.

"Who are you then?"

"I am The Honourable Adolphus Funnell. My family have great estates in Shropshire and Jamaica. Two of my cousins sit in Parliament. They have the ear of Mr Pitt."

"What are you worth then?"

"I hardly think my allowance is any concern of yours, Sergeant, but if ..." Adolphus put his hand inside his coat and pulled out a purse.

"What are you worth to your sitting cousins?" The sergeant snatched the purse. "A thousand francs? Five thousand francs? What do you think?" The coach was, by this time, completely turned about and waiting on the far side of the Corso. Adolphus looked at it and bit his lip.

"Put him in!" ordered the sergeant and, as Mother and I looked helplessly on, Adolphus was bundled back into his coach with two soldier for company and driven away the way he had come.

My heart sank. Of all the opportunities we had had to leave Rome in the past three weeks, Adolphus was the last and now he was gone. I sat down on a packing-case and put my head in my hands.

"What will they do to him?" asked Mother.

"Sell him, by the sound of it. You heard the sergeant."

"Poor Adolphus."

"Yes, poor Adolphus and poor us." A shiver ran through me. "The enemy is – quite literally – at our door." Mother shut the window.

"Then we must keep them there. We must stop them at the door. Fetch me my calash."

"Stop them at the door?" Mother never ceased to amaze me. One minute, she was in terror of the French and the next, she wanted to confront them. "Mother, they are a hundred drunken Jacobins with bayonets. You saw what they did to Mr Bertoni."

"Oh, Cornelia," Mother was rummaging through a packing case, "you are taller than they are." She found her calash bonnet and tied it onto her head. "Come along!" I leapt up from my packing case and went to block the door.

"Just think about this for a moment, will you? We are two unprotected women. You are seventy-three. How are we going to stop a mob of drunken soldiers? Think about it."

"Of course I have thought about it. We shall hail that sergeant fellow and tell him that we are old friends of General Berthier's mother." Mother looked at me as if it were so obvious – as if I were stupid to ask.

"But we are English. The enemy. You saw what they did to Adolphus."

"I am not going to tell them we are English. Really, Cornelia, what do you take me for?"

"But when you speak French your accent is horribly English."

"Is it?"

"Yes, it is."

"You have never told me that before."

"It never mattered before." Mother thought for a moment.

"Your French isn't horribly English."

"Thank you, Mother."

"You have a flair for languages. You get it from your great-aunt Louise." Mother took my arm and turned me to the door. "You go and tell them."

And so I went down into the street, on my own, in the dark, to ask a drunken mob if it would kindly leave us alone. I had no plan of my own as to how I might achieve this and so I fell back on Mother's. In the few seconds that I had to assert myself in the street, I could not see the sergeant and so fixed my sights on the least fevered face I could see and hallooed him. He was a youth, about half my age, with quite a nice face and I told him, in what I hoped would pass as socially-neutral Parisian, that Mother and I were indeed old friends of General Berthier's mother, adding that we hoped the association might command respect for our persons and property. I felt weak as I spilt out my words and my knees were shaking, but the young man heard me out and, when I had finished, went off for his sergeant. I don't know how long he was gone, probably only a few moments, but I was so frightened it felt like an age. The Corso – my home street – was in ruins. Broken furniture and clothes were scattered about and everywhere people were running. The apartments immediately opposite ours were being ransacked even as I watched and women were screaming and crying – women I knew – and any moment their plight could be mine but then, when the young man returned with his sergeant, I felt more frightened than ever. Viewed from close to, the sergeant looked like the very devil. He was short and square, like a Breton, with a cannonball head but his devilish feature, which I had not seen from our apartment window, was the sabre scar across his jaw that had cut away part of his lower lip, exposing his canines. It was not a face to which one would choose to plead. With my faith in my story ebbing, I repeated it to the sergeant while he, ominously, cast his eyes over our apartment building. When I had finished he said,

"Is that your Mother?" I looked up to where he had nodded and Mother's face was at the window.

"It is, yes." He turned back to me.

"Passports!" Why had I not expected that?

"I am sorry Sergeant," I extemporised, "but I am not sure that Mother and I still have passports. We have been resident in Rome for some years, you see." Other soldiers now gathered around us, curious, I imagined, to know what was keeping their sergeant.

"Names!" he barked, fixing me with his little black eyes. My entire body was now shaking with fear. Soldiers, some with torches, some with bayonets, had crowded round me. They smelt of sweat and stale wine and their dead eyes glowed yellow in the torchlight. Small women, I know, can feel vulnerable, but sometimes they should try being tall.

"Le Brun," I said, without a moment's thought, "Madame Louise and Mademoiselle Élisabeth Le Brun." I looked down at the sergeant and held his snake's eyes. I dared not blink. I would have been lost if I had, I knew, and, though my throat was dry, I dared not swallow. After what seemed an age, the sergeant turned away.

"Daub that door white," he ordered, and then he turned back to me. "Go back and stay there. Till we check with the General." And then, as he walked away, "Do not leave."

When I re-entered our apartment Mother's feathers were fanned like a peacock's.

"I told you," she preened, standing with her back to the windows, "when it comes to a crisis, you still need your mother." I felt weak.

"Mother," I sat down on a case, "that was the most stupid, dangerous thing you have ever made me do." I stared at her fiercely. I wanted her to know what she had done to me. "I could not have been more terrified if they had put a bayonet to my throat."

"*Fortuna audaces iuvat*, Cornelia." Mother wagged a finger at me. "Fortune helps the bold. Look down into the street. Thanks to your little chat, the Jacobins are passing us by." She took up a taper to re-light the candles, "Now, perhaps we can unpack."

We were at Angrisani's diligence yard by eight. I had indulged Mother for long enough and now, if I had to carry her, we were going to Naples, but we could not leave straightaway; the French were still in the street. I was on tenterhooks. Every second that we waited I expected the thud of an axe on the front door and boots on the stairs. Poor Mother went into a decline. The evening had been the climax of days of anxiety and now that I had wrested control from her, she withdrew into an absent sulk. I waited and watched the street in an agony until, eventually, the way appeared clear. I shouldered the bag and took Mother by the hand and hurried her down into the street. I'd decided against the Corso – I am too conspicuous – so we ran across it and entered the labyrinth of alleys that are the secret capillaries of Rome. We heard the French as we went – their shouts and their ugly songs – and we passed where they had been – over the debris of broken homes – but we did not meet them and, after fifteen minutes, we emerged into the Via Clementina and Mr Angrisani's diligence yard.

I had expected it would be busy and it was but I knew Angrisani's and what I must do. One of the advantages of being a tall woman is the ease with which physical dominance and men's deference to women combine to part crowds and I had no difficulty in attaining the inn at the top of the yard and the travel office inside it. The office was thronged with people, but it was no time for niceties, and I soon had the attention of the young clerk.

"Yes, madam," he said cheerfully, "what can I do for you?" Mother slipped from my hand and sank onto a bench beside the counter. She had resigned entirely. If we were heading for disaster, she was silently telling me, it would be my fault.

"My mother and I require passage to Naples," I told the clerk, whom I did not recognise, "and urgently … you know… the French." The clerk, who was well dressed with a jaunty soft cap on his head, gave me a curious look.

"Are you in trouble with the French?"

"No, no, not at all," I lied with a throw-away laugh, but the young clerk wasn't listening to me, he was watching me, assessing me.

"Fifty scudi," he said, then, with a wide smile, "each – and no dinners or beds."

"What?" I wasn't sure I had heard him correctly.

"Did you say fifteen scudi?"

"Fif*ty*," he repeated, emphasising the *ty*. "Each."

"But surely not," I replied, "it is usually fourteen scudi to Naples – including dinners and bed."

"Usually!" The young man laughed and threw out his arms over his crowded office. "But you said *urgently*. You want to travel *urgently*, you pay fifty."

I looked to Mother for support but she wasn't even listening. I was going to have to do this alone.

"It is a diligence, is it?"

"I am expecting a diligence from Gaeta at any time. When it arrives, we shall turn it round for Naples."

"But surely that will already be full." I indicated the throng. "All these people."

"Some will get on it, some will have to wait, but if you don't pay, you stay."

"You mean, all these people have paid?" He nodded. "When is the next diligence?"

"The one after this next one, you mean?"

"Yes."

"The way things are, it is hard to say," he shrugged, "even this one may not arrive, who knows?"

I looked again to Mother but her head was lolling in sleep. A hundred scudi was an awful lot of money, more than I could afford, but did I have any choice? We could not go home, I dared not return to the streets and Mother was exhausted. I didn't know what to do, but then, even as I fretted, I heard hooves and harness and a jubilant cheer rang out from the yard. Immediately, the office drained of people, leaving just Mother and me with the clerk. He folded his arms and gave me a wry smile.

"Forty scudi each," I told him.

"Ho-ho," he laughed, throwing back his head, "not so urgent now!"

"Yes," I told him, my blood starting to rise, "it is very urgent but we are two poor women and I resent being taken advantage of." He held up his hands.

"Wow, alright, alright," he stepped up to the counter, "I'll tell you what I can do. Because you are so beautiful when you are angry – forty-five scudi."

And so I paid the sharp young clerk his ninety scudi: a

king's – or a refugee's – ransom and, pulling Mother to her feet, I dragged her and our bag out into the yard.

The diligence was huge: the largest, most ramshackle thing I ever saw on four wheels. It had three separate compartments, space enough for twenty passengers, but there were a lot more than that wanting to travel and they were clambering on it like ants over a stag beetle. It was a scene of chaos and the throng too dense even for me to push through so I waited with Mother till someone brought order and we did not have to wait long. While the ostlers changed the horses, my young clerk came out into the yard with the fresh coachman and postilions and, with one high sweep, the coachman cracked his whip. It rang out like a pistol shot.

"All of you!" he cried. "Off!" and, flanked by his postilions, he marched towards the diligence. Some who had climbed on climbed off under the coachman's stare but others did not and the operation that followed had a precision I shall savour for ever. Working from his memory of faces, the young clerk instructed the postilions to remove certain persons to the yard floor and move others between seats in the mid-carriage, the coupé and the rotonde until he was satisfied that justice was done. Some of those ejected were grown men and, like everyone else, desperate to leave Rome but, so firm were the postilions in their work that not one dared gainsay them. Matelots dressing a packet boat could not have done a tidier job and when all was done to his satisfaction, the clerk looked at me and beckoned. I gathered my bag and my mother and ran to him.

"Urgent travel," he said with a twinkling smile and, with a sweep of his hand, he offered Mother the interior of the mid-carriage. I helped Mother in, it was a squeeze, and there was obviously no room for me. I looked to the clerk.

"Full." He shrugged. I looked into the coupé at the front and the rotonde at the back and they were full too.

"But I have paid you," I told him, "I have paid you a great deal of money for two seats. I will not be parted from my mother." He held my eyes but said nothing. His wry smile felt threatening now and the postilions, in their stiff thigh boots, were standing behind him. "No!" I insisted, "absolutely not. You led me to believe …" The clerk put up a finger and pointed to the banquette, the coachman's seat, on the roof of the coupé.

"You are too tall for the interior. You will sit with the driver." I looked up at the coachman already in his place. He was a very long way off the ground. I was not sure I could climb up to the banquette.

"But I am a woman."

"All the passengers are women, or children. You are the most suitable passenger for the banquette."

"But, but," I was thinking about the height from the ground and the exposure and the French sergeant with his frightening teeth, "I will be on open view up there."

"Ah, yes," the clerk remembered, "the French." I nodded. Again, he seemed to examine me, seeing, this time, my man's coat and my mass of woman's curls. He took off his cap and placed it on my head.

"Here, push your hair into this. My compliments." Then he placed my foot on the wheel hub and, with a hefty pull from the coachman, I was hoisted onto the board.

Our journey out of Rome was not one I should care to repeat. My nerves were taut before we set off and, sitting ten feet off the ground, in the dark, on that swaying behemoth, with only the bench to hang on to was frightening – and then there were the French. Three times they forced us to stop. Fortunately, the soldiers all seemed more ready for bed than picket duty and they accepted the coachman's call of 'all women for Naples' with a cursory glance into the compartments. In daylight, I like to think, they would have noticed how odd I looked beside the coachman but, sitting so far above them, in the dark, they seemed to accept that I was a relief coachman and so waved us on. That clerk's gallant gesture had served me well and I decided to think well of him – until I realised how many soft caps he could buy for the difference between twenty-eight and ninety scudi. I wondered, as we rumbled through the darkened streets, how much of my money Mr Angrisani would see, how much my fellow-passengers had paid for their *urgent* passage and how much all those others who we'd left behind. As the sharp young clerk might have said: 'unusual times'.

It was midnight by the time we got out of the city and onto the open road south. I was glad of my heavy coat and cap because it was bitterly cold on the banquette. The coachman had wrapped us together in a canvas apron that tied at the waist but my fingers were freezing and, once out of Rome, the ruts and bumps in the highroad were cruel. It was alright for the coachman: he had work to do and reins to hold but I was sat beside him like a sack of potatoes with only the seat to cling to. It is a humiliating fact of my life that, because I am taller than most men, I am assumed to be happy to be taken for one but I am not and those fifty-two hours that I spent hip-to-hip with that mastiff of a driver while he battled with his eight horses and two postilions were some of the most hateful of my life. It was February. The nights, especially, were bitterly cold and although, thank God, it did not rain, the road was mired from earlier rains and our progress was slow. Two days and two nights it took us to cover the hundred and forty miles to Naples, and we did not stop. Well, we stopped to change horses and let the coachman and postilions snatch an hour's rest but there was no accommodation to be had and, besides, some of us wanted to keep moving because we did not know if we were being pursued. I had pocketed some cheese and jars of potted beef before we left and, with some bread that we managed to buy at Fresinone, Mother and I were sustained and we pushed on. Mother, trapped in the middle carriage with a Piedmontese family, was warm at least but far from comfortable. Her companions were a matriarch in her fifties, her two daughters, their two toddlers and a babe-in-arms and what with the crush, the children's boredom and the infant's whining and mewling, Mother hardly slept – and then there was the smell, she told me. The family was well-provisioned and ate continuously so Mother was permanently assailed by the warm stench of garlic, rancid oil, foul breath and the emissions agitated from the women by the bumps in the road. By the time we reached Naples, at three in the morning on the feast of Saint Donatus of Zadar, Mother was in a state of collapse. I gave thanks to the good saint that we had managed to arrive alive.

CHAPTER TWO

We had lived in Naples before – thirteen years before – in 1785, until Mother's *contretemps* with the queen and our unseemly flight back to France. We lived in Marseilles after that for a while, then Avignon, and a year or two in Vienne, which was very nice, until '89, when our neighbours turned Jacobinical and we had to move on. That time it was to Genoa, and then, in '91, back to Rome, where we had lived before our first sojourn in Naples. For twenty-four years, Mother and I had been going round and round the Continent, eking out my inheritance from Father, but now, while I looked forward to re-acquainting myself with Naples, Mother declared that she'd had enough. Whether we could afford London or not, she decided, better to live like mice in a free country than be trampled by the Jacobins so, on the day following our arrival, our first call was upon His Britannic Majesty's Ambassador and Plenipotentiary to the Court of Naples, Sir William Hamilton.

"But, Lady Knight, there are no ships. The Mediterranean fleet was withdrawn two years ago. There hasn't been an English naval vessel east of Gibraltar since then." Mother and I were in Sir William's private study, the inner sanctum of the Palazzo Sessa. "I shall do everything in my power to assist you, of course, but there simply is not a ship I could embark you on."

"But you communicate with London," Mother insisted, perching on the edge of her chair, "you send your reports and receive your instructions. How is that managed? Not by post horse. All Europe is under the French." Sir William was sitting opposite us with one long leg lolled over the other and his hands in his lap.

"I do communicate with London," he agreed, "you are quite right, but you will understand, I am sure, that I cannot divulge to you how that is achieved." Mother, who is only small, drew herself up to her best height.

"And why, pray, can you not divulge that to us? Do you think that my daughter and I are Jacobin spies? I am the widow of Rear Admiral Sir Joseph Knight. Cornelia and I are daughters of the waves, our veins run with brine and rum and our hearts are of oak. The meanest of His Majesty's brigs would be to us a second home. You need have no secrets from us." Sir William opened his hands.

"Lady Knight. I can only repeat. His Majesty has no ships in the Mediterranean."

"An English merchantman then. Or a neutral." Mother was working herself up. "You must have a plan of evacuation, if only for yourself." Mother dabbed her cheek with her handkerchief, suggesting a pitiable tear, and Sir William rose and came to her. He rested his hand on hers on the arm of her chair.

"Dear lady," he smiled reassuringly, "you have suffered a terrifying ordeal and you are exhausted but you need not worry any more about the French." He smiled also at me but I was only half listening; I was more interested in the pictures on his walls and the contents of his cabinets. Sir William locked his hands behind his back and started to pace the floor.

"They were bound to take Rome and the Papal States. It was too easy for them and the symbolism, for their atheist philosophy, too powerful to pass up but they will not come here. The French have too good an opinion of the Neapolitan forces, their supply lines are over-stretched and remember, above all, that the Kingdom of Naples has a treaty of neutrality with France."

Sir William's study fascinated me. It was masculine and intimate, heady with the must of linseed, leather and books. The back wall was faced, from floor to ceiling, with a huge glazed cabinet that glowed with the gold and black glazes of a hundred Etruscan vases while, round the other three walls, there were glass-topped cabinets that I itched to get up to see. The furniture was extremely elegant; every piece a copy of one of those unearthed down the coast at Herculaneum, and the cornice moulding too was of a Roman design. Between the cornice and the cabinets, the walls were full of pictures: major works, like Da Vinci's *Laughing Boy* and a De Hooch landscape hung in jumbled juxtaposition with prints and Sir William's own studies of classical ruins, volcanoes and the male form, but of all the pictures on Sir William's walls, one in particular dominated: it was a portrait, hanging between the windows, of a beautiful young Bacchante. I was sure that the painter was Romney, and equally sure that the sitter must be Sir William's celebrated second wife, Lady Emma.

"France's economy is on the verge of collapse," Sir William was explaining. "Confiscations and high taxes have crippled her industries, inflation is out of control and her external trade is disrupted by our navy's blockades. It will be a year at least before the French can embark on another Continental adventure and in that time who knows what alliances might be struck." Sir William smiled and raised his eyebrows at us. "England is not the only power willing to take on the French."

"You mean Russia," Mother muttered, and Sir William shrugged.

"Study the map, Lady Knight. You can be sure that His Majesty's ministers do and, in the meantime, my advice to you is to regain your strength and enjoy Naples. I take it you have made your arrangements."

"Arrangements!" Mother bridled, adjusting her wig with both hands. "We sleep with fleas and cockroaches at the inn where we were dropped. We are two homeless women. We have no one to make our *arrangements*!" Sir William gave a nod.

"Then we must see what *I* can do. If you will excuse me for a moment." Then he walked from the room and left us.

I got up from my chair and went to look in the glass-topped cabinets. There must have been a dozen of them. One was devoted to samples of lava rock, another to sea shells, a third to insects pinned onto card and every specimen carefully labelled. There were drawers beneath the cabinets and, when I opened one, I found that it too was neatly laid out with specimens.

"What are you doing?" Mother hissed. "Will you learn to leave things alone?"

"Look here." I called Mother over. "Look at these cameos. They're beautiful. First or second century. Perhaps earlier." Mother came over to look and I moved on to a cabinet of Roman coins and medals. I knew of Sir William's reputation as a connoisseur of Etruscan vases but I had no idea that his interests were so wide. Mother had moved on to a cabinet beside the door. She'd gone very quiet but when I walked over to see what so interested her, she put up a hand.

"No, Cornelia, don't look, don't look." But she was too late. I could see quite plainly that the cabinet contained a collection of stone phalluses and, at that moment, the study door swung open. A young woman was standing there. She was wearing a Chinese silk dressing gown with a matching bandeau that held back her hair from the most strikingly beautiful face. It was oval, the eyes violet and large beneath dark, well-marked eyebrows. The nose was straight, the mouth full and curved and the complexion flawless as Carrera marble. This woman was older and heavier than the girl between the windows but there was no mistaking that this was Emma Hamilton. Embarrassed to be caught at the cabinet – at *that* cabinet – Mother and I froze. Lady Hamilton stood and watched us and then, barely perceptibly, her back straightened and her neck arched like a goose sensing interest. She tilted her head and pursed her lips.

"Great toes of the Priapus," she fixed her eyes on Mother, "from an uncharted region of the Abruzzo." Then her eyes turned to me. Half-smiling, with her pursed lips twitching, she watched me like an amused cat, daring me to speak but I could not speak and she knew I could not, but then – God be praised – we heard footsteps coming up the corridor and Lady Hamilton turned to them.

"Pliny!" she called out. "There you are. I need to talk to you about Saturday."

"Of course, my dear," Sir William replied, "two minutes. I shall come up and find you," then, as his wife slipped from the room, Sir William re-entered followed by a liveried servant.

"I am so sorry to have kept you waiting. This is Vittorio, my Head of Household." He put his hand on the man's arm and smiled at him. "If anyone can find a comfortable apartment in the Chiaia at a price Neapolitans would pay, then he is the man." Vittorio, a strikingly handsome fellow in his early fifties, nodded a bow. "Can I leave you with him?" With Mother still speechless, I answered for her.

"Thank you, that would be lovely," and Sir William turned to leave, but then he had an after-thought.

"I don't know whether it would be of interest to you, but we are having a musical evening on Saturday. Just a few friends. Informal. Would you care to join us?" I looked down at Mother, who was still struck dumb, so, again, I answered,

"Thank you. That would be lovely."

Vittorio Santino was as good as Sir William's word and within only a few days we were able to move into a suite of five pleasant rooms on the north-east edge of the Chiaia. The Chiaia is the best quarter of Naples, the area west of the royal palace, behind the sea-front promenade, that is home to the nobility and the *Corps Diplomatique*. The one drawback to our apartment however (and there had to be one at the rent) was its situation: it was up three flights of stairs in a barracks of a building right at the top of the hill but, to be positive, that also had its advantage because we had a panoramic view across the city of the bay and Vesuvius beyond – a view that is, as Goethe observed, one of the finest in Europe.

Mother and I had disagreed about Sir William's political analysis. I had been content to put my trust in him and enjoy Naples but Mother was adamant that the Jacobin juggernaut would continue rolling south all the way to the toe and to Sicily. Why would it not, she argued, when the French controlled the sea? She was determined to go home as quickly as possible but where was home to me? I was seventeen when Father died and we left England to live more cheaply on the Continent and now I was forty-one. London was not 'home' to me. My abiding memory of the place was that it was grimy, miserable and damp. I had no friends there and no brothers or sisters to go back to. The nearest thing I had to friends in London had been my tutors, who were legion, but now all probably dead. Studying was all I seemed to do in London, and it was all I wanted to do when the only alternative was sitting with Mother in Sir Joshua Reynolds' drawing room listening to Garrick and Sheridan scoring points off one another and Dr Johnson making jokes about the length of my legs and the cost of blue stockings. There was nothing in London for me. I wanted to stay in Naples and explore its treasures but Mother did not, her sights were set on London – only she did not know how to get there – until Sir William's soirée.

I would have preferred to stay at home that evening but we had accepted Sir William's invitation and so felt compelled to attend. I was tired. It was still less than a week since that ghastly journey and, in that time, we had had to establish ourselves with a banker and provisioners and move into our new home and now we must face society. We arrived at the Palazzo Sessa quite late, and when we walked into the long gallery, the chatter of some forty English was swamping the strains of a string trio coming out from the room beyond. I am not one for parties at the best of times so, once I had settled Mother with a glass of champagne and the Camerons of Droitwich and Rome, I left her and moved through to the music room. It was cool and spacious in there and the only occupants, apart from myself, were the trio of musicians playing in the corner. The violcellist, I was surprised to see, was Sir William's chief manservant, Vittorio Santino. I gave him a friendly nod and he smiled back over his instrument. The room was set out with rows of chairs and the walls were lined with portraits, only the extraordinary thing was, when I came to look, that they all were of the same sitter. There were more than a dozen of them and they were every one of Emma Hamilton. There was another Emma as a Bacchante, Emma as Circe, Emma as Sybil, as Hebe and I don't know who else from classical mythology. Some artists' hands I recognised; Reynolds and Kauffmann, because I had sat for them myself, Romney of course and a delicious Vigée Le Brun but, although this most beguiling of sitters was depicted by so many accomplished hands, not one, to my eye, caught her essence. The poses were perfect, wholly convincing, I could put a name to almost all of them but where was the sitter? Where Lady Emma? She seemed to have eluded them all.

"She is beautiful, isn't she?" A rather good-looking man in navals had come up beside me. "Or were you admiring Mengs' brushwork?"

"Is it by Mengs?" I looked more closely at the work and decided it could be. I looked again at the man. I did not recognise him, nor his uniform. He nodded me a bow.

"Forgive me, Miss Knight, but as there is no one here to introduce us, may I present myself? Francesco Caracciolo. I am a great admirer of your work."

My work! Had this man, whom I did not know, seen my drawings? I peered at his epaulettes and he added helpfully, "Admiral of the Neapolitan Navy."

"When you say 'my work' …?"

"*The History of Marcus Flaminius*. It is a fascinating exploration of the life of Imperial Rome." I was flattered. I was not often complimented on my books by handsome admirals.

"Well thank you."

"No, no…" he bowed again, "thank *you* for your scholarly insight into my country's history." The admiral had an open, friendly manner. He was tall for a Neapolitan; strongly-built and weathered, as a serving officer should be, and his hair was a mass of dark curls.

"The Roman Empire was the greatest civilization that Europe has produced," I told him, "it is so fascinating because its story is both a romance and an instruction."

"An instruction?" he looked surprised, "you mean for the future?"

"Rome's decline was not inevitable."

"No, Rome's decline was not inevitable, but the Roman Empire's was. Do you not think that when the emperors snatched power from the Republic they sowed the seeds then of their destruction?"

I warmed to this Neapolitan admiral. So few men take a woman's work seriously but this man evidently did. I could see where his argument was leading but I stood my ground.

"But Rome's greatest days were under emperors," I told him. "Nothing the Republic did was a match for the achievements of Augustus or Tiberius." The music room was beginning to fill. People were moving through from the long gallery and among them, glass in hand, was Mother.

"There you are, Cornelia. Will you please not abandon me in strange company."

"But you were with the Camerons, Mother."

"I didn't know that the Camerons would be the best of the company though, did I! A dozen tourists Suzie Cameron introduced me to, and not one of them of rank or title." Mother drained her champagne glass. "Apart from me." She looked round for a footman and, seeing the admiral at my side, for a second, I could see, she mistook him for one.

"Mother," I stepped in, "can I introduce you to Admiral Carocci … " The admiral bowed now to Mother.

"Caracciolo." He gave her a friendly smile. "In my experience, Mrs Knight, rank and title are poor indicators of worth."

"*Lady* Knight," Mother corrected him. She was still looking round for a footman.

"Francesco!" Sir William at last appeared. He gave the admiral a wave and came over to us. "I see you have found the Prince, Miss Knight."

"The *Prince*?" Mother, forgetting now the footman, drew herself up before Sir William.

"Oh, I am sorry," he added, "have you not been introduced? Lady Knight, Miss Cornelia Knight, both lately of Rome, may I introduce you to His Excellency Prince Francesco Caracciolo, Duke of Brienza and, as you see, Admiral of the Neapolitan Navy." Still clutching her empty glass, Mother lifted her skirts and lowered herself into a creaking curtsy. "Lady Knight's late husband was an admiral," Sir William went on, "In His Britannic Majesty's Navy. I am sure you will have much in common."

The string trio had finished its piece and Vittorio, laying aside his instrument, rose from his seat and walked over to us. He rested his hand on Sir William's back.

"When you are ready, Sir William." Sir William turned to him and smiled,

"Absolutely, my dear fellow," then he turned back to us. "If you will excuse me?" And he walked away with Vittorio, back to the musicians, where he picked up a viol and sat down to make the quartet.

I found another glass of champagne for Mother and we sat down with the admiral to what would be one of the strangest entertainments I ever saw. The music was not strange; it was a sweet piece by Boccherini and Sir William's ensemble played it beautifully, no, it was not the music that was strange, it was the Attitudes, Lady Hamilton's unique expression of the *tableau vivant* that was the talk of Europe but new to Mother and me.

Once the Boccherini came to its end, the musicians took their applause and then, after a brief hiatus of shuffling about, the audience's eyes were drawn to movement in a niche beside the musicians. The back wall of the niche began slowly to revolve and, as it turned, there appeared from its nether side Lady Hamilton, scantily draped in a diaphanous white shift and leaning on a half-column. It was an arresting vision. Her flawless, beautiful face, her arms and her feet were all white as marble and her eyes as large as fauns'. By the tilt of her head and the lie of her limbs she was, to an uncanny degree, the living embodiment of a figure from one of Sir William's vases. Mother, for whom prejudice always trumped experience, pulled a silly face at me but I was fascinated, and the audience around us broke into spontaneous applause. Then, while Sir William bowed on his viol an evocation of Olympus, Emma raised herself from her column and stepped onto the floor. She did not dance exactly, but moved with the nicest delicacy from one well-known pose to another: sometimes standing, then kneeling, sitting or lying prostrate on the floor, she managed, successively, to be wistful, arrogant, sad, childlike, exulting, grieving, seductive, menacing – her facial expression always matching the pose and utterly convincing. In the space of ten minutes and with only a shawl for a prop, Emma Hamilton was Hebe and Venus, then Helen, Cassandra and Andromache, every depiction perfectly executed, and then, when she was done, we had Emma. She took her applause with deep curtsies and a happy smile and then, to the audience's further delight, she entertained us with comic songs. Her voice was good and her delivery extremely animated. I enjoyed the songs, but when I turned to Mother to see what she had made of the performance, I found her fast asleep on the admiral's shoulder.

"Oh, I am so sorry," I said, embarrassed, and I pulled at Mother's arm.

"No, that's alright," the admiral smiled, "I am flattered that your mother finds me so comfortable."

"Mother!" I shook her arm and she raised her head, but her wig was caught in the admiral's braid and it was only with a quick tug and a pat that he set it back onto her head. Mother blinked at me through sleep-filled eyes.

"I think I should get her home," I said, standing up, and the admiral stood too.

"I shall help you." We each put a hand under Mother's arms and raised her to her feet. "Where is your carriage?"

"Oh, we shall get a hackney," I told him, trying to look collected.

"A hackney? On your own?"

"That is how we came."

"I shall not hear of it. I shall take you home."

And so the handsome prince-admiral did take us home, in a splendid landau bearing his arms and livery and, to my great mortification, he even helped me get Mother up the three flights of stairs to our apartment. Mother, *compus mentis* by then but deathly tired, thanked him for his kindness.

"Not at all, Lady Knight. I hope you will sleep well." Then, looking to me, he asked, "Might I call to see how she is in the morning?"

"No, no, I am sure there will be no need," I insisted, but Mother over-ruled me.

"Certainly you may, Excellency. Come at eleven." Then, with a parting bow, the admiral turned and went back down the stairs.

We were both too tired to speak while Maria, our new maid, undressed us, but once we were settled in bed and ready to snuff out the lamp, Mother nudged me.

"That prince-admiral likes you. You must cultivate him." I pulled up the covers.

"Good night, Mother." I was too tired for her barbed jokes.

"No, I mean it." I turned my head to her.

"But you always drive away Italian men, even princes."

"I don't want you to marry him! An Italian? A Catholic? I just want you to cultivate him. If he wants to see you, see him; to take you out, go."

"And why, all of a sudden, this particular Italian Catholic?"

"He has a navy-full of neutral ships."

CHAPTER THREE

Mother broke her big toe in the night. She had fallen asleep before me but then woken about three to get up for the pot. 'Get up' is probably the wrong expression because it was the great height of the strange bed from the floor that upended Mother when, committed to descent, she failed to find the floor and fell, stubbing her toe as she landed. I thought she was being murdered, the noise she made. It took Maria and me a full hour to re-settle her and in the morning the toe was blue and purple and three times its size. We left her in bed with a cold press.

Admiral Caracciolo arrived on the dot of eleven. Why he had wanted to come and see Mother, I had no idea, but then he had not really wanted to come had he? He would not have expected to be taken seriously, he was only being polite, but Mother had said 'yes please' so the poor man had had to come. Maria brought him into the morning room.

"You really should not have troubled," I told him, standing to receive him. He was wearing a navy greatcoat over his uniform and carrying his bicorn.

"I have not troubled," he smiled, "I only live at the bottom of the hill and, as your mother was unwell and you are new to Naples, I wanted you to know that you have a neighbour."

I felt embarrassed to be receiving this man – this prince – on my own, in our half-furnished apartment with bare walls and a floor full of boxes.

"Can I take your coat?" I suggested. "Will you sit down?" I pushed a chair towards him. "Would you like coffee?" He held up a hand.

"Thank you but no. I need to be in my office. Sir William and I are having a day out tomorrow on Vesuvius and there are things I must do before then." He glanced around the room. "How is Lady Knight?" Still gripping the chair I had offered him, I relaxed my weight onto it.

"I am sorry you asked that," I couldn't help but smile, "she has broken her toe." I nodded towards the corridor. "She's in bed."

"My God! How did that happen?"

"She fell out of bed." I tried to suppress my amusement but I could not and the admiral smiled too – it was a twinkling smile that showed, better than words, that already he knew my mother.

"Well, that will force her to rest at least. After everything you have been through, I'm sure rest is what Lady Knight needs."

The admiral had beautiful eyes: they were chestnut, warm and reliable, but I must have lingered on them longer than I should because he noticed.

"Well then," he said, turning away, "I must be about my business." But then the cry came:

"Cornelia?" The admiral turned back.

"Excuse me," I said, "just for a moment," and I left him fingering his hat. Mother was banked up on her pillows.

"Tell him you've always wanted to go up Vesuvius," she whispered, mouthing each word.

"But I haven't."

"Tell him!" I shrugged and shook my head and then Mother said again, this time loud enough for anyone to hear.

"How lovely for you, Cornelia. You have often said how you would like to go up Vesuvius." And she shooed me back into the corridor. When I got back to the morning room, the admiral threw out his arms.

"Of course you must come!" he declared with a wide smile. "The weather is set to be clear and cold, perfect conditions. I shall collect you at seven."

It was still dark at seven, and cold, with a chilly westerly cutting off the sea, but the sky was clear and twinkling with stars. I didn't have the wardrobe for scrambling over volcanoes, especially in February. I could find nothing decent to wear and ended up in my horrid old soldier's coat over a woollen cardigan and skirt with brown boots – appropriate, I thought as I looked in the glass; I looked like a refugee!

The admiral arrived in a fly. Not wanting to disturb Mother, I had gone down into the street to meet him and, once he had helped me up onto the board, he flicked off. Cautiously, on the brake at first, we descended the steep streets of the Chiaia to the Via Toledo where the ground levels out towards the harbour. I was still numb with sleep and only vaguely aware of how ridiculous my situation was: driving before dawn through Naples beside a man I hardly knew to spend the day with him on a volcano. In an hour or two, when the dawn had warmed my wits, I would blame Mother but, at that early hour, with the wind on my face and the smells of the sea and the city in my nostrils, I was, I confess, incapable of thought and content to be carried along. I was even content with the man at my hip. Admiral Caracciolo was no diligence driver; he did not drive with brute strength and the whip, he drove with a light rein and a whispered word – *this man*, I thought, *will know how to dance.*

We swept along the highroad, following the eastern shore of the bay with the houses giving way, by degrees, to workshops and makeshift huts until we left the city behind. It was still dark, and the sea, on our right, a brooding smudge, but the wind coming off it was bitter. I pulled my head-scarf over my mouth.

"Are you alright?" The admiral dashed me a look.

"Alright," I answered. "Cold." He took one hand off the rein and tucked my blanket in tighter.

"Not long now. Ten minutes." And on we flew to Portici and our rendezvous with Sir William.

Sir William kept residences at all the royal palaces and his Villa Angelica adjoined the grounds of the king's hunting lodge at Portici. It was a neat, two-storied house at the end of a wooded drive and its privacy was maintained on three sides by woodland and on the fourth by the sea. He had prepared hot coffee and cakes for us in his seafront saloon and so, while the men set to making their plans for the day, I left them to take a look round. The saloon was quite Spartan – not so much a reception room as an anteroom to the waterfront terrace on the other side of the French windows. Sir William's collection of marbles was arranged against the walls: heads, hands and torso fragments, and sections of pillars and capitals while, above them, on the walls, there was a series of studies of the male form. I went over to examine them. Most were posed on a waterfront terrace and were, I noticed, of the same sitter – a man that I recognised as Sir William's chief manservant, Vittorio Santino. 'Singular', was all I could think at the time, and I moved over to the French windows.

Dawn was lighting the bay by now and I looked out onto a terrace bounded by a low wall against the sea. The sea was still formless but the wave-tops were flecked with crimson and gold, heralding a fine day. I peered through the glass but still, in the glass, I could see my own reflection. I looked awful. My face was blotchy with cold and my hair would have frightened Medusa. *Did I really have to go up a volcano?* I asked my reflected self, *could I not stay here with a good book?* But no, that was not the plan.

We trudged off through the woods at the back of the house; the men in their well-cut coats and I resembling their porter. The trees gradually thinned as we walked, giving way to the vineyards and rough pastures of Vesuvius' lower slopes and, all the time, the gradient grew steeper. Sir William was sixty-seven years old but he had been up Vesuvius a hundred times and he climbed as he might his own stairs. The admiral too took the climb in his stride but I just hadn't the breath. I had to reach out to the admiral to help me over boulders and tuft grass while Sir William, oblivious to my difficulties, launched into a commentary on the geology and flora we tramped over and his theories on how they were formed. I felt completely out of my place and furious with Mother. It wasn't the admiral's or Sir William's fault that I was struggling up the side of their mountain; neither of them had invited me to join them; it was Mother. I felt wretched and, as the sun climbed higher in the sky, insufferably hot in that hateful coat.

But then, when, three hours later, we reached the summit, all was forgiven. The views were – well – indescribable. The air was so clear. It was like flying in a cloudless sky above the most beautiful coastline in Europe. We stood, side by side, on a ridge above Torre del Greco; Sir William and the admiral pointing out to me the towns and villages below us from Pozzuoli in the west to Sorrento in the south. The panorama embraced the entire bay – ancient and modern – mainland and islands – and though my delight had not figured in Mother's intentions, I had to forgive her. The other attraction of the climb, of course, was the enormous hole at our backs. The volcano's crater looked as if another gigantic mountain had been up-ended into it – or rather burned into it – because the whole cone was a desert of smouldering rocks. We walked around the crater's rim, Sir William drawing our attention to fossils and other geological minutiae, but the stink of sulphur on the leeward side was so awful that I hurried him along until he brought us round to windward again and a grassy hollow overlooking the bay. It was a sunny, sheltered spot and, it being about midday, Sir William threw out a cloth and unpacked a picnic. He had been trying to explain to us, while we were on the crater, his theory of volcanology and, as we settled down to the meats and cheeses, I tried to make sense of it.

"So, everything that we see in front of us, including this mountain, was once beneath the sea. Is that what you are saying?"

"You saw the marine fossils. There is no other explanation."

"Thrown up by the volcano?"

"Those fossils on this volcano, yes, but this entire region," he jutted his chin at the view, "right down through Calabria and the Sicilian islands, they are all, I am convinced, the products of countless volcanic explosions. It might be that every landmass on earth is too, but Southern Italy is younger than most regions, and so still active."

The admiral, lying with his head propped up on his hand, folded a piece of salami into his mouth.

"And how young is young?" he asked Sir William.

"That is the question, isn't it? I wish I knew, but if you take the soils on the plain, I calculate that it takes about a thousand years to lay down two or three inches so …" Sir William shrugged.

"And the soil can be feet deep."

"Yes."

"But your theory cannot be right," I put in, confused, "the entire earth is only six thousand years old."

"According to whom?" Sir William asked.

"The Bible."

"I think you will find that the Bible is non-committal on the question. What you are referring to is a later scholastic interpretation."

"Then someone's theory is wrong," said the admiral, leaning forward to pour us more wine. "But you are right," he sat up and pointed his glass at Sir William, "this entire region is on the move. Look at Monte Nuovo thrown up overnight at Pozzuoli, and the Calabrian earthquake."

"And our friend here only four years ago," Sir William patted the ground. "Torre del Greco was under forty feet of lava. I nearly lost my villa at Portici."

"Not a friend that I should want," I observed. Sir William leaned forward for the cheese and I passed it to him.

"That depends on your perspective," he answered. "This part of the Campania is one of the most fertile regions of Europe. You can grow anything here and it's because of the rejuvenating qualities of the volcanic soil. It is precisely the continual movement and activity that gives the region its character."

"Volatile!" declared the admiral. "Soil, people and culture!" Sir William raised an eyebrow.

"I couldn't possibly comment."

Our little hollow was shelter from the wind but, after sitting there for ten minutes, I began to feel the chill of altitude and I was, again, glad of my coat. I was glad too of the picnic after the climb and happy to 'mess in' with men like these – interesting, intelligent men who respected intelligence in women. We helped ourselves from the cloth-full of food, each thinking our own thoughts, and then, after a few minutes more, the admiral asked Sir William,

"Interesting isn't it that the progress of human society seems to follow your geological model?"

"Go on," Sir William said.

"Well, consider the super-heated lava of the new philosophy that is pouring out of Paris. Is that not rejuvenating old Europe with something more fertile?"

"What? Jacobinism?" I was shocked. "I hope you are teasing us. No one who has suffered under the heel of that murderous regime could possible call it *fertile*." Sir William smiled benignly and raised an eyebrow at the admiral.

"True," the admiral answered. "Fresh lava burns and destroys everything in its path but, as Sir William says, it is a matter of perspective, and though his Villa Angelica – and even all Naples – may someday be overwhelmed, it will be necessary for future fertility when the magna has cooled and settled."

"And you think that is an acceptable analogy for what the Jacobins are doing to Europe?" I asked him. "I think that is an outrageously cruel philosophy and, frankly, I am surprised to hear it from you." I looked to Sir William for support. He too was sitting up by now and resting his arms on his knees. He inclined his head to me.

"Francesco likes to provoke in debate, Miss Knight. You will only flatter him if he thinks he has alarmed you."

"Alright," the admiral conceded, "but did not countless thousands suffer in your own civil war against Absolutism? And is not England now, as a result, fertile ground for free men to think and write and invent what they please?"

"I think you will find," I told him, "that that particular flow of magna was swept back into the ground when our monarchy was restored. The revolution that secured England her liberties was bloodless. We progress by reform." The admiral smiled wistfully.

"How I wish we could too."

"We?"

"We in Naples. Do you think we have no educated and enlightened people who can think, write and invent? And I don't just mean artists. We have philosophers, physicians and technicians the equal of any in the world." The admiral looked to Sir William who nodded in agreement. "And shall I tell you where you will find these people, Miss Knight?" I waited. "Not far from your apartment – just ten minutes' walk – in the cellars of the Castel Sant' Elmo chained in the dark to the walls." The admiral locked his fists over his knees and looked down at the ground. I felt for him. I knew that, since the guillotining of her sister, Queen Maria-Carolina had come down hard on all free-thinkers in Naples.

"Is it not possible then," I suggested, "that the revolution in France has been the enemy rather than the friend of reform in Naples?" The admiral looked up and gave me a knowing smile.

"You know Edmund Burke."

"Very well. We met every week at Sir Joshua Reynolds' house when we lived in London. He used to dandle me on his knee. Why do you ask?" The admiral shook his head and laughed.

"Never mind."

"Don't patronise me, admiral. Why did you ask?"

"Forgive me. I would not patronise you, but I think you just quoted from Edmund Burke's *Reflections on the Revolution in France*."

"Did I? Well, there you are then. I must have learned it at his knee." The admiral retired, relieved, I thought, to have been so easily forgiven. Sir William got to his feet.

"I don't know about you two, but I'm getting cold. Shall we move?" We cleared the remnants of the picnic back into Sir William's bag and then, leaving all serious thought behind us, set off down the mountain for home.

I sat on the seaward side of the admiral on the drive back, glimpsing, between the flickering buildings, the declining disc of the sun to the sea. After the day's exertions, I was enjoying the drive – the speed, the wind and, I'll be frank, the admiral. I liked him. I could not have looked worse, nor imagined a less flattering situation for myself, and yet the admiral had been attentive, and if my clothes were a mess and my hair mad, I no longer cared because clearly he did not. *Yes,* I told myself, *I like him.* I liked his open mind and the breadth of his interests; so rare in a military man. I watched his hands as we sped along – his lightness of touch and sure control. *Strength and sensitivity* I thought. I liked that.

At the harbour district, the admiral did not turn into the town the way we had come but continued instead along the seafront.

"I hope you won't mind, but I need to call in at the naval dockyard," he said, "just for two minutes," and I told him, of course, I did not.

We turned in through a triumphal arch and, even as the admiral pulled up, a hand was on the bridle and every man within sight was saluting. He jumped down and disappeared into a building, leaving me on the board on my own. The dockyard was bustling. I looked out over quays crowded with chandlery, water butts and pyramids of ball; readiness, it seemed, was high but then, as I watched, I became aware that the eyes that had been on the admiral were now all resting on me. '*Who,*' I could see them all thinking, '*is that tousle-haired Amazon in the shabby old coat, and what is she doing with the admiral?*' It was a sweet moment.

On our way again, I put it to the admiral that his ships were preparing for war.

"Of course. Don't all fighting ships? *Si vis pacem, para bellum* – If you want peace, prepare for war." We were driving up the Via Toledo now towards home. I had seen men-of-war being prepared before, at Portsmouth and Chatham, and the activity I had just seen concerned me.

"Sir William is confident that the French have no ambitions on Naples and Sicily." I looked across at him. "Is he right?" The admiral kept his eyes on the thickening traffic.

"Sir William's intelligence confirms my own. There is no sign of the French breaking the treaty of neutrality. France has no significant land forces within striking distance of our borders and her Mediterranean fleet is moored up at Toulon with half its crews paid off, so yes, unless our queen does something completely stupid, the peace will hold."

"Why the queen?"

"Because Maria-Carolina is the government. Ferdinand hates affairs of state and she loves them so she sends him off hunting every day while she runs the country."

"Not unprecedented."

"No, history has plenty of competent queens. Our problem is though that Maria-Carolina detests the treaty of neutrality. Marie-Antoinette was her favourite sister and she has sworn to avenge her. That is why she might do something stupid."

"That must be difficult for you. Being in charge of the navy."

"Not really. I have made my choice: I shall serve my country. As to my philosophical meanderings," he looked over to me and smiled, "I am sure that whatever is said among friends on a mountain will stay there."

We climbed back up the hill towards our apartment building and I savoured those words *among friends*. If the admiral was prepared, on so short an acquaintance, to put his trust in me then I would be proud to honour it. He helped me down from the fly and offered to see me up the stairs but I declined. I was tired after a long day and I did not want him pestered by Mother.

"It's been a good day, hasn't it?" he said with a smile. "I've enjoyed it."

"Tiring," I confessed, "I am not used to climbing volcanoes but, yes, I have enjoyed it too."

"Then perhaps we might do it again, though not up a volcano next time." I was taken by surprise. I had not dared hope …

"Er, yes," I answered, "I should like that."

"Now, I sail on Tuesday with a small flotilla and I expect to be away for about a month, but if I might call on you on my return?"

"Well yes," I said, and, "thank you." The admiral climbed back on the fly.

"Give my regards to Lady Knight. Tell her to rest." Then he gave me a wave and flicked off back down the hill."

Mother was furious. She was sitting waiting for me by the fire, wrapped in a dressing gown with her bound-up toe resting on a stool.

"Where's he going with his flotilla?" she demanded.

"I don't know. I didn't ask him."

"You didn't ask him? The one thing you had to do all day and when you had the chance you didn't even ask?"

"I couldn't," I told her, unlacing my boots on the fender, "it wasn't appropriate."

"Not appropriate!" Mother threw up her hands. "Good God, Cornelia! Our lives depend on this!"

"No, Mother. I don't think they do. I asked the admiral about the political situation and he said there was nothing for us to worry about." Mother glared at me.

"Can we go home overland? No! Can we expect the Royal Navy? No! Can we stay here?"

"Well yes," I interrupted her, "as a matter of fact, I think we should. We are in no danger – and you really must rest."

"He sails on Tuesday you say?" Mother wasn't listening to me. "You must see him again." She raised a finger. "You must see him again before Monday and tell him we need passage to Gibraltar. It is within his power and he is a gentleman. He will not refuse you."

"No, Mother." The idea was just too embarrassing. "I cannot."

"Why can't you?"

"He's a busy man."

"Cornelia!" I had had enough. I was tired.

"If you want to embarrass yourself, Mother, you ask him yourself." And, picking up my boots, I went to see if Maria had my hot water.

Admiral Caracciolo was away for six weeks but it felt like six months. I missed him. It sounds foolish, I know, when I had known him for less than a week, but he was – I shall make no bones about it – a very attractive man, and how long had it been since an attractive, intelligent man had shown interest in me? Of course, Mother would not like it: an Italian and a Catholic. *They want only one thing and it is not what you think*, she had told me before we left England, *to a Continental, you are a woman of fortune. Show him the slightest interest and he will charm a ring onto your finger then set you to drudgery while he swaggers on your coin.* I didn't believe her and I'm not sure Mother believed herself really, bearing in mind that two of her dearest friends, Fanny Burney and Hester Thrale, had made happy marriages with a Frenchman and an Italian. I think I supposed then, at seventeen, that Mother was only looking after my best interests. I was a few years older before I realised who it was that really needed my coin.

I saw the admiral's sails from the morning room window. Our view over the bay was the same as Sir William's, only more elevated, and Sir William had lent me a telescope with which to enjoy it. Every day, I surveyed the bay. I don't think

I was actively watching for the admiral, but any strange ship brought him to mind and when, in mid-April, two 74s and a frigate came into view, each towing a prize, my heart rose – although it would be another week before we met.

The occasion was a conversazione hosted by the admiral's cousin, the Marchese di Gallo. Gallo was Naples' Minister of the Navy and Finance and he was about to leave on a diplomatic mission to Vienna. I was in two minds whether to go. I had hoped, every day, since the admiral's return, for a note from him – an invitation to the promised excursion perhaps or, at least, confirmation that he was back – but there was nothing. I knew that, as the Admiral of the Fleet, he would be attending Gallo's conversazione but, having heard nothing from him, I wondered if my presence would embarrass him, or if a wrong look or turn of his shoulder would embarrass me. I felt self-conscious about the whole thing and yet, I could not bear not to go.

The Neapolitan conversazione is an irritating gathering because you never know who will be there or when. On any night of the week, two or three *palazzi* would illumine their facades with torches, line their stairs with footmen and throw open their doors to their neighbours. The conversazione was a form both formal and informal. It was a promenade through enfilades of salons and galleries where one should be seen for an hour before moving on to a second conversazione and a third. Its purpose was not so much serious exchange as the opportunity to dazzle, gossip and flirt. I am sure that Mother and I, in our home-sewn ensembles, looked completely out of place but, after twenty-four years on the Continent, I really did not care. When we reached the top of the wide marble stairs, we were offered iced lemonade – the conventional refreshment at such gatherings – but lemonade did not suit Mother and, while she pestered a footman to bring her Champagne, Admiral Caracciolo found us.

"Lady Knight!" His face was tanned from his six weeks at sea and, in his dress uniform, he looked strikingly handsome. He gave Mother a bow. "I am glad to see you are up and about." He glanced down at her foot.

"Oh yes," Mother clucked dismissively, "that was nothing, nothing at all Your Grace – or is it Your Excellency?" She squinted at him. "Which form do you prefer?"

"Admiral will do," he told her, "it's the only title I've earned." He now turned to me and smiled. "Good evening, Miss Knight."

"Good evening, Admiral," I returned his smile, "I believe congratulations are in order. On your prizes?"

"There'll be a pretty penny there I dare say," Mother put in, "what's the going rate for a twenty-four gun galley? You took three, didn't you?"

"Enough that we liberated nine hundred pitiable Christians don't you think?" he answered her, "though the season is still young. The Musselman's economy depends on slaves."

"Nine hundred?" I was astonished.

"Rowers and fresh captives."

From the tail of my eye a familiar figure appeared. She was an apparition in white in a Grecian robe, a gold band beneath her bust and another tying her hair.

"Prince Caracciolo," Lady Emma pursed her lips at him, "I hope you are not avoiding me?" It was a cheap doxy's taunt, I thought, and the admiral ignored it.

"May I introduce you, Lady Hamilton, to two friends of mine: Lady Knight and ..."

"We've met." Emma stopped him. She looked at Mother, eyeing her up and down and then, rolling a champagne glass between finger and thumb, she raised an eyebrow. "I thought you were in bed. With a great toe." Mother flushed to her wig.

"No, perfectly alright," she fluttered, "a trivial matter."

"Then why haven't we seen you at Court?"

"At *Court*?" Mother coughed the word like a fishbone.

"Yes, Court. You cannot live as guests of Their Sicilian Majesties without presenting yourselves." Mother glared at me in panic.

"We are hardly nobility," I attempted but Emma scented sport.

"*Lady* Knight?" She leaned closer to her. "I shall introduce you if you like. The queen and I are extremely close." Mother turned now, in appeal, to the admiral who saw her panic.

"The custom is only a formality," he told Lady Emma, "it is not required of all visitors."

"No? And you would know about that would you? I don't know when we last saw *you* at Court."

"*We*?" Lady Hamilton?" The admiral fixed her with a level look. "Is that the royal *We*?" Lady Emma was not fazed.

"No. The *We* who serve the Sovereign."

"You mean the Sovereign's consort."

"The Sovereign," she repeated, holding his gaze but then, remembering Mother and me, the admiral yielded.

"I don't think the Marchese's conversazione is really the place to weigh the relative merits of Court attendance and military service."

"Then we shall toast the success of the Marchese's embassy to Vienna." Emma drained her glass. "We can all drink to that." But the admiral did not drink to that. Tension still sparked between them but then, just in time, it seemed to me, Sir William joined us.

"Lady Knight," he bowed to Mother, "Miss Knight. I see you are being entertained." He smiled cheerfully at the admiral.

"We were just toasting the success of the Gallo embassy," Emma told him while, at the same time, summoning a footman.

"Whatever that might be," Sir William observed opaquely but Emma was no longer listening; she was ordering more champagne, an order that Mother followed up with her own instruction for the footman to bring her the same. Sir William turned to me.

"How are your researches coming along, Miss Knight?"

"My researches?"

"Didn't you tell me that you were reading up on Neapolis under the Romans?"

"I was – I am – yes, and it is extremely interesting," I told him, "I had no idea how much of a pleasure-ground this bay was for the Emperors – interesting too how the culture of ease seems to continue."

"Posillipo," Said Sir William.

"Posillipo?"

"A Greek word meaning 'respite from care'. It's the name of an ancient Greek settlement just up the coast. I have a hide-away there." Sir William looked from me to the admiral, "perhaps you would like to see it?" and, raising an eyebrow at me, the admiral replied,

"I think that would make a wonderful excursion."

"Splendid!" said Sir William. "We shall all go!" He clapped his hands to seal the agreement and the footman brought up the champagne. Lady Emma and Mother each took up a glass.

"Mm ..." Mother whispered, "brandy in it."

It was the middle of May before Sir William and the admiral found a day in their diaries and, by then, the political ground had shifted. The rumour spread that Gallo's mission to Vienna was not to cement Naples' and Austria's neutralities, but to enter into a secret treaty of defiance of France. Mother had never had any faith in Neapolitan neutrality and she declared herself vindicated. This made her more determined than ever to quit Naples and she went herself to Admiral Caracciolo to beg him for transport to Gibraltar. I did not go with Mother so I do not know quite how the interview went but she came back empty-handed; the Neapolitan navy currently had no interests west of Sardinia and that was that. The admiral was sorry.

I felt sorry for the admiral. Was Gallo's embassy to Vienna the 'something stupid' that he had feared, I wondered? A vengeful queen's folly that could throw him and his beloved fleet into an unnecessary war? And I felt sorry for Sir William too, as the admiral's friend. England would take a very different view to the admiral's of an Austro-Neapolitan alliance against France and Sir William was her ambassador. And then, as we got into May, there were further rumours that the French were amassing a battle fleet at Toulon – and not just a battle fleet – but scores of transports and merchantmen besides, enough to carry an army of invasion and all it would need. They were dark rumours, but rumours were all they were and while Mother excited herself about thunder beyond the horizon, I confess that I was enjoying the Neapolitan spring – exploring – and not just the libraries and museums but the shops and markets as well because I was determined that, on my next excursion with the admiral, I would look my best.

Posillipo is about as far to the south-west of Naples as Portici is to the south-east. The two ancient settlements face each other across Naples' inner bay with the city at their nexus, but Posillipo is not penetrated by the city's sprawl as Portici is; it is much more secluded. Mother and I drove out there with the admiral in the back of his open landau. The drive itself was a pleasure; trotting along the seafront promenade with heads turning and sailors saluting our illustrious companion. Sir William had described the Villa Emma as his hideaway and so it proved to be. We eventually found it at the end of a dusty track that meandered for half a mile through groves of olive and myrtle that, on that May morning, were heady with the scent of their blossom. The villa was a plain, white-washed building of a single storey. It was very small, just three rooms and a kitchen, but when Sir William took us through them, to the terrace at the back, we saw why the place was so special to him. The terrace was the flat top of a great rock that overhung the sea, ten feet below. It was a spectacular situation and the moment I saw it, I walked over to the perimeter balustrade to look out at the view. Along the beach, to my left, Naples was screened by the romantic pile of the Palazzo Donn'Anna; to my right, empty shore stretched away to the Point, while, in front of me, with Vesuvius smouldering behind it, the emerald expanse of the Bay of Naples swelled and sparkled in the noon-day sun.

"Miss Cornelia isn't it?" I turned round. A little plump English lady in her early fifties was offering me a glass of lemonade. Clearly, we had never met and I did not recognise her. She had large, wide-set eyes and well-marked eyebrows. Her face was oval and her mouth generous but her nose, which was square as a tradesman's hammer, prevented her from being the beauty she might otherwise have been. I thanked her and took the lemonade and we looked out over the bay together. "Who would want England when we have this?" she observed.

"Who indeed," I agreed, "perhaps we should let all those ladies who are dying to go home get on with it and leave this for us." She laughed and turned to me.

"I am Mrs Cadogan, by the way. Sir William's mother-in-law."

We had lunch on the terrace beneath the shade of an awning. So much of Sir William's life was governed by convention that, whenever he had the chance, he dispensed with it. We ate picnic-style and the food, which Vittorio unpacked from hampers brought down from the Palazzo Sessa, was just perfect: *antipasti* of every sort; *frutte del mare* – crayfish, lobsters and crabs, with salad leaves and olives, and then cheeses and fruits – everything taken as each of us pleased and at leisure. We were only five to lunch; Lady Emma had been summoned to the queen at the last minute but I did not mind that, I did not find Emma the easiest of company and nor did Mother so it was a nice surprise for us to find her mother so agreeable. I would have expected Mother, whose prejudices are strong, to have bridled at being placed beside the mother of a woman with Lady Emma's history but not a bit of it. Mrs Cadogan was so open and so charming that she did not give Mother a chance to dislike her and they got on famously well. Their reminiscences of London in the 70s dominated the talk. Mrs Cadogan had known Sheridan and Garrick, Romney and the Reynolds and I don't know who else of our London circle. It was amazing that Mother and Mrs Cadogan had never met, they could have been firm friends, and Sir William and the admiral could only listen and watch.

By mid-afternoon, the sun had reached its zenith and even beneath the shade of the awning, it was hot. I didn't mind that. I liked the sun. I would not go out in it uncovered but I loved the sheer intensity of the southern light, and it is never more intense than when reflected off water. Mother's and Mrs Cadogan's chatter gradually wilted in the heat. The urgency of their delight with one another waned as the food and wine fatigued them and when Mother said she would retire indoors, Mrs Cadogan went with her. I closed my eyes and basked; listening to the wavelets lapping on the rocks, and the crickets' continuo in the parched grass, and I savoured the scent of myrtle mingling with the salt from the sea. Surely, I mused, behind my closed eyes, heaven has no more than this.

"This is an enchanting place," I heard the admiral say.

"I know. That's why I bought it."

"You really could believe that the lotus eaters lived here – if it were an island." I opened one eye. Both men had loosened their shirts and lifted their feet onto the vacated chairs.

"Well, perhaps it was, three thousand years ago," said Sir William. "Capri wasn't; it was still attached to the mainland. Much has changed." I too felt the connection with antiquity.

"I think Homer must have passed this way," I suggested, "isn't the island of the sirens in this bay?" Sir William pointed to the farthest headland.

"Just off Cape Minerva, beyond Sorrento. So legend has it."

"And the Elysian Fields are over beyond Baiae," the admiral added and then, as I languished in my chair, soaking up the sun and the romance of the place, I saw an extraordinary vision: a naked man of about fifty, but with fine musculature, walked out of the house and across the terrace. I blinked against the sun to be sure he was real. He stepped up onto the parapet and looked down into the sea and then, after adjusting his balance with his toes, he dived in and disappeared from view. It was Vittorio, Sir William's chief man-servant and, as neither of my companions blenched, nor did I.

All reveries must come to an end and horse's hooves broke ours. We heard them cantering up the lane towards the house and Sir William reluctantly rose.

"I had better see who that is." Buttoning his shirt, he went slowly into the house and the admiral and I exchanged looks. We heard Sir William talking in English with his visitor and then he re-appeared in the doorway.

"I am afraid you are going to have to excuse me for half an hour. One of my secretaries has brought me a dispatch." He gave us a wistful smile. "It seems important."

"Of course! Of course!" The admiral jumped to his feet but Sir William hesitated.

"It's just that the ladies are asleep ..."

"It's no problem," the admiral told him, "perhaps Miss Knight would enjoy a walk after that splendid lunch?" He held out his hand to me.

"Certainly," I too rose from my chair, "you must talk with your secretary here. I should enjoy a walk." I picked up my parasol from the back of my chair and, taking the admiral's arm, descended the steps to the coastal path and set off for an afternoon walk.

The path was little more than a goat track. It followed the margin of the rocky beach and the olive groves out to Punto di Posillipo. The air was hot and dry and a light breeze was loosening ringlets from my pinned-up curls but, as my ringlets had always been admired, I was content to let them fall. I looked down at my fluttering yards of almond-coloured muslin with the olive sprigs that Maria, our maid, had helped me to buy. I had made it up into an open robe with a half sleeve and shawl collar. I was pleased with it and pleased with myself but the admiral's eyes were on the path and I wondered what absorbed him.

"You are very quiet."

"Oh, I'm sorry." He looked up at me and smiled. "I was just enjoying the beauty of the place."

"Ah," I answered, "and there was I wondering if you were worrying about Sir William's dispatch." The admiral laughed.

"What passes between Sir William and his masters in London is no concern of mine."

"But it might be. If it involves your cousin's embassy to Vienna. Then it could be very much your concern." The admiral said nothing for a few paces, his head was down again and his brow furrowed but then, after a few moments, he stopped and looked up at me.

"Do you know, Miss Knight, where I learned to be a naval officer?" I did not. "In His Britannic Majesty's Navy. I learned my seamanship from Rodney, fighting the Americans, and the principles of command from Hotham, fighting the French in the Western Mediterranean. Everything I know about the principles and practice of naval warfare I learned from the English and the first principle, Miss Knight, as you will know if you are an admiral's daughter, is that an officer's duty is to serve. Politics is not his concern." His jaw was set and he was looking at me severely but he had no need to argue with me.

"I am so pleased to hear you say that," I told him, "it was my father's credo. But if a sense of duty is an English trait, it is one that we learned from the study of your people. Duty and Honour were Rome's foundations; they gave her stability and made her great. That is why we English are so interested in the classical texts; they offer a model of stability in our troubled times." The admiral looked puzzled.

"The *classical* texts? You mean Latin *and* Greek?"

"Oh, the Greeks had their genius, but for all their thirst for enquiry, they were too selfish to be great, too fond of themselves and disputation ever to create stability. The Spartans, I suppose, were the exception, but neither the Stoics nor the Epicureans understood the true path to happiness – it was too simple for them – *do what others expect of you – do your duty*. The Romans understood that, and it is all the fulfilment we can expect." I felt suddenly embarrassed that I had said too much. The admiral was watching me.

"I have read *Marcus Flaminius*," he said, "and duty is your major theme. Duty and discipline are indeed the absolute prerequisites for an effective fighting force but," he folded his arms and gave me a curious look, "what intrigues me is that *you* wrote *Marcus Flaminius* – you, a woman. I wonder that you are so passionate on so martial a subject."

"But are not duty and discipline essential for happiness in any walk of life?"

"I don't know," he shrugged, "I have spent all my life in ships. But you live under no discipline. You are a free agent, a woman of independent means. You come and go as you please. That does not sound like an unhappy portion."

"A free agent indeed!" I laughed. "That I am not! I do what is expected of me no less than you do, admiral."

"You mean by your mother?" He gave me that watchful look again. "And that is enough, is it? Fulfilling your duty to your mother is fulfilling for you?" His questions had become personal and I did not mind. In fact, I liked it. I liked being the focus of his attention. I liked his dark eyes examining me and I liked his concern.

"But my mother *is* my portion," I told him. "There is nothing to be gained in contemplating the impossible," I met his eyes, "not at forty-one." He moved not a muscle. He just watched me from over his folded arms and then he said,

"I am forty-six, and I think anything is possible."

I saw a lot of the admiral over the next two weeks. On the drive back into town, Mother had again pestered him about passage to Gibraltar but I stayed out of the conversation, I saw no imminent danger, I was quite happy in Naples and I wanted to stay. The admiral told Mother again about the limited deployment of his fleet but then Mother had suggested Syracuse where we might pick up a merchantman out of the Levant at which the admiral had cautioned against pirates. Mother worked herself up into one of her agitations about it and, in an attempt to appease her, and knowing our interest, the admiral invited us to look over his ships in the naval dockyard. With one voice I answered 'yes please' and Mother 'no thank you'. She fixed me, across the carriage, with an acid stare, trying to burn me into submission but I did not submit and the following morning, against Mother's direst imprecations, I went alone with the admiral to look over his ships.

I sensed no danger in Admiral Caracciolo. On the contrary: I felt peculiarly safe in his company; he had depths that transcended the petty fripperies of his Neapolitan peers and, with or without his titles, he would have made a nobleman in Athens or Rome. I cherished his friendship, and I cherished the chance of deepening it.

There was little to see in the dockyard that I had not seen already. Two ship-of-the-line, a frigate and some sloops and cutters were all that were carrying guns. Most of the home squadron was out on exercise, the admiral told me, but the ships I could see and the dock that supplied them were all in good order and the admiral's pride in them was clear.

When we had concluded the tour, we walked out along the mole. There was a lighthouse at the end and we sat down on its step to admire the view of the bay.

"Thank you for coming," the admiral said.

"Thank you for inviting me."

"I hope I didn't cause an argument between you and your mother."

"Mother and I never argue, Admiral. Mother will, from time to time, indulge in a diatribe but when she has finished I either acquiesce or ignore her, but I never argue." The admiral laughed.

"She is a funny woman, your mother."

"You could say that."

"No, I don't mean that unkindly. She is ..." he searched for the word, "eccentric?"

"You could say that too." He took off his bicorn to let the breeze ruffle his curls and, looking out to the bay, he asked me,

"Why is your mother afraid of the queen?"

"Afraid of the queen? Why do you say that?"

"Because, when Lady Hamilton offered, at Gallo's conversazione, to present your mother to the queen, she almost choked."

"Ah," I remembered, "you don't miss very much do you?" He raised an eyebrow. The queen was a sensitive issue, Mother didn't like me talking about her, but I was sure of the admiral's discretion.

"You know that we were in Naples in '85?" He nodded. "After we had been here for a little while, we were presented to Maria-Carolina at a ladies' levée." The admiral nodded again. "Well, Mother is never her best in the morning so she'd got herself into a terrible fuss and went completely over-dressed in a tall wig with a man-of-war on it."

"A man-of-war?"

"Yes, you know," I raised my hand a foot above my head, "one of those old-fashioned French wigs. They used to put all sorts in them. Mother had bought it years before for Versailles … anyway …" I waved the thought aside, "that is another story but, when Mother and I arrived at the levée, Maria-Carolina was, of course, in bed and looking … well … looking as you might expect Maria-Carolina to look in bed, first thing in the morning, and the vision threw Mother quite off balance. Every other woman in the room was wearing a day gown but Mother had on this evening Court outfit with the wig and Maria-Carolina set her eye on it as soon as we walked in. She called Mother forward before anyone else and straight away asked her where she had got that hat. *That hat*! Mother was mortified and she stumbled out some explanation about wearing it to Maria-Carolina's sister, Marie-Antoinette, at Versailles. Mother embellished her story – trying to explain the wig – with some Versailles anecdote in which she described Marie-Antoinette as 'the Ornament of Europe'. Well, Maria-Carolina took exception. '*The Ornament of Europe*', she repeated and then, very pointedly added, '*of all Europe?*' Of course, Mother and everyone else saw the implication of this and …" I put my hand on the admiral's arm, "bear in mind that the queen was sitting in bed looking far from her best – Mother tried to appease her by describing *her* as '*the worthy heiress to her mother, Maria-Theresa, the greatest statesman in Europe.*'"

"Oh no!" The admiral put his head in his hands.

"Yes!" I agreed, "Well, the queen must have been feeling off-colour or something because she got very cross. '*Statesman!*' she declared, and '*pray tell me who in your judgement is the Ornament of Naples?*' And, '*if she were a statesman what then was the king?*' Poor Mother was a sack of confusion and I had to hold her to save her from collapsing with shame but the queen didn't leave it there. She thought, she told Mother, that the ship on her hat had come on a friendly visit but now she saw that it had entered her port with all guns blazing." I stopped my story there and shook my head at the memory of it. It was just too mortifying to go on. The admiral eyed me wryly.

"You amuse me," he said.

"It was not amusing at the time, believe me."

"No. *You.*" He nodded at me. "You amuse me. Not your funny stories. *You.*" He was sitting forward over his knees, looking at me.

"Well thank you," I said, a bit embarrassed, "I suppose."

"We do not make women like you in Naples."

"No. I am twice their size."

"You are twice as interesting, twice as intelligent and twice as mysterious." We were sitting, side-by-side, on the stone step of the lighthouse. His dark eyes were resting on mine and, for a moment, I met them – and panicked.

"There is no mystery about me," I told him, turning aside. "I am plain as you find me. All five feet eleven of me."

"You know that's not true." I could feel him watching me. "You are a beautiful woman – and more – much more – but you take a perverse pleasure in denying it." He rose from the step. "And you can drop the five feet eleven nonsense because your inches are nothing to me." He stood over me, casting me into his shadow. Had he found me, this man? Where so few had even looked? He held out his hand and raised me from the step.

"Do you like Piccinni?"

"Piccinni?" I tried to think. "Some. Why?"

"There is a performance of *Pénélope* at the San Carlo on Saturday. It being a story from the *Odyssey*, I thought you might enjoy it."

And so the admiral took me to the opera. This extraordinary, cultured, unattached man – the scion of a princely house and commander of his nation's navy – escorted me in my opera pomp and, for once, without my mother. I felt liberated. With my hand on the admiral's arm, I carried myself at my fullest height with my hair tied high in a broad bandeau and all the way to the admiral's box the crowds fell away like the waves before Moses. It was an evening to remember but not, sadly, for the music, which may have been wonderful but could not be heard. From the overture to the final curtain, the audience chatted and picnicked and hallooed across the stalls. The purpose of the San Carlo, I learned, was less to watch and listen and more to be seen and heard – as it was at any Neapolitan gathering. As the admiral observed on our way out, to enjoy opera at the San Carlo, you must know the piece before you go in.

I accompanied the admiral to other social events during those last two weeks of May but they were less public than the San Carlo: afternoon gatherings over tea or soirées of just eight or ten. The admiral wanted me to meet his friends, to show me that Naples was not all frippery and empty heads, that there were intelligent and accomplished people who preferred discourse to display and I am so pleased that he did because I met some interesting people. Men like Baffi, the Greek scholar, Giaja, the poet, and the celebrated botanist, Domenico Cirillo. One memorable afternoon, I recall, was spent with the geologist, Duca della Torre, viewing his collections of curiosities and antiquities that rivalled Sir William's own. Nor were all these interesting people men. In that enlightened niche of Neapolitan society, the women were the equals of the men and the admiral introduced me to such literary luminaries as Eleanora Pimentel, Guilia Carafa and the Duchesses of Cassano and Popoli. Mother strongly disapproved of these visits of course. Now that it was clear that the admiral would not be evacuating us from Naples, she saw no reason in continuing in his company but I was drawn to him. He was the most interesting man I had met in a long time and, as I reminded Mother, I was forty-one and with my own money. Mother asked, rather hotly, if I were falling in love with the admiral. I told her 'of course not' but if I convinced her, I am not sure I convinced myself.

With Gallo still in Vienna and rumours about the Toulon flotilla growing evermore alarming, apprehensions darkened in Naples but the admiral was firm that we had nothing to fear. His information was that the French force was not being prepared for Naples but for Egypt, where its army would march to Suez to re-embark for India in support of Tipu Sahib's war against the English there. That scenario was too fanciful for Sir William who feared an invasion of Portugal, or even Ireland, in support of the United Irishmen's revolt, but for most people in Naples it was for their own safety that they feared and when hard news finally came, it did nothing to assuage them.

The occasion was the British Sovereign's Dinner when, on the fourth of June each year, Sir William entertained the English residents on the king's birthday. I could imagine that, in former years, the dinner would have been a grand affair but, by June of 1798, there were few English in Naples who did not absolutely need to be there and the dinner was quite intimate. Not that Sir William had spared himself. We had lobsters and oysters then woodcock and roast beef. The wines were of the best French vintage and the dinner culminated with individual ices in the shape of Britannia. The loyal toast too was drunk in French champagne and it was immediately after the toast that Sir William remained on his feet to give us his news. He had just received reliable information, he told us, that the French flotilla had left Toulon on 19th May. It was a force of one hundred and thirty merchantmen and transports escorted by twenty-two ships-of-the-line and associated frigates and cutters. The transports were carrying thirty-one thousand infantry and cavalry, twelve hundred horses, two hundred cannon and supplies for two months. The destination of this force, which was under the command of General Bonaparte, was still not known but it had not passed through the Straits of Gibraltar. The spirits of everyone around the table, that had been so cheerfully raised by the dinner, sank.

"However," Sir William's long, patrician face broke into a smile, "I also have other news." He looked around the table, feeding our anticipation. "On 8th May, a small reconnaissance squadron of three ships-of-the-line and three frigates, under the command of Rear-Admiral Nelson, entered the Mediterranean. Any day now, it will be joined by nine more ships-of-the-line under the command of Commodore Troubridge and this combined force, under Nelson, has orders to take, sink, burn and destroy the Toulon flotilla wherever it might be found.

CHAPTER FOUR

Mother was in no doubt about the outcome of an encounter between Nelson's twelve ships-of-the-line and the superior numbers of French.

"Cornelia, we are saved. Nelson is the most brilliant commander of his generation. He will seek out the French and destroy them and then he will take us home."

It was the morning following the sovereign's dinner and we were having our breakfast of anchovies and rolls in the morning room window.

"But Mother," I answered, pouring the coffee, "why would Nelson come to Naples? He is on the other side of the Mediterranean, hunting the French fleet which, in any case, is sailing for Egypt, not Naples."

"Bah!" Mother scoffed. "Who told you that? Your admiral, I suppose."

"He had it directly from the French ambassador. And his own intelligence supports it. There is absolutely no reason for Nelson to come anywhere near neutral Naples."

"Don't be so naïve, Cornelia." Mother reached out for the butter and I passed it to her. "Do you really suppose that the French ambassador would tell the admiral he is about to be invaded? This Egypt nonsense is a smoke screen, and a thin one, and if your admiral doesn't see through it, he is either more gullible than he should be or a traitor."

"Mother! That is outrageous!"

"Well," Mother buttered her roll, "everyone knows that the French invasion fleet is bound for Naples."

"No they don't. It's just a hysterical rumour. Even Sir William isn't sure where the fleet is bound."

"His wife knows." Mother bit into her roll.

"Oh, *his wife knows!*" I put down my knife and pushed back my plate. "And what superior knowledge do you suppose Lady Emma has that her husband does not? Is she a traitor too?"

"Very far from it." Mother sat up straight. "Emma Hamilton has the ear of the queen."

"You don't think it might be the other way round? That the queen has the ear of Emma Hamilton and is pouring into it any poison that she wants circulated? Admiral Caracciolo says the queen wants the world to believe Naples is under threat in order to lure Austria back into the war against France."

"And hurrah to that!" cried Mother. "If that is what Gallo is plotting in Vienna, then all power to him!"

"I'm sorry, Mother, but do you hear yourself? You want Naples' neutrality to be deliberately violated and thousands here slaughtered?"

"Ah," she pointed her knife at me, "but that will be after Nelson has sunk the French and taken us off."

Mother had become more generously disposed to Lady Emma since she became friends with her mother. There being so few English left in Naples, Mother's acute sense of the social order had had to lose its edge. But then, if she had taken a broader view, Mother might have recognised that Mrs Cadogan's Flintshire farming roots were only a little lowlier than her own Harwich packet boatman's. I wonder if she also recognised that they both lived off their daughters? Probably not. Anyway, I was glad that Mother had a new friend, and glad too of the liberty that their friendship afforded me because, while Mother and Mrs Cadogan passed their afternoons playing cards at the Palazzo Sessa, I was free to pursue my own interests which, increasingly that spring, involved the admiral.

The sailing of the French fleet made waves in Naples and the admiral was called to a number of high-level meetings at which his own counsel seemed to prevail: the French were bound for Egypt, Naples was neutral, the war between England and France was none of Naples' business and a show of inactivity was the appropriate response so, during those first weeks of June, the admiral had time on his hands and much of it he spent with me. Our round of visits to his friends and sites of interest continued but then, on 17th June, the political wind shifted again.

I think I must have been the first to see the blue ensign entering the bay. I had seen the ship coming round the Punto di Posillipo during the morning and, recognising it as a man-of-war, I set my glass on it. It was an English 74, the ensign aft was unmistakable. I called to Mother to come and look and when she had seen for herself, she wrapped her arms around me.

"You see," she triumphed, "didn't your old mother tell you?" She lifted her tear-filled eyes to me. "We shall go home."

Mother sent me down to the harbour to find out the news and as my hackney approached the mole we joined a swelling tide of people all moving in the same direction. The shouts were all for Nelson and the English and snatches of *Rule Britannia* kept bursting from the crowd like explosions of birdshot. At the Castel Nuovo, we could go no further, but the word was that the warship was the *Culloden* and her jollyboat had landed an English commodore with a guard of marines who'd gone straight to the English embassy. I told my driver to turn back to the Palazzo Sessa but before we had got even close, we found the streets sealed off by the English marines and so I returned home empty handed and, that evening, *Culloden* sailed. It was only the following morning, when Admiral Caracciolo called, that we learned what had happened.

Nelson's squadron, the admiral told us, was standing off just beyond the horizon and it still had not found the French. After hunting them for a month, Nelson had less idea where they were than when he set out and he had dispatched Commodore Troubridge to ask Sir William if he had heard anything. Sir William had not, but then the commodore had made a second request and with that he had more success. By the time he had regained his jollyboat, the admiral told us, Troubridge had in his hand written permission from the Neapolitan government for Nelson to avail himself of any facilities he might require in any of King Ferdinand's ports. This permission was in direct contravention of Naples' treaty of neutrality with the French and Admiral Caracciolo was livid.

"They have betrayed their own people," he told Mother and me as he paced our morning room floor.

"Well the people don't seem to mind," Mother observed.

"That is because the queen's agents have been lying to them – putting it about that the French are sailing to invade us when they are not. The Lazzaroni are fooled blind. They love the English sailors now because they think they are their saviours but they are not, they will bring the world down on their heads, but anyone who tries to tell them so risks getting his throat cut."

"So what will you do?" I asked him.

"My duty. I shall prepare for war. But who I shall be fighting … I shall have to wait for orders."

Two days later his orders came. He was to sail south to visit every major port on the Tyrrhenian and Ionian seaboards to confirm Nelson's warrant and inspect shore defences. Before he left he came to say goodbye.

Mother and I had been in Naples for four months by late June. In that time, we had decorated our rooms with the furniture and pictures that Angrisani's had forwarded from Rome so that we were, once more, among our own things. I stood in the morning room, waiting for the admiral, and I thought about that first time I'd received him. Then, the walls had been bare and the floor full of boxes. I had felt self-conscious then – gauche even – thinking that Mother should have been receiving the stranger but the admiral was no stranger now; I was looking forward to receiving him and I had chosen a time when Mother would be out. In my buttercup print with the maroon sprigs, and my hair tied up in a maroon bandeau, I had dressed to look my best – for the admiral and for myself.

The admiral declined afternoon tea but accepted my offer of lemonade which Maria brought to us sitting in the chairs by the hearth. He was in his summer whites, looking tanned and handsome but he seemed ill-at-ease.

"I did not want to leave without saying goodbye," he said

when Maria had left us. "I have enjoyed these last weeks." He looked up at me. "I shall miss you."

"I shall miss you too." I felt the colour pricking my cheeks. "You must take care of yourself. These are troubled times."

"Bah! Troubled times!" He twisted away in his chair. "Don't you go believing any of that nonsense about invasion. The only foreign warships you will see in Naples will be English ones so that will please your mother at least." He took a quick draught of his lemonade then slammed down the glass on the wine table. This business with Nelson's ships was nettling him but he had no need to be angry with me. If he valued me, he would have to learn to trust me. I decided to draw him on the ships.

"Are you afraid that English ships in your ports will provoke the French?"

"The English are at war with France." He opened his palms. "They have been for years. What I think about that doesn't matter, my country is neutral – or she was – only now she has taken sides so, yes, I am worried." He leaned forward to me with his hands clasped over his knees.

"The whole purpose of my life, Cornelia, has been to defend my country. My training, my years at sea, my decision to forego a family life – these things I have given for the honour of serving my country at the highest level – defending her against any aggressor that might threaten her – but when my country is the aggressor, when she violates her own treaty to support the enemy of her co-signatory, that is not in my philosophy." He looked down at his hands, like a bewildered schoolboy who has learned for the first time that even honour can be compromised. I looked down at the lowered head and strong shoulders and my heart went out to him. I wanted to raise him up and hold him in my arms and draw his cares to myself but, of course, I could not and so I rose from my chair and walked over to the window.

"Still," I said, turning the conversation, "this cruise down the coast should be peaceful. If Nelson does catch up with the French, it will not be in Neapolitan waters."

"That is true." The admiral too now rose from his chair. He crossed the room and joined me at the window where we looked out, together, over the bay. "The next few weeks will be peaceful." He turned to me and attempted a smile. "I might even take my paints." But his eyes were not smiling, they were anxious, and he saw that I saw. He looked back to the bay. "And what about you, Cornelia? What shall you do while I'm away?"

"Oh, I shall keep busy, I also have a commission. Sir William has asked me to catalogue his collections for him, to make an inventory."

"Has he?" The admiral was surprised. "And which is it? A catalogue or an inventory?"

"Aren't they much the same?"

"One is a record for the sake of scholarship and the other a record of ownership." He remained looking out at the bay for a few moments and then he said, "perhaps Sir William is worried too," he looked back to me, "for his collections?" Again, he attempted a smile but it only made him look sad. I met his sad eyes. *You should not be going away,* I thought, *not at a time like this.* His whole manner spoke of foreboding, of fears too deep to express. I willed him to reach out to me, to take me in his arms and hold me so he would know that, whatever his fears, he could share them with me but he remained where he stood and a wave of despair swept over me. My heart rose in my chest but I was determined he should not see my tears so I turned away and said as firmly as I could,

"God speed you then, admiral, and bring you safe home."

He reached out to me now and took my hand. His was strong and dry, and when I turned to him he said,

"Admiral is my rank, Cornelia, my name is Francesco."

"Francesco," I whispered, struggling to hold back my tears, but he just stood there examining me – my face, my hair and down the full length of my robe.

"You look beautiful," he said, "this is the picture I shall take with me to sea." Then he lifted my hand to his lips. "God bless you."

The news that Nelson could use the ports electrified Naples. To the Lazzaroni, those vulgar hordes of the streets, it was final confirmation that the French must be coming, only now, at the eleventh hour, their heroic Ferdinand had enlisted the greatest sea power in the world to defend them. Their conviction was cemented in mid-June when word came that the French fleet had finally appeared, capturing Malta, only two days' sail from the Sicilian coast. Nelson now knew where the French were – or so the Lazzaroni supposed – and he would attack and destroy them and the man the muddle-headed simpletons credited with this fond hope was their king. Misplaced though their gratitude was, Ferdinand basked in it. He went down to the fish docks in rustic garb, moving among them, joking and bantering in their own rough tongue. He even accepted a rowing match from a burly young fisherman, a match that he won to everyone's, especially his own, delight. But if Ferdinand could take pleasure in uncertain times, the queen could not. It no longer mattered whether Maria-Carolina believed in a French invasion; she had violated a treaty and thrown in her lot with the English – or, at least, with Nelson – and her fate now rested with his.

June slipped into July. The French fleet departed Malta, leaving only a small garrison behind and, as the days went by and it failed to appear in the bay, Naples, by degrees, began to relax and return to its summer torpor – and it was hot – I had never known such heat. It poured off the house walls and up from the setts, raising the smells of dung, brick dust and stale wine that are the signature essence of Naples. The nights were suffocating and the days enervating so I was glad of the diversion of Sir William's inventory. Over those long weeks of summer that Francesco was away, I catalogued four hundred pictures and a thousand Greek vases and hundreds more items besides. Sir William himself I rarely saw. After thirty-five years' service, he occupied a unique position at Court as the king's favourite diplomat and wherever Ferdinand went, Sir William was expected to follow. That summer, while so many important matters pressed, Sir William had to spend days at a time simply sailing in the bay with Ferdinand or fishing or going off with him to inspect his hunting estates in readiness for the new season. The time wasted frustrated Sir William, I knew, but I did manage to win some of his time and, when I did, I enjoyed him. Sir William was witty and urbane and one of those men with whom a woman can feel entirely at ease and when, in mid-July, he told me he could spare me a couple of hours, I assembled my queries in his study. He surveyed them and sighed.

"Is this then the sum of all my happy summers?"

"Hardly," I told him, "a mere sample. And isn't your first collection now gracing the British Museum?"

"Ah yes." He smiled and cast his eyes over the tables, the floor and the walls, taking in some of the most precious relics of our civilization. I knew what he was thinking.

"You are worried that the French will come and this will all to go Paris."

"They have plundered every major art work in northern Italy and, even as we speak, they are systematically removing the best from Rome. The Louvre is to be the sole repository of all Europe's art."

"Perhaps we should be thankful that the Jacobins value former civilisations at least, if they do not value their own."

"Their own?" Sir William put back his head and looked down his long nose at me. "What civilisation is that?"

"Our shared European civilisation. The one they trample and crush with their armies and their Reign of Terror." Sir William pursed his lips.

"An Enlightenment philosopher might argue that their revolution is intended to advance European civilization."

"Anything can be *argued*," I told him, "and look where that got Socrates?"

"Well, I think you can fairly mark a trajectory of European thought from Socrates and his pupils through Thomas Aquinas to Bacon and Descartes right up to the Jacobin's favourite *philosophe*, Voltaire – of whom so many English Whigs were once fond."

Sir William leant forward to examine a tray of specimens on the table. I wondered if he had found something amiss but then, when his attention moved to the next tray and then to the one beyond, I realised he was merely distracted.

"I visited him, you know," he said, without looking up, "in Switzerland, with my first wife."

"Voltaire?"

"Yes. A great privilege."

"Then what went wrong? How is it that an enlightened philosophy has plunged all Europe into darkness?"

"How is it?" He stood up from his specimens and looked at me. "Because all Europe unleashed the dogs of war, that is how, and look where it has brought us: Britannia defending superstition and tyranny against the sons of Voltaire."

Francesco finally came home during the second week of August and, within hours, I received a note from him suggesting a day out to Pompeii. My heart leaped. Pompeii would be perfect: alone together, away from Naples, exploring an ancient site. Mother was sniffy of course. Pompeii was too arid for August, too unwholesome and simply too far but I was having none of it; I would not be harassed by Mother any more – although she did try to harass Francesco.

"But, Lady Knight, all those rumours about the French and Naples are nonsense," he told her, "Bonaparte's army will be in Egypt by now, fighting its way to the Red Sea and embarking for India."

"Huh." Mother, still in her morning wrap, stiffened. "So, you still hold to that fanciful theory, do you? You surprise me, Admiral."

"Mother!" I despaired of her. Francesco had barely crossed the threshold and she was nipping at his heels but Francesco was not fazed.

"It was never a theory, Lady Knight. My information from the French ambassador was supported by my own intelligence from Toulon but, if you wish to remain sceptical, you might ask yourself where, after three months in the Mediterranean, a flotilla of one hundred and fifty ships might be. There is a limit to how long thirty thousand men and horses can remain cooped up in ships in high summer and, even sailing at one knot, they would be in Egypt by now." Francesco, tanned and handsome in his whites, gave Mother a rueful smile, "Nelson has lost them. I am afraid he has been wasting his time, and a great deal of his country's resources."

"But you don't know that," Mother bridled.

"I'm afraid I do. I met Nelson in Syracuse three weeks ago."

"You met Admiral Nelson?"

"He was availing himself of my country's hospitality there, revictualling his ships, while I was conducting my survey. He told me that he had less idea where the French were then than he had when he set out."

"And your intelligence about Egypt; what did Admiral Nelson make of that?"

"I didn't share it with him."

"Oh?" Mother affected disbelief.

"He asked me what I had heard, but I had to tell him that, as a neutral, I was not at liberty to say." Now, Mother affected shock.

"Less than civil, don't you think?"

""That was what Nelson said – in a sailor's usage." Francesco flashed me a twinkling smile. "He was not best pleased."

It was going up to nine before I managed to get Francesco away. He had come in his open landau and, once the footmen had settled us in and the coachman faced downhill, he flashed me a happy smile.

"You look pleased with yourself," I told him, happy, myself, that we were at last alone.

"I am." He stretched wide his arms. "Look at me! Home from the sea and you at my side – you look lovely by the way – I had been wanting to say – those colours," he cast his eyes over my robe, "maroon and cream are perfect for you." I gave him a doubtful smile.

"Your being so happy has nothing to do with Admiral Nelson's discomfort then?" He threw back his head and laughed.

"Oh dear! Did it show?" I raised an eyebrow. "I'm afraid that might have been personal but, well, Naples is still neutral you know, Cornelia. I know that you and your mother are English and your country is at war with France but *my* country is at peace, and I want to keep it that way."

"I understand that. I really do," I put my hand on his arm, "and you know that I respect you for it."

"The trouble is though, my government seems not to be interested in peace."

"The concession to the English ships?"

"My government is playing a double game, which is dangerous, even with a fistful of cards, but with the hand that Naples is holding …"

"A player with a weak hand has few options," I suggested.

"He can pass. Sit back and watch the big boys play it out, but to think he can win by cheating and lying," we were down on the waterfront by now and Francesco looked out over the bay, "he won't and he shouldn't." The sea and the sky were one blazing haze and I put up my parasol.

"Is Naples cheating and lying?" Francesco set his jaw.

"I have been instructed, since my return, that I have not, for the past seven weeks, been inspecting shore defences, I have not been to Salerno, Messina or Syracuse and I did not meet Rear-Admiral Nelson." He looked at me angrily. "I have been nowhere in particular failing to catch pirates." I closed my hand round his arm.

"I'm sorry. I know what Naples' independence means to you." Under my hand, his muscles relaxed.

"It is sixty-four years since King Charles gained our independence from Spain," he rested his head on the folded hood, "and in that time I don't think we have done a bad job. Thanks to Charles, we have our beautiful carriage drives, our public buildings and squares. He defended our borders and our rights, refusing the Inquisition and the excesses of the Curia. His enlightened rule allowed art and science and commerce to flourish and although the son may not be so active a monarch as the father, Ferdinand has, at least, the good sense to maintain the liberties of his people and for that his people love him. Ferdinand may never be great but he is honest and he is generous."

"Perhaps there lies the problem," I suggested, "that Ferdinand has been too generous." Francesco looked puzzled. "To his wife? He has rather given her the kingdom."

It was fifteen miles from central Naples along the coastal highroad to Pompeii and we arrived covered in white dust. Mother had been right: Pompeii is a long way, it was hot and the landscape arid, but what of it? Francesco was back and we were together. We left the servants and horses at a nearby farm and then dusted ourselves down and set off for the site. The sun was at its zenith by then, beating down on the parched landscape of broom and drooping eucalyptus and the only sounds in the deadening heat were of crickets and the crunch of our shoes. We were the only people there. After a word and a coin to the gate-keeper, Francesco showed me the principal sites: the Herculaneum Gate, the Necropolis and the Temple of Isis. We wandered through the ruins of bathhouses and bakeries and people's homes and down the paved streets with their precipitous pavements, I, in my diaphanous cream robe with my parasol, and Francesco in his shirt-sleeves, carrying his coat. Francesco knew something about everything we saw. I had read Pliny's account of the explosion of 79AD but Francesco's knowledge went deeper than Pliny. I loved that he took such pride in his forebears, all Italians should, but too many so bow to the Rites of the Church that they miss all the treasures beyond them.

Francesco wanted to make some studies of the Temple of Isis but I declined to join him. There was no shade where he wanted to sit and I had had enough of the sun so I walked over to the shade of an arch and sat down on a fallen capital. I had a clear view from there down the street to where Francesco was sitting on the pavement with his feet in the road. I don't think he could see me in the deep shade of my arch but I could see him, looking intently at his subject then sketching on his pad. Francesco had the tight curls of the ancient Romans and the physique of the athletes on Sir William's vases. The musculature of his thigh, on which he was resting his pad, was clearly discernible through his white breeches and the straight lower leg was in perfect proportion. Francesco was sitting three-quarters away from me so I could see through his tightened shirt that his back muscles were well-defined too. I saw him, in my mind's eye, unclothed, absorbed and unaware of me. I took out my pad and, for the next half-hour, in the heat and the quiet and the bright yellow light, I made my own studies of him.

"Had enough yet?" Francesco called when he evidently had. He walked over to me and I slid my pad into my bag.

"Yes," I called back, "I am ready for a drink."

"I am ready for food, I'm hungry." He came into the shade of my arch and held out his hand. "There's a picnic in the landau. We can have it down at the farm." I took his hand and he pulled me up but then I let my hand linger in his and he let his linger in mine. He shouldered my bag with his own and his coat and then, hand-in-hand, we walked back to the farm and our picnic.

Three more weeks would pass before the suspense of the French fleet was finally over. It was a Monday morning, the 3rd September. I was reading to Mother in the morning room when, from the window, my eye was caught by a sloop coming into the bay. I put aside my book and, saying nothing to Mother, went over to the telescope. I set it on the sloop, a sloop-of-war of about sixteen guns and she was flying the blue ensign.

"What are you doing, Cornelia? This is no time to leave off the story."

"There is an English sloop." Mother lifted herself out of her chair and came over to me. She pulled up a stool and climbed up to the eyepiece.

"It's an English sloop-of-war," she confirmed, "no pennant, no sign of damage." I took back the telescope and followed the sloop's progress towards the harbour. A small boat with four oarsmen and two men in the stern-sheets put out to meet her and when the sloop dropped anchor she pulled alongside. Mother took back the glass.

"Two officers have come on deck," she said, "and they both have gold epaulettes."

"Dispatches?" I suggested, thinking aloud.

"Surely so," agreed Mother, "two captains. One, the commander of the sloop and the other carrying the dispatches." Mother turned from the telescope and frowned at me. "What do you think?"

"I don't know." Something had happened, I felt sure. Something important. "Let me see." I took back the telescope. The officers were in the boat now being rowed ashore. One of them was sitting with a bag on his lap while the other waved his arms about, telling something to the men in the boat. He threw up his arms into the air demonstrating surely, I thought, a great explosion, and then his hands went down, as if pushing under the sea. "There has been an action." I stepped away from the telescope and turned to Mother. "There has definitely been an action."

"Maria!" Mother called out and Maria came through. "Lace caps and parasols please, then go find a hackney. We are going to the Palazzo Sessa."

The arrival of an English warship had again brought Naples out onto the streets and our progress was arrested in the Via Toledo. Our driver told us he could go no further, he would have to turn back, but Mother was not for turning back. She pushed her head out of the hackney's window and hallooed a pair of ruffians. She showed them a ducat and promised it would be theirs if they could conduct us unharmed to the Palazzo Sessa. I will not pretend it was the pleasantest quarter mile I ever walked but, with their strong arms and loud voices, the ruffians delivered Mother and me to the palazzo where Sir William's footmen brought us in through the cordon.

Before ever we had reached the top of the stairs, we knew what had happened. The noise of excited chatter spilled down from the long gallery and the shouted words of 'victory' and 'Nelson' left nothing to doubt. It was not a large crowd making all the noise – there could not have been more than fifty English present – but their halloos and laughter resounded all round the room. Nelson's squadron, we learned from a Mr Thomas, a merchant, had surprised the French at anchor in Aboukir Bay near Alexandria and sunk or captured twelve of their fourteen ships-of-the-line. Bonaparte's army had been landed but was now marooned, the commander of the escort squadron, Admiral Bruyes, was among the thousand killed when his flagship exploded, and although many English ships had been battered, all would repair and fight again. The victory was complete. Mother cried and hugged me and did a little dance.

"We are going home – home – home ..." she sang as she danced and then Mrs Cadogan appeared. Mother gave her a big hug. "And where is the captain of this sloop?" Mother asked her, "is he here in this room?"

"Captain Capel?" Mrs Cadogan was surprised at the question. "No. Sir William has taken him to the palace to deliver his news to the king and queen."

"But he will be bringing him back here?" Mother asked her, "before he sails?"

There was a loud 'bang – bang' and all eyes turned to see Vittorio Santino bang his staff on the floor.

"My Lords, Ladies and Gentlemen." His smooth Neapolitan baritone stilled the room. "Pray silence for the king's messenger." He stepped aside to reveal a dapper little fellow dressed head to toe in the king's livery.

"Subjects of his Britannic Majesty, King George," he proclaimed in courtly French, "His Sicilian Majesty King Ferdinand and Queen Maria-Carolina request your immediate presence at the Royal Palace to receive their majesties' congratulations and gratitude on the recent success off Alexandria of King George's ships under the command of Rear-Admiral Nelson." A great English cheer flew up to the covings and I was as thrilled as the rest: a royal celebration, in a foreign land, of an historic English victory, and we the first to know of it. It would be a day to remember for the rest of my life.

"We cannot go," Mother snapped and, as our fellow-countrymen moved towards the stairs, she pulled me aside. "Stay back." Her eyes were flicking in panic. It was the old nonsense.

"Mother!" I drew myself up and towered over her, "you are being ridiculous!"

"We must find this Captain Capel."

"He is at the palace. Mrs Cadogan just told you. Anyway, why are you interested in him?" Mother gripped my arm and pulled me down to her.

"He has the London dispatches and he will not delay. As soon as he is out of the royal palace he will be back to his sloop and gone, and we must go with him."

"What?" No one, except I who knew Mother so well, could have believed she was being serious. "Sail for England? This afternoon? In what we stand up in?"

"It's the first chance we've had. And when will we get another?"

"And what about our things? My drawings? My books? Money? And we would need passports." And then I realised that I was taking her seriously. "No, Mother," I told her. "I don't want to leave Naples, and anyway, hasn't Nelson just destroyed the French threat?" Mrs Cadogan returned to take Mother's arm.

"Come along!" She pulled at her. "We have all to be presented to the king and queen." I took Mother's other arm but she held back and, in mortal alarm, appealed to Mrs Cadogan,

"But first you will present me to Captain Capel?"

"If you like. If he's still there." And so we went to the palace.

None of us was in court dress of course, the invitation was so impromptu. I was still wearing the simple muslin robe I had put on for a quiet day at home, as was Mother similarly attired, but as everyone else was taken by the same surprise no one seemed to mind. We were shown up a wide sweep of marble stairs to the *piano nobile* and then along a corridor to a reception room. The room was not large by palatial standards but it was more than adequate for the hundred or so English present. The walls were decorated with frescoes of fealty and benignant conquest, while, on the ceiling, there was an apotheosis of victory – apposite, I thought, for the day's event.

The band struck up with *Rule Britannia* as we walked in, which heightened the air of excitement, and as the trays of canapés and champagne went round, Mother and I toasted with the rest the health of King George and the victorious Nelson. We remained thus entertained, chatting cheerfully with our fellow countrymen, for about fifteen minutes before the double doors flew open and King Ferdinand and the queen strode in. I say 'strode in' because the king did, but his queen fairly ran.

"God bless and save you, sons and daughters of Albion!" she cried aloud, flinging her arms in the air, "God bless and save King George and Queen Charlotte and George the Prince of Wales." The English parted before her as the heavily pregnant Maria-Carolina, with Lady Emma in her train, rushed through the room. "And God bless and save brave Sir Horatio Nelson and his good wife in Norfolk." The queen spied a young man standing in the crowd and she stopped to accost him. "He has delivered my family from the Regicides," she shouted into his face, "and delivered my country from the murderous fleet." She thrust out her chin at the young man and then, turning from him, she clutched her breasts in her hands and offered them up to the ceiling. "What do we not owe him? What do *I* not owe our saviour? Nelson! Nelson! Nelson!" And she swept on.

Mother, stricken by the memory of her late embarrassment with the queen, tucked herself behind me, hanging on to the back of my robe. Hiding was not an option for me, even if I had wanted to, but when the queen advanced on me, I made sure my curtsy was wide.

"God bless you, Mrs Cadogan." She said to our companion beside me. "What a day was that when you brought forth this dear child." She took Lady Emma's hand. "England is in her debt you know, it was your daughter's counsel that secured our assistance for Nelson's ships." The queen smiled fondly upon her protégé, "and was she not right?" Now, she thrust a fist up to the ceiling. "Victory!"

The queen's face had been a yard from my own but only now did she seem to notice me. She blinked her pug's eyes and her jowls wobbled.

"Ma'am," said Mrs Cadogan, "this is Miss Cornelia Knight. Her late father was an admiral in King George's navy."

"Splendid!" The queen shouted, then, "Did you say 'Miss'?" She screwed her face at me. "*Miss*? You cannot find a naval officer of your own?" She looked at me, demanding a response but I could not think what to say. She stepped back a pace and looked me up and down. "I have seen you before," she decided. "Long time, but I have seen you before. I don't forget. You must be the tallest woman in Europe."

"We … *I* was in Naples in '85, Your Highness." I was not going to lie to a queen. "I had the honour of being presented to you then." The queen looked at me closely for a moment and then stabbed me with her finger.

"I remember you! You were with your mother weren't you? A thin little woman with a hat with a ship on it. Is your mother dead?" I felt the weight of Mother tugging at my back.

"No. Thank you Ma'am. My mother is well." The queen seemed ready to move on but then had a thought.

"Tell her to find that hat with a ship on it. It will be the very thing when Nelson arrives."

King Ferdinand too was passing through the room. He had Sir William at his side, who was presenting to him some of the English residents. Striking though Ferdinand was with his opaquely pale blue eyes and pendulous nose, he did not command a room as his queen did and he confined himself to stamping his feet and barking odd words such as 'capital', 'hah' and 'kaboom'. A posse of his ministers had followed him into the room and, bringing up its rear were two naval officers: one, an English captain, whom I took to be Capel, and the other Francesco. I caught his eye and he brought the captain over to me.

"Captain Capel?" Francesco rested his hand on his arm, "may I introduce you to Miss Cornelia Knight? Resident of Naples." The captain nodded me a bow. "Captain Capel has the dispatches from the engagement in Aboukir Bay and he has just been ..." Mother leaped out.

"How do you do, Captain?" She was on him like a cat on a mouse while Francesco, unaware that Mother had even been there, could only add,

"and ... Lady Knight."

"One of the Essex Capels I dare say?" Mother gripped the captain's arm and thrust her face into his.

"Er yes," Captain Capel replied, "my father is the fourth Earl."

"Ah, how lovely." Mother drew – or pulled – the captain aside. "Tell me about your service. My late husband was in the service you know – Rear-Admiral Sir Joseph Knight – you will have heard of him." Mother manoeuvred Captain Capel away into a corner where she could have him to herself while Francesco looked on, bemused.

"Your mother knows Captain Capel?"

"No, not at all. She is trying to ingratiate herself with him. She wants him to take us to England."

"To England?" Alarm shot through his face, "But I always thought ..."

"*I* don't want to go to England, no, but Mother does." His alarm turned to amusement and he broke out a smile.

"Well, she is going to be very disappointed. Captain Capel is carrying the dispatches overland and he won't be taking passengers." I looked over to the corner of the room where Mother was still harrying the captain. She did not know yet but she soon would. I looked back to Francesco.

"Oh dear!"

"Oh dear!" he agreed and we both laughed. I took Francesco's arm and drew him aside. I did not want to talk about Mother.

"But what about you?" I said. "If congratulations are about, surely some are due to you."

"To me?"

"Yes. You were right all along about the French going to Egypt. No one else was." He raised his eyebrows and sighed.

"The French never were a threat to Naples. Your mother had no need to worry, but now, if Nelson brings his squadron here, as Capel tells me he will … then we shall have cause to worry."

CHAPTER FIVE

Three more weeks were to pass before Nelson's ships began to arrive in the bay and, in that time, Naples threw caution to the wind. Banquets, tableaux and balls were prepared, miles of bunting and lanterns slung along the waterfront and private and public buildings emblazoned with the names of Britannia and Nelson. Lady Emma assumed charge of all these arrangements, setting everyone to their tasks. Mine was to compose the panegyric to Nelson, drawing comparisons between his victory and the feats of the heroes of antiquity. Sir William declared himself so pleased with my effort that he insisted I join him on the embassy barge so I might declaim it to Nelson myself. Francesco's task was to skipper the royal barge, taking Ferdinand out to Nelson, and quite how all these demonstrations of delight at the defeat of the French were to be squared with the French ambassador was left till another day.

Nelson was coming to Naples to avail himself of the naval repair yards at Castellamare and his most badly damaged ships limped in in dribs and drabs. *Alexander*, with her main and mizzen masts shattered, and *Culloden*, with a lashed hull, were the first to arrive, on the 16th, and then, six days later, came three more: *Minotaur* and *Audacious*, both under some sail, and then, under tow, the un-masted wreck of *Vanguard*, Nelson's flagship, and all Naples went out to greet her.

It was a day I shall never forget; a day of pure emotion when all thoughts of politics or sympathy for a brave foe defeated were swept away on a wave of Britannic pride. We, in the embassy barge, were supposed to be the first out to *Vanguard*, with the king following on, but several thousand Neapolitans thought differently. Everything that floated was put into the water. There must have been five hundred boats around us, all overloaded, flag-bedecked and flailing their oars like so many waterboatmen. Skiffs, painted guzzi and rude fishing vessels jostled with the gorgeous barges of diplomats, princes and mitred bishops. Boats were rammed and gilding scraped, and pennants, too long to be held on the breeze, snagged on the oars of neighbouring boats and the shouts of laughter and recrimination rose with the music in a cacophonous din. The embassy barge – a baroque pleasure craft of eighteen oars that Sir William had hired for the day – was towing its own eight-piece band that played *Rule Britannia* and *See the Conquering Hero Comes* but none could have known because their efforts were drowned out by trumpets and drums and a thousand hearty voices singing their own Neapolitan songs. Even the king, whose own band was following the state barge, ran the same noisy gauntlet but what the cacophony lacked in musical precision, it more than made up for in unalloyed joy.

I had run up a navy and white robe for the occasion with the initials HN and GR embroidered with laurels round the hem but if, for a moment, I had thought it too showy, I soon changed my mind when I saw what Lady Emma was wearing. She was *alla* Nelson from head to toe. Her robe was white with gold buttons embroidered with the letter 'N'. Gold anchors dangled from her ear lobes and more gold anchors decorated her blue shawl while, across the breadth of her forehead, her bandeau proclaimed the legend 'Nelson and Victory'. Lady Emma was almost beside herself with excitement. While Sir William and I sat with his secretaries beneath the canopy in the barge's stern, she danced around the deck, waving and bantering with the Lazzaroni, joining in their songs and accepting their acclamations all the way out to *Vanguard*. It was an exhibition of Lady Emma's theatricality that I was having to get used to but it did not prepare me for what was to come: the moment her feet touched *Vanguard's* deck, Emma flew at Nelson.

"Oh God, is it possible?" she shrieked, flinging herself at the waiting admiral. "I am delirious with joy." Nelson, who was a good two stones lighter than she and with only one arm to support himself, staggered under her weight. "How many months have I been in fevers of dread and of joy anticipating this moment?" She pulled him to her bosom, tears flooded her eyes and then, loosening her hold, she slid down his be-medalled chest. "I fainted when I heard the news," she went on, now breathless, "I fell and bruised all up this side." She took Nelson's hand and pulled it up her thigh. "I should have been glad to die in the cause except then I could not have embraced thee, Victor of the Nile." She slid from his chest to his legs, the register of her voice sinking as she went. "How I glory in the honour of my country – and of my Country*man*!" she growled. "Oh England! You have made an immortal." Then she slid to the deck as if dead at his feet.

No one moved. The officers of the ship's company, drawn up against the gunwale, looked on, unsure what to do. I looked to Sir William's secretaries, Messrs Smith and Oliver, but Mr Oliver shrugged and so I looked to Sir William. He was standing apart, looking splendid, I thought, in his powdered wig and the brocades and buckles of his best Court dress. He was smiling benignly upon the crumpled heap at Nelson's feet, apparently enjoying the moment, but then, when Nelson looked to him in appeal, Sir William remembered himself and went to him. The two knights shook hands and exchanged a few words over Lady Emma's prone body and then, with a nod to me that I should follow, Sir William coaxed his wife off the deck and, with Nelson's help, carried her through into *Vanguard's* great cabin.

They set her down on a chair beside the dining table where she threw herself back demanding air. 'Air' evidently meant something more substantial in the Hamilton household than the benign aeriform because Sir William took a glass of champagne from a steward's tray and asked for brandy to be brought. The aperitivo revived Lady Emma but not sufficiently for her to be left apparently and the two knights drew chairs up beside her. I stood back by the door and looked on. Nelson was, after his many adventures, already a national hero and his portraits were familiar to me but if those portraits had been taken from the life, they must have been drawn long ago. He was a year younger than me but looked ten years older. His grey hair was tousled and lifeless, his braided coat, weighed down with medals, was too big for him and his white stockings were crumpled. He looked frail, I thought, and tired. His face might have been beautiful once: his blue eyes were keen, his nose strong and straight and his mouth sensuous but his face was lined with thirty years of hard weather, war and the weight of command and then, of course, he had suffered – his right eye, blinded by the French in Corsica, and his right arm, lost to the Spanish at Santa Cruz, and now, from Aboukir Bay, that livid three inch gash above his right eye. But for all the wear and tear to his meagre frame, there was a hardness about Nelson; it was there in his steel blue eye and in the stiffness of his bearing and even watching him from the back, while he talked with Sir William and Emma, I could see that he should not be crossed.

King Ferdinand arrived to a twenty-one gun salute in the gaudy confection that was the Neapolitan State Barge. His entourage was small: just half a dozen courtiers, and Francesco of course, playing the boatman. Ferdinand was an unpredictable monarch at the best of times and, that day, he did not disappoint. Displacing one of their number, he had rowed all the way out to *Vanguard* with the naval cadets in the galley. He arrived at the gunwale gate dishevelled and sweating and putting on his coat but, when Sir William introduced him to Nelson, he clasped the hero's hand.

"My deliverer!" he thundered at him. "My preserver! God, I wish I could have been there. Blasting those Regicides to damnation! That must have been a day." Nelson was smiling graciously, awaiting the return of his hand.

"A night, actually, Your Majesty," Nelson corrected him, "it was a night action."

"Was it by God?" Ferdinand gazed into the middle distance as if visualising the scene. "A night action eh!" Then, returning to Nelson, "Well, my family is in your debt. The queen should have been here – wanted to – bit unwell." He let go Nelson's hand. "Lost a child." He sniffed and pulled at his nose – an inadequate memorial, I thought, to the death of a son.

Ferdinand walked over to the ship's officers drawn up along the gunwale and then, after barking a few words at a couple of them, he descended the companion way, with his entourage in tow, to take a look round the ship.

"What a very odd king," said a young commander standing next to me.

"Very odd," I agreed, "even for a king."

"May I?" He offered me his arm and, as Francesco had not yet appeared, I took it and repaired with him to the great cabin.

Fresh trays of champagne were circulating through the officers and their guests and my escort took two, handing one of them to me. He offered up his glass and I chinked it.

"To victory!" I toasted, and we drank. "So," I offered, keeping an eye on the door for Francesco, "you are a hero of the Battle of the Nile. You must feel very proud."

"Oh no, not me. I wasn't in the battle." He took another drink of his champagne.

"Oh?"

"I command a frigate – *the eyes of the fleet* – only Nelson lost us back in June, which is why it took him so long to find the French."

"But you are here."

"We caught up with the squadron after the battle."

"Aah," I gave the young man a knowing smile, "so, Nelson lost you – or did you lose Nelson?" The commander – who was only about twenty – looked down into his champagne and a lock of dark hair flopped over his eyes.

"It doesn't matter."

"That's alright," I shrugged, "it was you who opened the subject." Still looking into his champagne, the young man thought for a moment, then drained his glass and exchanged it for another.

"Last May," he decided to tell me, "when we were off Toulon watching for the French fleet, a storm blew." I nodded that I was listening. "Most of us rode it out on bare polls but *Vanguard* set heavy storm sails and ended up losing her main mast and top-mizzen. I and another frigate had got separated and knew nothing about it so, the next day, when the storm passed, we sailed for the rendezvous station. We waited there for a week and then, with none of the others appearing, we opened our 'failed rendezvous orders' and sailed south to patrol between Sardinia and North Africa. We stayed there for two months completely wasting our time."

"So what had happened to *Vanguard*?"

"They towed her to some remote bay in Sardinia and spent two weeks fishing up her masts, by which time, the French fleet had sailed, so had we, and Nelson was left with only one frigate for a dozen ships-of-the-line."

"No wonder it took him so long to find the French."

"Six weeks too long. He could have had them on 21st June but, for want of frigates, he missed them by three leagues."

"I'm sorry," I said, growing uncomfortable now with this vehement young man, "but one hundred and fifty ships cannot be missed by three leagues."

"They were. Nelson crossed the flotilla's stern at night, a hundred miles south of Syracuse. Lookouts saw their lights but the only frigate they had was away scouting elsewhere so they couldn't confirm it and Nelson decided to leave them. We could have had the entire French invasion force at sea: the army, Bonaparte, the lot. We'd have gone through them like dolphins through herring."

At last, Francesco appeared at the door. He had an English captain with him and I gave him a wave.

"Cornelia!" he smiled, "how are you?"

"Oh, well enough," I returned his smile, "this young commander has been looking after me." The English captain frowned at my companion and at his empty glass. I had thought the junior officer might have come to attention for his superior but he did not.

"May I present Captain Berry to you?" Francesco said, "Admiral Nelson's Flag Captain. He has been briefing me on the action."

The commander, beside me, shuffled his feet and muttered 'bravo' at that but I don't think the captain heard him.

"Miss Knight is resident in Naples," Francesco went on, "she is Sir William Hamilton's right hand."

"Ha!" the young commander now cried out, "we should get you attached to our Rear-Admiral!" There was a stunned silence. I don't think any of us quite believed what we had heard. Captain Berry turned puce.

"Mr Nisbet!" He spat out the name like pips. "Being the Admiral's son gives you no licence …"

"Stepson," Nisbet corrected him. "Nelson is not my father. He is merely the man who married my widowed mother." Berry was livid.

"Get out," he hissed, and the young man, his empty glass dangling in his fingers, left the cabin, passing Nelson, the king and the Hamiltons without pause or a salute. It could have been a difficult moment but then the king noticed his own admiral in the room and made straight for us. I dropped into a curtsy and the men bowed. King Ferdinand was built like a small bull and he snorted down his pendulous nose.

"Seen over the ship yet, Admiral?"

"No, not yet, Sir," Francesco answered.

"Good. Full of men. See it better empty." He turned to Nelson. "Show Admiral Caracciolo your ship, Nelson, when the crew's ashore."

"It will be my pleasure, Sir," Nelson replied and then, turning to Francesco, "don't leave it too long though, Admiral. As soon as I have my masts, I shall be back at the French." I expected some comradely response from Francesco but none came, he merely held Nelson's eye, and for so long, it became uncomfortable.

"Admiral Caracciolo?" Lady Emma suggested. "Surely you will want to congratulate Admiral Nelson on his triumph?" Still Francesco seemed reluctant – until Ferdinand gave a hefty cough and then he said simply,

"Congratulations, Admiral, on your decisive action." It was the very least he could have said and he did not offer Nelson his hand.

"Congratulations accepted." Nelson gave him a wry smile. "My captains are all masters of cutting in and cutting out." Francesco stiffened, again, offering no response, and this time Sir William broke the silence.

"If you would care to breakfast perhaps, Sir?" He indicated to the king the enormous table, the width of the ship, that was laden with victuals from the embassy kitchens and, upon that lead, we all moved to our seats.

I had been embarrassed by Francesco's rudeness and wanted to know the reason why but, as I was seated in the centre of the table, between Messrs Smith and Oliver, and Francesco was at the bottom, as far away as he could be from Nelson, the Hamiltons and the king, I had to bide my time. The breakfast was raucous, as might be expected with Ferdinand, Lady Hamilton and two score of sailors all drinking their endless toasts, but my panegyric went down well and the mood – save Francesco's – was merry. I tried to catch up with him when we rose but he shot off, while I was herded up with the Hamiltons and Nelson to the embassy barge. Nelson was, by his own admission, exceedingly tired and suffering from the wound to his head so when Lady Emma offered him a warm bath and a feather bed he did not demur. Lady Emma was starting with Nelson as she meant to go on. On the barge back, she requisitioned every cushion on board and piled them together to make Nelson a couch and then proceeded to flatter him with Attitudes of obeisance and ministration. Sir William was, at first, admiring of her exhibition – as he ever was – but I found it too sickening to watch and, after a while, even Sir William was looking out over the side.

As we pulled ever closer to the Great Quay between the Royal Palace and the Castel Nuovo my heart began to rise. The sight was barely believable. Neither in Paris nor Rome had I seen such crowds. The full length of the promenade, the mole, the shore down into the sea and the hundreds of boats bobbing on it were all packed with people. The bunting already hung was augmented by hundreds of other flags: the Union Flag, the Neapolitan and the flags of societies and princely houses unknown to me, but also Russian, Austrian and even Turkish flags. *Where now*, I wondered, *is the alliance with France*? As our gallant oarsmen pulled for the shore, the cheering grew louder. Nelson rose from his couch – indeed, we all rose – how could one not, faced with that? Lady Emma took possession of Nelson. She played to the crowds, offering the hero theatrical curtsies and holding his hand up in triumph while Nelson, his pains forgotten, happily acquiesced. Sir William too waved and smiled and so did I – why not? – I was there, at the making of history.

As we drew near to the quay, the noise became deafening. "Viva, viva, viva-viva Nelson!" was repeated again and again, the synchronicity sharpening as we drew closer. We saw soldiers clearing a landing space and, behind them, a military band. "Viva, viva, viva-viva Nelson!" The chanting battered our ears. I looked at Nelson, wondering what all this must mean for him and he caught my eye. His smile was as wide as a child's and his cheeks were streaked with tears and then, as our painter was thrown ashore, the massed band struck up with *Rule Britannia* and ten, twenty, fifty thousand voices lifted to the sky with whatever words they knew and thousands of caged birds were released to fly with them.

We were put into an open landau from the royal mews and escorted by a troop of King's Dragoons back to the Palazzo Sessa. All along the short route, foot guards held back the cheering crowds, people and flags hung out of the windows and at every house corner there was a decorated motto: 'Vittoria', 'Viva Nelson' and 'Nostra Liberatore'. When we reached the Palazzo Sessa, Mother and Mrs Cadogan were waiting for us. So overcome was Mother with the emotion of the day that when she was introduced to Nelson she forgot even to mention my father. All afternoon, the crowds remained outside, dancing and chanting and singing songs and then, after dark, there were fireworks and illuminations across the city and on every ship in the bay.

Over the next few days, Nelson was fêted by the great and mobbed by the poor. He was desperate to expedite the repairs to his ships and get back among the French but the invitations were too grand to decline. On the second day, the Neapolitan government hosted a banquet in his honour. It was attended by every government minister and every military and Church leader but neither the king nor the queen was present. The queen was still mourning the loss of her sixteenth child while the king stayed away on account of the alliance with France. That seemed, in the face of everything else that was going on, an extremely slender nicety and one that was further eroded two days later when the Austrian ambassador, Count Esterhazy, hosted a ball for Nelson. The count took the opportunity to announce publicly, for the first time, that during Gallo's mission in May, Austria had promised sixty thousand troops to Naples if she were attacked by the French. Russia and Turkey had both declared war on France since the Battle of the Nile and it really did seem that Nelson's victory might have turned the tide of the war, and now all eyes were on Naples. There could be no doubting what the British government wanted of Naples, nor what the Neapolitan people wanted.

"Where is the threat from France?" Francesco asked me. We were sitting in the library of the Palazzo Sessa, enjoying a few minutes peace before the next Nelson celebration: his fortieth birthday party hosted by Lady Emma.

"I am not going to rise to it, Francesco. I know you enjoy an argument but I think we have exhausted that one."

"No, listen to me a moment. France's armed forces were over-stretched before the Battle of the Nile. Now, her navy is seriously depleted, Bonaparte's Army is marooned in Egypt, Russia and Turkey have declared war on her and the Austrians are about to. Why would France want to turn on a peaceful neutral like Naples? I have no argument with the English navy but the sooner Nelson's ships are out of Naples the better it will be for us."

We were relaxing in the cool quietude of Sir William's library; Francesco in his best dress uniform and I complementing him in ivory and cornflower blue.

"Are you sure you have no argument with the English navy?" I asked him.

"Of course not. I was brought up in it. It's the best in the world."

"Then why were you so ungracious to Nelson?"

"When?"

"*When*!" I laughed. As if he didn't know! "On *Vanguard*, when you refused to shake his hand." Francesco shifted in the deep library chair.

"He hasn't got a right hand. I wasn't going to hold hands with him." Francesco was being evasive and that interested me.

"Did something happen between you two in Syracuse?"

"No," he said, tight-lipped, but he wouldn't look at me.

"Then where? Something happened somewhere. You don't like Nelson do you?" He crossed his long legs at the ankles and gave me a twinkling smile.

"Is it so obvious?" I raised an eyebrow and waited. Francesco joined his hands in his lap and looked up at the bookcase in front of him. Like every other square inch of the palazzo it had been decorated by Lady Emma with victor's laurels and blue ribbons embossed in gold with HN.

"We were in an action together three years ago," he conceded, "before the treaty with France. I was commanding one of three Neapolitan ships attached to a dozen English under Hotham when we engaged a French fleet off Genoa. My ship, the *Tancredi*, was a 74, and Hotham ordered me to attack a damaged French 80, the *Ça Ira*." Francesco uncrossed his ankles and sat up in his chair. "Bear in mind that this was a great opportunity for me. The Neapolitan navy offers few chances for major action so I grasped at it but, before I had hardly put on sail to bear down on *Ça Ira*, Nelson, in *Agamemnon*, broke from the line – contrary to orders – and cut through to attack *Ça Ira* himself. *Agamemnon* is a 64, lighter and faster than a 74, and Nelson cut across my wind and bore down to take her."

"And you haven't forgiven him?"

"It was typical Nelson bravura," he opened his palms, "successful if he is successful."

"And you cannot forgive that?" Francesco got to his feet.

"I would have forgiven and forgotten." He clasped his hands behind his back and went over to the window. "I am not a schoolgirl. But when Hotham asked for his explanation, Nelson told him that he believed I lacked the stomach for close engagement and needed his help."

"On what evidence?"

"None." Francesco turned to me. "On no evidence. Hotham reprimanded him and cleared my name but I never got another opportunity to prove myself and mud sticks. That is what I do not forgive."

We left it as late as we reasonably could before going up to dinner because it was going to be a long night. The Hamiltons had invited eighty to dine with them, seventeen hundred to the ball afterwards and eight hundred to late supper. Lady Emma had requisitioned the state rooms of every neighbouring palazzo for Nelson's birthday party and

I dared not think what it was all costing Sir William. Mother came and found us in the library and I thought she looked wonderful. She had told me what she was intending to wear but I did not think she would. I was sure that, once she had looked in the glass, she would have lost her nerve but 'no', there she was, resplendent and defiant in the Versailles wig. It was at least eighteen inches tall and the sixteen-gun frigate on top was, after thirteen years in its box, still in splendid condition. Francesco was delighted with the wig and that delighted Mother so we were a happy trio that trooped up to dinner.

The dinner was served in the long gallery which had been transformed for the occasion. Two parallel tables had been set up, connected, at the top, by a shorter top table and behind that stood a faux triumphal column reaching to the ceiling. The column was Ionic and bore, on its shaft, the names of the victorious English captains while, across its pediment, the words 'VENI VIDI VICI' had been inscribed. The gallery's walls were festooned with swags of fresh flowers and wreaths of laurel framing the letters HN. The tables sparkled with silver centre-pieces and tall candelabra while arrangements of peaches and roses, nectarines, salvias, grapes and dahlias filled the spaces between. HN was embroidered into every napkin and embossed on every plate and beside every name-card there was a button on a silk bow embossed with HN that we were all expected to wear.

We found our places at the bottom of the table on the left. I was at the end with Francesco next to me, while Mother sat across from him between two English officers. The one on Mother's left, I recognised as the young Commander Nisbet whom I had encountered on *Vanguard*, but I did not know the officer at the table-end opposite me. As we took our seats after grace, he examined my name-card.

"Miss Knight," he read, and looked up at me. "Not the Ellis Cornelia Knight who penned the panegyric?"

"The same," I acknowledged, taking up my napkin. I was having to get used to celebrity since Sir William printed a thousand copies of my ode.

"Then you are the author of *Dinarbas*."

"I am, yes." Francesco was leaning against me while a footman poured him wine.

"What is *Dinarbas*?" he asked, and the officer – a Captain Gould – answered for me.

"It is an oriental tale, a romance, and it is an answer to Dr Johnson's misanthropic tale, *Rasselas*. Miss Knight's piece asks us – and Johnson – to take a more positive view of life."

"Johnson of the English Dictionary?"

"Yes."

"I didn't know he wrote romances."

"Only the one," I told Francesco.

"Ah," he remembered, "you knew Johnson in London."

"He thought the world of her," Mother chimed in. "What did he call you, Cornelia?" I shook my head, preparing to be embarrassed again. "'Inordinately tall and odiously accomplished!' That was it." Mother laughed at the memory of it. "And then, when we were leaving for the Continent, he said, 'Good! Cornelia is far too large to be contained by an island.'"

"Yes, well," Captain Gould offered, giving me a friendly smile, "it was a point well made."

"This is very intriguing," said Francesco, "you never told me you had written a second novel."

"Did I not?" I was now leaning away from Francesco so that my wine might be poured.

"And what *is* the point in this novel," Francesco asked Captain Gould, "that Miss Knight makes so well?" Captain Gould looked over to me.

"Miss Knight will correct me if I am wrong but, précising hugely, Dr Johnson's characters manage to conclude to their own satisfaction that human happiness is unattainable in this life while, in *Dinarbas*, Miss Knight's characters find happiness, and they find it by knowing the limits of their place in the world and doing, within those limits, what the world expects of them."

"Aah ..." Francesco smiled and raised his eyebrows, "now where have I heard that before?"

The salvers of meats arrived and one of them was placed before us. The oval dish was a yard wide and in its various compartments there were pâtés of cheese and macaroni, smoked and boiled fishes, pots of ragouts, game, fried and baked meats and Périgord pies.

We each helped ourselves to whatever we chose and, continuing the Dr Johnson theme, Mother asked Captain Gould if he had known any of Johnson's circle.

"No, I am afraid not, Lady Knight. My life has been spent either at sea or in Somersetshire. I have little experience of literary salons, but I enjoy books. I think they are in my blood."

"Gould..." Mother mused, holding up a fork, "Gould... Isn't Sharpham Park in Somersetshire?"

"Why yes," Captain Gould was impressed, "that's my family's seat. I was born at Sharpham Park."

"Then," Mother wagged her fork at him, "I see why ink is in your blood. Was not the great Henry Fielding also born at Sharpham Park?"

"He was my cousin," the captain was amazed, "or half-cousin, but yes, his mother was a Gould. You are very knowledgeable, Lady Knight. Perhaps you've also heard of my uncle, The Reverend William Gould? He is quite well known in philosophical circles." And so Mother and Captain Gould chattered on about another of the captain's illustrious relatives: a reverend connoisseur of the habits of ants.

Lady Emma was progressing down the room, introducing Nelson to her guests. Aware of her acid humour, I watched warily as she moved towards Mother's wig but she stopped short at Commander Nisbet. Nisbet had not noticed her approaching and, when she covered his eyes and bent to his ear, he leaped up.

"Lady Hamilton!" Emma flung out her arms.

"Come here!" She pulled him to her bosom, holding him there for a moment before setting him at arm's length to examine him. "Do you remember? When you were here with your father five years ago?" She struck an Attitude of such maternal pride that I thought she might burst into tears. "And now you are a man!"

Nelson, at Emma's side, gave a loud 'Huff!' at that and Emma turned to him.

"Leave him with me for a month, Sir Horatio, and I shall make him a man."

It was such a cheap, crass remark. I felt so embarrassed for Nisbet and when he regained his seat I saw him mouth the word 'bitch'.

Now, Emma saw the wig. She peered at it and into it and at the little frigate on top of it but before she could think of a cutting remark, Nelson had moved on and her moment had passed. He was at the foot of the table, between Captain

Gould and myself. He nodded me a polite 'Miss Knight', which I returned, and Captain Gould and Francesco both rose for him. Captain Gould congratulated Nelson on his birthday but Francesco did not. Nelson gave him a wry smile.

"Not long now, Admiral," he told him, "you crack the whip in the repair yards and I'll soon be gone. I have unfinished business with the French," he flashed Captain Gould a cold smile, "haven't I, Mr Gould?" Captain Gould shifted awkwardly and said nothing. The remark, it appeared, was barbed. I had watched Nelson on *Vanguard* and again at the table, and I was beginning to understand where that frail little man drew his power: he knew his men; their strengths and their weaknesses.

As the meal progressed, Mr Nisbet's mood did not improve and he drank heavily. Mother seemed quite taken with him. She chatted away to him about I know not what (I could no longer hear for the din) but I would give short odds it was genealogy or my father's service in the American War. Mr Nisbet was being polite enough with Mother but she did not have his attention: his eyes were on the top table; on Nelson and Lady Emma who was fawning all over her principal guest, cutting his meat and ordering champagne while Sir William, on her right, conversed, oblivious, with the Princess Colonna. By the time the meats were cleared and the desserts brought, the room, dominated, as it was, by jubilant sailors, was as noisy as a tavern and licence being sanctioned from the top table down. Lady Emma, whose ample décolletage was falling dangerously low, was now feeding Nelson with sweetmeats and iced fruits – an indignity that Nelson seemed happy to bear. The hostess's behaviour to Nelson was sliding below the threshold of decency and it was too much for Mr Nisbet. Suddenly, without a moment's warning, he sprang to his feet.

"Sir!" he yelled, but not loud enough to still the room and so he yelled again "Sir," and this time he got quiet. All eyes turned to him. His face was flushed and his breathing heavy and he steadied himself with one hand on his chair.

"I have a mother at home," he declared, looking up at Nelson. "Your loyal and faithful *wife*." His arm was shaking on the chair back and sweat was beading his brow. He lifted his chin at Nelson. "Have you a message for her, on your birthday? That you would like me to pass on?" The room had gone deathly quiet. On the top table, Lady Emma moved, as if to speak but Nelson, his face like iron, checked her. "No?" Nisbet looked round the room. "Very well." He feigned a smile. "Then it must fall to me to give Lady Nelson my own account of your *pathetic* …" he spat out the word, "*public* …" his voice broke, "*debauch* …" and he jabbed a finger at Lady Emma, "*with that fat whore.*"

The room exploded. Everyone was shouting at once. Lady Emma, open-mouthed, blinked in disbelief; Sir William took hold of her hand, while Nelson's face drained to the colour of stone. Captain Gould got up and went to Nisbet. He put his hands on his shoulders, reasoning with him, but Nisbet seemed spent, his head lolling as if he were about to faint. Captain Gould sat him back on his chair, talking urgently to him but then, above all the noise, Nelson himself yelled out,

"Get him out!" Captain Gould continued talking to Nisbet and Nelson yelled again, "Mr Gould! Get him out!" But the captain took no notice. Mother was talking to Nisbet too by now, resting her hand on his, while around the room, the shouting raged.

"Troubridge! Berry!" Nelson called out, this time as an order, "*Get ... him ... out!*" Troubridge and Berry, who had been sitting together at the top of our table, now rose and came down the room. Captain Gould stood up to meet them and, as he approached, Troubridge called to him,

"Get out of the way, Gould," but Captain Gould did not, he stood his ground, protecting Nisbet. He said something like,

"Troubridge, this is completely unnecessary," but Troubridge took hold of him and thrust him aside while Captain Berry took hold of Nisbet's arm. Now Mother got to her feet.

"Unhand him!" she cried, and Berry, with his free hand, tried to sweep her aside but Mother resisted. I got up and went to Mother and Francesco came too but by the time we arrived, Troubridge and Berry had Nisbet by an arm each and Mother was blocking their way.

"Unhand the boy you brutes!" she cried again, and she punched Troubridge in the chest. Troubridge sneered at her,

"You set a toy frigate against me?" And he knocked Mother down. Well, to be completely fair to him, he swept his arm against Mother and I think she lost her balance but the effect was the same; Mother fell against the edge of the table and onto the floor, banging the side of her face and losing her wig. I was incensed.

"You lout! You are not fit to wear the uniform! My mother is seventy-three!" He dashed me a look.

"And what are you then? The spare mast?"

I bent down to Mother to see if she was alright and Troubridge, who had Nisbet's head under his arm by now, strode over me dragging Nisbet and Berry behind him but that was as far as he got. Francesco put his hand on Troubridge's chest. Troubridge was about to respond but then Captain Gould appeared at Francesco's side blocking Captain Berry. Troubridge hesitated.

"Apologise to Lady Knight," Francesco told him, his eyes blazing, "and to Miss Knight." Troubridge looked murderously at Captain Gould, but Gould agreed with Francesco.

"That was a bit much, Troubridge," Gould told him, "I think you should apologise." Francesco kept his hand on Troubridge's chest but then, while his captors hesitated, Nisbet freed himself and stumbled off towards the stairs.

"Come on, Troubridge," Berry said, although whether he wanted Troubridge to apologise or withdraw was not clear. I got Mother onto a chair and reset her wig on her head. She was moaning and rubbing her ankle which looked to be swelling. Francesco, still holding Troubridge, said to him,

"*If* you are a gentleman ..." but Captain Gould interrupted him.

"Come on now, Troubridge," he urged him, "think of our hosts." Troubridge glared at Francesco for a few moments more but then, with a snort down his nose, he backed away and turned to Mother and me.

"Ladies," he said with a mocking bow, "on behalf of my uniform, I apologise." Then, without troubling to know whether Mother or I accepted his apology, he returned with Captain Berry to the top of the room.

CHAPTER SIX

Mother's ankle was so painful that Francesco and Captain Gould had to carry her down to the carriage, sitting on their locked hands with her arms around their necks – a position that, in happier times, she might have enjoyed. Together, they settled her into Francesco's coach from where we all, I think, expected Captain Gould to leave us but he did not. He insisted that, as Mother had been injured by an officer of the service, he, representing the service, had a duty of care and he would discharge it. Francesco paid no heed to Captain Gould – his sole concern was for Mother. He tucked her into a corner of the coach with a blanket and then told her plainly that, in his opinion, she was not fit to mount the stairs to our apartment and she must go home with him to the Palazzo Caracciolo. He looked to me for confirmation. I had never been inside Francesco's palazzo but I knew it as one of Naples' most noble; Mother would be cosseted there by an army of servants, so I thanked him and accepted.

We rumbled through the narrow streets in our cramped dark box; I with my arm around Mother while the men filled the seat opposite.

"Troubridge has something to answer for," Captain Gould growled from his corner, "and he will. You shall have his apology." Francesco raised his eyebrows and gave me a weary look.

"We already have Troubridge's apology," I told the captain, "I think we can leave it at that."

"That was no apology," Gould persisted, "it was a compounding of the insult, but you shall have it, Miss Knight. I shall see to that."

And so the man bore on. He had never seen such behaviour from King's Officers, he told us. He was going to demand apologies from all of them – Troubridge, Berry, Nisbet and Nelson. Nelson! 'And what do you want Nelson to apologise for?' Francesco asked him. 'Why, his behaviour,' replied Gould, and Francesco asked him if he really thought it a kindness to Mother and me to involve us in Nelson's behaviour. The captain really was very tiresome and I could feel Mother getting agitated. I put it to Captain Gould that the greatest service he could do Mother just then would be silence – which set him off apologising for himself. I thanked God when we reached the palazzo.

We drove through an arch into a square courtyard lined with Romanesque colonnades. Torches were blazing in brackets between the arches and even before we'd pulled up, a footman was opening the door. Francesco jumped down and helped Mother and me out but when Captain Gould tried to follow, he stopped him. He instructed his coachman to return the captain to the Palazzo Sessa and then call for Doctor Pico on his way back. I was so glad Francesco did that. Captain Gould, I am sure, meant well, but he didn't have to parade it.

Francesco and his footman got Mother into the palazzo and sat her down on a seat in the hall. Poor Mother. Her ankle was swollen and a bruise was developing on her right cheek. Francesco squatted down to her. He squeezed her hand and gave her a warm smile then he looked up at me.

"Are *you* alright?" His frown was full of concern. I loved that; to feel his concern. I wished *I* were in his care and could tell him that *no, actually, I'm not alright. I have just been humiliated in front of a group of men for whom I have the highest regard. I want you to tuck me in with a blanket and squeeze my hand* but, of course, I just said,

"Yes," and he rose from his haunches.

"I have sent for my physician and your rooms are being prepared. If you would just wait here for a moment?" then he walked away across the hall, disappearing through a door behind the stairs.

I sat with my arm round my little broken mother and looked round. The hall was a cavernous white space dominated by an elaborate marble staircase that divided both ways at its turn. The floor and walls of the hall were of marble – the floor white, and the walls creamy-blue with panels of applied stucco framing the portraits of generations of Caracciolos. Francesco was only gone for a few moments and, when he returned, he had a lady with him.

"Mother," he said, as they came to us, "this is Miss Knight." The lady held out her hand and I rose to take it. "This is my mother, Cornelia. The Dowager Princess." I bobbed her a curtsy.

"I hear you have been in the wars," she said, with her son's firm smile.

"My mother has." The princess was a striking vision in ice blue and grey, the colours of her eyes and hair. She must have been well into her sixties but when she squatted down before Mother, she was as supple as her son.

"Do you think you have broken anything, Lady Knight?" she asked her, and for the first time in half an hour, Mother spoke.

"All down this side," she rubbed her right hip, "and my ankle." She thought for a moment, "I don't think so." The princess nodded and smiled.

"My parlour is just across the hall. I have ordered sweet tea; it's the best thing for shock." Mother thought for a moment more then suggested,

"Cognac?"

Doctor Pico arrived a few minutes later. He examined Mother in the princess's parlour and confirmed that no bones had been broken. He recommended bed rest for at least a week and so footmen were summoned to carry Mother up to a second-floor room where two lady's maids were already waiting. They helped Mother through to a dressing room and I gladly relinquished control. I was tired. I stood, all alone, and looked round the room: it had oak beams in the ceiling, oak boards on the floor and an ancient oak bed with rich hangings and rugs. It was reassuringly homely and, in the candlelight's glow, the strains of the day drained from me.

"Poor Cornelia, you look tired." I turned round. Francesco was in his shirt sleeves, leaning in the doorway.

"I am tired," I told him.

"I am so sorry about tonight. Sailors celebrating their victories should not invite ladies to join them."

"Nor gentlemen."

"Nor gentlemen."

"Still," I told him, "you shouldn't be apologising, you have been kindness itself." I felt awkward, standing, on my own, in the middle of the floor while Francesco leaned in the doorway. I wanted him to come to me but instead he said,

"Let me show you your room."

"*My* room?"

"It's next door. All prepared." A shiver of panic shot through me.

"No, thank you," I told him, "I could not leave Mother, not tonight."

"That's alright," he stood up from the doorframe and came to me, "whatever you wish. I'm only happy to have you here under my roof." He took both my hands. "There will always be a room for you here, Cornelia. My home – and I – will always be at your disposal." His eyes were steady and deeply sincere. Was it my tiredness, I wondered, or the candlelight's glow in that mellow room or was I losing my heart to this man? He drew me to him and I closed my eyes then, very gently, his lips brushed mine.

"Sleep well," he said, then he let go my hands and left.

I did not sleep well in that big feather bed – I was too hot, Mother too restless and my mind awash with Francesco. That kiss! – or near-kiss – an *hors d'oeuvre*, an *aperitif*, a promise of a kiss to come – and more – there was intent in those lips and in Francesco's eyes. How little more he needed to do to bear me away! Did he know that? And if he did, what did he intend? I slipped my hands under my head and peered up through the gloom at the bed's deep-carved canopy. '*There will always be a room for you here.*' What did that mean? Was he thinking of Mother? If her fall had been worse and she had died. '*Always a room for you.*' But as what? A patronised old spinster? Passing my days in sequestered retirement like some pensioned retainer? Surely not that. '*Always at your disposal.*' He had said that too – and meant it – it was there glowing in his eyes – and that kiss wasn't patronising, it was a promise of passion. '*A room for you here.*' Did he want me for his mistress? No, never, that wasn't Francesco. Mother's arm flopped over my face and I laid it back on the sheet. He couldn't be thinking of marrying me, could he? The offer of accommodation would be an oblique approach to a proposal of marriage and Francesco is never oblique so, what then? I turned away from Mother to try to get some sleep. Mother would not approve – an Italian and a Catholic – but would she scorn palaces in Naples and Avellino? Doctors, servants and security? Her daughter a duchess, a princess …

It was gone ten by the time I went downstairs. Mother had woken up stiff and aching but the Caracciolo maids had soon made her comfortable and I left them giving her breakfast. I decided against breakfasting with Mother myself; I thought it better form to join the household and, as I passed the state rooms on the stairs going down, I ran into the dowager princess.

"Ah, Miss Knight," she gave me a breezy smile, "I hope you slept well."

"I did, thank you, Ma'am."

"And how is your mother?"

"Bruised," I told her. "Aching. But she slept. Your maids are giving her breakfast."

"Good. Rest is what she needs. I believe Doctor Pico is planning to call in later." She looked at the clock at the head of the stairs. "Have you breakfasted yet?"

"No. I thought your maids had enough to do with Mother."

"Lovely," the princess declared, "then you and I shall breakfast together." She took my arm and led me across the top of the stairs to a more domestic-looking corridor where we turned through a door on the left. "This is the family breakfast room." She held open the door for me. "We are quite informal here. You must treat it as your own."

The room was charming. Not over-large, just big enough to accommodate a broad sideboard and a table and chairs for a dozen guests but it was not the furniture that was charming, it was the frescoes. All four walls, beneath a celestial sky, depicted a single panoramic landscape, as viewed from the table, across *trompe l'oeil* balustrades on which people and pets sat admiring the view.

"My goodness!" I exclaimed. "Al fresco frescoes! How delightful!"

"It is nice, isn't it? To be in town and start the day in the countryside? They are views of our estate at Avellino. Francesco did them."

"Francesco?" I was amazed; they were beautiful. "Francesco, your son?"

"Yes."

"I didn't know he could paint fresco. It takes years of training." She gave me an indulgent smile,

"It was an interest. He made it his business to learn."

Just two place-settings had been laid at the top of the table which made me suspect, rightly or wrongly, that the princess had been waiting for me.

"Coffee and rolls?" she asked, "or some kind of tea?"

"Coffee. Thank you." I reviewed the cold meats and fishes, the eggs, cheeses and fruits on the sideboard and a footman appeared at a serving door.

"Both coffee," the princess informed him, in a manner suggesting that he too had been expecting us together. I helped myself to some sardines and anchovies and a piece of Burrino and went and sat down. The princess also took sardines and anchovies and, once the coffee had been poured and she'd given thanks, we took up our knives and forks.

"It really is very kind of you to take us in," I told her, "I am sure we would have managed but Francesco was adamant." I broke open a warm roll and took a knob of butter from a silver dish.

"Francesco thinks a lot about you and he has a generous heart," the princess raised her eyes to me, "and it is nice for me to meet you after these months." *After these months.* I wondered how much Francesco had told her about me. I decided not to respond. "Your late father served in the English Navy, I understand."

"Fifty-two years, mostly in the West Indies. He retired as Rear-Admiral when King George was gracious enough to knight him. He lies in the Chapel Royal in St James's Palace."

"It is a demanding career, the navy. Your father will have earned his honours, I am sure." Again, I did not respond. I was beginning to feel that my place was to answer questions, not make conversation. "You know that Francesco has dedicated his life to the Neapolitan navy?"

"He loves his ships and his crews," I agreed, "anyone can see that." The princess took a sip of coffee, eyeing me over her cup, and then, returning the cup to its saucer, she dabbed her napkin to her lips.

"The Caracciolos – I can say this because I am one only by marriage – have a strong sense of duty." She sat back and rested her hands in her lap. "Francesco counts among his forebears generals and ambassadors, a Field Marshall of France, a Viceroy of Sicily and even a beatified Saint of the Holy Church – San Francesco Caracciolo – you must visit his shrine at the Church of Santa Maria di Monteverginella;

it is rather beautiful." She gave me an indulgent smile. "It is what attracted me to Francesco's father, the sense of duty, and, I think, you to Francesco." Another veiled question?

"Yes," I answered, "I believe that the fulfilling of the responsibilities laid upon us is the path to our own personal fulfilment. And I admire those that follow their given path."

"Then you admire my son's devotion to his duties?" Now what did that question mean? It sounded like a trap but I decided to stand my ground.

"Yes," I told her firmly, "absolutely I do."

"You will recognise then, from what you know of his background, that Francesco bears a range of responsibilities besides those of his chosen career. To his inheritance," she spread her arms over the frescoes of the Caracciolo possessions, "to family." I nodded, unsure of where this was leading and she sat up and straightened her cutlery.

"Francesco is now forty-six," she proceeded, "and he has yet to fulfil the first responsibility of a first-born son," she fixed me with her ice-blue eyes, "to produce an heir." My face coloured; I could feel it. Despite the force of my will to deny the princess any show of emotion, it was plain as the pink in my cheeks.

"It is not impossible," I heard her say while my mind spun, "that he could sire a child ten, even twenty years hence – although that would do no kindness to the infant, nor its mother, and none to me," she put a hand on her chest, "I don't want to die without seeing my grandson. No. Francesco needs to marry, and it must be soon."

Why was she telling me this? My mind was in turmoil. Men proposed marriage to women, young men sought the permission of their intended's fathers and parent's consulted together, but was this a mother cutting in on her son? Proposing marriage to a prospective daughter-in-law because she did not think he would do it himself? These, I confess, were the unbidden thoughts that flooded my muddled mind but how foolish they were! How laughable in the face of what followed.

"There are a score of eligible girls in Naples in their teens and early twenties who would swoon to be chosen by Francesco. All it needs is for him to be bent to the task; for those who care about him to get him to shift his attention from his ships for a couple of months and secure the family's future." She gave me an unanswerable smile. Had she really no idea how I felt about him? Or was she just cutting me out with the cold steel of the dynastic imperative? I felt humiliated and needed to get away, away from her, the table and the room. I think I blustered some words like 'indeed' and 'I'm sure' and I thanked her for breakfast and then, on the pretext of seeing to Mother, I left her.

'Left her!' '*Fled*' was more like it. I needed to get away from the princess and away from her house. I ran up the two flights of stairs to Mother whom I found back under the covers. I put it to her that, with nothing worse than bruising, she did not need to stay at the Palazzo Caracciolo and we should return straight away to our apartment but Mother would not hear of it. She sighed and groaned and looked pathetic. 'A week's bed rest at least', she quoted Doctor Pico, and I was to go home and fetch her toiletries and a change of clothes – she was immovable and, with no concrete argument to resist her, I went and took a cab to our apartment – that, at least, got me out of the house.

Maria was pleased to see me. She hadn't known why we hadn't been home but then, while I was telling her about the brawl and Francesco, I suddenly burst into tears. I couldn't help it. It was a reaction to my talk with the princess, I knew, but I couldn't tell that to Maria. I let her assume I was upset about Mother. My tears distressed her and their vehemence surprised me myself. What had I felt for Francesco before that breakfast? It was difficult – because of the breakfast – to remember. We had been friends, certainly, and, yes, I think I was falling in love with him but how brightly shine our deepest hopes when once they have been exploded! Francesco's mother had shown me, as in a flash of reflected light, how much of my hopes I had pinned on Francesco and now she had smashed the glass. I sat on the window seat with Maria and quietly wept out my tears and then, together, we collected what Mother and I might need for a few days and packed a bag.

The palazzo was quiet when I got back. A footman was on hand to take my bag but neither Francesco nor his mother was about, for which I was glad. I felt incredibly tired. I had barely slept the night before and since then my strength had drained from me. I mounted the stairs, thinking only of removing my clothes and going to bed for the whole 'few days' but when I opened our bedroom door, who should I see sitting with Mother but Captain Gould. My heart sank. Of all the people I did not want to see that afternoon, Captain Gould was top of my list.

"Cornelia!" Mother cried from her bank of pillows, "Captain Gould is giving me his first-hand account of the Battle of the Nile. *Grrreat events!*" She threw out an arm and beckoned to me. "You must join us." Captain Gould stood and drew up a chair beside his.

"Miss Knight," he bowed, "I cannot tell you how sorry I am about last night. It was unforgivable," he shook his big round head, "really unforgivable. I trust you are feeling better than your poor mother." I raised my hands in appeal.

"Please," I asked, walking round the bottom of the bed, "let us hear no more about last night." And I took the seat nearest Mother.

"I have told him," Mother said, her right cheek now purple and blue, "he has nothing to apologise for. He was the gentleman. He showed that ruffian how an officer behaves." She leaned across me and patted his hand, "We are in the captain's debt, aren't we, Cornelia?"

"Captain Gould was very kind, I am sure," I agreed, "now, can I ask once more that we put last night behind us?" I looked to the captain. He was a similar age and build to Francesco but his curls were fair and his round face as ruddy as a Somerset farmer's. He put a finger to his lips.

"You shall hear no more from me."

"That Commodore Troubridge ..." Mother began, and I despaired.

"Mother!"

"No," she put up a hand, "listen, this is nothing to do with last night. That Commodore Troubridge – Captain Gould has just told me – played no part in the Battle of the Nile." Mother set her jaw and gave me an emphatic nod.

"But he commands *Culloden*. One of the 74s."

"And he ran her aground," Mother nodded again, "as he came into the bay. He never fired a shot and *Leander* and *Mutine* had to waste their time trying to pull him off." Mother chuckled with delight. "There'll be no medal for Mr Troubridge. No wonder he was cross." Mother looked to me to share in her delight at Troubridge's misfortune but really I could not – my head felt like lead – yet still she bore on, "Tell Cornelia how you captured the *Conquérant* Captain," but the captain, bless him, could see what Mother chose not to: that I was dropping with tiredness.

"Perhaps another day, Lady Knight." He gave me a sideways glance and got to his feet. "I will not be accused of tiring you when your doctor has ordered rest." He picked up his bicorn from the bottom of the bed and Mother whined,

"Oww ... but you will come and see us again? I do so want Cornelia to hear about ..."

"I shall be delighted," the captain assured her, and then he looked over to me, "if Miss Knight will also permit it?" I believe I gave him some sign of support which satisfied him then he left.

I slept the clock round that night, but fitfully, drifting in and out of the tangled weed-beds of my folly. A princess and a duchess indeed! Me! An impoverished Protestant Englishwoman already at the limit of her fertility. The idea was preposterous – laughable – if I could laugh – if I did not feel so wretched at my stupidity, for had not the dowager princess, in the gentlest way that she could, done me a kindness? She had not challenged me or banished me; she had invited me, as one intelligent woman to another, to see the reality of Francesco's place in the world and his obligations to it. Why had I not understood that for myself? I was forty-one years old; an educated, travelled, woman of the world, not an empty-headed slip of a thing with no wit to know better. I saw them in my mind's eye, the score of pretty Neapolitan girls with titles as long as their lineages, laughing and dancing in beautiful clothes around a maypole and the maypole was me. Was that then always to be my place? The passive support of others' brighter lives? The dowager princess would be talking to Francesco; telling him as reasonably as she had told me that it was time for him to attend to his duty. I would lose him. We could not remain friends when I loved him.

I woke the next morning to the sound of bells: tinny bells, squeaky bells and loud, booming tenor bells all summoning Naples' monks and nuns to their morning office of Lauds. The bed smelt stale so I drew back the bed curtain and got up and opened the shutters. The sky was already blue and the air fresh, but a golden glow on the mountains threatened another baking day. I stood and looked out over the roofs of the monasteries and palaces and gleaming white churches and the patchwork of ten thousand homes. That kiss. Its promise. Was Francesco deluded then, as well as I? His meaning had been far from clear but his mother's was clear – she had made herself very plain. I looked out over the roofs to our apartment at the top of the Chiaia and I knew that was where I should be. I could not stay another day in Francesco's house. As soon as Mother was awake, I decided, I would tell her that we were leaving and, this time, I would brook no argument.

"What time is it?" Mother was awake.

"Six. A little early but I wanted …"

"I'll just use the pot." Mother rolled off her side of the bed to the floor. I stayed where I was by the open window and waited until she had finished and then, while she rearranged her nightdress back over her ankles, I said,

"You look to be moving better this morning."

"Do I? I don't feel better. I've got a huge bruise." She lifted her nightdress again and looked at her thigh."

"Yes, but you are moving better. I think we should go home."

"Oh no, Cornelia. It's much too soon. Doctor Pico said a week." And she climbed back into bed.

"A week's bedrest, yes, but you don't have to be in bed here." I walked over to the sofa and put on my wrap. "You will be much better in your own bed with Maria looking after you and your own things about you. I shall tell the maids we are leaving." And, ignoring Mother's wails of protest, I went out to look for the maids.

Mother did not go quietly. She feigned fainting and flouncing and stamped her feet but I made it plain, while I dressed, that I was leaving whether she came with me or not. As ever, in such crises, once Mother had accepted that I was adamant, she sullenly acquiesced. Over a simple breakfast in our room, I scribbled a note for the princess and then, with the maids' help, got Mother down a back stair and departed the palazzo unseen. It was an ungracious exit, I know, but through all my confusion, the one thing that I did know was that I must be away and at home.

Our apartment was like a morgue when we got back. Thinking we'd be gone a few days, I'd let Maria go to her family so I had everything to do for myself – the unpacking and putting away, settling Mother and then thinking about what we might eat – but it was no bad thing – occupation is balm to a troubled mind – and when Sir William called in the afternoon, he too was a welcome distraction.

I took him into Mother while I made us some tea. She would give him her version of Saturday night's events, which

I did not want to hear so, when the tea was made, I took it into the morning room and waited for Sir William there. When he came through, he pulled the door shut behind him.

"Lady Knight is settling down for a rest."

"I thought she would. She has just had her posset and it soon sends her off."

Sir William came and took the wing chair across the hearth from me and I poured the tea. I did wonder what Mother had said to him after being knocked to the ground in his house while defending a drunken youth who'd insulted his wife. What could she have said? I hardly knew what I could say. I passed Sir William his tea and we drank in silence and then, both at once, I said something like 'she'll soon be up and about' and Sir William said 'thank God she is no worse' whereupon I gave him the floor.

"Tell me about the rest of the evening. We left early of course."

"Oh," Sir William stroked his fingers across his forehead, "long. I am no slouch at entertaining, Cornelia, but really," he shook his head, "the ball – three orchestras in three ballrooms – went on until after three and then there was supper. I saw dawn in; whenever that was."

Though my mind was still fogged with Francesco, I was determined to show a firm front.

"So, everyone enjoyed themselves." I took up my tea.

"The fracas was unfortunate, but spirits were high weren't they, and our victorious officers were not going to let young Nisbet spoil their celebration."

I marvelled at Sir William. The 'fracas' as he styled it was the direct consequence of his own wife's licentiousness and yet he seemed untroubled by it. I marvelled even more when next he said,

"I was so pleased that Emma managed to enjoy it. She really did put an enormous effort into all the events of last week – and the fortuity of Sir Horatio's fortieth birthday …" he smiled and opened his palms to me, "it was the fitting climax." He reached for his tea and took a sip.

I was incredulous. Emma? Enjoy it? I had never seen a woman so publicly humiliated but Sir William hadn't finished,

"Emma is rather enjoying the whole thing, you know, organising great events, being the centre of attention. That kind of thing means a lot to a woman of Emma's background and now, with the hero of all Europe in her lap, I think she finds the whiff of high influence quite heady." He shook his head and chuckled. "I look forward to seeing where it leads."

There was a knock at the front door. I got up and went out to the lobby to answer it while Sir William, unsure what to do in a house with no servants, hovered on the rug with his cup and saucer.

It was Francesco.

"Cornelia. What has happened?" He burst across the threshold into our little lobby. "I thought you were staying till your mother was better. I went up to see you. They said you had left without a word, by a street door." His questions cannoned off the walls like trapped birds – too many – too quickly – in too small a space – I could not think what to say, then Sir William appeared with his cup and saucer.

"Francesco, my dear fellow," he gave him a cheery smile, "well met, well met!" Francesco was taken aback – he had not expected Sir William – there was a hiatus until Sir William said, "Should we not invite him in?"

"Yes, of course, both of you ..." I pushed my fingers through my hair, trying to gather myself. "Go through, go through," and I ushered them into the morning room.

"I think your journey might have been wasted," Sir William told Francesco, "the patient is taking her nap."

"But she is alright? Lady Knight?"

"Mother is very tired," I told him, "she will get the rest she needs here, in her own bed." Francesco looked baffled. His face was full of questions that I was not going to let him ask. "I have just made some tea," I told him, "if you will sit down with Sir William I shall fetch you a cup."

I left the men and hurried down the corridor to the sanctuary of the kitchen. I felt shaky. I could not face Francesco alone, not today, not in that questioning mood. I took down a cup and saucer, taking my time so that the men might engage in conversation, and it was only when I was sure that they had, that I felt safe to re-join them.

"I sail for Malta on Thursday," Francesco was telling Sir William, "sent in support of the English blockade. I wish to God Nelson would go himself and take the rest of his ships with him. Naples' neutrality is in tatters."

I poured Francesco's tea and put it on the table beside him. He shot me an urgent look but then Sir William said,

"Hear, hear! Get Nelson back at the French. Leave Naples in peace," and I went and sat in the window, out of Francesco's line of sight.

Sir William chatted on, unaware of how one-sided the conversation was but I was aware of it; I could feel the power of Francesco's attention – even sitting behind him – he was desperate to turn round and interrogate me and only waited for the chance. It thrilled me to feel Francesco's power –

thrilled and frightened me because I doubted my will to resist him. I watched him from my window-seat, listening to Sir William: the straight nose and firm jaw, the weathered face and dark, tight curls. He was beautiful, but my attachment ran deeper than that. If his nose had been broken and his hair gone, I should still have loved him because he had captured my heart. Wherever Francesco went for the rest of his life, I knew, my heart would go with him – but the rest of me could not. In a few days' time, he and my heart would sail south, our parting would be complete, and the rest of me would have to endure.

"No, the Austrians won't," Sir William was saying, "I am quite sure of that. Not unless Naples is attacked first."

"Then that is the hope I shall cling to." Francesco rose from his chair and turned to me. "Shall we see if Lady Knight will receive me now?" His face was set and his eyes spears but I was determined to withstand him. My story about Mother wanting her own bed was my only excuse for leaving the palazzo and I was not going to let Mother explode it.

"She will still be asleep," I told him. "She always sleeps for an hour after her posset." Francesco's eyes were so fierce I turned from them. "I will not wake her."

"Quite right, quite right," Sir William too now rose to his feet, "I think we should leave the ladies in peace, eh Francesco? I shall walk down the hill with you. Or are you in your carriage?"

"I am, but I must go on somewhere." Francesco's eyes remained on me.

"That's quite alright. I prefer to walk." Sir William smiled and looked about him. With no servant in the apartment, he was now unsure how to leave.

"Let me get you your hat." I led him out to the entrance hall and gave him his hat and Francesco followed us. I opened the door and thanked Sir William for calling and, while he descended the stairs, I stood with my hand on the door, waiting for Francesco to follow but he didn't, he remained in the hall.

"We have to talk, Cornelia." I stayed holding onto the door and I think I said,

"Do we?"

"Why did you run away like that?"

"We did not *run away*." I tried to laugh but the attempt sounded foolish.

"What is it that's upset you?"

"I am not upset. It is just that Mother likes her own familiar bed and, now that we know nothing is broken …"

"Cornelia, please, do not dishonour me by lying to me." He moved towards me and I averted his eyes. "Let me help you. Whatever it is, just tell me." He lifted my chin and made me look at him. "If something happened to you in my house then I need to know." His closeness was unbearable – his concern was unbearable – his tenderness … my heart heaved, my tears spilled and the words,

"Ask your mother," burst from me.

"Ask my mother?" He let go my chin. "What do you mean, 'ask my mother'? Ask her what?"

"Please." I could not see for my tears. I put my arm across his back and pushed him towards the door. "Please, leave us, please." I could not speak to him. All I wanted was to get him out before he could say any more.

"Cornelia! Don't turn from me." He tried to resist but I pushed him out of the door. "Let me put things right.

Whatever it is, just tell me and we shall make it right." Then, as I shut the door against him, he called back, "Please, Cornelia, I love you!"

I ran into the morning room and shut the door. Then I ran up the corridor, shutting each door behind me until, in the kitchen, where no voice could reach me, I sat on the stool and wept at my folly.

CHAPTER SEVEN

Francesco called again the following day but I told Maria not to admit him. Then, on the Thursday, when he sailed for Malta, there was a letter from him which I burned without opening because there was nothing Francesco could say that would not hurt me. *He loved me*! He should not have said that. And what had I been thinking all summer to fall in love with him? We were both in our forties! We were not children, blind to the consequences of flights of passion, we were supposed to know better, and we did know better, so what were we both thinking of? The answer is that we were not thinking at all. We had, like children, merely sauntered onto a bowered path without bothering to see where it led. *Cornelia, I love you*. Those words he shouted through the door were not just words, I knew that, but there are only two consequences of falling in love: one is marriage and the other is ruin. I had seen it too many times. Europe is littered with ruined women who had allowed themselves to be loved by men who could not marry them – or worse – men who should not but did marry them, like Prince Augustus and Augusta Murray in Rome, and his brother George and Mrs Fitzherbert in London – and they, men at the pinnacle of society. No wonder the nobility and their lessers feel free to love where only ruin can follow. I must have been sleep-walking to have travelled so far with Francesco. Perhaps, in my defence, after a lifetime of disappointment, I had felt free to flirt with happiness, confident in the knowledge that it would, as ever, elude me. Such a yielding fatalism is, I would contend, permissible in a spinster but in a man who commands the consequences of his actions there can be no such excuse, and the declaration of a love whose outcome could not possibly be marriage is a cruelty. And marriage between us was impossible; his mother had been right; his duty to his family was inescapable. He did not have the liberty to fall in love with Cornelia Knight. He needed to find a wife appropriate to his station who would bear him sons and whichever way you look at it Cornelia Knight could never be that wife. Set aside religion – if you could – and social background – I was forty-one years old and, surely, beyond the time when I could bear children. I will not pretend that when I heard the words *I love you*, I was not affected; the words hit me like a cannon ball and, had I been weaker, I might have succumbed, but Francesco's love, however genuine, could never bring me anything, in the end, but despair and so I resolved, as he sailed south, to detach myself from him and return to the life I had known.

I spent most of that October in the cellars of the Palazzo Sessa. With the political ground weakening and Naples' neutrality tottering, Sir William decided to pack up his treasures and he asked me to help. All his pictures and collections from the palazzo and other properties were assembled in the cellars and, for several weeks, I checked the items against the inventory and directed a small army of packers. It was a practical absorption for me but the mind runs deeper than the practical and all the time I was working I was thinking of Francesco – where he was and what he was doing and whether he was thinking of me. I didn't enjoy being so consumed by him; it was a torment. Whatever I was doing, he was a film on my eyes, a humming in my ears and his essence misted the air – I loved him – I could not help it and, with the political clouds darkening, I feared for him. I ought to have feared for myself as well, and for Mother, but somehow I did not. One day at a time was as far as I could see.

"A damnable business!" Sir William came down, one day, to see how I was getting on. We were standing beneath one of the iron grilles that light the former monastery's labyrinthine undercroft and, as we surveyed the shambles of timber, straw and antiquities, he gave me a tired smile. "It really is very kind of you to do this for me, Cornelia. I should have attended to it weeks ago and now it's to be done in a rush." He folded his arms and frowned at the scene.

"You are expecting the French to invade." He lifted his head and looked down his nose at me.

"You don't think we have given them sufficient cause? France sees the fleet that destroyed her own given shelter in Naples Bay and she follows Naples' preparations with Austria for a joint declaration of war so why should she not strike first? Such a shame. Such a beautiful land." He cast down his eyes over his folded arms and I felt for him: a long and fruitful part of his life could be drawing to its close.

"I think you love Naples better than England, don't you, Sir William?"

"No, no, no," he tutted, "I could never say that, no, England is my home." He thought for a moment. "Shall we say, Naples has been my garden? Yes," he agreed with himself, "my walled garden in which I have passed my happy days peaceably cultivating its beauties while, beyond its walls, the world sinks into madness." He looked up at me. "I get a sense that you understand Naples too, Cornelia – how special it is."

"Yes, it is special, and I hope there won't be war." I sat down on the edge of a packing case and Sir William joined me.

"I was a soldier once, when I was a young man," he confided, "in the Foot Guards, fighting the Dutch. I don't think I was particularly talented but I saw action and valour; I also saw cruelty and depravity sufficient to make me try, in my small way, to devote the rest of my life to peace." He gave me a sad smile and I returned it. "You know what is the magical thing about Naples, Cornelia? In the thirty-five years that I have been here, I have entertained most of the crowned heads of Europe and their Grandees – English, French, Russian, Prussian and the rest – when, at any one time, one of them was at war with another and yet here, in Naples, they were as peaceful as the lotus eaters of old." He smiled now with pride. "That is the magic of Naples: she makes people nicer. It is something in the climate and the sheer beauty of the place; Naples deserves to be left in peace but …" and now he frowned, "shall I tell you the worst of it? Poor Naples, innocent Naples, after her decades of tranquillity, is to be put to the sword because of the actions of my own countrymen. Nelson is ordered to make his headquarters here, use it as a base for harrying the French, besieging Malta and, most ominously I fear, giving support to Naples' connection with Vienna." He looked out across the packing cases. "So ends the career of a peacemaker."

With the threat of war gathering daily, Mother was more determined than ever to quit Naples and Sir William packing his treasures suggested an opportunity: *were the cases to be shipped to England? If so, how?* And, *how could she get to go with them?* Dutiful daughter that I was, I put Mother's questions to Sir William but he had shaken his head; he was making what preparations he could but Nelson had promised him nothing. This was not the answer that Mother had wanted, of course, and, though her bruise still glowed on her cheek, she got dressed and went down to the Palazzo Sessa herself. She took up her vantage point again with Mrs Cadogan at the card table looking out into the hall. Mother did not know many of the officers – Troubridge and Berry she avoided – but then when Nelson himself came through, she pushed Mrs Cadogan out, hoping that she, Emma's mother, might have some sway, but Nelson gave her the same answer that he'd given Sir William: he had no ships bound for home. Again, this was the wrong answer for Mother so when, a day or two later, Captain Gould walked past, Mother hooked him with a loud halloo and decided to play him long: she invited him to dinner.

"What on earth did you do that for?" I asked her, because we had never had gentlemen to dinner before, not in Naples at least.

"Because he has a ship."

"No he doesn't have a ship. He commands *Audacious*, one of King George's ships; it is hardly the same thing. If Nelson says that none of his ships are going to England, I don't think your giving Captain Gould dinner will persuade him to cut and run with you."

"Cornelia!" Mother snapped back. "I am doing what I can here to save our lives. It would be nice if you did not resist me. Captain Gould likes you, you are the same age and you both like books. I shall expect you to be encouraging of him."

Encouraging of him! That was a euphemism I didn't wish to unpick! I could abide Captain Gould in general company but I had no wish to know him better – and I hoped he would not discover how much fuss Mother was making. Deciding upon a traditional Englishman's dinner, she had persuaded Mrs Cadogan to prepare a steamed beef pudding for him – and a custard – and a simnel cake – with instructions to Maria on how they should be served. Then, on the evening of the dinner, Mother laid out my buttercup print with the maroon sprigs and my maroon bandeau – *tints to set off my chestnut curls* as she told me. The ghost of Adolphus Funnell shimmered before me!

Captain Gould wore his dress uniform and, seeing his big face wedged into his collar, I could see what had inspired Mother's menu. He seemed a little unsure of himself at first, as well he might, not knowing why he had been invited, but after a glass of dry Marsala and Mother's customary opening on the parallels between an officer's career and my father's, he began to relax and his eyes to move towards me. I pretended not to notice. As long as Mother kept talking, I decided, I could sit quietly by. I might have been dressed to impress Captain Gould but I would not be offering him encouragement, I had made up my mind about that, Mother could manage him herself.

Mother was still talking when we moved through to dinner. I was never quite happy with our dining room: it was too small and too plain and our second-hand furniture from Rome too severe for Naples, but our bits of silver looked well, Mother had done her best, but, when we sat down, it seemed her efforts might have been in vain. In answer to Mother's tentative enquiry about the future movements of *Audacious,* Captain Gould told her briskly,

"We sail for Malta on Monday, to join the Valetta blockade."

"The Valetta blockade!" Mother exclaimed. "But blockades last for months, sometimes years." We were eating the beef pudding, which looked awful but tasted divine.

"I think I am being punished for *Guillaume Tell* and *Généreux*," said the captain, sprinkling salt over everything.

"The ships that got away from the Nile?"

"Yes, *Guillaume Tell* is trapped in Valetta harbour and I think Nelson wants me to stand off looking at her, contemplating my sins."

"Your sins?" asked Mother, "surely Nelson does not blame *you* for her escape?"

"He has to blame someone. He says I robbed him of his victory."

"And did you?"

"No."

"Then why does he say that?"

"I will not bore you with the entire battle," the captain took a drink of his wine, "it raged all night, but during the morning, Nelson saw *Guillaume Tell* and *Généreux* setting sail and he signalled me to give chase. I was taking the surrender of *Conquérant* at the time and though I set what sails I still had, I was on the landward side of the action and boxed in. There was nothing I could do."

"Hardly cause for blame," I suggested.

"Very harsh," Mother agreed, "but then Nelson does seem to be a demanding officer; demanding of his men and of himself – I mean, look at him – the poor man is a ruin."

"Then perhaps Admiral Nelson takes on too much to himself," I suggested.

"By which you mean, dear?"

"Trying to get Naples to declare war on France. It's not his business. I would have thought he had enough to occupy him without playing politics."

"We must throw everything we can against the French," said the captain, who was enjoying his beef pudding, "it all helps."

"Helps who?"

"Helps us." He jabbed the heel of his fork against his chest. "Helps the fight against the Regicides."

"But war won't help Naples."

"It will help the Queen of Naples. She needs to avenge the murder of her sister."

"But that's exactly my point, Captain. Don't you see? That has nothing to do with the Neapolitans?"

"She is the Queen of the Neapolitans," he answered, his mouth over-full, "she and Ferdinand rule. They have the right to do what they wish with their forces and if Nelson can persuade them to throw them against England's enemy, I say that's good use of his time."

"But is it, Captain?" I persisted, "a skilled naval commander Nelson may be, but he is no diplomat, diplomacy is another business entirely, and he should know that."

"Well, our ambassador here has failed in that department, don't you think? From what I hear, he has been too soft for too long with these people and the strong language of an English admiral might just be what's needed."

"So," I said, feeling the heat rising in my cheeks, "Nelson is now representing the British government here is he?"

"Er, Cornelia dear ...?" Mother kicked me beneath the table. "I am sure Captain Gould thinks politics poor talk for the dinner table and, in any case, best left to the men."

"I agree," I told her, "please tell that to the queen and Emma Hamilton." Mother, fuming, returned to her guest.

"I think what my daughter is trying to impart to you, Captain Gould, is that we are worried; terribly worried. We are just two poor ladies you see – the daughter and widow of an English admiral – stranded far from our home. This talk of war is frightening to us; we do not know what we should do." Mother put her hand to her breast and fluttered her eyelids. "Should we feel safer now that our ships are here? Or more fearful? Should we remain in Naples, or flee? We are completely unprotected, Captain, and helpless to know." She put her free hand on his. "You will have a mother I am certain, do you also have a sister?"

"Only brothers, Lady Knight, and my mother is dead."

"Oh. Oh dear. I am sorry to hear that, but can you imagine, Captain, if my daughter and I were your mother and sister – if you had a sister – what then would be your advice to us?" Captain Gould took up his napkin and wiped his mouth.

"Unless you have very strong connections here, Lady Knight, I would advise you to leave, and the sooner the better. Let us not beat about the bush: Naples will soon be a theatre of war." My heart stopped. He was so emphatic – and in a position to know. Suddenly, as an overwhelming need, I wanted Francesco. He would settle this madness. He had always insisted that Naples need not go to war and he had argued it in the councils of state. Was that then why he'd been sent away? So the queen and Nelson could prepare a war?

"But how can we leave?" Mother gripped the captain's hand. "Sir William and Admiral Nelson both say there are no ships." The captain hesitated.

"Well, as you are navy," he dashed me a guarded look, "there is the wounded ship. Sir William probably won't know about it and Nelson won't want to arouse any impossible hopes among you ex-patriots but a ship will be taking our wounded home, within the next two or three weeks." Mother flashed me an excited look.

"Which ship?"

"It isn't decided yet."

"But when will it be decided? Who should I speak to? Admiral Nelson?"

"No, don't say a word to Nelson. You would get me into terrible trouble and he would deny it anyway. Leave it with me. I will see what I can do."

And so Mother achieved her purpose. How many times in her life had she not? She was a tiny little mite of no great education or family and yet here she was at seventy-three battling alone in some corner of the world against the Fates, ambassadors and the navy and, it would seem, winning. But it was not the victory that I wanted. Passage to England would be Mother's hopes met but not mine. What was England to me? My heart, even my broken heart, was in Naples.

With the hunting season started, Sir William was away with the king for days on end and, in his absence, Lady Emma had the palazzo transformed into a military headquarters. Nelson's most private audiences were held in his suite on the top floor but Emma had also cleared ground floor rooms for the more general use of his staff. English and Neapolitan officers, naval and military, tramped in and out at all hours and their boisterous swagger left no doubt as to the imminence of action. I was at the palazzo when General Mack arrived. Lieutenant-Marshal Carl Freiherr Mack von Leiberich, to give him his full style, was a gift to Maria-Carolina from her son-in-law and nephew, the Emperor of Austria, while he made up his mind what to do. When I heard his cavalcade thunder in, I ran up from the cellar to watch. Five gorgeous carriages flanked by a troop of caparisoned outriders delivered Mack and a score more Austrian officers to parley with Nelson. This was not, as the world might have supposed, an Austrian military delegation; it was the arrival of the men who were to take over from the Neapolitan generals the leadership of their own army. After placing her trust in the English at sea, this was Maria-Carolina's final insult to Naples' military elite.

Sir William was increasingly impotent against the hastening tide. I know, because he told me. With no other sympathetic ear to turn to, he shared his anxieties with me. The Turks, he told me, were embarking ten thousand Albanians to join a Neapolitan invasion of the Papal States and a Russian fleet was on its way to defend Sicily. London was not willing to commit her ships without an Austrian declaration – which was still not forthcoming – but in Naples the die had been cast: with or without direct orders, Nelson had promised support.

I was proud to have Sir William's confidence and, in return, I shared one with him. On one of his visits to the cellar, I told him about the wounded ship.

"We could embark your collections on it," I suggested, "short of burying the crates in the ground, it could be our last chance to save them."

"I don't think the saving of my collections will be much of a priority for Admiral Nelson," Sir William observed, gazing out over the crates.

"Surely so, if he knows how important they are to you, and to England, to the British Museum?" Sir William shook his head.

"No. Admiral Nelson is not susceptible to antiquity's charms."

"Nor to Lady Hamilton's?" I was surprised I'd dared say that but a twinkle entered Sir William's eye and he gave me a boyish smile. He pondered for a moment.

"Two weeks you say?"

"That is what I'm told."

"Then we must catch that ship, and you and your Mother go with it." He took my hand between both of his. "This adventure of theirs will end in disaster, I'm sure of it." His brow darkened. "It will be terrible. Thousands in Naples will die. No one will be safe. You must settle your affairs, Cornelia. If I can get my crates onto that ship, you and your mother must sail with them."

I walked home that afternoon. It was nearly November and a cold mist was creeping into the city from the sea but I needed to walk to clear my head. The narrow canyons of the Chiaia were thronged with people – more peddling their wares than buying them, it seemed to me – each raising his voice above the rest until it took flight into song, always, in Naples, there was song. Is it ironic or obvious, I wondered, that the teeming Lazzaroni, who had nothing, should be happy? Some said they were a distinct race, like gypsies, whose origins were unknown. They disdained possessions, living in winter in the catacombs and in summer al fresco on the Mergellina waterfront where they basked and fished and groomed each other while all the time they sang. They were a rabble, the Lazzaroni, but a rabble constrained by two passions: their love of the Church and of their king.

Sixty thousand happy rogues! Would they be happy next month, I wondered, as I walked among them? Or at the turn of the year? And would they still be sixty thousand? *Thousands will die*, Sir William had said. *Die.* Such a limp word; as if dying were as peaceful as closing a book but if the French came, how would those thousands die? Should not that thought be on the minds of those preparing for war? And for their own sakes too? How many of those young officers with their pretty uniforms were facing ugly deaths? And Francesco ... Francesco ...

Five weeks had passed, by then, since he had left and every minute I still ached for him. Did I want that, I asked myself, as I turned out of an alley into the Via Toledo? Always to carry that ache? Because, however much I wanted Francesco, I knew that I could not have him. There was nothing left for me in Naples now except heartache, loneliness and the real possibility of a violent death. Sir William had been right: I had to leave, and for Mother's sake too. Even if I wanted to stay in Naples, I could not, because Mother had made up her mind to leave and my duty was to her. By the time I had reached our apartment, my mind was clear: if we were offered passage to England, we would take it.

The army was assembled on the plain outside St Germano, sixty miles north of Naples. In a matter of weeks, Naples' fifteen thousand regulars had been augmented by thirty-five thousand recruits – some forced levies, the rest from the gaols because the queen did not trust volunteers.

Conjuring up what justification they could for attacking an ally, the Court and Church declared the adventure a Holy Crusade, its rightness was proclaimed from every pulpit in the land and sufficient fervour generated to excite several hundred young gentlemen to purchase commissions in the new army. Ferdinand, so necessary for popular support, was also pressed into the venture. He was proclaimed Defender of the Faith and Champion of Italian Liberty and put into uniform at the army's head. He, the queen and the Hamiltons all decamped to St Germano to watch the army being worked up, leaving Naples to worry and Mother and me to start packing.

I saw *Colossus* coming into the bay through the telescope. The arrivals and departures of English 74s were such a familiar sight by then that I thought little of it, until the evening, when two notes arrived at our door. One of them was in Francesco's hand and addressed to me; the other was in an unknown hand and addressed to Mother. Mother opened hers and read it to me.

Dear Lady Knight,

I am arrived at Naples from the Malta blockade where I received representation from Captain Gould of *Audacious* that you and your daughter require passage to England. I understand that you are widow and daughter of the late Rear-Admiral Knight. If you are requiring such passage, it might be practicable, if you could confirm it to me in person, on *Colossus*, by tomorrow dusk – and in the strictest confidence.

I am & c.
Murray

"There," Mother thrust the note at me, "what did I tell you? He has done it again! Our guardian angel, Captain Gould, has saved us again!" I slipped Francesco's note into the book I was reading and took Mother's from her. I tried to make sense of Captain Murray's words but the presence of the note in my book so flooded my mind that I found it hard to focus. *Passage might be practicable.* So, there it was. After the weeks of conflicting fears, hopes and anxieties, there in my hand was our passage home. It read like a sentence of death.

Captain Murray was brisk but courteous. He made it plain that his priority was the comfort of the hundred or more wounded seamen he was transporting home but he showed us a cabin that he said could be cleared for us. It was situated off the wardroom on the gun deck and no bigger than a cupboard but its partitions were of timber and it would suffice. Captain Murray could not say exactly when he would sail because *Colossus* needed repairs, but he hoped by the end of the month, which was three weeks.

Before we left *Colossus,* I scribbled a note for Sir William and dropped it in at the Palazzo Sessa on the way home. I wanted him to know that the 'wounded ship' had arrived, but when I got home, there was a note from him offering me the same intelligence. I walked over to the morning room window and looked down at *Colossus* in the naval dockyard. Was Murray Charon, I wondered, and our passage across the Styx? It felt so. My fate was slipping away from me, our departure was a looming fact and there could be no turning back. That evening, I opened my note.

Dearest Cornelia,

I met Captain Gould today in conference on *Audacious* with other captains on the blockade – including Murray. I listened to their conversation with disbelief. I cannot believe that, after my letter, you want to leave Naples. I know that you received my letter because I delivered it myself. Every day I have waited for your reply until now I am sick with worry. I know that you will have replied – it is not in your nature not to – I can only blame the English navy, which has frustrated this voyage from the start. Even the orders were strange. Transporting arms and foodstuffs to the Maltese nationalists was never a task for a flagship. Naples has no interest in Malta and the orders were not signed by the Navy Minister, as is usual, but by the queen herself. Since I arrived on station, my attempts to land my cargoes have been frustrated time and again by the English staff. I am sent to rendezvous where there is no one to meet me, or to another where it is impossible to land. Their intelligence tells them that such-and-such partisans are infiltrated, so for yet more days I am told to stand off. I have serious questions about this voyage. Mine is the only Neapolitan vessel among a dozen English, I am doing nothing they could not do themselves – and this while my country is being dragged into war. Believe me, Cornelia, I will be home the minute I have delivered my cargoes and you must wait for me. I love you and believe you love me. I can offer no more than I did in my letter and implore you to do nothing precipitous.

Wait for me. I beg you.
Francesco

I never read Francesco's first letter so I did not know what it contained. This second letter upset me – as I knew it would – but it only confirmed that nothing had changed: I knew that Francesco loved me and I loved him but, whatever had been in his first letter, he could not marry me because his duty to his family forbad it and Francesco would do his duty. I folded the note and put it back into its envelope. It would be my departing memento.

A few days before we were due to sail, the Hamiltons and Nelson returned to Naples from reviewing the troops at St Germano. It was a low time: Sir William foresaw only disaster and I was still dreading leaving but Nelson at least was cheerful; he had just received news of his elevation to the peerage and, to mark it – and also Mother's and my departure – Sir William hosted an impromptu dinner. Nelson's elevation was not unexpected after his victory at the Nile but, after Sir William had made the toast, Lady Emma fizzed with indignation.

"A barony!" she exclaimed as we regained our seats. "If I was King George, I would make you the most puissant Duke Nelson, Marquis Nile, Earl Alexandria, Viscount Pyramid and Baron Crocodile so that posterity might honour you in every degree." Lady Emma was flushed with the heady mixture of hubris and wine and Nelson too was expansive.

"I would never disdain any seat in the House of Lords," he replied, smiling across Sir William, at the head of the table, to Lady Emma opposite. "No officer of my rank has ever been awarded a barony before so I am content with that, and," he raised his glass as if in toast, "let us also remember that if this wound in my head had been any deeper, Westminster Abbey would have been my abode so I give thanks to King George and to God."

"Well said, Nelson!" Sir William again stood up and raised his glass. "The loyal toast!" And again, we all rose,

"The King!"

Lady Emma's and Nelson's high spirits did nothing for my own nor, I was sure, for Sir William's and, as the Marsala and chocolates went round, I wondered about him. It intrigued me how easily Nelson had elided into his family. There Nelson was, at Sir William's right hand, like an adopted son, while, across from him, sat Emma, playing a role very different from that of an adoptive mother – that role taken up by her own mother sitting next to her. It was an unorthodox family but, it appeared, a contented one – so long as Lady Nelson were ignored.

Nelson was on his feet again. He raised his glass to Sir William, to Emma and then to us all,

"To friendship!" he declared, and then, as we rose once more to join him, the doors at the bottom of the room flew open. Sir William, facing them, was the first to see him.

"Francesco! What timing! Please, come in. Come and join us." Francesco, still in his seaboard uniform, hesitated. Whatever he had expected to find in the dining room, this gathering wrong-footed him – until he saw me. He glared at me so fiercely, I couldn't face him. I regained my seat with the other ladies and gave him my back.

"Yes, Admiral," Nelson agreed, still standing with Sir William, "join us. Tell us how the blockade fares." On Sir William's nod, a footman drew out the chair beside Mrs

Cadogan but Francesco ignored it and advanced instead up my side of the table, halting behind me.

"Your blockade is starving the three thousand French very nicely," Francesco's voice was like flint, "and also every man, woman and child on the island. Your blockade is so successful, Nelson, it is a damned disaster. You either attack the French or you leave them be." Very carefully, Nelson put down his glass.

"Thank you for your advice, Admiral. I am sure I shall consider it." The room went quiet. It was the old antagonism. Sir William reached out to Francesco.

"My dear fellow …" but Francesco gripped the back of my chair.

"It is Miss Knight I have come to see." His coat was brushing my hair and I could feel his breathing. The women, sitting, and the men, standing, all looked at me and I looked up at Francesco. His eyes were spears. I picked up my reticule and rose, whispering to Mother,

"Excuse me a moment," and I followed Francesco out.

He led me downstairs to the small parlour that Mother and Mrs Cadogan liked to occupy. Apart from the glow at the window from the torches in the courtyard, the room was in darkness. I went and stood by the window while Francesco remained by the door.

"Why?" he said. I didn't know what his question meant and didn't answer. "Is it your mother? I know that she wants to go back to England, but I thought you wanted to stay." Francesco's manner was fierce. I did not know what he was thinking but he had mentioned Mother so I hid behind her.

"It is getting too dangerous here, and, yes, I owe it to Mother."

"And to yourself?" He took a step forward. "What do you owe yourself? What about *you*, Cornelia?" He was so intense and so close, he was frightening me. I blurted out,

"We have had this conversation before."

"No, we have not had this conversation. We have not spoken since my letter – to which you never replied – or, if you did, I never got it." He lifted his head at me. "Did you reply to my letter?" I looked away and shook my head. "But why?" He stepped forward again and opened his arms. "I don't understand. It is not like you …"

"I burned it!" I threw the word at him. "I never read your letter."

"But why?" His eyes were wide with disbelief. I tried to answer.

"I will not be your mistress. We cannot be just friends." I met his wide eyes. "And so I must leave."

"Then marry me. That was what was in my letter. I asked you to marry me. And you never replied." He stepped nearer. "I see I must ask you again: Cornelia, will you marry me?"

Was I dreaming? *Marry me*? My head spun. I felt I would faint. I looked round the room for support – for some third party or inanimate sign that might tell me if this was real – and then I remembered what was real. I gripped the back of a chair.

"Did you speak to your mother?" For the first time, Francesco's shoulders relaxed. He dropped his arms and leaned his weight onto one foot.

"I did." He smiled. "I had some very strong words with my mother – and that too was in my letter – I am sorry you burned it – it was well composed." Again, he reached out to me. "Cornelia, I am forty-six years old and master of my own house. It is normal that a mother should want grand-children, I understand that, but I acknowledge no obligation. I have nephews and nieces. My mother has plenty of grand-children already without my giving her more." He gave me a knowing smile. "I'm afraid my mother was being mischievous, and a bit selfish."

"But your mother and you, you are not a normal family. You are the heir to ancient titles and privileges that you have to pass on." I fixed him squarely. "I cannot bear your heirs."

"I don't want heirs," he laughed, "I have never wanted or expected to have children, and as to the titles and privileges, they will pass, on my death, to one of my nephews or nieces. Naples is not like England, you know. Neapolitan titles can pass through the female line as well as the male. That is why we have so many. They hardly ever die out." I looked through the half-light at this man; this lovely man with the hopeful eyes and I grasped, for the first time, that this was real; he could be mine.

"Ask me again," I told him.

"Ask you what?"

"To marry you. You haven't asked me properly." He smiled broadly and threw out his arms.

"Cornelia Knight, please will you marry me?" My heart soared.

"Yes!" I told him, "I will!" and I went and fell into his arms.

We agreed that Francesco would not go back to the dining room and, when I returned, no one mentioned him. Clearly, the other guests' witness of his behaviour had excited more speculation than they cared to share with me and soon afterwards Mother and I left. In the cab, she was less reticent.

"What was that about?" she asked flatly and I told her. There was no point lying or putting her off. If I had tried she would have relentlessly pestered me and why would I? Our engagement was a fact. Her brow had darkened.

"Why?"

"Don't be so silly, Mother. I am not seventeen. He has asked me to marry him because he loves me." She turned in her seat and stared at me.

"But why?"

"Good God, Mother, is it really so hard for you to believe that a man might love me? You try me sometimes, you really do."

"No," she conceded, "but he has been gone for weeks, and he just walks into the room like that … has he been writing to you?"

"No," I fibbed. Mother sat back in her seat.

"Very singular!" She pondered for a few moments while we rumbled along through the darkened streets and I waited for the inevitable next question. She turned to me again, only this time, she looked fearful. "What did you tell him?"

"I told him I would."

Mother slumped back in her seat and looked out of the window. I knew what she was thinking; and once she'd assembled her thoughts to respond, I wasn't sure how I'd reply. She'd be dead set against my marrying a Catholic, she always had been, and the only reason she had allowed my friendship with Francesco was because she thought he could find her a passage, only now, she had found her own passage and, within the week, we would sail. And all the arrangements had been made – our furniture sold and our things packed – and then there was the war. Francesco and

Sir William both foresaw a disaster and, while I was happy to throw in my lot with Francesco, was it right to ask Mother to? All these things, I knew, Mother was thinking but then, when she eventually turned back from the window, she managed to amaze me.

"Prince Caracciolo."

"Yes, Mother."

"He does not seem to practice his religion."

"He is no more religious than we are."

"He doesn't want children?"

"No."

"Then he must love you very much. Why else would he want you?" She rested her hand on my arm. "Marry him, Cornelia. We could do with a wealthy protector."

"But you want to go back to England."

"Did you see the size of that cabin Captain Murray showed us? Six weeks below decks with five hundred crew and a hundred groaning wounded? The Bay of Biscay in December? I should be dead before we arrived."

And so Mother accepted Francesco and *Colossus* sailed without us. I was so proud of her. She would never admit it – she stuck with her own rationale – but she had made her decision to stay for my sake; for my future and my happiness, and I shall always love her for that. Over the next few days she reset her sights onto Naples – reading up on the Caracciolos and making friends with the dowager princess. Any disappointment that the dowager might have felt about our marrying she quietly subsumed beneath her innate good manners and her faith in Francesco's judgement. She invited Mother and me to move in with her but that was not what I wanted. I did not want the world to see me under

Francesco's roof until I had his ring on my finger and so I declined and we stayed on in our bare apartment. It was a tumultuous time and, for Francesco, not just personally. A few days after his return from Malta, he attended a meeting at the Navy Ministry. He went into the meeting elated, but he was not so when he came out. When he came up to our apartment, his face was like thunder.

"This is why they sent me to Malta!" He stalked back and forth over the bare boards. "They have sacked Gallo as Minister of Finance and the Navy and brought back Acton." He darted me a frown. "Another damned Englishman! We Neapolitans are becoming a minority in our own Council of State." I reached out and took him by the arm.

"Please will you calm down?" He stopped his pacing and dropped his head.

"I'm sorry."

"Come and sit down and tell me properly." I drew him over to the window-seat and took up his hand. "Now, who is Acton?"

"I'm sorry, Cornelia, I rave about the English but you know …"

"Yes, of course I know. You are marrying one and your best friend is another, so go on – who is Acton?"

"He's a warmonger, despises the French, a confidant of the queen for donkey's years. She had to drop him when we signed the treaty with France and now she has brought him back to Navy and Finance and they're sending me away again."

"Sending you away? But you've only just got back."

"I know. It's deliberate." He put his free hand over mine, holding it between both of his. "They're keeping me out of

Naples, away from the decision making. If I were not so effective with the crews, they'd probably sack me along with Gallo."

"So, where are they sending you now?"

"Up to Livorno with his lordship."

"You mean Nelson?"

"Mack and Ferdinand are marching the army out tomorrow. No declaration of war or any formality like that, just setting off to invade the Papal States and Nelson is transporting four and a half thousand troops up to Livorno to open a second front. English ships for the troops and me to carry the horses."

"Why do they need you to carry the horses?"

"They don't. It's like Malta. Showing the Neapolitan his place."

"You ought to refuse."

"What?" He gave me a wry smile. "Refuse an order?"

"Did you say Livorno?"

"Yes."

"But Tuscany has a treaty of neutrality with France. Is she too complicit?"

"No. The Tuscans are in for a surprise. But do you think the French will believe that when four and a half thousand troops cross her border?"

The following day, the decision finally came through from Vienna: Austria would stand by her commitment to support Naples if she were attacked, but she could not support Neapolitan aggression. Her sixty thousand troops, that the queen and Mack had confidently expected, would not be put in the field – and nor had Turkey's ten thousand Albanians materialised. Mack's army was on its own but the die was cast, the Livorno flotilla had sailed and there could be no turning back. At dawn on Thursday 22nd November, Ferdinand showed himself before his troops and Mack ordered the advance.

In Naples, we women could only worry and wait. Maria-Carolina gathered the Court and the Hamiltons around her at the royal palace which left the Palazzo Sessa eerily quiet for Mrs Cadogan and Mother and me. The mothers were established friends by then and they passed their time sewing and playing cards but I could not apply myself to anything; I had only one thought and that was Francesco. I paced the floor of the long gallery, or gazed from its windows to the rain-swept bay until, on the sixth day, his sails appeared off the Punto di Posillipo and he came back. He looked better than when he had left. The troops and horses had been successfully landed, the voyage had been uneventful and he'd had time to think.

"Do you remember, in June, when we walked by the sea at Posillipo?" We had just finished dinner in the dining room of the Palazzo Sessa. Mother and Mrs Cadogan had retired to the small parlour, leaving Francesco and me to ourselves.

"Of course. I shall never forget that day." He gave me a warm smile.

"Nor I." He was relaxed after his first meal ashore. He leaned back in his chair, fingering the stem of his wine glass. "We talked about politics, do you remember?" I nodded. "And an officer's duty."

"I remember the conversation very well; duty above politics."

"That's right. Duty to country above politics." He lifted his glass and took a sip of his wine. "But what if my country were usurped?"

"You mean a coup d'état?"

"No, no. That would be straight forward, unlawful, indefensible." He put down his glass on the table and looked at it. I could see where his thoughts were leading: to his being side-lined by Nelson, and Mack taking over the army. I sat and waited for him to tell me but he did not, he remained staring at his glass, so I helped him.

"It is a common enough thing for states to employ foreign officers," I told him, "Ferdinand is at the head of his army, he is not usurped."

"And who is at the head of his navy? Acton? Nelson? It certainly isn't me. Is the navy not usurped?" I laid my hand on his on the edge of the table. "I'm sorry, Cornelia," he shook his head, "but everything about this campaign is so completely illegal."

"I know," I squeezed his hand, "the whole adventure is a great folly but doesn't Nelson's folly in getting involved in politics reinforce the officer's code?" Francesco looked puzzled. "Don't do it? Stay out of politics? Do your duty in whatever circumstances? No one told you it would be easy, Francesco." He smiled, then leaned over and kissed me.

"I love you, Cornelia Knight."

"Thank you. And I love you too."

Two days later, we received the dispatch we'd been waiting for. It was not the official dispatch; that arrived a day or two later, it was a letter from a Neapolitan officer friend of Francesco's and Francesco brought it to me at the Palazzo Sessa.

My good friend.

I write from Rome! I rode in triumph this morning into the Eternal City only four horses behind King Ferdinand. The joy of the people and their acclamations had to be seen to be believed and I shall count this day as one of the greatest of my life – but it is how we achieved our success that is the real story – the people here are calling it a miracle.

The opening of the campaign (can it be only one week ago?) could not have been less auspicious. Some of us thought that the withdrawal of the Austrians would have been enough to abort, or at least postpone the advance but not a bit of it; we marched as planned on the 22nd. And then there was the weather: steady rain all day and then, in the afternoon, we came to the River Malfa. I am not on the staff, so I don't know how it happened, but I would have thought that fifty thousand men and their baggage crossing a major river, on the very first day of a campaign, might have warranted a military bridge but 'no', we were ordered into the swollen waters. The troops were up to their necks and the new recruits in particular were scared out of their wits. The cavalry had to cross too, but it was with the waggons that we really struggled. Both the king's and Acton's carriages got bogged and it took a tremendous effort with relays of mules to pull them across by which time it was dark and we had to leave the baggage waggons on the south bank. No change of uniforms and no hot food. It was a most miserable first night to a campaign – and without troubling the French!

The second day was just as bad: forced march in wet clothes leaving the waggons further and further behind as they struggled, one at a time, to ford the river. Another miserable night, and another forced march and then we met the French. General Championnet, with a light escort, came out to meet our vanguard. The formalities were observed and General Mack requested the French to withdraw all their forces to a position north of Rome and – and this is the miracle – Championnet agreed! On the 29th, exhausted and foot-sore though we were, we marched into Rome without a shot fired! Even as I write, the bells of Rome are ringing and Ferdinand is standing with the Grand Constable Colonna on the steps of the Villa Farnese receiving 10,000 cries of *Long Live the King of Naples*!

Tell all Naples of our success, my dear friend. I go to celebrate now with brother-officers. We can hardly believe it is true!

Yours ever & c.
Luigi di M.

CHAPTER EIGHT

And, as the world now knows, Ferdinand's triumph was not true, it was a chimera, the result of Championnet's tactical withdrawal to buy time to reorganise his forces before chasing the parvenus out. Nor did Ferdinand's brief stint as a conqueror bring him credit. While he and his amateur officers paraded and partied and issued proclamations, the rabble soldiery they had conscripted from the gaols ran amok as despicably as the French had before them. Ferdinand had promised protection to all who submitted to his rule and yet hundreds who had offered no offence to him – French, Jews, Roman Jacobins – were robbed and butchered by his men. Ferdinand himself ordered the pillaging of art treasures not already stolen by the French, and their removal to Naples. Was that then all the invasion had been for?

In Naples, Ferdinand's victory was received with rapture by the Court and the Lazzaroni who danced in the streets and thronged the churches to sing their Te Deums but their joy was remarkably short-lived. Just one week after Ferdinand's triumphal entry into Rome, France formally declared war on Naples and Championnet's hardened veterans swooped. They retook Rome in a day without the slightest difficulty. By good luck or some inkling, Ferdinand was out of Rome at the time, visiting the Duke of Ascoli at his villa at Albano and, when the news was brought to him, he was, by his own admission, terrified. Jettisoning all responsibility for his fifty thousand men, he donned the garb of a lackey and rode pell-mell out of Albano to the waiting carriages where he crouched in the corner of the meanest-looking and ordered it south with all speed.

Championnet took the Neapolitans completely by surprise. Division after division of Mack's army simply collapsed before him. The ten thousand in Rome were taken prisoner on the first day; General San Filippo, commanding nineteen thousand Neapolitans, fled in the face of three thousand French and, in short, it was a rout. The Neapolitan troops, abandoned by their officers and starved for want of supplies, deserted in droves and straggled homeward ravaging the country as they went. The news reaching Naples was received with disbelief but the rout of the army was only part of it: as Championnet swept south, taking town after town in the Abruzzo, hordes of refugees swelled the tide of soldiers heading for Naples with Championnet in full cry behind them. The queen was filled with dread. She had been brought up to expect courage in her family's armies so she was at once bewildered and enraged at Mack's performance. His officers had shown themselves to be inept cowards, her glittering vision of glorious retribution against the Jacobin Regicides had been exploded and she found herself facing her worst nightmare – a second flight to Varennes and all its frightful consequences.

Ferdinand arrived back in Naples on 15th December with Sir John Acton, in whom he had vested emergency powers over every department of state. Their first act was to issue a bellicose edict. All Frenchmen were banished from Naples and their property sequestrated. 'I shall hasten with a mighty army to exterminate them,' the king's edict ran, 'but in the meantime let the people arm, let them succour the Faith, let them defend their king and father who risks his life, ready to sacrifice in order to preserve the altars, possessions, domestic honour and freedom of his subjects. Let them remember their ancient valour.' This potent rallying cry was music to the ears of the Lazzaroni who swarmed in their thousands to the gates of the royal palace to offer themselves to their king. They demanded weapons with which to defend Ferdinand, but the view from the palace windows, of a mob demanding arms, was too much for Maria-Carolina. It evoked too powerfully in her imagination the scenes that had preceded the downfall and violent death of her sister and she refused to let Ferdinand stand by his call. For her, the only option was flight.

Of course, we were not supposed to know that the royal family was planning to flee. If the people on the streets had known, they would have rioted as the queen feared so those of us who did know were sworn to secrecy. Sir William told Mother and me when he asked us to call on him at the Palazzo Sessa. With Nelson back in his top floor suite and the Court in turmoil, the palazzo was again a bustling war room and Sir William conducted us through a mêlée of uniformed officers to the relative peace of his study. With its collections, books and pictures stripped out, the room was a sad sight – an empty shell with the life that had created it sucked from it.

Sir William closed the door and offered us seats on a couple of dining chairs he had brought in and then, as Mother and I sat, he clasped his hands behind his back and started to pace the floor. He had become thinner recently and more stooped and his usually tanned face was grey with worry.

"My dear Lady Knight," he began, "Cornelia, thank you for coming," he frowned at us as he paced by, "you may have heard rumours."

"The city is a hive of rumour," I told him, feeling his discomfort.

"Quite. Yes. It is, isn't it?" He seemed to be struggling to say what he had brought us to hear and Mother shot me an anxious look.

"Do you mean about the army's retreat?" I suggested.

"That is it." He raised a finger at me. "That is where we start. The army, as you say, is falling back quite rapidly, and in disarray. General Mack sees no realistic possibility of rallying it to defend the city." He dashed us a severe look. "My understanding is that the French could be at the gates in a week, so the decision has been made: the royal family, the Court, the Diplomatics and the English community are to be evacuated to Palermo."

"To Palermo!" I don't know what I had expected but I did not expect that. "Does Francesco know about this? Has he approved the plan?" Sir William put up his hands.

"That I cannot say, Cornelia. My concern is only for the English."

"But when?" Mother asked him. "How?"

"There is a plan," Sir William went on, "and three things I must tell you. Firstly:" he raised a finger, "please tell no one," he glared at me as he paced, "*no one*. You shall receive your instructions in due time. Secondly:" his eyes were now on the floor, "be ready: either here at the embassy, or in your own apartment with just one trunk and, please, from now on, go nowhere else; if you need for anything, send a servant. Thirdly:" he raced now to be rid of the words, "transportation.

You will be conveyed to Palermo with the royal family and Lady Hamilton and myself aboard *Vanguard* so," finally, he stopped pacing and attempted a smile, "I hope you will see that Britannia is doing her best for you."

"But how will we know?" Mother asked him.

"From me." Sir William placed his hand on his chest. "*You*, Lady Knight, and you, Cornelia, are, I assure you, my first concern. If you can bear with me for a day or two, all will be revealed and, I am sure, be well." Clutching her reticule in her lap, Mother frowned up at Sir William.

"I do not doubt your goodwill, Sir William, but you have so many other responsibilities: the king and queen and their children, their possessions, the Court ..." but Sir William waved this aside.

"No, no, no, not at all, Lady Knight. Those matters are in the safe hands of Lady Hamilton and Lord Nelson. They are looking after the royal family and the Court, my responsibility begins and ends where it always did – with the English community, and it is one that I shall discharge."

Mother was agog with questions after Sir William had left us; questions that I could not possibly answer and which, in any case, were of no interest to me. I was not interested in Nelson's and Emma's sordid little plans for saving the wretched king and queen who had brought this disaster to Naples; I wanted to know what Francesco thought and what his plans were so I put Mother in the small parlour with Mrs Cadogan and hurried down to the dockyard to find him. He was in his office, his orderly told me, but in conference, so I had to sit and wait in the outer office for half an hour before a dozen officers finally trooped out and I could go in. I threw my arms round his neck and held him to me.

"Hey now, what's this?"

"I need holding." He put his arms around me and we held one another until, slowly, my tensions ebbed and I eased back from him. He put his hand to my cheek.

"Has something happened?"

What could I say? Sir William had told me I was to tell no one. But Francesco? The head of the navy? For a marine evacuation?

"Sir William has offered to evacuate us to Palermo. Mother and me, and the rest of the English community." Francesco raised an eyebrow.

"On an English ship?"

"*Vanguard*."

"*Vanguard*! The flag ship! Then Nelson's going too?"

"I don't know. Don't you know about this?"

"So, it's true." He leaned back onto the edge of his desk and folded his arms. "If Nelson is going, they must be evacuating the Court."

"So, you do know."

"Nobody has told me anything but I guessed, it's written all over their faces. Ferdinand failed his army very badly. The campaign was a disaster – worse – a fiasco, but I never thought he would run away."

I wasn't interested in Ferdinand.

"But where does all this leave us? You – me – your navy?" He frowned and took my hand.

"Sir William's offer is a good one. If the French do take Naples, it could be difficult for anyone with English naval connections. You and your mother will be safer in Palermo."

"And you too? Will you be taking your ships to Palermo?"

"I have no orders and the navy no money. Acton is now Minister of the Navy and Finance and he has emptied the naval treasury and run home to pack. The navy is completely forgotten." He squeezed my hand. "Isn't it incredible? The Court is evacuating *en masse* to Palermo, I have thirty ships in the bay and no orders."

"Then how will they manage it?"

"Nelson's ships and merchantmen I suppose."

"But why?" He shrugged and shook his head.

"I am cut loose – the ghost admiral of a ghost navy – the queen seems to prefer the English."

"But that is insane." Francesco shrugged again.

"It is insane – she is insane – and I really don't mind. In fact, I'm relieved."

"Relieved?" I was astonished. "How, relieved?"

"Well, think about it." He stood up off the desk and took my hands again. "Look what happened to the army. The king and queen gave it to the Austrians who immediately destroyed it. What do you think would happen to the navy if its ships and crews went to Palermo?"

"They would be saved from the French surely." He shook his head.

"There is another way of doing that. No. If the Neapolitan fleet were in Palermo, do you not think that the queen's party would hand it over to Nelson, as they handed the army to Mack, so that Nelson could use it to retake Naples? I shall never let my ships be used against Naples. The ships and Naples are safer staying together."

"Then what is the other way?" He looked puzzled. "You said there was another way of keeping the ships from the French."

"The crews. If the king and the Court are going to look to themselves and their families, I shall advise my crews to do the same – go home – I cannot pay them anyway – melt away and look after their families."

Mother and I did not need Sir William to tell us to keep indoors. The Lazzaroni, enraged at the disgrace brought upon Naples by an army that barred them from its ranks, were determined to show what Neapolitans could do. They took the king's edict at its word. The French embassy was sacked; suspected Jacobins and French citizens too slow to leave were beaten to death or lynched in the street and every day, as more and more refugees poured in, the clamour grew louder for arms to defend the king and themselves. One incident in particular, at the palace gates, seemed to justify the queen's terrors.

On the Friday of the second week of December, another large crowd had gathered at the palace, chanting against the Jacobins and demanding arms. The king's personal messenger, one Ferreri, needing to gain access to the palace, made his way through the crowd to the gates where he made a fatal mistake. He addressed the officer of the guard, on the inside of the gate, in his customary Court French which, being overheard, marked him to the Lazzaroni as French and they attacked him. He was brutally beaten and then, in his maimed state, dragged across the front of the palace to beneath the king's balcony, where, under the king's horrified gaze, he was butchered with knives and his corpse offered up for royal approval.

Mother and I had felt safe at the Palazzo Sessa for the first few days but then the mob turned its appeals to Nelson and the embassy too came under siege. Nelson posted marines with fixed bayonets around the building, day and night, because, if those outside had known what those inside were planning, they would certainly have stormed it. Nelson and Lady Emma were secretly preparing every detail of the royal family's evacuation. At night, after the crowds had dispersed, cases of jewels, plate and money were brought over from the palace for re-labelling as 'salt pork' or 'biscuit' before being forwarded to the English ships. It was an alarmingly risky business. Neither Nelson nor Emma dared to go out, least of all to the palace, for fear of raising suspicion, so a constant flow of secret notes passed between the two buildings – a proceeding about as prudent, it seemed to me, as passing a lighted taper back and forth over an open powder keg. As the tension mounted, Mother and I felt less safe at the Palazzo Sessa and decided we'd be better at home.

Maria had stayed on to look after us but it was a Spartan existence. We had sold most of our furniture when we thought we were going to England and our most necessary clothes and possessions were packed into our single trunk. All we had left to sit on while we waited were the window seats and the wooden chairs from the kitchen but we still had the bed – no one had wanted that – and Mother passed those last days laid in it. I felt awful about Mother. She did not say, but she would have been as aware as I that if it had not been for my love for Francesco, we would have been half way to Gibraltar by then with Naples and her troubles behind us. But Mother did not complain and, when Francesco called to see us, she was welcoming, so perhaps she really did trust him as much as I.

She was taking her nap when Francesco called on the fourth day of our confinement and, as Maria was down in the town, I opened the door to him myself. His face was set and, without a word, he drew me to him and wrapped me in his arms.

"Is Maria out?" he whispered. I nodded.

"And Mother's having her nap."

"Good." He released me and gave a sad smile. I led him through to the morning room where I closed the door to the corridor. When I turned back, he was standing at the window looking down over the city. I joined him, slipping my hand into his.

"Everything is unravelling so fast," he said, looking out. "Ferdinand has locked himself away. Since his fatuous edict he has said nothing, done nothing, no one has seen him. He told the people to fight for him but without arms and without him, so, until the French arrive, the mob has to guess who his enemies are and vent their frustration on them." He turned from the view to me. "It's a slaughterhouse down there, Cornelia. No one with any reputation for enquiry is safe. If you are not of the queen's party, you are a Jacobin, and the queen herself is the worst: every day, she has scores of good, intelligent people arrested, which excites the Lazzaroni to yet further excess. They will be storming the armouries next and who will stop them?"

"Are our friends all safe?"

"No. Jacopo Gianni is arrested, and the Barinelli brothers," he shook his head, "many are arrested."

"And your family?"

"We have closed the palazzo. Mother has moved the household up to Avellino. How safe it is there, we shall have to see but Naples I am afraid …" he broke off, too overcome. I made him sit down with me on the window seat.

"And what about you Francesco?" I took his hand into my lap. "How safe are you?"

"No one is safe. That is why you must leave, Cornelia, and the sooner the better."

"And you must come with me." I needed to force his decision. We were engaged to be married, after all, he had a duty to me.

"I cannot." He looked down at our entwined hands.

"But why? The king and queen have abandoned you, the navy board has abandoned you, you have dismissed your crews, you could be set upon and murdered at any time and the French army is about to sack the city." He looked up at me.

"Will they sack the city? And if they do, won't the city and its people survive it? Life goes on, Cornelia, even through disasters, and what concerns me is what happens to Naples," he let go my hands and stood up, "what happens once the Bourbons are gone and the Lazzaroni's fever burned out. If the French come, they will create order, a rational order, maybe not in a month or six months but," he took my hands and lifted me from the seat, "if the future for Europe is going to be a republican settlement, which seems likely, in whose interest, I ask myself, is it to fight it?" He looked at me with hopeful eyes.

"And your duty?" I asked him.

"Absolutely, Cornelia! Isn't that the entire question – the question I have been struggling with these last weeks and now these events make it clear. I am sworn to the service of my country but what is my country?" His eyes were bright as a schoolboy's. "Is it the half-Spanish, half-Austrian family that has drawn down disaster on Naples and is fleeing with the nation's treasure? Or is it Naples herself and her people? It is a reasonable question to ask, don't you think?"

"A treasonous one."

"No. Not if the Bourbons run away and abandon Naples. That is why I must stay. To do my duty to my country." I looked at this man, this exhilarating, heroic man, so determined to stick to his principles.

"I shall stay with you."

"No." He drew back. "We cannot be sure what will happen. The French may or may not come. Naples could be facing a brilliant future or a calamity." He took up my hands again. "If you love me, Cornelia, then keep yourself safe for me. With a fair wind, Palermo is only two days away and with no French at sea, for the time being, safe for you." He affected a jaunty smile. "Besides," he nodded towards the corridor, "you have your mother to think of. It was generous of her to let *Colossus* sail but I don't think we can ask her to do that twice." He was right about that. Always, there was Mother, but what about him? What about us? A wave of despair swept over me.

"But I might lose you." My voice sounded thin and tearful. He took my face in his hands and brushed my tears with his thumbs. I closed my eyes and he kissed me, and then he said,

"Here, I have something for you." I opened my eyes. He was holding up a ring between his finger and thumb. It was a large ruby set within an oval cluster of diamonds with a halo of small rubies around them. "It had to be rubies," he smiled, "nothing else would do for you." He slid the ring on my finger. I could not speak. I threw my arms round his neck and kissed him.

"Thank you," I whispered, "thank you."

Francesco left me before Mother woke, with the promise to return in the morning but, that night, as Mother and I were preparing for bed, they came for us.

CHAPTER NINE

"Lady Philippina Knight?" The midshipman looked too young to be in uniform.

"No, *Miss* Knight, Lady Knight's daughter." I held up my lamp and saw that he had four seamen with him. They each wore a cutlass, and the midshipman a pistol. I looked down at it.

"No cause for alarm, Ma'am," he reassured me. "I am sent by Admiral Nelson to escort you and Lady Knight to the boat."

This was not what I had expected. I don't know why, but I had imagined it would be Francesco who would come for me, not one of Nelson's midshipmen.

"But my mother and I are getting ready for bed. What time is it?"

"Gone eleven, Ma'am." He looked past me into the morning room. "Do you have your trunk packed?"

"We do, yes, but…" I scanned the sullen faces of the war-hardened sailors and felt a flutter of fear. "Does Admiral Caracciolo know about this?"

"Admiral who, Ma'am?"

"Admiral Caracciolo. The Head of the Neapolitan navy."

"This is nothing to do with the Neapolitans, Ma'am, don't you worry about that. You are in Nelson's hands now."

In Nelson's hands! I did not want to be in Nelson's hands, I wanted to be in Francesco's. I wanted Francesco to take me to Palermo, either that or stay with him in Naples, I could not leave him now. I twisted the ring on my finger and looked down at the midshipman.

"I don't think we will be going."

"Cornelia? Who is it?" Mother, already in night gown and cap, came up behind me. "What is the matter?" She saw the midshipman. "What do you want?"

"Come to take you to the boat, Ma'am. The evacuation. If you would get dressed quickly please." I turned to Mother.

"I cannot go with you; not without Francesco." Mother stiffened.

"Don't talk so soft, Cornelia. This is not the moment. Francesco told you himself, only this afternoon, that you had to leave and the sooner the better."

"How do you know that? You were in bed. The door was closed."

"And I was behind it. You accepted his ring; now do as he told you."

"Madam, I am going to have to insist," the midshipman said, "we do not have much time."

"Of course young man," Mother assured him. "We shall be ready in five minutes. You may come in and close the trunk."

How could I argue? Mother was right. Francesco had told me to leave and he had meant it. I felt the whole tide of events was flooding against me but how could I resist? Mother, Francesco and Sir William were all urging me to leave so I had no option but to wrap myself up in my refugee clothes and submit.

It was not a good night for a sail. A Tramontana – Italy's bitter north wind – was cutting down from the Apennines, spattering raindrops and threatening worse which, I decided, was a good thing: it would keep the Lazzaroni indoors. The prospect of being confronted by a pack of them while we were scuttling through the darkened streets with a trunk and armed guards was one I preferred not to face. I was frightened, as was Mother, I could tell from her silence, and the sailors were silent too. They hurried us along down the steep empty streets to the naval dockyards: two of them supporting Mother and the midshipman me while the other two struggled with the trunk. All I could think of was Francesco. If he was not collecting me, I told myself, he would be on the quayside to say a proper goodbye but when we got there, he was nowhere to be seen. The dockyard was in darkness but, along its quays, I could dimly see groups of figures being embarked into boats so I ran to them, asking each in turn if they had seen Francesco, but none had. I walked back, dejected, to Mother. I did not blame Francesco. If he had known tonight was the night, he would certainly have been there, but for me to leave without saying goodbye was to leave too much of myself behind and that hurt me.

I found Mother on the east quay, huddling for warmth with the rest of the *Vanguard* party – Sir William's secretaries, Smith and Oliver, whom I recognised, and six noble-looking women whom I did not. The wind off the water was bitterly cold. It whistled in the lanyards and tossed the dark smudge of the launch at the bottom of the sea steps. We watched anxiously as the men carried down our trunks and then it was our turn. The secretaries and I were taken down first but the steps were so slippery and the night so dark that the old ladies had to be man-handled down and the transfer at the bottom into the pitching launch was a feat none will wish to repeat. The men sat us down in the stern-sheets, five either side of the tiller then, when all were aboard, the midshipman took his stand.

"Cast off!" he called, buttoning his coat to his chin, and the oarsmen pulled away.

Cast off! How many times had Mother and I done that? Too many to count but, every time before, there had been some new place to explore and nothing to leave behind but this time I was leaving everything behind. I had needed a proper goodbye – to hold Francesco so close and so hard that I would imprint myself on him as deeply as he was imprinted on me because all I could see in the future was darkness. I twisted my ring on my finger and huddled down in my coat, but if I thought I should brood on my miserable lot, the storm soon knocked that out of me.

Pulling out from the shelter of the mole, the wind blew up to a storm. It whipped our faces and buffeted our ears and the waves, in the dark, were alarming. We plunged and rose and plunged again and all credit to our young midshipman that he kept with the wind because, had he not, I am sure we should all have perished. I had no idea if it were raining – the spray from the waves and the splashing oars soaked us whether or not – and as frightening as the waves was the dark. Within ten minutes of our setting out, the lights of Naples had disappeared and we did not see another for a full half hour. My respect for our midshipman soared that he managed to find *Vanguard* at all but he did, and, when we drew alongside, it was the flag-captain himself who was down on the ladder to greet us.

"I am sorry, Mr Tanner," he shouted against the wind, "you cannot board your party. We can take no more passengers. Return them to Naples." The midshipman was dismayed. He called back in appeal,

"One of the merchantmen then, Sir?" But the captain shook his head.

"No. The whole flotilla is full. Return them to Naples." The midshipman sagged with exhaustion and the oarsmen audibly groaned. The journey they had just made was not their first that long day and now they were faced with two more. I could not believe it. To be returned to Naples! I couldn't have hoped for more but the protests from the others exploded like grapeshot:

"But we are the ambassador's secretaries …"

"This lady is the Archduchess of Metekerenberg …"

"We are French émigrés of the royal blood …" but it was all to no avail. Sir William was not to be consulted; such authority as he had on land was trumped by an admiral at sea and that admiral had been trumped by the king and queen who wanted our berths for more of their Court and retainers. None of us was going up the ladder.

The journey back was worse than the journey out because we were heading into the wind but the waves and spray didn't frighten me now, I was exhilarated by them, and thanked God for the turn of events but my companions were not so pleased: the oarsmen, battle-hardened though they were, pulled into the wind with fixed stares and gritted teeth while the sleep-deprived midshipman jumped up and down to stay awake. And the passengers: would Sir William's secretaries be abandoned to the Jacobins? And the Russian Archduchess and the French ladies of the royal blood? None of them wanted to go back to Naples and then there was Mother. She had huddled inside her cloak on the way out but now the continual rising and plunging was churning her stomach and she was sick over the side several times. By the time we were back on the quayside, she was chilled to the bone and worryingly pale.

My one thought now was to find Francesco so I left Mother in the care of the others and set off to look for him. I ran along the darkened quays to the naval dockyards but the gates at the entrance were locked. I hailed the sentry pacing behind them and, stung by my urgency, he went off to find the officer of the watch. I stood and waited looking in through the gates. The windows of the buildings were dark and there seemed to be no one about but then, after a minute or two, the sentry returned with a lieutenant and, thankfully, he recognised me. As far as he knew, he told me, Francesco was staying at The Officers' Club. I knew the building, it was back along the seafront promenade, so I ran back the way I had come and, passing the others, called out,

"Wait there, I'm going for help."

Three in the morning and the seafront promenade was deserted: not a soul to be seen nor a light in a window. With the wind at my back, I felt I was flying. Not since childhood had I felt so free. All Naples was mine and the wind was mine and the jingling strings of lanterns and the crashing surf beyond the sea wall – all were mine – I felt more alive than any time in my life and, as I burst through the doors of The Officers' Club, the night-porter shrank back from me.

I sent him upstairs to rouse Francesco and while I waited in the white marble hall, I caught sight of myself in a mirror. Never before, I felt sure, had so wild an apparition disgraced that gilded space – not so much a bumpkin this time as a rain-sodden soldier returned from the front. I took off my clerk's cap and shook out my hair. That, at least, was dry and I arranged it as best I could so as to look a bit less of a fright.

I heard a door close on the landing above me and men's boots click-clack down the stairs and then, still buttoning his coat, Francesco appeared and I threw my arms round him. I had never been so happy. The last terrible hours had wrenched me from him and cast me on the seas not knowing if I would see him again and now I was back in his arms. It was a turn too fantastic for gothic romance and yet here I was, it was true.

I told him quickly what had happened and, without a word, he took my hand and we ran out of the club and back up the promenade. Passing the others, I called to them, 'five more minutes' then, at the dockyard, the gates fell open and instantly all was activity. The guard was turned out to fetch Mother and the others and orderlies sent to build beds. I felt so proud of Francesco. The task was nothing to him, I knew that, but it was everything to me because he was doing it for me, affirming, in a man's concrete way, that he was glad I was back and he loved me. Mother and I were billeted in the mess library with the Russian archduchess and her companion and, while the orderlies made up our pallets, we sat together in front of the fire, drinking hot chocolate and eating pastries and with warmth there soon advanced sleep. The young Russian settled her archduchess and I Mother, then we snuffed out the candles and joined them. I was utterly happy and asleep within seconds.

I woke to the sound of shouting. I had slept heavily and, for a moment, didn't know where I was. I looked at Mother, beside me, and the Russians, opposite, and they were all still asleep so I rose and went to the window. I lifted back a curtain and looked down. The street was seething with people, all shouting – artisans, clerks and clerics – but also wealthy people, struggling with bags against the buffeting wind, and the focus of all their shouting was the dock gates. I let fall the curtain and turned back into the room. 'So,' I thought, 'Naples now knows that the Bourbons have fled.'

I noticed a folding screen that had appeared overnight. I looked behind it and found water-bowls and towels so I quietly washed and then dressed and slipped out to the corridor. I recognised it as Francesco's own so I walked to the end and knocked on his door.

"Miss Knight!" His young orderly opened it. "You slept well I hope?" I had no wish to be rude but I was acutely aware that we were in the midst of a crisis.

"I did, thank you," I told him. "Is the admiral in?"

"He is, yes, but …" I walked past him into the outer office.

"Please tell him that I am here." The orderly hesitated, but only for a moment because he could see that, on that particular morning, I would not be detained.

"Just a moment." He knocked lightly on the inner door and put his head round. There was a brief exchange then the door opened and three lieutenants came out followed by Francesco.

"Cornelia!" He smiled to see me and drew me in. "How well you look. Did you sleep alright?" He was ungroomed and unshaved but his eyes were ablaze.

"I did, I slept heavily," I told him, "but look at you; you don't look to have slept at all." He raised an eyebrow.

"I have been busy!" He was beginning to worry me. This was not like Francesco. We were in the middle of a national crisis and he was grinning like a school boy.

"Francesco, there is a crowd in the street. What is happening?" Still smiling, he took both my hands.

"No more than we should expect, my dear. The word is out that the Bourbons have fled and those people down there want to go with them." He lifted my chin with his finger. "Don't look so worried. Everything will be fine – for us and for Naples – only, just now, we must get you to Palermo." He gave me a kiss then let go my hands and went over to his desk piled with ledgers.

"Since I left you this morning, I've been sending out for volunteers to crew *Sannita*." He was leafing through the books. "I already have a full complement of officers and three hundred men which, if I get no more, should be enough to get us to Palermo." He gave me another wide smile. "I intend that we sail this evening." I was incredulous.

"You would do that for me? The *Sannita*? She's a ship-of-the-line."

"Of course I would do that for you. Aren't we to be married? But I would not entirely make free with my country's flagship. My officers are busy as we speak, screening all those people down there. We shall take as many as we can – innocent foreigners that the French might harm, and certain of Ferdinand's office-holders who might suffer for his cowardice. I'm tidying up after Nelson and his new friends."

"And your own friends?" I asked him, barely believing what he was saying.

"My Neapolitan friends?"

"Yes. Will you be taking Baffi, Cirillo, Della Torre?" Francesco laughed.

"Now why would my friends want to go to Palermo? None of them has anything to fear from the French."

By seven that evening, Mother and I and another hundred refugees were safely aboard the *Sannita* and her ladder drawn up. It had been an extraordinary and exhausting day. Our little party of *Vanguard* rejects had been the first to be rowed out through the wind and the waves and Francesco had charged me with the care of the ladies. This, with the help of his First Officer, I tried to fulfil but the facilities were so basic that, as every new boatload arrived, my available space grew smaller and my need to assert myself against some formidable women grew greater. I had been given Francesco's great cabin but that soon filled and I had to haggle with the First Officer for space in the wardroom that he had allotted to the men – and it was not just space – there was only one bed in the great cabin (which I secured for Mother and the archduchess) and not enough palliasses to go round so bedding had to be made up from stores of canvas and wadding while all the time *Sannita* rolled and pitched making Mother and others sick, which was just something else for me to contend with until, at about seven o'clock, Francesco finally arrived and the ladder was raised. I was out on the wheel deck to greet him, hanging onto the poop steps newel post, and, when he saw me, he swayed towards me.

"How are you managing?" he shouted against the wind.

"It's mayhem," I shouted back, holding down my hair. "They are packed like slaves in there. Not enough palliasses, not enough pots, not even enough bowls to be sick in." He rocked back and laughed.

"Never mind. You've done well. Now they will sort themselves out. How is your mother?"

"Not too good, I'm afraid. She hasn't recovered from last night's boat trip and she's a poor sailor."

"Then go to her," he pulled his shore cap down to his eyes, "I'll come and find you later." Then he squeezed my arm and lurched off down the companion way to the lower decks.

We couldn't sail that night. The gale was too strong so, as Francesco had predicted, my sixty or seventy women and children made their own nests in what space they had and huddled together for warmth. Mother, with the archduchess beside her, was, at least, warm in the bed but when the stew was brought she was sick just from the smell of it. Francesco came in at about nine with a rummer of brandy and warm sugar-water which Mother took.

"That's good," she nodded, licking the rim.

"I'm sorry to be putting you through this," he told her but Mother shook her head.

"You have nothing to be sorry about, Admiral, you are our saviour." She gripped his hand. "Turned back from the side of one of King George's ships! In a storm! At night! The widow and daughter of a decorated admiral with fifty-two years' service! What kind of an admiral does that? You will do for us, Admiral, " she told him, "you will do for us very well." Then she settled down into her bed.

I slept on a palliasse next to Mother, fully dressed, in my soldier's coat. I thanked God for my strong sailor's stomach. The continual pitching and rolling at anchor in the dark was a torment to many of my ladies but I found it quite soothing. Even so, my sleep was fitful and, at first light, I rose and picked my way out to the quarter deck. Francesco was already there, standing alone at the gunwale with his coat collar up and his shore cap pulled down to his eyebrows. I lurched over to him and put my arm through his.

"Cornelia!" He still had to shout. "What are you doing up?" I kissed his cheek.

"It's morning." I pointed to the glow behind Vesuvius.

"The best time of day, at sea," he said, "alone with the elements. Collecting your thoughts and assessing the weather for the day."

"And what of the weather?"

"The Tramontana's still stuck in the north. Clouds too high for rain."

"Shall we sail?" I pulled my clerk's cap further down on my head and Francesco laughed. "Why are you laughing?"

"You in that cap and coat."

"It's my refugee outfit." I gave him a playful smile. I wanted him to kiss me but, of course, he would not on deck and anyway, he'd been distracted.

"Look at that." He pointed over the gunwale towards the town. I looked to see what he was pointing at but the air was so filled with spray, I saw nothing.

"Look at what?" He took his eye-glass out of his pocket and extended it for me.

"Look off the mole." I found the mole and, just off it, saw half a dozen small boats struggling through the waves.

"Fishermen?" I returned his glass.

"Not in this weather." He put the glass to his eye. "Oh," he said, "there are more of them. A lot more of them." I was beginning to make them out myself now. Dozens of small boats were putting out from every part of the waterfront. Most of them were heading towards Nelson's flotilla, at anchor on the eastern side of the bay, but some were heading for us. Francesco turned and looked up at the top gallant. His pennant was horizontal, rigid as a weather vane and pointing south. He snapped shut his eye-glass and smiled. "Ready for a cruise? I think it's time we weighed."

I went back to the poop deck steps and hung onto the newel post to watch. It had been thirty years since I had last stood on the deck of a ship-of-the-line while she was getting under weigh. Back then, I had been an eleven-year-old girl, proudly watching her admiral father put his flag-ship through her paces in the English Channel. I had thought then that my father must be superior to all men: in command of the most powerful invention of human ingenuity – a man-of-war – capable of destroying a town in any corner of the globe, powered by the wind and the brawn of five hundred men and all of them subject to him. I had found the experience exhilarating then and I did now. From the shelter of the wheel deck, I watched, not my father, but my husband-to-be, calling out his officers, setting hands to the capstan and top-men aloft and, if all this were being done in the teeth of a gale, so much the better. I loved it. The elemental force was transcending and, watching Francesco, I saw how completely that element was his. On that first day, when he had taken me out on the fly, I had admired the lightness of his touch on the reins and so, here, on a sixteen hundred ton ship-of-the-line, he commanded with that same ease of control. A 'cruise', he had called it. Well, why not? If Francesco could be phlegmatic, so could I.

We bore away on just topsails and gallants, heading due south to leave the bay round Capri. *Vanguard* and her flotilla of chartered merchantmen were moored to windward of the island and, as we passed her, Francesco re-joined me on deck and we looked out together at the scores of small boats bobbing round her.

"All those poor people," I shouted against the wind, "so desperate to get away." He shook his head.

"They don't want to get away. None of them is trying to board. Look." He pointed to the boats. "They are all Lazzaroni. They have come to beg Ferdinand to stay."

"But why?" I asked. "The king and queen have failed them."

"They don't see that. They are simple people. Ferdinand has been their king for forty years – he's their father, their saviour, their godhead. The Lazzaroni don't distinguish between Religion and Monarchy, and the Church feeds off it. Look. There's a priest in every boat."

"They might yet prevail," I suggested, "and Ferdinand will stay."

"Why do you say that?"

"Well, he and his family have been embarked for two nights and a day and they haven't sailed yet." Francesco laughed.

"They haven't sailed because they can't. Nelson has moored his flotilla too close up behind Capri. He will never get away on this wind without being dashed on the rocks. No Neapolitan would have moored there."

The 'cruise' was terrifically rough. Francesco told me that he had never known a Tramontana blow so hard for so long and it only eased when we were approaching Palermo, by which time, many of my ladies were distressed. My main concern was for Mother, of course. She was a frail little thing at the best of times and for the forty-eight hours that we had pitched and rolled in *Sannita*, she ate almost nothing and was frequently sick. Francesco was worried about her too; so much so that, when we dropped anchor in Palermo Bay, he handed command to his captain and carried Mother in his arms to the boat himself. The wind had slackened by then but it was still bitterly cold and snowflakes were flurrying out of a scudding grey sky. We huddled Mother between us in the stern-sheet and then, when we arrived at the quay, Francesco picked her up again and carried her across the road to the harbour master's office. It was, he said, the nearest fire he knew of in Palermo and, with only a nod to the surprised harbour master, he carried Mother through to a small back room where a fire was burning in the hearth. He set Mother down in a battered armchair and then, with a promise to return, he went back to speak with the harbour master.

I banked up the fire from a pile of kindling I found behind the door. The only furniture in the room – apart from the battered armchair – was a rustic round table and wooden chairs and I pulled one of them up beside Mother. I rubbed her cold hands between mine. She looked pitiful. Her thin grey hair was flat to her skull, her cheeks were hollow and her skin as lifeless as crumpled parchment but, worse, she wasn't speaking. We sat by the fire for about ten minutes before Francesco returned with a serving woman. She was carrying a heavily laden tray which she set down on the table.

"Beef broth," Francesco announced cheerfully, "strained, no lumps." The woman filled a bowl and passed it to me. I tested it to make sure it was not too hot and then offered it to Mother. She smelt it, cautiously, then gave me the nod and I gave her a spoonful. She chewed it round her parched mouth, screwing her face and frowning then, with an effort, she swallowed it. Again, she paused for thought and then, for the first time in twenty-four hours, she spoke:

"Some more."

Francesco's family – or a Sicilian branch of it – had a house on the Marino, the elegant promenade that sweeps south and east from Palermo's harbour district. The Marino was the summer resort of the Sicilian nobility and the Villa Caracciolo was one of dozens of handsome palazzi set back, behind walls, from the road. It was a baroque, cream-washed house of seven bays on three floors and, inside, we found it in turmoil. The maggiordomo, whom Francesco introduced as Luciano, was still in his own clothes; piles of white sheets from the furniture were littering the floors, and footmen, also undressed, were up ladders putting candles in sconces. While Francesco went off to find the housekeeper, Luciano showed Mother and me to our room. It was on the first floor, overlooking the formal gardens at the back. It was pretty and light, the wallpaper and hangings rich with plants and exotic birds in pinks and greens and, in the room, were two lady's maids, Valentina and Valeria. They had already begun to unpack our trunk, warming pans were in the bed and a bathtub and jugs standing by the fire. I passed Mother into the two Vs care and left them. After all that had happened, I needed to be with Francesco.

I could hear his voice from the corridor. It was coming from the ballroom, opposite the top of the stairs, and, from the doorway, I saw he was with Luciano. He was wearing his sea coat and carrying his cap.

"You're not going out again, surely," I said, and he caught my alarm.

"Yes, I need to get my land legs back." He abandoned Luciano and came to me. "I was hoping you might join me. Along the promenade?"

"But it's dark, and snowing."

"Better wrap up then. Back into that horrible coat."

It was seven when we walked out through the villa's gates. We crossed the wide carriage drive that, on summer evenings, would have been bustling with gleaming carriages and high-stepping horses but now, in December, was quiet. We crossed the linear gardens, also stripped bare for winter, and then, at the seafront promenade, we turned east, walking away from the town. The wind was no more than a zephyr by then, quietly wafting snowflakes in from the pitch-black sea that settled on the virgin white carpet. I put my arm through Francesco's.

"Thank you," I said.

"For what?"

"For this. Bringing me here. The two of us staying together – and for being good with Mother." I smiled at him. "I think she's falling in love with you too."

"I'm sorry about your mother. It was a rough passage."

"Oh, she will bounce back."

"Well, I hope so, because I feel responsible – my passenger – my ship."

"You mustn't say that. Do you suppose passage would have been any easier on *Vanguard*? She wouldn't have had the cabin, and certainly not a bed – and she would still be at sea now – whereas look at her: tucked up in a warm bed in a warm room with maids attending to her every need." I gave his arm a squeeze. "Mother was right: you've been our saviour." The snow was settling on the frozen path, crumping under our shoes.

"You know it was a spur-of-the-moment decision."

"I know, and I can still hardly believe you did it. You rescued more than a hundred people."

"I had made up my mind to stay."

"But you saw what was needed and you did it." I squeezed his arm again and he halted, turning to me.

"Cornelia, you do know that I shall have to go back."

"But why?"

"For the same reason that I'd decided to stay: to serve my country. I don't want to have anything more to do with this discredited Court."

"But you said yourself; you don't know what will happen in Naples. We don't even know if the French will come. They have chastised Ferdinand for his folly but everyone says they are over-stretched so perhaps they will stop short, and then where will your enlightened friends be?" Francesco was frowning but listening. I went on. "The Lazzaroni won't forget Ferdinand overnight and nor will the Church. All sorts of different parties will feel aggrieved and if the French don't come and impose some order, there could be civil war – and then which country will you serve?" Francesco's frown deepened. The snow had settled on his cap and his shoulders. I did not want to upset him but we needed to be honest with one another. I brushed the snow from his coat. "Wait on events Francesco, for a week or two at least, until we know what is happening."

"I cannot stay in Palermo with that corrupted Court."

"Then stay in Palermo with me." I put my palm to his cheek.

"But we don't know what will happen in Palermo either. I might have no choice but to go back."

"A day at a time then."

"Yes," he conceded, "a day at a time."

We walked as far as the botanical gardens then back, hand in hand, through the quiet white snow, to the villa where supper was waiting. A table had been set up in a cosy little parlour on the ground floor and we ate in front of the fire. We had crayfish and lobster followed by cheeses and dates and Marsala wine. It was the most perfect night of my life.

I awoke to the sound of coughing – a hollow, dry cough from deep in Mother's chest.

"I'm sorry," she croaked, "I did not mean to wake you." I turned and looked at her sitting up beside me. I pulled myself up and drew back the bed-curtain.

"It sounds as if you've caught a chill." She coughed again, nodding her head.

"Yes," she wheezed, "being bathed on a weak stomach. I shouldn't have let them do it."

"What nonsense." I got out of bed and went to open the shutters. A pink glow was haloing the mountains so I guessed it must be gone seven. I looked down into the garden. The statues and seats were evenly covered with an inch of snow and I remembered last night.

"What are you looking at?"

"Nothing," I told he, "just opening the shutters." I went round to her side of the bed and drew back her curtain. "You were two days at sea, Mother, sick and cold with nothing to eat. That is why you have a chill." I put on my morning wrap. "You need hot honey and lemon. I'll go and find a maid."

We were fortunate with the two Vs. They took to Mother. She amused them with her brusque northern ways and, in the depths of winter, they were glad, I'm sure, to have full employment in a warm house. The infusion of honey and lemon relaxed Mother's cough and I stayed with her for breakfast but she ate only little. Despite her two days of starvation, she still had no appetite. What she needed, she insisted, was only rest so I left her in the care of the maids and went downstairs.

I had hoped in the night (or dreamed?) that I would breakfast with Francesco – break bread with him again in that cosy parlour – but, when I got to the turn in the stairs, I saw that he had already breakfasted: he was standing in the hall in his dress uniform and carrying his hat.

"Good morning," he called up cheerfully. I descended the stairs and he came and kissed me. "You look particularly charming this morning."

"So do you." I cast an eye over his uniform. "Are you going somewhere special?"

"*Vanguard* came in last night …" he screwed up his face, supressing a smile.

"And?" I asked him. "Why are you smirking? What is so funny?"

"I should not be laughing, but Nelson made such a terrible fist of the voyage. He's lost *Vanguard's* fore-yard, her sails are in shreds and her shrouds hanging in strings. A coastal patrol found her struggling in the roads and towed her in." He stroked his hand down his face to wipe off the smile. "I'm sorry. It's not funny. The passengers took a hell of a battering – and there was a casualty I'm afraid." A chill shivered through me.

"Not Sir William I hope?" He was the one person on *Vanguard* for whom I had any affection.

"No, not Sir William. Prince Albert. He was terribly sick and died of convulsions – in Lady Hamilton's arms apparently. The queen was too ill to see to him."

"Which one is Albert?"

"The youngest boy. He was only six, poor little chap."

He gave a resigned shrug. "Anyway, Ferdinand and Acton are making a grand landfall at nine and I ought to be there to explain why *Sannita* is here so …" he spread his arms to explain the dress uniform.

"And where is Sir William now?"

"He went straight to the Colli Palace when they landed, with the queen and the children."

"And is he alright?"

"I don't know, this is all second-hand, but we could go and see him when I get back if you like."

"No, I'll wait. He'll be exhausted."

At the end of the hall, the front door opened and a footman appeared.

"Your carriage, Excellency."

"I must go." Francesco kissed me again. "Have you had breakfast?"

"I have, yes, with Mother."

"A pity." He looked disappointed. "Never mind." He started to walk backwards towards the front door. "Pop into the small parlour anyway." He lifted his hat, "Compliments of the season. Happy Christmas!" then he turned and disappeared through the door.

I followed him out to the steps and waved him off, then I came in and went through to the parlour. A fire was burning in the hearth, the table was laid for breakfast for two and, in the middle of the sofa, there was a large parcel tied up with a bow. I looked for a note but none was attached so I pulled loose the bow and opened it. Inside, there was a box and in the box there was a heavy velvet cloak, lined with fox, in a rich shade of plum. I shook it out and put it round my shoulders. It had the fashionable shallow collar fastened with a gold clasp and it was exactly my length. I twirled around looking for a mirror and only then did the note fall to the floor. I picked it up and read it: 'Never more the refugee: I am your refuge.'

The Colli Palace too was a shambles. If it had been stampeded by a fleeing army it could not have looked worse – and this was two days after the royal family had arrived. The only visible security was maintained by Nelson's marines and the palace itself, though extensive, was a summer palace in the Chinese style with ill-fitting French doors and there were few fireplaces. The king and queen had not used the palace in decades and, arriving without notice, in the middle of the night, with the greater part of their Court, they had given the small caretaking staff no time to prepare or even find furniture, most of which had disappeared in their long absence. I struggled through corridors and salons choked with Neapolitan refugees and Palermitans eager to empty their pockets but no one seemed to know who occupied what rooms and I must have been in the building a quarter of an hour before I found the second-floor room allotted to Sir William. When I knocked on the door, it was opened by a doctor. He was in his waistcoat with his sleeves rolled up and holding a bowl of blood.

"Oh, I'm so sorry," he said, "I was expecting the maid." I looked past him to Sir William who was sitting up in bed with another doctor bandaging his arm.

"Cornelia!" he cried, "oh my dear! Come in!" He was wearing a voluminous night-shirt and cap. He had lost weight and his long, gaunt face, usually so tanned, was yellow. His wasted appearance was accentuated by the size of the bed he was sitting in – it was enormous; too enormous evidently for anyone to make off with – but, apart from the bed, the room was unfurnished. I felt I was intruding.

"Perhaps I should come back."

"You shall do no such thing," Sir William insisted. "These rogues are just going. Come here and sit with me." He patted the further side of the bed and, as I walked round, the doctor glowered.

"You know you must rest Sir William. Always, after bleeding, you must rest." The doctor picked up his bag and moved towards the door.

"Rely on it," Sir William told him, "what strength I might have had to do otherwise, you have carried away in that bowl." The doctors left, closing the doorbehind them, and I sat on the edge of the bed.

"How are you?"

"Weak," he attempted a laugh, "bilious fever. I'll be alright." He reached out and took my hand. "But what about you? I was so angry when I heard you'd been turned back from *Vanguard*."

"You heard about that?"

"Smith and Oliver came to see me yesterday. Thank God for Francesco, eh? Didn't he save the day?" He saw my ring. He went quiet for a moment and looked at it, then he raised my hand to his expert eye.

"Francesco's ring?" I could not help but smile. "When?"

"The day before we sailed." Sir William opened his arms and I leaned into him. If ever a girl needed a father, I had him in Sir William but, my goodness, he felt frail. His face against mine was stubble and bone and I could feel every rib in his back. I released myself and drew back.

"But what about you? Poorly and alone in this huge empty room?" I looked round it. "Did Vittorio not come with you?"

"I'm afraid he did not. He could have – I wanted him to – I begged him to, but he has a family and he wanted to stay and look after them."

"And Lady Emma, where is she?" He nodded beyond the door.

"Further down the corridor; also poorly. She went straight to bed when we arrived and slept for twenty hours. It was the first chance she'd had in two weeks, what with the packing for the queen and the children and the voyage – Cornelia –" he sat forward and glared at me proudly, "Emma was a Titan on that voyage! When the queen and her children were in despair, it was Emma and her mother who looked after them – no one else could – I couldn't – I was as sick as the rest." He sat back on his pillows and frowned. "And you'll have heard about little Albert." I nodded. "That was really terrible." He shook his head at the memory of it. "We all thought we would die. Some were crying, others praying – I loaded a brace of pistols. I wasn't going down gurgling salt water into my lungs – I was quite resolved to blow out my brains – even Nelson said it was the worst storm he'd known." He nodded to beyond the door again. "He's in a room next to Emma's; prostrated with fever and headaches. The truth is, Cornelia, that the last few weeks have been hell and that damned voyage has done for us all."

The door suddenly flew open. An Irish wolf hound bounded in followed by two more and a couple of spaniels and they all leaped onto the bed. They meant no harm, I could see, they wanted to fuss Sir William, but I feared for him; just one of the hounds would have weighed more than him and I tried to pull them away, but then I saw there was a man in the room and that man was King Ferdinand. I climbed off the bed and dropped into a curtsy and Sir William also made to move but the king stopped him.

"No-no, my dear fellow. Stay where you are. Thought I'd bring some old friends to cheer you up." Sir William fussed the five dogs and then, when they had all been greeted, he ordered them down. I had remained standing at the side of the bed while Ferdinand, at the foot of it, stared at me.

"Your Majesty," Sir William offered, "I think you know Miss Knight?" Ferdinand, who was wearing a battered old shooting coat and muddy boots, sniffed.

"No. Don't think so. Wouldn't forget. Not that big and that handsome."

"Miss Knight was a great help to me cataloguing and packing my collections, Sir."

"Huh!" the king huffed. "Accomplice eh! Helped you spirit away my country's treasures!" His hands were fidgeting in the huge game pockets of his coat and he rocked impatiently on his heels. "What brings you here then, Miss Knight?"

"I came down with my mother on *Sannita*, Your Majesty. We arrived on Christmas Day."

"Then weren't you the lucky ones! I wish I'd been on *Sannita*. Francesco knows how to handle the Tyrrhenian Sea a lot better than any Englishman. Any damage?"

"No, I don't think so, Sir."

"There you are then!" He pulled a knot of string from his pocket and, as he absently fiddled with it, I remembered what he had lost on *Vanguard*. On top of everything else, that must have been the cruellest blow. I felt I must say something.

"May I offer you my sincere condolences, Sir, on ..." he sniffed fiercely and pulled at his enormous nose then turned from me to Sir William.

"That great wind we've just had," he said, "I've been talking to Georgio about it – you know – game-keeper Georgio?" Sir William nodded and Ferdinand, thrusting the string back into his pocket, started to pace the floor. "It's been a damned good woodcock season this year, as you know, and Georgio thinks that that wind will have blown thousands of 'em down from the mainland to Sicily. What do you think?"

"Could be," Sir William offered, and the king wheeled on him.

"Brought your guns?"

"They might be somewhere I dare say," Sir William put up his hands in a show of impotence, "we haven't unpacked yet."

"Come with me then." Ferdinand's eyes were ablaze with excitement. "I have taken a park and lodge fifty miles to the south-east. First class woodcock country. We need to get at 'em while they're still here – too good a chance to miss. What do you think?" Sir William – gaunt, yellow-faced and in night-shirt and cap – simply opened his palms to the king. He did not need to say more, even to a fool like Ferdinand. "No," Ferdinand agreed, "still – when you're stronger." With a click of his tongue, he brought up the dogs. "You know, there's a lot of good sport on this island, and as we're not going anywhere else too soon, we might just as well enjoy it. Get better old friend." And he left.

Over supper that evening I told Francesco about my encounter with Ferdinand. He had spent the day with his officers in the naval-yard and Ferdinand's behaviour had not surprised him.

"That's Ferdinand," he said, putting down his napkin, "he's a child. Give him his friends and his toys and enough money in his pocket for his amusements and he will be happy in Naples or Sicily or Timbuctoo – and as to Albert: for how long does a small boy mourn the passing of another small boy? I have known him all my life, Cornelia, and, I am sorry, but I have learned to expect no better."

It was the third evening of our occupation of the Villa Caracciolo and our third supper in the small parlour. The room had become our own: our private bower where, with Mother confined to her bed, we could spend our evenings together.

"Hard on the queen though," I suggested, "Maria-Carolina might be a tyrant but she is a devoted mother and she deserves better from her children's father."

"Well," Francesco pushed back from the table and crossed his legs, "she has put up with him all these years but now that it's all over, perhaps she will feel free to leave him."

"Really? Surely that's not possible."

"She has lost two children and a country in the last three months. She is defeated, humiliated, exhausted, and she despises Sicilians even more than Neapolitans. Rumour has it that she has asked the Emperor to take her in. Settle the girls with good marriages and then retire to Linz or Salzburg or somewhere."

"So it really is all over for them?" Francesco picked up his wine glass.

"Yes." He raised it, as in toast, and drank.

"I wonder what Sir William will do."

"You didn't ask him?"

"I didn't get the chance."

"Well," Francesco uncrossed his legs and drew back up to the table, "the word in the wardrooms is that Nelson has applied to his Commander-in-Chief for permission to take Sir William and Lady Emma to England on *Vanguard*, then they can all retire."

"Oh, I hope that's not true. I should hate to lose Sir William. Naples would not be the same without him."

"Naples will not be the same again with him or without him, but I too hope he stays: I want him to see what free Neapolitans can do."

CHAPTER TEN

It continued to snow throughout January. Such weather, we were told, was unheard-of in the long Sicilian memory and that superstitious mind put the blame at the door of the visitors. Sicilians, I quickly learned, held Ferdinand and Maria-Carolina in as deep a contempt as any other authority set over them and now, with their two thousand unwanted guests pushing food and fuel prices through the roof, the Palermitans took to the streets. The royal party, with no troops of its own to defend it, feared for its safety. Maria-Carolina, still waiting for news from Vienna, resorted to isolation and opiates while her husband, according to Sir William, was toying with the idea of sailing with him into an English exile. There was the whiff of a dynasty decaying in Palermo – or more – perhaps even of the monarchical epoch decaying because the news from Naples offered nothing to the royal family.

On 18th January, the man whom Ferdinand had left as his regent in Naples, General Pignatelli, turned up in Palermo after fleeing disguised as a woman. Less than a month into his thankless post, he had signed an armistice with the French, abandoning all territories north of the Voltera, banning English ships from the ports and committing the state to an indemnity of ten million francs. The Lazzaroni were incensed. They stormed the forts and marched on the royal palace demanding the heads of those who had sold

Naples out. There was anarchy, the French were at the gates and then we heard that someone had fired Francesco's ships. We had the news in a letter from Francesco's friend, Carlo Lauberg, that arrived just after Pignatelli.

My dear Francesco,

I hope this finds you safe and well. Was that not a terrible storm? You could not have chosen a worse night to sail on your errand of mercy but now, more than ever, we need you back in Naples.

My dear friend, it is with a heavy heart that I write to inform you of the destruction of your ships. Three seventy-fours, *Partenope*, *Tancredi*, and *Guiscardo*, and the sixty-four, *San Giovacchino*, are burned at their moorings along with five frigates and a dozen each of galleons and corvettes. It is a monstrous act of wanton destruction. Your navy was the pride of the nation and everyone here from the most enlightened to the basest is incensed and in grief at our loss. And who, you will ask, is the perpetrator of this crime? There seems little doubt that the leader of the gang was one Commodore Campbell, a Scotsman in the Portuguese service, but on whose orders he went to his work can only, for the moment, be guessed at and the man himself has sailed. It was the most heinous of many senseless acts of destruction during that dreadful interregnum but now, though your ships are lost, I can tell you that the worst is over and a new epoch has dawned.

Francesco, we have achieved our revolution! After the flight of Pignatelli, we had a week of mob rule. The Lazzaroni occupied the forts and, for a week, ran amok. No one with an education was safe. There were terrible scenes and we have lost friends but I will not burden you with more heartbreak now, sufficient to tell you that the good people of Naples turned against the Lazzaroni's tyranny and invited the French in to help us. We now have – and I marvel I can write this – a republican government and I am asked to be its president. The best of Naples are stepping up to take the seals of office: Mario Pagano, Domenico Cirillo, Prince Moliterno – and Generals Massa and Federici have agreed to re-organise the army with French help – so now all that we need is you. We have lost most of our navy but there are still ships scattered around the coast and I ask you, as your president, to come home to rebuild the navy. The day for which we have so long dreamt has arrived! Join us, and long live the republic!

Your good friend and President
Carlo Lauberg

I read the letter and passed it back to Francesco. He had turned aside from the breakfast table and crossed his legs. He was toying absently with a teaspoon, waiting for me to finish, waiting to talk, but I hardly knew what to say.

"Francesco, I am so sorry about your ships." I rested my hand on his, stilling the spinning spoon. He gave me a firm smile.

"It is done. It is a rule of command that you understand your situation and work with it. I shall not weep over burned ships." These were brave words, but could the disaster be so quickly dismissed? Francesco should have been in Naples that night, he could have saved his navy but instead he was in Palermo with me.

"But if you had been there …" I began, but Francesco stopped me.

"No, no, there are no what-ifs," he drew up to the table and put his hand over mine, "there is only what is and look what *is*." His eyes were wide and shining. "Look at *us*: happy. Look at the queen's party: destroyed by its own hand. Look at that letter. A republic is born in Naples and her best minds are stepping up to nurture it. That is what *is*, Cornelia," he gripped my hand, "and isn't it good?" He was being so brave. I could not believe he was being so positive.

"But your life's work," I insisted, "you were so proud …"

"I am proud, yes, and now, again, I have a country that I can be proud of." He let go my hand and picked up the letter, "and as Lauberg says, there are still ships – at Salerno and Taranto – there is a squadron in Messina of two ship-of-the-line and four frigates. Much is lost, yes, but very far from all." He fell silent, chewing his lip, and I knew what he was thinking.

"You must go back."

"*We* must go back." I shook my head.

"You forget that I have a mother. She has only once ventured out since we arrived here and the cold almost killed her. She cannot possibly face another sea voyage until spring."

"But I will not go without you. I will not leave you here on your own."

"I won't be on my own. I have Mother and the servants, and Mrs Cadogan calls most days."

"You know what I mean."

"Francesco, I have looked after myself and my mother all my life, and in less comfortable surroundings than these." He got to his feet and went to the hearth.

"Then we must get married. I do not want you to have to look after yourself any more. If I must leave you here in Palermo then it shall be as the Princess Caracciolo with all the protection of my name." I felt a smile twitch at my lips. Sometimes Francesco could be so gauche.

"Of course I want that too," I told him, "but why the haste? I don't want to be married here in some hurried little ceremony where no one knows us. What would your mother think? Or the rest of your family? Or our friends? They would think you were ashamed of me and that is not how I want our marriage to begin. No, Francesco, we should marry properly in Naples in your family's church. Spring is only three months away. It is not too long to wait."

Francesco, in the end, acquiesced. He would go to Naples and assess the situation while I stayed with Mother, waiting for the spring and his call. He planned to slip away quietly, saying nothing to anyone, but there was one leave-taking that he had to make, and that was to his old friend, Sir William.

The Hamiltons and Nelson had moved out of the Colli Palace at the beginning of February and taken up ambassadorial residence in the Palazzo Palagonia not far from the harbour. The palazzo was a rambling confection of fifty painted rooms and the day they moved in, Francesco and I paid a call. It was another palazzo in turmoil. In the great frescoed entrance hall, decorators were working on scaffolding and servants and tradesmen of every description scurrying over the floors. No one seemed to know if Sir William were home but Lady Emma was, we were told, and a footman conducted us up to her in the ballroom. She was swathed in furs, poring over plans with tradesmen and she was not pleased to see us.

"Admiral!" she called across the floor. "What are you doing here? We are still in disarray." Francesco and I were standing in the doorway: he, in his winter greatcoat and I, in my new plum cloak.

"We wondered if Sir William were home," Francesco told her and she looked to the footman.

"Is he, Claudio?" The footman shrugged. "If you would try to find him then?" The footman disappeared down the stairs leaving Francesco and me in the doorway. Lady Emma might have come over to us or invited us in but she did neither; she remained where she was, flanked by her tradesmen, watching us.

"Miss Knight isn't it?"

"Lady Hamilton," I sighed, "you know that you and I have met many times." She lifted her head as if to see me more clearly.

"It must be that cloak you are wearing," she looked at Francesco, "someone has taste." Her eyes rippled over him and a smirk twitched her lips. She was thinking of something pointed to say about our being together but, before she could choose her dart, Sir William came in from the stairs.

"Francesco, my dear boy!" He embraced him warmly. "Congratulations!" Then he turned to me and kissed both my cheeks. "Congratulations to you both. I am so pleased. It's a match made in heaven."

"Not in the Palazzo Sessa?" I suggested.

"Ah yes," his eyes twinkled, "well, there you are then." He looked into the ballroom where Lady Emma's attention had returned to her plans. "Emma, my dear, is there any chamber in this house not tenanted by workmen where one might take some tea?"

"I don't know, dear," she replied, without looking up, "it is your house as well as mine, take tea where you like." Sir William cast about the enormous ballroom. At either end, there were large white doors with elaborate gilded mounts that, in such a house, must have led to enfilades of salons, music rooms, drawing rooms and dining rooms down the full length of the house.

"No," he muttered to himself, "they'll every one be full of drapers and decorators." He gave me a wistful smile. "Where is Vittorio when we need him, eh? Come on." He turned from the ballroom and led us back down the stairs.

"Not got your bearings here yet then?" Francesco suggested.

"I have not. I go off hunting with the king for a few days and, when I get back, I'm moved here."

"Not your decision?"

"No, not my decision. Emma found the place. It's convenient for Nelson and his officers and, as he is paying the rent ... you there!" A liveried footman, with his arms piled with fabrics, was passing the foot of the stairs. "Where is the maggiordomo?" Without breaking his stride the footman replied,

"Gone out," and Sir William exploded.

"For God's sake man, stand still when I speak to you!" Taken aback, the footman halted. He looked at Sir William and then, with no better grace than the other, asked him,

"And you are?"

"I am the owner of your damned livery you scoundrel. Now, put down those bolts and take me to the housekeeper."

The good lady, when we found her, soon smoothed Sir William's feathers. She was sorry for all the turmoil, she told us, it was in preparation for a supper and ball to mark Nelson's granting of the Freedom of Palermo and the only quiet room she could offer was her parlour. Naturally, we all protested, but she insisted and showed us into a simply-furnished room looking out onto a back court. There was an armchair by the fire and a table and chairs, two of which she brought forward, and then, once she had settled us, she left with the promise of tea. Sir William spread wide his arms.

"Welcome to my home!" After the recent annoyance, it was hard to tell whether he were being funny or bitter. "So," he declared, smiling across the hearth at us, "Tell me about your exciting news." Francesco rested his hand over mine on the chair arm.

"We want to be married a soon as we can," he told him, "but I have to return to Naples and, while Lady Knight is unwell, Cornelia must remain here so …" he smiled and shrugged, "as soon as we can." Sir William frowned.

"Are you sure you have to go back to Naples dear boy? That sounds like a dangerous undertaking to me."

"Yes, I do. My country has been abandoned by its sovereign and government and that vacuum must be filled." Sir William shifted in his chair.

"But why you, Francesco? And why now? There is anarchy in Naples."

"No. The anarchy is quelled and, with the help of the French, a new government already sworn in," Francesco let go my hand and reached out to Sir William, "and it is the best government we could have hoped for: Pagano and Cirillo are in it, Prince Moliterno, Vittorio Russo and the Duke of Roccaromana. These are some of the best minds in Naples but, being the best, they are necessarily few and it is the moment for all who can help to step forward." Sir William raised an eyebrow and Francesco put up a hand. "I know what you are thinking; that Ferdinand is sovereign, but he has abandoned Naples with no thought of returning and my duty is to Naples not to an abdicant." Sir William looked to me.

"He has to go," I agreed, "you know how patriots are. Francesco could never rest if he thought he was failing his country."

The door opened and the housekeeper came in carrying the tea things on a large tray. I jumped up from my chair.

"Let me help you." I pulled forward the table and, taking the cloth from the housekeeper's arm, spread it out and she put down her tray. "This looks lovely," I told her, "thank you so much."

"Shall I serve you, Madam?"

"In your own parlour? I should think not, no, I am sure we can manage." Together we unloaded the things from the tray then the housekeeper slipped from the room. Sir William and Francesco drew up their chairs and, while I poured the tea, they made their selections from anchovy rolls and savoury pastries, pistachio biscuits and sweet almond cakes. Sir William took a pastry and sat back in his chair.

"I know that patriotism is supposed to be the *sine qua non* of the man-at-arms," he observed, "but I was never a particularly warm patriot myself, even when I was a soldier and, as the years go by, I grow less so." Francesco took up his tea cup and regarded Sir William over its rim. "It is the duty of the patriot to support his own country," Sir William went on, "above all others, for a good cause or a bad. Patriotism was to the Romans the noblest of the virtues but the Greeks favoured also philosophy and the grasp of the broader view," he reached forward for his tea, "and we are all children of the Greeks as well as the Romans you know – Sicilians, Savoyards, Saxons and Scots – we are all children of that broader Greek republic."

"Yes!" Francesco put down his cup, "and now we can share a political republic too! Three-quarters of Europe is now republican thanks to the French – and on the principles espoused by the Greeks. I wonder, Sir William, that you cannot support that."

"Support it? All I support is peace dear boy and if you can achieve your ambitions without war I wish you well."

"Do you, Sir William?" Francesco asked him. "It would be important to me to have your blessing."

"Then you have my blessing, for what it is worth – you *and* Naples – for I love you both."

"Speaking of blessings," I put in, seizing the moment, "I have a request of you, Sir William, and you do not need to answer me now." The men looked at me. It was a matter I had not shared with Francesco, a privilege that I wanted to exercise for myself. "Will you give me away?"

"Oh, my dear girl." Sir William slid his cup and saucer back onto the edge of the table. He dabbed his mouth with his napkin and sat back on his chair. "I hardly know what to say." Francesco smiled at me, obviously pleased, but Sir William seemed overcome. He raised his napkin to his face again, this time to dab at his eyes.

"You could say 'yes'," Francesco suggested, but Sir William was shaking his head.

"Oh, how I should love to, Francesco, Cornelia, for I am so happy for you both but shall I ever see Naples again? You know how it is, Francesco. For as long as Naples lies under the influence of France, my government will not reopen the embassy and how long will that be? And who can say that there will not be conflict? I could not bear to see war between England and Naples, let alone be a party to it. No. I'm afraid my life in Naples is over."

"But if we could find a date," I suggested, "and you were still here?"

"Yes, of course, my dear. Should it be at all possible, I shall be there and be honoured but did you know I have asked to go home?" I had heard the rumour. "I am sixty-eight years old, exiled from my adopted home of thirty-five years, out of strength, out of spirits and out of money too – my debts are beyond ignoring and are another reason why I must go home."

"You are in debt, Sir William? And you have taken this place?" Francesco waved an arm at the enormous house.

"No, no," Sir William answered, "Nelson has taken it. He is happy for it to serve as my embassy but he will be paying the bills. Nelson is a wealthy man since the Battle of the Nile." Now Sir William indicated the house. "This seems to be the way he likes to spend his money and Emma is happy to help him but, for myself," he popped a piece of almond cake into his mouth, "the time has come for me to face my creditors."

"Then what will you do?"

"Go to England, if someone will take me. But don't look so worried; the vases will cover my debts. I came to a very satisfactory arrangement with the British Museum over my first collection and the vases aboard *Colossus* are of a far superior quality. No. My retirement will be comfortable."

I had supported Francesco to Sir William because how could I not? If I had insisted that Francesco remain in Palermo he would not have been able to live with himself and so I had to support him, but I was frightened for him. It was alright for Francesco to accept Lauberg's view of events but Lauberg was excessively partial and from different sources with different partialities I heard stories of lawlessness and duplicity even in the ranks of the republicans. And then there was the French. General Championnet was an uncommonly enlightened commander who, by all accounts, was treating the Neapolitans well, but for how long? He could be replaced at any time, or ordered by Paris to pillage and subdue, as had happened in the rest of Italy, but Francesco was not open to these doubts, his schoolboy's optimism coloured his vision and I knew, as I loved him, that whatever was happening in Naples, Francesco must find out for himself and so, though it wrung my heart, I kept silent.

The date of his departure was fixed for the day following Lady Emma's grand ball. I say 'Lady Emma's grand ball' because although it was ostensibly to mark Nelson's promotion to Rear Admiral of the Red and his award of the Freedom of Palermo, everyone knew who would be playing hostess and claiming centre-stage. Francesco and I had not wanted to attend. Neither of us was particularly comfortable with Nelson's and Emma's increasingly public *affaire* but Sir William, we knew, would want us there and besides, the ball would be a rite of passage: Francesco's final departure from the *ancien regime*.

I would challenge any woman present at the Palazzo Palagonia that night to say that Francesco was not the handsomest man in the room. He was wearing his evening dress uniform: cream waistcoat, breeches and stockings beneath the Italian blue swallow-tail with gold epaulettes, froggings and cuffs. Any man is improved by a uniform but Francesco's dark complexion, rugged features and tight curls set him apart from the ruddy-faced English officers and a world apart from the pale and diminutive admiral on Lady Emma's ample arm. I too was wearing cream with Italian blue edgings to my robe and bandeau. Francesco and I were a couple, and I wanted the world to know it.

We arrived as late as convention allowed, about midnight, and the dancing was in full flow. A couple of hundred dancers in groups of eight were dancing a Neapolitan cotillion and Francesco and I edged our way round them to reach the refreshment room beyond. Nelson was in there, surrounded by a coterie of admirers, and there was also a group of Neapolitans who drew us into their circle for champagne and small talk. I was dying for Francesco to ask me to dance. We never had danced but his long limbs and the graceful economy of his movements had always suggested to me that he would be a dancer and I wanted to see if I were right. After a few minutes Sir William appeared with a party I did not know but took, from their hauteur, to be Palermitans. He brought them over to us and introduced us which generated more small talk and I began to wish we had stayed at home. I still had not seen Lady Emma, and when I asked Sir William where she was he had answered with a 'not long now' that I took to mean an Attitude.

And we did not have to wait long. After the cotillion set was finished an usher came through and called everyone into the ballroom where we stood round a space by the doors. A spinet struck up and rattled away at a hectic pace, raising our expectations until, when the time was deemed right, the double doors flew open and in ran Lady Emma, barefoot and wearing nothing but a diaphanous shift and a crown of gold laurels. Bending this way and that, she rushed across the floor, fending off a blow here and taking one there and throwing up her big white arms while the spinet sped on through its scherzo. She rose and fell and spun round the floor in a tragic tarantella until, in a climactic convulsion, she dislodged the laurels from her head and slid in a swoon to the floor.

"Beloved Naples!" she wailed, as the music slowed, "where is the hero who will restore my laurels and my innocents to their ordained inheritance?" She cast about the room in appeal, "Is there no man left in the world with the stomach and the heart?" Her big doe's eyes rolled from man to man until finally they rested on Nelson. He was standing between fellow-officers, leaning against the wall. Emma, the prostrate apotheosis of Naples, summoned the last of her strength and, propping herself on one hand, reached out to Nelson but, though he gave her an appreciative smile, he did not respond. The laurels lay halfway between them. A dead silence hung in the air. Emma's arm stayed out-stretched to Nelson and her eyes implored his response but, beyond the light smile, he did not respond and after what seemed like an age she released him from her gaze and collapsed on the floor as if dead. It was another bravura performance, it drove the audience wild and it changed the whole mood of the evening. Suddenly, small talk was abandoned and all the talk was of politics. Had Emma deliberately provoked the debate? Was she so clever? Or so bold as to champion a cause that even her royal mentor seemed to have abandoned? Emma too was the talk of the room and, as we made our way back to the refreshment room, a loud voice called out,

"Francesco!" We both turned to be met by a giant of a man whom I vaguely recognised. He was in his mid-fifties with golden hair and a nose to rival the king's.

"Cardinal!" Francesco greeted him. "How are you?" The man was wearing a purple suit and a big silver crucifix hung on his chest.

"They tell me you are going back to Naples tomorrow." The big man's fore-knowledge startled me but Francesco was not fazed.

"Have you met my fiancée? Miss Cornelia Knight?" The man lifted my hand and pressed it to his lips. "Cardinal Ruffo is the Prince of Castelcicala in Calabria, and sometime War Minister to Pius VI." The cardinal stood back, still holding my hand.

"Miss Knight and I once dined together at the table of Cardinal Bernis," he reminded me, "when Rome was a happier place." He gave me a warm smile and I did remember him. "And now you are to marry our admiral," he closed both his hands over mine, "may God bless you and bring you both much happiness." Then he turned back to Francesco. "So, Naples. Reconnaissance is it?"

"I shall see what I shall see," Francesco told him opaquely and the cardinal's eyes narrowed.

"Secret business, eh?"

"For the time being." The cardinal's eyes remained on Francesco's until, at last, he seemed satisfied.

"Good!" he declared. "It's time something got moving. It's just a pity it takes a half-naked dancing girl to tell us."

"*Half-naked*?" I had seen Lady Emma and Nelson approaching, but from behind the cardinal's back. He spun round.

"Uh!" he exclaimed, "Lady Hamilton! Good for you, good for you! Just the fork up the bum that's needed round here."

"I should dance fully naked if that was what it took to rally the cause of the king and queen." She had changed, since her dance, into a full length robe but it was cut so low as to leave little to the cardinal's imagination.

"Well," he drew himself up to his full height and pulled at his nose, "I, for one, will spare you that indignity, madam. I have already decided to go."

"Go?" Francesco asked him. "Go where?"

"Calabria." He gripped his crucifix. "I have the legitimacy of my ancestry there and of the Holy See. I shall, if God wills it, raise an army for Christ and take the fight to the Atheists before they get any further south. If Ferdinand isn't ready to counterattack, some of us are." And he gave Lady Emma a decisive nod.

"Bravo," muttered Nelson, standing at Emma's side, and the cardinal leaned to him.

"And you will support us with your English ships. Your Mr Pitt has cemented this new alliance; Austria is now committed with Russia and Turkey to the aid of England and Naples. If there is a push, you will support it." Nelson gave a sardonic laugh.

"I would not rely on that if I were you, Cardinal. Not in the foreseeable future. I have a dozen ships-of-the-line at my disposal with which I am ordered to disrupt communications between France and her army in Egypt, besiege the island of Malta, assist the Russian and Turkish squadrons in the Adriatic and the Archipelago and defend the coasts of Sicily and Naples."

"There you are then!" declared the cardinal, and again Nelson laughed.

"Do you know that I currently have one ship patrolling the entire coast of Sicily? There is the world of difference between defence and the support of an attack."

"But we supported an attack last autumn," Emma cheerfully reminded us and Nelson's face set. He looked down at the buckles on his shoes for a moment, then back up at Emma.

"And look where it got us." His gaze was cold as steel. Emma's mouth twitched, unsure how best to reply but then the cardinal answered for her.

"Ah well," he harrumphed, "we are all allies against the Jacobin and when it comes to it, I expect you will be there, Admiral." Emma leaned to Nelson and closed her hands round his arm.

"*The world* will expect him to be there, Cardinal. This man does not baulk at the chance of glory."

And so the guests dispersed to the refreshment rooms, to eat and drink toasts to Emma's patriotism and Nelson's new honours while Francesco and I remained at the ballroom door. The room had emptied but the orchestra still played; some old-fashioned tune that meant nothing to me but Francesco knew it.

"Isn't that a danse-à-deux?" he asked me. "Do you know the danse-à-deux?"

"I learned it at Versailles years ago, but nobody dances it now."

"Then, as we seem to be out of step with everyone else here, perhaps we should." I looked into the ballroom.

"But there is no one dancing."

"Could there be a better time?" He offered me his hand and, under the eyes of none but the musicians, we took to the floor. I had not danced the danse-à-deux in twenty years but my master was at my fingertips. Francesco moved a minim ahead of the music, leading me into the dance, until after a few rounds I felt the steps come and he dropped back into my time. We turned and passed in flawless euphony, owning the whole of the floor, and the more we danced the more I lost myself in Francesco and he in me and the musicians smiled us their blessing.

We did not re-join the party. Emma's voluptuous call to arms and that bullish cardinal frightened me. Could a force be mobilised for Ferdinand, I wondered, in spite of his indifference? And what about Naples? What awaited Francesco? He was excited to go but I feared for him, and while I wanted to protect him from my fear, I also wanted him to know that he took with him my heart and so, that night, I pledged him it with my love.

We breakfasted together but he wouldn't let me go to the docks. His mind was already on his ship and the crew and the business ahead so we said our goodbyes on the doorstep – I, shivering in my thin morning wrap, and he in his winter greatcoat. We kissed and I held him and, when we parted, my face was streaked with tears and my heart too full to speak. He turned and climbed into his carriage and, a moment later, was gone.

It was a quarter past noon when the *Sannita* sailed past the mole. Two days later, Cardinal Ruffo sailed for Calabria.

CHAPTER ELEVEN

I was worried about Mother. After that sunny day in late January when we had wrapped her up and taken her out for the breath of air that almost killed her, Mother had not left her room. Our bedroom was re-ordered over the weeks of our occupancy around her needs. The chest and armoire were removed with our clothes to an adjoining room, which became our dressing room, and comfortable chairs and a tea table brought in so that Mother might entertain. They were not many who called: Francesco had sat with her before he left, and Sir William when he could but, for female company, our Neapolitan acquaintances proved faithless and Mother's only regular visitor was her old companion of the *rouge et noir* table, Mrs Cadogan. Emma's mother was twenty years younger than mine and of sturdier stock but, marooned with the rest of us on that sullen island with the old certainties crumbling, she found as much comfort in Mother's company as Mother found in hers – she proved a godsend and, after Francesco had left, our principal source of news.

It was from Mrs Cadogan that we heard about Sir William. I had been incredulous at the time – so much so that I had left the tea table, donned my cloak and run all the way to the Palazzo Palagonia to hear it for myself. The moment I arrived, I dispatched a footman to announce me to Sir William and, while I waited in the hall, Lady Emma found me.

"He does not need vultures circling," she'd snapped – her rudeness fuelled, no doubt, by fear – but she was too late; when the footman returned to tell me Sir William would see me I brushed her aside and followed him up to the second floor room. Sir William was in bed, raised on a bank of pillows and wearing a day shirt. He looked gaunt and grey and dark bags sagged beneath his eyes. Once the footman had left us, I took Sir William's hand.

"I am defeated, Cornelia."

"Then it is true?"

"Ruined."

"But how did it happen? When? Where?"

"She was almost home. Off St Mary's in the Isles of Scilly. A storm blew up and the captain took shelter in St Mary's harbour but, for want of an anchor apparently – that Nelson had taken – she was driven out of the harbour and onto a reef where she foundered. The good people of St Mary's managed to rescue all but one of those on board – all the Nile wounded were saved – but the cargo is lost," he opened his arms, "all of it, lost."

"But how can you be sure? If she broke up on rocks so close to the land? The waters cannot have been deep and those cases are very strong. Seawater is nothing to terracotta and marble."

"Oh I am sure." He lifted himself up on his pillows. "I have it from my nephew, Greville, and he has investigated thoroughly. Our cases were stowed deep in the bottom of the hold and, as *Colossus* broke up, a couple of hundred tons of shot and cannon tumbled through crushing everything beneath it."

"Oh, Sir William." I sat on the edge of the bed and stroked his skeletal hand. His eyes were moist with tears and I did not try to hold back my own. "They were such beautiful things." I remembered the weeks I had spent recording and supervising the packing of those priceless antiquities – and there were so many of them. That every one was now destroyed was too awful to take in. "Such a tragedy for scholarship too."

"Well, yes – or it would be if scholarship knew about them."

"But scholarship will know about them. You had every piece meticulously drawn, and Tischbein has the engravings. You will salvage some of your investment when they are published."

"Have you heard from Tischbein since we left Naples? I haven't. The engravings are probably on their way to Paris by now. No, Cornelia, let us not grasp at straws; the plain truth is that I am £15,000 in debt with nothing to cover it."

I leaned to Sir William and kissed him. I loved that man, that gentle man in debt after a lifetime of selfless generosity.

"What will you do?" I wiped my cheeks and he shrugged.

"Let it sink in." He gave an acid laugh. "*Sink* in! I shall sleep on it."

"And I shall sleep on it too." I stood up from the bed. "If there is anything that I can do for you. I share this loss with you, you know – not the financial one of course – although I dare say I might spare one or two hundred pounds without too much pain."

"Oh no, no, no," Sir William laughed, "God bless you my child, it shall never come to that! God forbid that I should ever descend to beggary! No, let our first response be the wise one. We shall sleep on it and see how the world looks tomorrow."

I returned along the corridor and descended the broad marble stairs towards the first floor landing. What plans we make for our lives, I thought, and how little they relate to those of Providence. What was it some ribald youth once told me? 'If you would make God laugh, tell him your plans.' How profound is the wisdom of fools! As I descended the stairs my mind was awash with sad images: hundreds of Grecian urns, every one a masterpiece, crushed under guns off St Mary's; *Colossus* herself, wrecked on the reef, and the wounded of the Nile, some blinded, some limbless, struggling in the storm-tossed sea, and Sir William, skeletal and sad, sat up all alone in his bed – all these images swirled while I tried to gather my thoughts and then, as I turned at the first floor landing, I heard from behind me,

"Miss Knight?" I stopped and turned.

"Lord Nelson!" He was coming along the corridor with his secretary carrying his papers.

"Have you been visiting Sir William?" I was taken aback. The encounter was so unexpected.

"I have, yes."

"And how is he? He has taken his loss hard." The little admiral, with his right sleeve pinned across his be-medalled chest, was watching me gravely.

"Well, yes, he has taken it hard," I told him, not really wanting to talk to him, "how could he not?"

"Because he has lost only money?"

"No, he has not!" Sometimes, Nelson's Philistinism astounded me. "He – we – civilisation – has lost hundreds of the most exquisite works of art ever produced; objects of great antiquity that Sir William has spent half his life excavating, researching and cataloguing. His loss is incalculable."

"Is that what you were talking about then? Jugs and vases?" I did not like his tone, and I did not want to talk to him about Sir William, but then he rested his hand on my arm. "You mustn't worry about him, you know; we'll not leave him in want. The queen is always very appreciative of Lady Emma's services, and my country and others have been generous to me. Sir William will be well looked after."

I could not believe what I was hearing from this man. I was still trying to absorb the St Mary's disaster and Sir William's desperate situation and now this upstart usurper of his marital bed dared patronise him. There were many things I could have said to Nelson at that moment but instead I asked him,

"Did *Colossus* not have an anchor?" My question surprised Nelson, as I supposed it might.

"Yes, she had an anchor," he let go my arm, "and it was out, as I am informed, in St Mary's harbour, but it was not adequate to the gale and the condition of the harbour-bed. Why do you ask?"

"Because Sir William said something about your taking *Colossus's* anchor when she was at Naples."

"I took her second anchor. I needed it to replace one we'd lost in Aboukir Bay."

"And that second anchor, if she had had it, would have held *Colossus* in St Mary's harbour, wouldn't it Admiral?"

Nelson, and his secretary behind him, both smiled indulgently at me. I was on the brink of an argument with Nelson but I realised that it would only be acrimonious and serve no good purpose so I turned away from him, back towards the stairs.

"Do you know how many judgements I make in a single day, Miss Knight?" Nelson called after me, and his words hit me like a club. I spun round.

"No. But I am sure their quantity is great. It is only their quality that I might question." And I hurried away down the stairs.

I should not have been so hard on Nelson – it was bad-mannered – but I was upset about Sir William's plight and annoyed that Nelson took it so lightly. I did not regret my parting shot though. It was discharged in passion but it was the truth, and I was not the only one questioning Nelson's judgement that winter. There were questions over his seamanship when he lost his masts and his frigates off Corsica, and again, during the flight from Naples, when he lost his rigging and Prince Albert. And was it not an outstanding mis-judgement to encourage Naples to attack the most powerful land force that Europe has seen in a thousand years? In his own words, 'look where that got us?' And now he was being led by the nose by Emma Hamilton, the some-time courtesan and confidante of a cruel queen whose policies had failed Naples and England. Apart from all considerations of morality, decorum and bilateral diplomacy, did he not consider what his officers felt about that? Their leader? The heroic icon of the entire navy and nation, panting like a puppy after such a woman as Emma Hamilton? He was a laughing-stock in the wardrooms and, if he did not see that, he knew his men less well than he should. *Lady Emma and I will look after Sir William!* The audacity! Standing beneath Sir William's own bedroom and to me whom he knew loved him. I wondered at Nelson, I wondered at Emma, and I wondered at the effect of their *affaire* on Sir William.

"An unforeseen consequence. Don't all experiments have unforeseen consequences?" I was sitting with Sir William in his improvised study, a small baroque corner room with disproportionately tall windows on two walls and a disproportionately large stove throwing out heat from another. It was only forty-eight hours since he had received his fateful news but in that time he had recovered himself and was groomed, dressed and back at his desk.

"Your marriage was an experiment?" I was a little shocked. I was sitting on a sofa next to the tiled stove while Sir William sat alongside his desk. "Whatever do you mean?"

"Not our marriage as such," he explained, "I had known Emma for five years before we married, the solemnisation was just a formality."

"A formality?" Sir William's candour astonished me. Our talk had until then been all about Francesco and me and our compatibility but then Sir William had turned it to his own marriage to Emma and their perceived incompatibility. "So you did not love Emma when you married her? Though you had known her for five years?"

"Yes, I loved her," Sir William twisted in his chair and crossed his long legs. "I love her now, very much, she is a dear and fascinating creature but I could not love Emma in the way that I loved my wife – my late wife that is, Lady Catherine." He turned his face to the window, drawn, I supposed, by the memory of Lady Catherine. "She passed away in '82 you know. We were married for twenty-four years."

I watched Sir William, staring pensively out of the window. His marriage did intrigue me. He and Emma seemed so mismatched and now he was telling me that his first marriage was the more important. So, why Emma? I wondered. Sir William was not the ageing roué who would take a young wife just for vanity. Perhaps Emma was a remembrance of Catherine? Or the daughter that they never had.

"Did Lady Catherine not have any children?" I asked him, "no infants … no still-born …"

"Oh, no, no, my dear," Sir William turned back to me, "there was nothing like that, the procreation clause in the marriage contract was one that both of us were happy to disregard, no, Catherine was my companion, my soulmate and my friend. Emma was never going to take her place but, if you are interested in Emma, as I see that you are, I shall tell you about her." He rose from his chair and went to look out of the window.

"When I described Emma's attachment to Lord Nelson just now as the unforeseen consequence of an experiment, I think I was trying to be clever." He turned to me. "You know – skimming over a difficult truth with a smart remark but, thinking about it, it has a ring of truth." I settled myself by the stove while Sir William turned back to the window.

"Twelve – no – thirteen years ago now, Emma was abandoned to me." He looked round to make sure I was listening. "She had been kept by my nephew, Greville, since she was sixteen, at his house in Edgware Row, but then, when it came the time for him to think about marrying, he decided he had better tidy up his domestic arrangements and so looked to place Emma elsewhere. I think it occurred to him that the tidiest possible arrangement, one putting Emma beyond London gossip, would be to place her abroad and he thought of his old Uncle William. He asked if I would look after her for six months, show her the sights and give her a little polish that might improve her future prospects and – accustomed as I am, to playing the host – I agreed, just so long as she came with a chaperone. What Greville did not tell me, and which came as a shock to us all, was that he would abandon Emma and her mother in Naples, leaving me to decide what to do with them."

"But that is appalling! Your nephew is a scoundrel!" Sir William laughed and turned back into the room.

"Maybe, maybe. I certainly felt ill-used at the time and so did Emma but then, what were Emma's prospects at home? Greville was not going to take her back and, with no other connections, her chances in London could have been bleak.

"And so you took her in?"

"I felt I had no choice and, besides, after knowing her for six months, I was intrigued with Emma, she was no ordinary English visitor. Her background could not have been more humble – raised in the Flintshire bog, fatherless and coarse-tongued – she had no education but that which she needed to survive as a child courtesan but for all that, I could see she that had qualities. Emma Hart, at twenty-one, was a woman of surpassing beauty, as lovely as any depicted on a Grecian vase, but there was also a pliancy about her, a willingness to please and learn that I felt should be encouraged."

"So you decided you would have her educated."

"No. It wasn't like that. I did not want to educate her, my interest was – my experiment, if you like – was to see how far she might educate herself, if she had the opportunity." Sir William leaned his back against the window sill and folded his arms. "Even in London, Emma had been in demand as an artist's model. She had sat scores, probably hundreds of times, for Romney, Reynolds, Fuseli, Lawrence – even the

Prince of Wales commissioned her – it was an almost full-time occupation and so it became for her in Naples." Sir William put up a finger. "The thing that you must always remember about Emma is that she wants above all to please. It is the legacy, no doubt, of her years as a courtesan, and she had an intuitive grasp of what it was that an artist wanted in the cast of an eye, the curve of a shoulder or the line of the fall of her hair. By the time she arrived in Naples, she knew who were Medea and Circe, Agrippina and Andromache, without ever reading any of the texts – the posing came naturally to her and as the artists queued to paint her so their clients and their friends queued to watch."

"Which led then to the Attitudes." I saw now where the story was leading.

"Yes. Which led then to dance, and dance to song – Emma has a beautiful voice – whatever she did was applauded and what audiences enjoy, Emma is pleased to serve.

"But you did give her singing lessons, Mrs Cadogan told Mother."

"I did, but they were at Emma's request, and some Italian and French lessons too, again, at her own request – do you see the point – I suggested nothing, I merely gave her the space and the means."

"But then, after five years, you married her. If you were as detached as you say, how would that enlarge her space?"

"That too was at Emma's request. As she grew into Neapolitan society, she became sensitive to the whispers about a young woman living under the roof of an ageing widower and she wanted the situation righted. I saw no reason to refuse her and, besides, she was more than capable by then of playing the ambassador's wife."

"And playing *your* wife?"

"Playing *my* wife?" I felt the colour rise in my cheeks. Sir William had volunteered so much. "What do you mean?" He was smiling at me with such dispassionate, intrigued interest, I could not withdraw.

"I just wondered," I told him, meeting his interested gaze, "whether Emma was as happy as Catherine to be selective with the wedding contract?"

"Aah," Sir William's smile broadened and a twinkle entered his eye, "now there, my dear Cornelia, you have grasped the unforeseen consequence."

The Palazzo Palagonia was rapidly becoming the *de facto* Court. While the queen wept and wailed at the Colli Palace and the king went off hunting, the Palazzo Palagonia blazed every night with a thousand wax candles and rang with music and song. After the fateful flight from Naples, Lady Emma's position as Queen's Favourite had become unassailable. Emma was the queen's rock in a rising tide of suspicion and duplicity and if she was also well-placed to secure the protection of Nelson's ships, then that too was a reason to cherish her. The queen showered Emma with gifts – gold, jewels and trunks of robes – Emma was growing rich on the queen's favour and, for as long as it lasted, she was determined to enjoy it.

Every evening she hosted a banquet followed by music and gambling into the small hours. There was no shortage of pretexts: Nelson freshly honoured by the Czar or the Sultan or the Cities of Palermo or London. Jewels and gold were pouring into Nelson's coffers too and he, in his infatuation, fawned on Emma at her banquets as slavishly as she fawned on him. It was a nightly spectacle of mutual admiration that all who had the stomach were welcome to watch. Two dozen to dinner was normal and twice that, not uncommon. Cohorts of servants laboured in the kitchens and footmen lined the bright stairs. Excess was the norm: excess of food and champagne and cheaply-bought friendships and, at the card tables, while the servants ached for their beds, hundreds of pounds would be risked on the turn of a card. If Emma had grown under Sir William's liberality, she fairly ballooned under her own. Her appetites were great, and Nelson, besotted though he was, struggled to keep up with her, generally retiring after supper. Nelson was, after all, much more than Emma's trophy; he was the commander of a powerful squadron with all the logistical and political problems that that position entailed, and besides, he still was not well.

"I don't think he has recovered from the head wound he received at the Battle of the Nile," was Mrs Cadogan's analysis. "Emma says he weeps with the pain in his head and sometimes it's so bad he is sick. Emma is so good to him. I don't think he is an easy man." We were taking tea in our bedroom in the Villa Caracciolo. Though the worst of winter was behind us, Mother was still too weak to go out but she dressed now every day and put on her wig and some paint.

"You might be right," Mother told Mrs Cadogan, "but he has his worries too, and they would be more than enough to give a man a headache."

"Oh, I accept that," agreed Mrs Cadogan, "such a weight upon one man's shoulders! A score of ships! Thousands of men! Victualling! Repairing! Not to mention the politics – and he has it all to bear on his own – weeks and months away from his masters. Yes. It would challenge the strongest man."

"I was not thinking about his command," Mother replied. "My late husband had command of a squadron in the West Indies – much further away from his masters – and he did not have headaches. English admirals are trained from boyhood for command, no, the worries I had in mind were those within Nelson's conscience: he made a terrible mistake urging the Neapolitans to attack the French – what does an admiral know about armies? There are no two ways about it: Nelson lost the Bourbons their thrones and he is feeling the weight of it."

The mothers could while away their afternoons putting the world to rights but, without Francesco, Palermo was a desert to me. I had Sir William, of course, but from the morbidity of the Bourbons to the vulgarity of Lady Emma and the sullen hostility of our Sicilian hosts, Palermo was Golgotha, Sodom and Hades and I ached to be back with Francesco. Our separation, so rationally agreed, pained me more than I had ever imagined and, on top of the pain, I worried about him. He had sailed away to … what? A city ravaged by the French? At war with itself? Or shining with justice and liberty? Accounts were so mixed there was no way of knowing the truth but then, on the twelfth day, his letter arrived and the worst of my fears were dispelled.

My dearest Cornelia,

We arrived safely after a good passage and to a warm welcome. Mother came down from Avellino, and Naples seems just what it was but how deceptive appearances can be: politically, it is transformed.

The new provisional government has had a shaky start – as you might expect – but the direction of change is all positive. Already, we have a draft constitution and it looks very well. The monarchy, the Church tithes and the whole feudal system are abolished. Radical change! I am proud of this draft constitution and while I have no illusions about the task of weakening entrenched loyalties, we have the powerful support of General Championnet and that, I believe, will be key.

I know, Cornelia, that you think me blinkered about the French – that I am less critical than you of their treatment of conquered territories – but Championnet is no Berthier and Naples no conquered territory. Once the Bourbons had fled, the provisional government opened the gates to Championnet and together they subdued the Bourbon rump. I know that you were there when the French occupied Rome, and that it is a bitter memory, but let me tell you what is happening here. When those same French agents who directed the plundering of Rome arrived in Naples, Championnet would not admit them. He sent them back to Paris with the clear message that Naples is an ally and not to be disturbed and so we remain.

Cornelia, you must come to Naples and smell this fresh air. It was never so sweet and, with spring around the corner, it will, I am sure, be the tonic that your mother needs. Hurry to me, my love, I miss you terribly but know that we will be happy – Naples will be happy – the future is bright. As to the navy … sufficient for now to say that she keeps me busy and the charred hulks are a sad sight. Let me know the moment that your mother is fit to sail and I shall send a sloop.

Keep well. Keep safe.
Francesco

P.S. As things stand in Palermo, it might be prudent to write to me care of a friend with royalist connections – the Duke of Bagnara at the Palazzo Bagnara. The Duchess is Ruffo's niece.

He was happy. It shone from the page and that lifted my heart. I knew that Francesco was partial and that he flew on the wings of his enthusiasm but he was not alone in his optimism, others too were noting Naples' tranquillity and the competence of her new government. Two English travellers in particular, who arrived in Palermo from Naples, confirmed Francesco's view.

"I applaud the republican regime. Every Englishman should." Lord Montgomery and his companion were Grand Tourists, a rare breed in those war-torn times and, knowing my need for news, Sir William had invited me to dine with them. It was – for the Palazzo Palagonia – an intimate gathering: just Lady Emma and Nelson, Sir William and his principal guest (a Turkish envoy), Lord Montgomery, his friend and the Camerons and me. Nelson had scowled at the young peer.

"They want only what we have," Montgomery told him, "an elected parliament, free movement of labour, an independent judiciary. I wish them God's speed."

"Hear, hear," I agreed and Nelson shot me a look.

"And to whom do these republicans pay allegiance?" Nelson asked Montgomery.

"Well, not to any king. Theirs has run away."

"Run away!" Lady Emma, who had been occupied with her ice cream, slammed down her spoon but Nelson covered her hand.

"Like the French then," Nelson suggested, "allegiance to no one, which is why France is a wasps' nest." Lord Montgomery shook his head.

"Naples is no wasps' nest. Quite the opposite. We found it the most peaceable city in Italy."

"Peace at the point of French bayonets," Nelson persisted, "take those away and your republic will crumble. It is the monarch that cements a country. All history affirms that, and it is the law of God."

"Yes," Emma agreed, "kings are ordained by God!" She was ready to do war with the peer but Nelson's hand still held her.

"I don't see the United States of America crumbling for want of a monarch," Montgomery continued lightly, "or the United Provinces of Holland. They haven't paid allegiance to a king for two hundred years." Nelson shifted in his seat and growled.

"I must say, Lord Montgomery, for an English peer, you have a singular sympathy for King George's enemies."

"Well, the world is changing, Nelson – oh, congratulations by the way, on your elevation, deserved I am sure – the world is changing and concepts of patriotism are changing with it. Look at you," the young nobleman extended a hand to Nelson, "recognised across Europe as the model patriot, and yet which monarch have you been serving these past months, and does he even have a country to cement?" Around the table, there was an audible intake of breath. Lady Emma, already suffused with wine, went puce while Nelson's colour drained. He dashed a look at Sir William, demanding his support, but Sir William was engaged in translating the exchanges for the Turkish envoy and so missed Nelson's appeal. Nelson glowered round the table, assessing the disposition of support, but then he seemed to collect himself.

"Did you happen, while you were in Naples, to meet General Championnet?" he asked Montgomery.

"We did," Montgomery told him, "and I have to tell you that, whatever we might think of his uniform, he seemed a most intelligent and generous-spirited man. I do assure you, Nelson, that his influence upon the Neapolitan Republic is far more benign than a bayonet's tip."

"And did he tell you, during your conversation, that he was being recalled?"

"No, he did not." Montgomery looked surprised. "Is he?"

"He is. For insubordination. The Directory in Paris does not take kindly to generals who turn back their booty agents. He is to be replaced by General Jacques Macdonald – don't be fooled by the name; he's as French as the rest – Miss Knight?" Nelson turned to me, "I think you will remember MacDonald, he was General Berthier's second-in-command in Rome, in charge of the plundering and sequestering and confiscating." He looked back to Montgomery. "I look forward to having this conversation with you again your lordship, when Naples is wrung dry."

"Ah! Ha!" The Turkish envoy, seized by something Sir William had translated, suddenly leapt to his feet and pulled out his scimitar. He was a moustachioed brute of the warrior type and he set to declaiming in his native tongue and brandishing his sword over the table. I leaned to Sir William and asked him what the man was saying but Sir William seemed reluctant to tell me, fobbing me off with,

"He doesn't like the French," which Emma overheard.

"Well hoorah for him!" she shouted and she too rose to her feet. "Thank you Excellency! It takes a Musselman to speak sense! I salute you!" and she drained her glass of wine. The Turk, still declaiming, rested a finger on his scimitar's tip and held the weapon up to his face. He seemed to be addressing it, and now Nelson called to Sir William,

"What is the man saying, damn it?" and Sir William felt obliged to explain.

"He is saying – and I hope I have this right – that with this sword, in one day, he beheaded twenty French prisoners. He is pointing out the bloodstains." A groan of revulsion rolled round the room. Only Emma was unmoved, apparently fascinated by the Turk and, while everyone else shrank in dismay, she held out her hand to him.

"Let me see that sword." She took it by the hilt and tip, just as the Turk had done, and then, to everyone's horror, she lifted it to her lips and kissed it once, twice, three times along the blade as tenderly as if she were kissing a child, and then she offered the sword to Nelson. He, for his part, was not even looking at Emma, he had turned aside to help Suzie Cameron who had fainted and slipped to the floor. I jumped up and ran round to her, skirting Montgomery and his friend who were leaving in disgust. Nelson was struggling, with only the one arm, to help Suzie so I stepped in and, with Mr Cameron's help, got her to her feet. We decided to take her out for some air but then, as we manoeuvred

Suzie through the dining room doors, I caught sight of Sir William, himself on his feet by now, staring after us with a look of the most abject sadness. We carried on down the stairs, behind Montgomery and his friend, and it was from there that we heard Lady Emma declare,

"Well, that shook out the damned Jacobins!"

"Another unforeseen consequence of your experiment?" I suggested, and Sir William laughed. I had asked him to walk with me along the Marino promenade after spending an hour with Mother. The sea was sparkling in the spring sunshine and, in the gardens, blossoms of orange, oleander and pomegranate were beginning to burst into life.

"I have given up worrying about consequences, Cornelia, and only charlatans claim to foresee."

"But you were shocked by her brutality," I told him, "I saw it in your face." Sir William looked down, pensively, at the gravel path. This was not an easy conversation but, because I cared for him, it was one that I needed to have. "Lady Emma is so much changed," I went on, "does she not worry you?"

"You think her changed?"

"Well, she certainly is not the captivating hostess that I knew when I arrived in Naples, nor the heroine who brought the queen and her children to Palermo."

"Interesting," Sir William mused, "so, what is it in Emma that you think has changed?"

"Her coarseness, boorishness even. You saw her last night. You cannot tell me that you were amused." We walked on in silence, shoulder to shoulder, and then, after a few moments, Sir William asked me,

"Do you remember my telling you a week or two ago that Emma wants, above all, to please?"

"Yes, I do."

"And do you remember also what I said about my allowing her to be whatever she wanted to be?"

"Yes," I said again.

"Well, I am beginning to think, in hindsight, that though I tried not to influence Emma, everything that she chose to do in those early years was, in fact, only to please me – to help her become the woman she thought I wanted her to be – just as she had tried, for my nephew, to be what she thought he had wanted her to be. Greville's and my Emma were the same woman but she behaved with each of us only as she thought we each expected."

"Striking Attitudes," I suggested.

"Well, yes. What an interesting idea. Adopting a persona, you mean?" Sir William seemed pleased with this matching of Emma's different facets. "And then, similarly, with the queen," he went on, "Emma had always admired Maria-Carolina but when events so fell out that Emma was, of a sudden, useful to her, Emma responded with that same instinct to please that she had shown to Greville and me and the more the queen asked of Emma the more Emma gave."

"But can Emma please you and the queen at the same time?"

"Of course. Why not? I am the British Ambassador to the Court of Naples and Maria-Carolina is the Queen. Where is the conflict?" I stopped on the path and turned to Sir William.

"But now it is Lord Nelson that Emma is anxious to please."

"Indeed, the military hero," he gave me a sad smile, "and now she disguises fair nature with hard-favoured rage. She didn't learn that from me, did she Cornelia?" He looked away to the gardens and the vivid hues of the blossom. "I am glad that Emma has fallen in love – found someone who wants to please *her* for a change – we all need that. I just wish she hadn't fallen for such a consummate dog of war."

Nelson had frightened me with his talk of Naples being ravaged. I did not doubt what he had said about Championnet's recall, Nelson was not a man to tease or trade in gossip, but how significant the change of command would be to the new republic must surely be open to question. As Francesco pointed out in his letter, the Neapolitan Republic was not subject to Paris, she was her ally, so why would the French want to plunder and weaken her? General Macdonald may not have been as enlightened a commander as Championnet but his reputation was more for cunning than brutality so perhaps Nelson's judgement was wrong – I hoped so, but still worried.

I wrote again to Francesco – mostly small talk. I had so many questions I wanted to ask about the French and the reforms but I was afraid that if I asked I would betray my anxiety and I did not want him worrying about me so I kept it bland. What I really wanted, of course, was to hear from him. I had only received the one letter and that, too, worried me because Francesco, I knew, must have written more. I needed reliable news, so when a card was presented by an old name from Naples, I made sure I was home to meet him.

Captain Gould had been away on the Malta blockade since October but now he was recalled for fresh orders.

Mother was still unwell – the spring weather had not, so far, improved her breathing – but she liked Captain Gould and insisted on receiving him, even propped up in her bed. I curled her thin hair and put her pearls round her neck and her pashmina over her shoulders. She looked pretty, I thought, despite her thinness, and, while Captain Gould and I took tea with her at her bedside, Mother asked him about Nelson's recall.

"Oh no, Lady Knight, there is no question of his going home now, the French are back in the Mediterranean." Captain Gould took a small piece of almond cake. He looked tanned after his months at sea, and fitter than I remembered him. "Twenty-five French ships-of-the-line have broken the Brest blockade and passed through the Straights of Gibralta. Lord St Vincent's squadron is pursuing them but we do not know where they are bound – it could be Minorca or Malta, or they may try to re-embark Bonaparte's army and invade Sicily, we don't know. Nelson is ordering all the ships he can spare back to Sicily, just in case: Foley and me from Malta, Troubridge from the Bay of Naples and others from Leghorn and Alexandria. We are to rendezvous off Cape Maritimo to try to defend Sicily and the routes to Malta and Egypt."

"I am sorry, Captain Gould," I had to ask him, "but did you just say Troubridge was in the Bay of Naples?" Captain Gould nodded as he took a drink of his tea. "But what is Commodore Troubridge doing in the Bay of Naples? How long has he been there?"

"He has been there since the beginning of April, re-capturing the islands and some mainland forts." Gould put down his cup and gave me a curious look. "I am surprised you don't know that."

"Oh, we hear nothing here, do we, Cornelia?" Mother told him, "we might as well be in a nunnery."

"I mean," Gould explained, looking at me, "that I am surprised that you, Miss Knight, did not hear it from Naples." He looked down at my ring and a shiver ran through me. Captain Gould knew something about Francesco. It was there in his raised bushy eyebrow. I put down my cup.

"I know nothing about Troubridge's activities," I told him, fingering my ring, "but if you have any news of Admiral Caracciolo, Captain, I would be obliged if you would share it with me." Captain Gould shifted awkwardly in his chair. He had news, I could tell. He ran a finger under his collar.

"I don't know how else to say this, Miss Knight," he shot me a worried look, "but Admiral Caracciolo engaged Commodore Troubridge."

"Engaged him?" My head swam. I knew what Captain Gould meant by 'engaged' but I did not want to believe it.

"One of the forts that Troubridge captured was Castellamare. After a few days, the republicans mounted a counter-attack and Admiral Caracciolo sailed out in support with a frigate and half a dozen corvettes. He fired on the English ships laid at anchor."

"But you cannot be sure that Admiral Caracciolo was involved in the engagement." Mother's eyelids were closing and Captain Gould took her cup.

"Troubridge saw him on the frigate's quarter deck, directing the action." I imagined the scene: the smoke and the noise and Francesco on deck for everyone to see.

"And were there casualties?" I asked, my heart in my mouth.

"Some, of course, on both sides, but Admiral Caracciolo went home unscathed." Captain Gould leaned forward and clasped his hands over his knees. "Miss Knight," he hesitated, "I know this is not my place but do you realise how dangerous this is for the admiral?" Captain Gould was so close and so large I felt hot. I got up and walked over to the window.

"You just told me he was unscathed."

"I mean politically dangerous." I turned round to him.

"Politically dangerous? How so? From your own account, he, the commander of a sovereign navy, defended his own fort against a foreign aggressor. I could not think of anything more honourable or legal."

"I think you know what I mean, Miss Knight."

"I am afraid I do not, Captain, you will have to explain it."

"It was an act of treason."

"No, it wasn't! Admiral Caracciolo's loyalty is to Naples, not to King George."

"But King George's ships were acting on behalf of King Ferdinand, Admiral Caracciolo's sovereign lord …"

"Who abandoned his throne!" My heart was thumping in my chest. "Francesco was defending his own country!" Tears welled in my eyes and my legs went weak. Captain Gould got up and came to me.

"Miss Knight. I tell you this because I want to help you and, if it is not too late, help Admiral Caracciolo as well, for your sake." He took hold of my arms. "If you want to save the admiral you must persuade him to get out of Naples and quickly. The republic's situation is hopeless. The combined Austrian and Russian armies have entered Italy and are sweeping south. The French are drawing all their forces north to meet them, including from Naples, they have abandoned the city, it is wide open, Ruffo can retake it for Ferdinand any time he chooses."

"Ruffo? *Cardinal* Ruffo?" I had not heard his name in weeks. "Did he raise a force in Calabria then?"

"Did he raise a force! He landed with half a dozen men and within three weeks had an army of seventeen thousand. He is an impressive character; a Prince of Calabria and a Prince of the Church and recruits flood to his banner every mile he moves north – and now Russia and Turkey are landing forces to support him." It was too much for me to take in.

"But are you sure? I have heard nothing of this."

"You won't have, because timing and surprise are everything. Ruffo doesn't want the republicans forewarned of his advance and he doesn't want the Lazzaroni running amok either before the king returns."

I saw Francesco again, alone on his quarter deck, defending the republic against impossible odds. I grasped at a straw.

"But the republicans have the sea. You just told me that Nelson has recalled Troubridge from the islands to await the French fleet off Sicily."

"The islands are immaterial." The captain's eyes were pleading with me. "The English ships are immaterial. The French have marched out of Naples, and Ruffo, the Russians and the Turks will, any day, march in. I tell you this because I worry for you, Miss Knight. I don't want you to do anything rash."

CHAPTER TWELVE

I went to see Sir William. He was the British Ambassador, a friend of the king, and his wife a friend of the queen. He must have known about the Austrians and the Russians and Ruffo and Troubridge attacking the forts. He was Francesco's friend, and my friend. I could not believe that he had kept so much from me.

"There is no secret about the coalition, Cornelia." I had walked in, unannounced, to his office. My obvious agitation must have startled him because he rose from his desk and crossed to the window. "It is months now since Austria joined Russia against France."

"But I did not know they were in Italy already and pushing south. Did you know that the French had abandoned Naples? And that English warships were back in the bay?"

"I try not to involve myself in the minutiae of naval manoeuvrings. Warfare is not my strong suit." It was a lame answer and Sir William knew it. I stood and waited for him to do better and when, after a few moments, he turned to face me, his eyes were full of sadness.

"I am afraid Francesco is in terrible trouble." He stroked his long fingers across his forehead. "You heard about the engagement with Troubridge?" I nodded. "Well, now, he has attacked *Minerva*, one of Ferdinand's ships attached to the English flotilla, and mounted a concerted attack on our forces on Procida."

"Our forces on Procida? I thought Troubridge had been recalled to face the French fleet."

"Yes, Troubridge has, but he left garrisons in the forts and one or two smaller vessels to protect them."

"Against Neapolitans? But they are Neapolitan forts. Francesco is defending his own territory." I took a step closer to Sir William. "Why is England making war on Naples?"

"We are not making war on Naples, quite the contrary, Nelson is trying desperately to support Naples, our ally."

"Support Ferdinand you mean, who forfeited his legitimacy when he abandoned his country." Sir William shook his head and sighed.

"Oh Cornelia, Cornelia," he held out a hand to me, "this business pains me as much as it pains you. I have known Francesco since he was a boy and he is the best of Naples – intelligent, active, passionate about his country – and I could name twenty more like him whom I am also proud to call my friends and now face this terrible peril." He glanced across at the sofa and then at me.

"Won't you sit down?" I went and sat next to the cold stove and Sir William sat down by his desk.

"Perhaps," he mused, leaning back and examining the ceiling, "when the French had their revolution, if we and the other monarchical powers had let them be, their republic might have blossomed," he gave me a sad smile, "and perhaps other European states, like Naples, might have peaceably followed their example and proved the excellence of Voltaire's ideas, but the fact of the matter is that France was not left alone, all Europe went to war with her, and the hard reality that I have to face is that Naples' young republic is the child of the French and my country is at war with France."

"But the French are not in Naples anymore," I reminded him. "They have withdrawn, so, surely, now, if we are not at war with Naples, England too should withdraw her forces and besides, what about Francesco? With Ruffo and the Russians and the Austrians getting closer, the sea is his best means of escape." Again, Sir William looked to the ceiling.

"Your logic has power, Cornelia, and who knows, the British government might someday be persuaded by it, but policies cannot be changed and communicated back to an ambassador in a few days or weeks and besides, you tell me that your hope for Francesco rests with the sea but who controls the sea?" He looked at me but it was a rhetorical question. "However you slice Nelson's orders, after those two hostile actions, he cannot regard Francesco as anything other than an enemy." Sir William sighed deeply. "I am sorry, Cornelia, I really am, but I just don't see what either of us can do for Francesco."

Sir William's despondency upset me but I tried not to show it. He too had his problems – I understood that – he had lost everything and waited only for passage to England and retirement. But I was not ready to retire, my life was just beginning and I needed to hear from Francesco. This latest intelligence frightened me. Too many powers were gathering against the young republic before it was even weaned and with its wet-nurse, France, abandoning it, I needed to know what Francesco thought. Did he still have faith in the republic? Was there enough life in it to warrant his continuing? Or was the situation as hopeless as Captain Gould said and he should get out? It was impossible for me to know from Palermo but of one thing I was sure; whatever Francesco was thinking, he would be thinking of me. He would not throw himself away on a lost cause leaving me to grieve for him – he loved me too much for that. If I had not heard from him, I told myself, it was not because he had not written; it was because his letters had not got through; there was something wrong in the line of communication but what could I do? I wished that Sir William had been stronger. He was Francesco's most powerful friend in Palermo and, if he had stirred himself, surely, he could have done something. I was disappointed in him, and at a loss as to know what to do.

Cardinal Ruffo's Calabrian adventure had been astonishingly successful. Landing almost alone, he had, with messianic brio, conscripted every vassal from his family's estates, promised freedom to the felons in the gaols and, in a passionate encyclical proclaimed from every pulpit in the province, promised absolution to all who rallied to Cause. In a culture where hatred of foreigners was matched only by its devotion to a vengeful god, the cardinal's appeal was electrifying and thousands upon thousands brought their guns and daggers to his banner. It was a motley and ill-disciplined band that soon slipped from the cardinal's control. Their conquests were brutal and their atrocities music to a vengeful queen.

'*God speed Your Eminence to that Monstrous Sodom,*' she urged Ruffo in an open dispatch. '*Impose order on her ungrateful citizens. Accept no conditions. Set your heart against pity and hunt down the wicked. Chastise them. Annihilate their leaders – a massacre will not displease. If you love God and your King leave Naples with nothing but her eyes that she might weep.*'

It was the uncurling of a viper that had lain dormant in her lair for the past six months and my blood ran cold. Captain Gould's and Sir William's talk of ships and troop movements had been worrying but cerebral; Maria-Carolina's intervention was visceral and Francesco had to be warned. Her message was unambiguous: forget principle, philosophy and the weighing of conflicting loyalties, bestial vengeance was to stand for law and the good would go down with the bad. There was no point in my writing to Francesco; I had written to him a dozen times since his letter to me. Something was wrong in Naples and if Francesco was to know how I feared for him, I would have to tell him myself.

Mother – as wise mothers will – appeared sympathetic.

"There is no more powerful emotion than love, my dear, and you must not let your duty to your decrepit old mother prevent you from following your heart, but have you thought what Francesco might think about your going to Naples?"

"I cannot ask him, Mother. That is the point."

"And you think, do you, that he would sanction your voyaging alone into a theatre of war? With bandits poised at any moment to invade? The poor man will have enough to do looking after himself and his family and all those who come under his command without having to worry about you. No, Cornelia. Francesco is a resourceful man. Have faith in his ability to manage his own affairs and, if you love him, put his care for you above your impatience with yourself."

Sir William called the following day. Mother was not feeling so well, her breathing was short, so he did not stay long but, as I walked him downstairs to the door, I asked him what he thought of my going to Naples. At the foot of the stairs, he had given me a severe look.

"I think it would be a mission fraught with danger."

"But from all that we hear," I argued, "Naples is quiet. You heard Lord Montgomery; he said it was as peaceful as any city in Italy."

"When his lordship was there perhaps – and maybe even today – but, with the French gone, Ruffo's brigands, I am afraid, are approaching an open city."

"But I could be there in forty-eight hours. And Francesco is a public figure. I would find him – or news of him – the minute I landed." Sir William looked doubtful.

"And how would you get there in forty-eight hours?"

"I would charter a ketch."

"You really have been thinking about this, haven't you?"

"I have, yes."

"Have you thought about the English ships in the Bay of Naples? What if you were intercepted? What would you tell the English officer? I am sorry, Cornelia. I don't think it is possible." I could not conceive of it not being possible; the idea was too fixed in my mind. Another thought came to me.

"There will be sloops supplying the English ships in the Bay of Naples."

"From Palermo, you mean?"

"Yes."

"I don't know. There could be." He gave me a smile and touched my arm. "Let me see what I can find out." Then he left me and walked out to his carriage.

Six more English ships-of-the-line arrived in Palermo at the beginning of June, all sent to reinforce Nelson's defence of Sicily and the routes east. The threat from this latest French fleet was being taken seriously. A thousand English soldiers were landed on the island and local militias hurriedly levied. For a third time in eighteen months I was facing a French invasion but I was not worried about that; for me, the French fleet was a distraction from my greater concern about Naples and, after my talk with Sir William, I went to see Captain Gould.

"Oh no, Miss Knight!" You would have thought I had stabbed him with a dagger. He got up from his chair in *Audacious's* great cabin and staggered to the windows. He looked down at the quayside where his ship was being revictualled. "You promised me you would not do anything rash. If you go back to Naples now …" he turned back, his face wrung with worry, "we may never see you again."

"But would such a passage be possible?"

"Well, physically, yes. We have courier boats passing between here and the Bay of Naples every day but, unless you are planning to stow away, you would need permission. No captain would take you without the proper permission; it would be contrary to regulations."

"And who could give me such permission?"

"From here? It could only be Nelson." I thought he might say that. My heart sank. "But please do not think of asking him," Captain Gould went on, "between you and me, he is already driven sick by the queen and Lady Hamilton trying to divert him to Naples. If you were to add to his worries …"

"The queen wants Nelson to go to Naples?" I was astonished. "When a French fleet is bearing down on her here?"

"Please, Miss Knight. This is not common knowledge …"

"But why?"

"She thinks that, with all that is happening on the mainland, the time is opportune to retake Naples from the sea."

"But what about Sicily and the French fleet?"

"I don't think she gives three farthings about Sicily. The queen and Lady Hamilton are trying to persuade Nelson there are laurels for him if it is he who restores the monarchy."

"But it is not up to the queen or Lady Hamilton, is it? Nelson will have his orders."

"He does, and they are to keep station off Sicily, off Cape Maritimo."

"Well then. That is what he will do."

I walked home from *Audacious* feeling utterly dejected. It was hopeless. Asking Nelson to help me find Francesco – the old rival who was now attacking his ships – was unthinkable. I had finally to accept that my hair-brained scheme was just that and, in the clear light of day, I could accept that Mother was right and Francesco would not, in any case, have wanted me to take such a risk. I would have to stay in Palermo until I had some firm news but then, only two days later, Captain Gould's words proved prescient. I had it from Sir William when he called on us.

"Lady Knight. Cornelia. I call to bid you adieu." He sat down beside me at Mother's bedside.

"*Adieu*, Sir William?" Mother asked him. "You are leaving us?"

"Only for a short while." Sir William shot me a nervous glance. "Lord Nelson has decided to take his squadron to Naples to secure the capital for King Ferdinand and, as my masters in London will want my assessment of the political situation there," he lowered his eyes and stroked his brow, "I feel I should go along."

"Nelson is taking his squadron?" I could hardly believe what I was hearing. "How many ships?"

"Fifteen, sixteen, something like that."

"His *entire* squadron?"

"Almost."

"But what about the Cape Maritimo patrols and the French fleet?"

"His Lordship expects only to be away for a few days – put in an appearance as it were – a show of strength – deter resistance." Sir William attempted a smile but nerves or guilt or simple cowardice turned it sour."

"Is he taking the king?"

"Err, no. Not at this stage."

"The queen?"

"No, no, but Lady Emma is fully acquainted with the queen's views on Neapolitan matters."

"Lady Emma? Is she too sailing with Nelson then?" Sir William shifted uncomfortably.

"My wife will be accompanying me, yes."

"Or will you be accompanying her?" I should not have said that. I had embarrassed Sir William and I immediately regretted it but by then greater matters were worrying me.

"Then I shall come too."

"Cornelia!" Mother protested, but I ignored her.

"I shall sail with you," I repeated. "You know what this means to me, Sir William – and do not tell me that I shall not be safe – I shall be surrounded by nine hundred English canon."

"Cornelia," Sir William cooed in appeal, "I only wish that I could, but you know I shall do everything in my power to protect Francesco …"

"No," I told him. "I am coming with you. If you are my friend, you will arrange it."

I went as Sir William's second secretary. I appreciated that he was already heavily burdened with more than his fair share of worries but while he was battling with disappointments in his life, I was battling for the hope of mine and once he applied himself, it proved easier for him to take me than he had thought. He needed two secretaries, and he needed to leave someone behind so, while Mr Oliver manned the Palermo office, I took his place on the voyage with Mr Smith. It was an arrangement that suited us both: we had worked together before and Sir William knew my strengths while I, for my part, was glad of occupation that might distract me from constantly worrying about Francesco.

I wrote to Francesco to tell him I was coming. I no longer expected him to receive my letters but better, I thought, to write than not. Mother was sanguine. She was not going to worry about me sailing with such a force in such company and it was, we were told, only for a few days. Mrs Cadogan promised to call on Mother every day and the two Vs, I knew, were a solid support so I kissed Mother goodbye in full confidence. We sailed from Palermo in *Foudroyant*, a brand new eighty gunner to which Nelson had transferred his flag. It was the twenty-first of June, the feast of St Rufinus, the first Sicilian martyr.

CHAPTER 13

I was given Nelson's secretary's cabin in the corner of the wheel deck, just outside the doors to the great cabin. It was little more than a cupboard but it gave out straight onto the quarter deck and it was a pleasant thing, after Palermo's torpid heat, to stand on the deck of a fine new ship, beating into a north-west wind under full sails and a high sky. Men-of-war are not built for comfort but the great cabin, immediately behind my own, was a commodious space and Nelson had had the hinged partitions swung down to divide the dining cabin in the fore section from his private cabin behind it. The dining cabin made a comfortable, private space for us passengers, a place where we could read and write our letters for dispatch on the daily courier boat. Most of the communication was back south to Palermo but, on the afternoon of the second day, a boat hove to from the north with a dispatch for Nelson from Naples. He took it into his cabin and closed the door, but he was soon out again.

"Damn Cardinal Ruffo!" he exploded, "and damn Captain Foote! We do not treat with Republican traitors!" He thrust the dispatch into Sir William's lap. "Your opinion if you please, Sir William. Quick as you like!" And he strode out to the quarter deck calling for his flag captain.

Sir William and I exchanged a look, then he drew up his chair to the table and set to reading the dispatch. I moved up beside him.

"Does it mention Francesco?" Sir William stopped reading and leafed through the pages.

"Err ... yes it does ..." and he read, "'Admiral Caracciolo, commanding seven gunboats, bombarded the loyal positions in the Castel del Carmine and the Marinella but failed to dislodge the occupiers. His crews are now fled and the admiral himself gone to ground."

Fled. Gone to ground. The words stabbed my heart.

"What action was this? You said *loyal* positions. Has the cardinal entered Naples?" I needed to know more. "What else does it say about Francesco?"

"Cornelia, please!" Sir William pleaded. "Glancing through it, I can see no further mention of Francesco but if you will let me read the dispatch properly I might then answer your questions." I got up from the table and walked over to the double doors that led out onto the quarter deck. Half of me wanted to go through them and feel the wind on my face but the other half would go no further away from that dispatch so I stood and stared out at nothing. After what seemed an age, Sir William called me back.

"Ruffo's forces have taken Naples." I sat down beside him, my legs trembling. "Over a week ago. The Republicans still holding out are occupying the two seafront forts, the Uovo and the Nuovo."

"Is Francesco with them?" I was desperate for firm news but Sir William just sighed.

"I have no idea. I have read to you the only reference there is to Francesco. The important thing here," he tapped the dispatch with his forefinger, "the issue that has angered Nelson, is the armistice. Cardinal Ruffo has signed an armistice with the forts offering the Republicans either safe passage to Toulon or liberty to return to their homes. Nelson's senior officer in the bay, a frigate captain called Foote, has appended his name to this armistice and Nelson does not approve."

"But why not? That sounds perfect. You would agree to that wouldn't you, Sir William, and Nelson has asked for your opinion." Sir William sat back on his chair.

"It sounds humane, yes, and honourable. But if those sentiments prevail in Nelson's philosophy, they do not in Maria-Carolina's."

We were two more days, beating against contrary winds, before we passed Capri's Punta di Carena and entered the bay. Fifteen warships in line astern with their guns run out was a sight to strike fear into the boldest foe but there was no foe to be seen. On the contrary: just as when Nelson last sailed in, the bay was littered with little boats, their flags flying and lanterns dancing, coming out from the shore to greet him. Nelson and Sir William and the secretaries were out on deck and I with them but not to enjoy the boats. Shading my eyes against the sun, I scanned the vast city of Naples: its patchwork of azure and ochre roofs that pile in steps up the hillsides, its churches and palaces and the seafront forts where the Republicans were said to be. Was Francesco in one of those forts, I wondered, or was he alone, hiding under one of those roofs? I saw the white flags flying over the forts, and another on a frigate moored off the mole.

"Damn him!" Nelson said through his teeth. "Signal Captain Foote to remove that white flag please, Mr Tanner, and attend me here." The midshipman at Nelson's back ran off to hoist the signals and, at that same moment, Lady

Emma appeared. She came out of the great cabin, swathed as Britannia in navy and white, and walked over to the gunwale. She waved down to the people in the hundreds of boats, whipping up their cheers and then, when she had gained their attention, she thrust out an accusing finger.

"No armistice with Republicans and traitors!" she shouted. "Tear down those flags of truce!" Of course, as Emma well knew, her words fell on the Lazzaroni like fire into a tinderbox and their roar came back in reply.

"Long live the king!" they shouted, "Long live Ferdinand and long live Nelson!" Emma's words were passed from boat to boat, raising waves of men to their feet all stamping and cheering and chanting for the king. Such approbation was meat and drink to Emma and she mounted the steps to the poop where a wider audience might see her strutting her Attitudes of victory and vengance. Nelson and Sir William, whatever they might have thought, were powerless to intervene, she was beyond either's control, but it was too much for me. Somewhere beyond those boats was Francesco. Was he scanning the English ships, I wondered, as I scanned the land for him? If he were, the sight of them must surely spell the end of his republic. A wave of revulsion swept over me. I could see and hear no more. I went back to my cabin and covered my ears with my hands.

I lay in my cot but I did not sleep. I was trying to gather my thoughts – or *thought* – I had only one: how to get ashore. Nelson had ordered that no one was to leave the ship, but was there a way? I could not lower a boat, nor climb down the side on my own, and who would help me? Sir William was the only one on board who knew my true mission but this was no time to compromise him, he was already too compromised already. I lay with these thoughts muddling my head until, at about four o'clock, I heard the unmistakable sound of the boarding steps being lowered. I leaped from my cot and went out on deck. I looked over the side but the steps were not down for anyone leaving, they were down to receive Captain Foote, come to explain himself to Nelson. I stood aside and watched as a lieutenant conducted the captain across the deck and into the great cabin where the doors were closed behind them. I wondered about Captain Foote. He had been in the bay for weeks now, directing operations in Troubridge's absence. He must know something about Francesco – not where he was of course – but he would know more than any other English officer and his white flag suggested a flexible attitude so I decided I would button-hole him. The doors to the great cabin were guarded by marines but, as these men were the same who guarded my own cabin, they knew me well enough and they did not prevent me from putting my face to the windows. Sir William was in there with Nelson and the secretaries, Campbell and Smith. Was not I also a secretary? Should I not be in there with them? I put my hand on the door handle.

"No, Ma'am!" One of the marines stepped sideways to block me. "Orders, Ma'am. No one goes in."

"But I am Sir William Hamilton's secretary."

"His Lordship's orders, Ma'am. If you'd step aside." The marine's expression was fixed. No one who valued the flesh on his back contradicted Nelson's orders, I knew that, so I gave way and returned to my cabin in the corner of the deck.

It was gone six by the time I heard the conference break up and straight away I went out on deck. Captain Foote, dispatch case in hand and head down, was already striding towards the steps and I tried to catch up with him, even calling his name "Captain Foote", but he did not turn round and in a moment he was gone down the steps. Mr Smith then came out, clutching his papers.

"Mr Smith, good evening," I greeted him as naturally as I could, "how was the meeting? Is there anything that I should know?" Mr Smith looked puzzled.

"That you should know, Miss Knight?" My mind was spinning. I could think of nothing that I had a right to know and so, without a thought, the truth spilled out.

"About Admiral Caracciolo, perhaps?" Now I had embarrassed him. Smith knew that I was engaged to Francesco and my question was improper.

"Don't you think you should ask Sir William about that?" He gave me a reproving look then set off down the companionway to his cabin on the gun deck.

It was another half hour before Sir William emerged and I was out on deck waiting for him. His shoulders were down and his face grey. He looked terribly tired but when he saw me, he knew I'd been waiting and so said simply,

"Shall we go to your cabin?"

Two tall people in a cabin eight feet by five make an intimate gathering and I sat on the small chair while Sir William sat on my trunk. He took off his hat and laid it on my cot.

"You will want to know about Francesco," he said, and I said,

"Yes."

"Captain Foote does not know where he is. I had the opportunity to ask him. Most of the leaders of the republic are thought to be in the forts and Francesco may be with them in which case, as things stand …" Sir William lowered his head and stroked his brow.

"In which case what?" His hesitation worried me. "What is it you are trying to tell me?" Sir William sat up and looked me in the eye.

"You know this armistice they have signed?"

"Yes. You explained it to me from the dispatch. Cardinal Ruffo has signed an armistice with the Republicans in the forts and offered them freedom to either return to their homes or go to France."

"Yes, that's broadly it, and it was signed by the leaders of the Russian and Turkish contingents as well, and Captain Foote for the English." I nodded that I understood this and that it must be good news. "But Nelson disapproves of the armistice, in fact he more than disapproves of it, he has told Foote that he is rescinding it."

"But he cannot do that."

"No, I don't think he can, and I told him so. Foote was the senior officer in theatre and if Nelson considers him too junior to be signing such a document then he should not have left him in charge."

"You told Nelson that?"

"I did – once Foote had left us – and besides, I think this armistice is rather a wise move for the royal party. Taking the forts by storm would be bloody and recriminations would be divisive but shipping the republic's leaders off to France would effectively clear the kingdom of Ferdinand's most disaffected citizens. I don't see what there is to object to."

"And you told Nelson that?"

"I did."

"And did you persuade him?" Sir William leaned his head against the bulkhead.

"He said that he is not here to negotiate. He is sent with instructions to accept nothing from the republicans but their complete submission to His Majesty's clemency."

"But that is only Nelson's view," I insisted, "what about Ruffo and his allies who re-took the country for Ferdinand? They have the greater right to decide and they take a very different view." Sir William opened his palms.

"Ruffo will be here in the morning. Let us see who prevails."

Cardinal Ruffo and his ADC arrived to a thirteen gun salute and were received on deck by Sir William and Nelson. Lady Emma and I were also in attendance because, on this occasion, we were to be at the table: Emma to translate for Nelson, and I to take the minutes because the cardinal was notorious, after his years in the Vatican, for deploying several languages at once. The cardinal was much altered since I last saw him: he looked ten years older and three stones lighter and his formerly full face was now gaunt – the result, I supposed, of his arduous campaigns. We repaired to the great cabin and took our seats either side of the long table and then, the cardinal declining refreshments, Sir William opened the subject of the armistice. Nelson, who was suffering a head pain that morning, soon interrupted.

"Our arrival changes all that," he snapped. "Fifteen English sail-of-the-line in the bay completely alters the military situation and as to treating with republican rebels – King Ferdinand does not, never would, and never will. He requires only their unconditional surrender." The cardinal shifted in his chair.

"You speak with great authority for a naval officer, Lord Nelson," he coolly observed. "May I ask if your view is shared also by His Britannic Majesty's ambassador to the Court of Naples?" The cardinal looked to Sir William, sitting at Nelson's side, but before Sir William could shape his reply, Nelson answered for him:

"This is not a matter for the ambassador, Cardinal, nor for me. I speak for King Ferdinand." The cardinal pushed back, scraping his chair across the boards.

"No, no, no, no, no!" He shook his head. "The world knows that you are bold, Lord Nelson, but that is impertinent." He fixed Nelson with a searing glare. "Pending the king's return, I am His Sicilian Majesty's Vicar General and Plenipotentiary on the mainland. *I* speak for the king. There is my warrant," and the cardinal's ADC pushed a document across the table. Nelson picked it up and looked at it but, it being in French, he passed it to Sir William.

"Yes," Sir William confirmed, "Vicar General and Plenipotentiary pending His Majesty's return. Signed and dated 25th January 1799." He smiled at the cardinal and passed it back to him.

"Well, that is as maybe, historically," Nelson sniffed, "but my orders were given to me by the king himself, just five days ago. I do assure you, Cardinal, I speak for him."

"Then show me those orders," said the cardinal. "As the king's Vicar-General, I cannot simply accept the word of a foreign naval officer. The matter is too important." Now Nelson shifted in his chair.

"My mission here does not require specific orders," he attempted, "it is merely an extension of the service that my squadron has been providing King Ferdinand for the last nine months." The cardinal pursed his lips and shrugged.

"You are the professional, Lord Nelson, I am merely an amateur in these matters but do not all military actions require orders? I understood that yours were to stand off Sicily, to defend the island and the routes east against an expected French fleet." Nelson's patience snapped.

"Then why do you think I am here?" he thundered, "if not for King Ferdinand? He – and *I* for him – will not permit the republican rebels to walk free. Believe me, Cardinal, I shall take their surrender."

The cardinal looked down, dropping his chin on his chest and examining his hands in his lap. The next word would have to be his but he was in no hurry to speak and it was a long time before he finally sighed and said quietly,

"I shall have no more blood spilled over this." He looked up at Nelson. "God knows, I have waded through enough these past five months and – yes – I am to blame." He rolled his eyes to the rafters and crossed himself. "I raised the banner of the Holy Faith. No one can say that it was not the right thing to do against that wave of atheism that was sweeping south – and it was what the people wanted." The cardinal drew back to the table. "Men flocked to me from the moment I landed, swords in their hands and the fire of faith burning in their eyes. The cry was for Christ and the king against the sworn enemy of both – was there ever a more noble cause?" The cardinal opened his palms and gave a sad smile. "But I had no officers." He looked from Nelson to Sir William to Lady Emma and me. "No training. No logistical support. No intelligence beyond gossip and prejudice," again he lowered his eyes, "and vendetta." He fell silent. Lady Emma, in low tones, was still translating for Nelson and Campbell, who leaned into her from either side. Once he saw that she had finished, the cardinal continued.

"By the time we got to Naples I was only too aware of what I had unleashed and I did not want the barbarities committed against Calabria and Basilicata visited upon the city. I tried to hold the line at Nola, waiting for orders from the king, or better, for the king himself to come and impose his authority, but the pull of the final prize was too great and when the accursed Turks broke ranks, the rest, and mayhem, followed. Anyone they suspected of being Jacobin they regarded as legitimate prey. I am not proud of this." He looked sternly at us each in turn. "In fact, I fear I have forfeited my immortal soul, but I tell you this to warn you – against the rule of that mob. Victims were stripped and dismembered alive; their roasted flesh was eaten; their severed heads borne on pikes or kicked about as footballs. Ladies," he shot Emma and me a sharp glance, "innocent or guilty, republican or what, were chased through the streets, undressed, submitted to every outrage and forced into Jacobin postures for hours on end while the men – *my men* – pelted them with filth and obscenities." The cardinal hung his head. I wondered if he were overcome, perhaps needing some help but, as I put down my pen to rise, he lifted his head again. "But," he raised a finger at Nelson, "terrible as those two days were on the 13th and 14th, and guilty as I stand, I prevented the larger outrage – the one that would see Naples consume herself completely: with the help of the Russians, I kept the Lazzaroni in check. *I*," he glared fiercely at Nelson, "with my men and the Russians. You will not do that with all the ball in Chatham and Portsmouth."

Nelson shuffled, irritated but glad, I thought, that the cardinal had finally finished.

"And I am sure we can rely on your keeping them in check," he told him. "We are both here to serve the king's cause." The cardinal sat back in his chair.

"Yes we are," he agreed, "and we have a joint armistice to prove it." Nelson's face set.

"Cardinal Ruffo. You have been eloquent on the sacrifices that you personally have made in the king's service but now let a naval officer be plain with you." Nelson leaned to Sir William and whispered something to him. Sir William's brow clouded and he whispered something back, whereupon Nelson nodded, and Sir William turned to me.

"It might be better, Cornelia," he said in a low tone, "if you left us for a minute or two."

"Why?" I asked him, surprised.

"Nelson has a letter from the king, bearing on the armistice, that he wants to read out. It refers to Francesco and he thinks you would prefer not to hear it."

"About Francesco? Of course I want to hear it. I will stay." Sir William looked pained. This was not the answer he had wanted but, as he drew breath to appeal, I said again, "Tell Nelson I will stay," and, reluctantly, Sir William passed back my answer.

"Mr Campbell!" Nelson called to his secretary. "The king's copy letter dated the 20th if you please." Campbell passed him the letter.

"Now Cardinal." Nelson cleared his throat and held the letter in front of him. "I promised you I would be plain. I have here a translated copy, forwarded to me by the king's secretary, of a letter that His Majesty wrote to you five days ago. I quote from paragraph three:

'It is bruited abroad that in the surrender of the castles, all the rebels shut inside them will be allowed to leave safe and sound, even Caracciolo etc, and proceed to France. This I shall never believe, because God preserve us from them. To spare those savage vipers, and especially Caracciolo, who knows every inlet of our coastline, might inflict the greatest damage on us.'

The words landed like nails in my heart. I felt sick and my head spun faster and faster. I dropped my pen. I thought, *I am going to faint. I might even die,* and then Sir William and the cardinal were at my sides, lifting me from my chair and bearing me over the spinning floor on legs I could not feel to my cabin where they laid me down.

"I shall send a steward with brandy and water," I heard Sir William say and then, as he left, the cardinal put his face to my ear and said in a low tone,

"Francesco is safe Cornelia and waiting for you. He is not in the forts. My niece knows where he is. She can arrange for you to meet if you can get ashore."

"Francesco?" I barely knew what the cardinal was saying, or if I were awake or dreaming. "Where is he? How can I get ashore?"

"I shall be back again tomorrow. Nelson is not going to agree to the armistice today. Find a way of getting ashore and tell me tomorrow. I must go. Talk to Sir William." And he was gone.

The spinning of the joists in my cabin's roof gradually slowed and when the brandy arrived, I drank it. I no longer felt nauseous; just empty, calm – dead-calm – and I slept. Sometime about two in the afternoon a steward woke me with a dinner tray and I sat up in my cot. The tray was well presented with a napkin and finger bowl and silver cutlery, and the cold dinner itself reminded me more of the Palazzo Sessa than naval fare: three baked sardines with sweet onions, herbs and peppers, served with rosetta rolls. I did not feel hungry but I nibbled around my plate, enjoying the association with happier times at the Palazzo Sessa more than the food itself. *Find a way of getting ashore.* How could I do that? The cardinal should have taken me with him! Whisked me away, there and then, while I was in my dizzy spin, because his boat and Captain Foote's had been the only ones I had seen against the ship's side and Nelson's embargo was absolute. I set the tray aside and settled down with Gibbon. He was a shrewd observer of politics and war. Perhaps he could illuminate Naples' agonies.

At about four, there was a knock on my door: Sir William.

"How are you, Cornelia?" I sat up and laid down my book.

"I don't know," was my honest answer, "numb." And for the first time that day, a wave of despair surged through me and tears pricked the backs of my eyes. Sir William sat down and took my hand.

"What can I do for you, Cornelia?" His pale old eyes were full of concern.

"This is what you can do for me," I told him, my tears now spilling down my cheeks, "just be here." He gave my hand a squeeze.

"I just wondered what the cardinal had meant," he went on. "As I walked with him to the steps, he said 'speak to Cornelia. She needs you to do something.' I wondered if you knew what he meant."

"Did he not tell you that Francesco is safe and that his niece knows where he is?"

"There was no time for him to tell me anything. Just that I should speak to you." I looked down at our combined hands, knowing how hopeless this all was.

"The cardinal thought that you might be able to find a way of getting me ashore," I looked up at Sir William, "but of course I know that that is impossible, and the cardinal needs to know by tomorrow morning when he comes back for more talks." Sir William sat back and leaned his head against the bulkhead.

"That will be difficult," he agreed, "but not necessarily impossible."

"You think you *could* get me ashore?" With a sideways look, he drew my eyes to the remnants of my dinner on the chest.

"I got Jean-Carlo aboard, didn't I? Things are bad enough without us having to live on boiled pork and biscuit." He slapped his hands onto his knees and rose to his feet. "If I got him on, I dare say there'll be a way of getting you off." He bent down and kissed my forehead. "Let me think about it."

Supper was difficult that evening. All I really wanted was to stay in my cabin but I was stuck on *Foudroyant* with Nelson and Lady Emma and it was better to face them now than become the butt of their mocking gossip so I tied up my hair in a pretty bandeau and put on a light summer robe. Sir William and Nelson were standing talking over a glass of champagne when I entered the great cabin while Lady Emma entertained them on her harp.

"Miss Knight," Nelson greeted me, "you are well rested I hope." A steward offered me champagne and I took it.

"Thank you. I am, yes."

"I am sorry that you ..." Nelson went on but I stopped him.

"Do not apologise, you have your duty and you did warn me." I took a sip of my champagne and walked away from the men to watch Emma at her harp. Her body was rolling behind her large white arms, rippling over the strings and she gave me a harpist's fey smile. She played well, I will admit. It was a skill she had acquired during her Flintshire childhood and one of which she'd a right to be proud.

The table had been reduced to a small square for the four of us and the meal was vintage Jean-Carlo: linguini with *frutta del mare* followed by a fowl baked with rosemary and lemons. Conversation was necessarily stilted with Lady Emma confining herself to twitchings of the lips and the raising of eyebrows – how could it have been otherwise? I had publicly exposed the rawness of my anxiety for Francesco – a rebel – when the issue on everyone's minds was the rebels and what to do with them. But then, at least, I told myself, I knew what Nelson did not: that Francesco was beyond his reach. That thought sustained me, though I still did not know how to reach him.

Over the chicken, Sir William raised the question of the embassy. He told Nelson that he had learned from Jean-Carlo that the palazzo had suffered damage and he was anxious to have it assessed.

"Perhaps," he asked Nelson, with a quick look at me, "a marine escort might be found to accompany Mr Smith and Miss Knight on an inspection?"

"Hardly woman's work," Nelson replied as he chewed.

"Miss Knight's knowledge of the palazzo's contents is second to none," Sir William reminded him. "She undertook the inventory you know." Nelson shook his head.

"Not yet," he skewered more chicken onto his fork, "the city is not safe." I caught Sir William's eye and he raised his eyebrows. That was it, they were saying, he had tried.

There was no thirteen gun salute for the cardinal's second visit; just the boatswain's pipe and a quick stride across the quarter deck to the great cabin and business. Sir William and I, Nelson, Lady Emma and Campbell were ranged, as before, across the table from the cardinal and his ADC and the cardinal came straight to the point. He had conferred with the leaders of his Russian and Turkish allies and they were as adamant as he that the armistice agreement was useful, necessary and honourable. They insisted that it stand, and the cardinal added for good measure that whoever dared to violate it would be responsible before God and the world.

I don't think Nelson had expected anything other from the cardinal because he was ready with his response. He passed him a declaration, which he asked to be delivered to the occupants of the Uovo and Nuovo forts, ordering them to surrender themselves immediately to the cardinal's forces and the king's mercy. The cardinal flatly refused and then raised the stakes by telling Nelson that if *he* did anything to break the armistice he, Ruffo, would withdraw his forces and leave Naples with him. Nelson was furious. He glared angrily at the cardinal but before he could frame a response, the cardinal and his ADC were on their feet and making for the door. Sir William and I rose with them and escorted them out but the others did not, they remained in their seats in a belligerent show of ill-temper. On the quarter deck, the cardinal shot me a look.

"Well?" I did not know what to say. The cardinal was so fierce. I did not want to be part of these great events.

"Quickly," he insisted, "what have I to tell my niece?" And then I realised that he was talking about Francesco.

"I still can't get ashore." I was hurrying along to keep up with him.

"That is a pity," he growled. "Francesco has sacrificed much to meet you. I offered him safe passage out but then he got a letter from you saying you were on your way so he said he would stay and wait." We reached the top of the steps. "Don't let him down."

I stood at the gunwale with Sir William while the cardinal descended the steps and was aware of being watched. I looked over to the great cabin and Nelson was there in the doorway, staring at me. How long had he been there? And what did he think he had seen? When our eyes met, he averted his and returned to the cabin.

I walked back to the great cabin with Sir William and, when we entered, Emma was in full cry.

"He is bluffing!" she was shouting, gripping the back of a chair. "It would be treason. Ruffo knows full well that the queen – and the king – want those rebels, only he hasn't the stomach to take them."

"Oh, the cardinal has the stomach, my dear," Sir William told her as we walked in, "you heard him yesterday. He just doesn't want any more blood."

"Emma is right," said Nelson, collecting his papers from the table, "that letter from the king could not have been plainer. Ruffo has been ordered to annul the armistice and deliver the rebels to the king's justice. If he refuses, it will be a gross dereliction, and if he withdraws his troops, well, yes, that would be tantamount to treason."

"Can we arrest him?" asked Emma.

"I don't think that would be helpful," Sir William told her, sitting down on one of the chairs, "his Turks and Calabrese wouldn't like it; they'd tear Naples apart." Nelson handed his papers to Campbell and started to pace the floor.

"We have a couple of thousand marines, and I could match that with seamen but they could not hold the city, not *that* city."

"Oh, let Ruffo go," Emma decided. "If he wants to disgrace and humiliate himself, the king has other friends."

"By which you mean?"

Sir William asked her.

"Egidio Pallio has been asking to see Nelson ever since we arrived. Perhaps it is time we gave him an audience."

"Who is Egidio Pallio?" Nelson asked her, still pacing.

"The leader of the Lazzaroni."

Sir William laughed.

"I am sorry my dear but the Lazzaroni do not have leaders. They are a rabble and any encouragement from us would create more mayhem and misery than the Turks and Calabrese together."

"I have met him," Emma persisted, "and I was impressed with him. He has sixty thousand loyal subjects, all anxious to take up arms for the king but arms they do not have. If we can supply them then Pallio will guarantee the peace until Ferdinand arrives." Nelson stopped pacing. He looked across the room to Sir William, who shook his head, then to Emma, who fixed him with her most dazzling gaze. After a second's beat, Nelson called to Campbell,

"Send for him."

That evening, scores of boxes of muskets, powder and ball were collected from the English ships and delivered to Pallio.

I was sure, like Sir William, that it was a desperate move. King Ferdinand himself, when the French were at his gates, had refused to arm the Lazzaroni – so nervous was he of their capricious temperament – and, sadly, the next day, Sir William and I were proved right. Pallio's hordes had swept through the city like locusts, arresting and molesting whoever they pleased. Cardinal Ruffo's stern edict, forbidding the molestation of non-combatants, was torn down wherever the Lazzaroni found it and, within the space of a night and a morning, they undid all the cardinal's work and let loose on the city their own brand of anarchy. Inevitably, Pallio's men clashed with the cardinal's and when, during the afternoon, they delivered Nelson's surrender demand to the forts, the cardinal fulfilled his promise and withdrew his troops leaving Naples to the mob and to Nelson.

My heart sank. If Naples had been too dangerous for me to go ashore before, then what chance had I now? Every report that came aboard was of a city descending into chaos – and under the supposedly commanding guns of Nelson's ships. This was not the effect that Nelson had intended with his 'quick show of strength'. He could not fire on the people he had just armed, nor could he force the surrender of the forts because the moment that he breached their walls, the Lazzaroni would swarm in and rob the king of his justice. All these things were discussed over a sullen supper to which I contributed nothing. I made an excuse and retired early, leaving Sir William long-faced and Nelson and Emma cursing the cardinal and Naples.

I had never expected such chaos. All I had wanted was passage to Naples and Francesco – and I was close to him, I could feel it, and the cardinal had confirmed it. I slept fitfully that night, wondering if and how, in the morning, I might get ashore but, by the morning, everything had changed. At some hour in the night, Nelson had allowed Sir William to write to the cardinal telling him that he now accepted the armistice and would do nothing to break it. It was a complete *volte face* and the letter went further, asking the cardinal to facilitate the release of the Republicans to their homes or the ships bound for France. Nelson's only addendum to the original armistice was a request for the names of those leaving 'for the king's and the public record'.

The night must have been busy ashore as well because, by the time I walked into breakfast, we had the cardinal's reply. He welcomed Nelson's change of heart and told him that he would move immediately, under cover of night, to secure the environs of the forts and the docks. By dinner-time, we could see for ourselves the boats full of men being rowed out to the transport ships and by supper-time the deed was done: the Republicans were all embarked or gone home, English marines were in the forts and Nelson had his names.

The mood at supper that evening was very different from the evening before. Nelson had invited half a dozen of his officers to join him and while they seemed wary of their admiral's change of tack, Nelson himself was expansive.

"I dare say you will be asking to inspect the embassy again," he suggested to Sir William and Sir William was taken off guard.

"Err, yes." He dashed me a quick look. "If you think the Chiaia safe enough."

"Mr Smith and Miss Knight again, is it?" Sir William looked to me again, but how could I respond? I had no idea what his plan involved, nor if it were even still valid.

"Yes, thank you, Nelson," Sir William said, "if you think it safe."

"Oh, I doubt there are more than a handful left who are not for the king but, just in case, I shall send a double guard." He called down the table to his Captain of Marines, "If that is convenient to you Captain Shand?" and Captain Shand returned him a nod.

I went out on deck as soon as the meal was over and Sir William followed me. It was dark and we stood at the gunwale together, looking out over the lights of Naples flickering on the water.

"So," I asked him, "what is it you have planned for me?"

"Nothing," he answered. "Nelson took me completely by surprise. Going to the palazzo on the pretext of assessing the damage seemed like a good idea two days ago when the cardinal was coming and going and we could give him a message for Francesco but now I don't know." I turned and looked at him.

"There must have been plenty of comings and goings with the cardinal last night." Sir William looked puzzled.

"The letters, you mean?"

"Yes, the exchange of letters. Tell me there isn't a boat on stand-by right now."

"There is, yes. A bag is going to the cardinal later this evening."

"Then put a note in it, in any code that you like, telling the cardinal to tell his niece that I shall be in the cellars of the Palazzo Sessa tomorrow morning."

CHAPTER FOURTEEN

I scribbled a note to Mother, bringing her up to date and then, at seven, I went down into the launch with Smith and the marines and the oarsmen pulled us away. I felt light-headed after a sleepless night and butterflies danced in my stomach. Why would they not? Within the hour, I would be with Francesco. I dangled my hand over the side and trailed it in the water. Would he look well, I wondered, after his adventures? Or would he look war-ravaged like Cardinal Ruffo? Would he even be there? A coded message sent at night through two messengers to a man in hiding is not guaranteed to arrive. The oarsmen pulled east into the rising sun that sparkled in shards off the sea so I brought in my hand and put up my parasol. Fear, too, can agitate butterflies. Naples was a hostile city and we would have to be careful but, I told myself, Francesco still had friends, we would be safe, and then, when we were alone … what then? It occurred to me that I had no idea what the rest of my life would be.

We passed by the transport ships – a dozen polaccas in line astern – and the Republicans were out on the gunwales.

"Look after Naples for us," one of them called, "we'll be back soon," and they all laughed and waved. Not understanding Italian, some of the marines waved back but their captain understood them; he stood up and cupped his hands.

"Enjoy the day!" he called back in Italian and then, regaining his seat he added quietly, "it's the last you will."

"How is that, Captain?" Mr Smith asked him. "Aren't these the Republicans bound for France?" Captain Shand tapped his nose and winked.

"Watch and wait, Mr Smith. Watch and wait."

A crowd had gathered to see us come in and, at the harbour steps, Captain Shand sent up men to clear the way. I had been in Neapolitan crowds before and they had not bothered me but – perhaps because of my jangling nerves – this one did: its faces were uglier, its chanting more raucous and its bantering humour darker. I was glad when we arrived at the Palazzo Sessa but then, when we did, I was shocked at what we found. Every pane of glass in the building was shattered, the front door sagged off its hinges and there was a ragged hole between two of the first floor windows where a ball had smashed through. We waited in the sun in the courtyard while Captain Shand made sure the building was safe. Mr Smith was to make his inspection from the attics down while I was to start in the cellars, ostensibly then to work my way up. Was he down there, I wondered as I waited? Would we be able to talk? And when we had talked, what then? Captain Shand appeared in the doorway; he waved Mr Smith up and I went down to the cellars.

Two iron grilles lit the outer edge of the former undercroft but, beyond that, there was darkness.

"Francesco?" My voice echoed in the fathomless gloom.

"Cornelia?"

"Francesco!" He emerged as a smudge and enveloped me. "Thank God," I whispered. "Oh, how I've missed you!"

"And I have missed you." He held me and kissed me, the bristles of a beard brushing my face, and then he drew back.

"Let me see you." He took my hand and led me to the stone seat that ran round the walls. I could see him now. His face was deeply tanned, his beard and hair were dishevelled and he was dressed in the clothes of an artisan but it was him, Francesco, his unsullied soul shining from those warm, brown eyes.

"I got your message in the night," he said as we sat down, "I knew you would come. Ever since I got your letter I've been waiting, but I knew you would come." His smile was as wide as a schoolboy's but worry-lines furrowed his brow.

"How are you?" I asked him. "You look tired." His smile slipped but he gave a firm nod.

"I'm alright. Better than most."

"Cardinal Ruffo was worried about you. He said something about your making sacrifices to meet me. What did he mean?"

"Sacrifices!" He coughed out a laugh. "Is that what he said?" He dropped his head and stared at the flags. He looked at them for a long time – too long a time.

"Francesco, are you sure you're alright?" He turned up his face to me.

"You never did like the French did you?"

"The French?" The question surprised me. "I never liked the Jacobins." He sat up now and leaned his head back against the wall.

"They abandoned us." He gave me a resigned smile. "We knew it would take time to establish a republic – old loyalties run deep in Naples – but we had made our plans: the French would take care of security while we tackled the politics and the arrangement began well." He took my hand into both of his. "In just the first month, we trained three thousand commissioners to go out to the Lazzaroni in the streets and the peasants in the countryside, to explain the benefits to them of the new constitution – equality under the law, free movement of labour, the end of Church tithes – big concepts, not easy for the illiterate to grasp but the work was under weigh." He stroked my hand and his smile sagged. "But then the French left us, just when we needed them, when the cardinal's hordes arrived." He looked up to the vaulted ceiling. "You talk about sacrifice, Cornelia, they slaughtered hundreds when they came in, thousands perhaps, but I don't blame Ruffo." He looked back at me. "He is a victim in all this too – another enthusiast trampled by events – and he has been incredibly kind to me – offered me a passport and safe passage to Rome – but then I got your letter telling me you were coming ..." he broke off and frowned, "did you get any of my letters?"

"I got one, soon after you left, full of optimism." I rested my free hand on his. "Were there others then?"

"Many others. I don't know what could have happened to them. I won't blame Maria. She's been wonderful."

"Maria, the cardinal's niece?"

"Yes. She helped get the passports for Rome." He tapped his pocket. "I have them with me."

"Them?"

"When you said you were coming, I asked her to prepare two, just in case."

"Just in case what?"

"I don't know." He gave an embarrassed laugh. "You won't be able to come immediately, obviously, you have your mother to think of – how is she by the way?"

"Not good. Still weak."

There was a footfall on the stairs. We looked up and saw Captain Shand bending forward and looking at us.

"Everything alright down there, Miss Knight?" he smiled, then, feigning surprise, "Ah! You have a friend!" He descended the rest of the stairs and came towards us. He was relaxed and smiling with his left hand steadying the hilt of his sword. "Perhaps you would like to introduce us." I did not know what to say. The captain was so affable; an introduction seemed so natural but …

Francesco leaped at him. He struck him with his fist on the temple and knocked him to the ground.

"Come on!" He gripped my hand, "Keep close. I know the way," and he pulled me towards the darkness. I panicked.

"Come where? It's pitch black."

"I have the passports. Stay with me."

"I don't think I can." The captain groaned from the floor and lifted his head.

"Sergeant Morris!"

"Yes, you can!" Francesco shouted at me but, after only a few steps, we were in total darkness. "This leads to the catacombs," he was saying, "Trust me, I know the way." Marines were clattering down the steps, some carrying torches. I froze. I could not enter that darkness. I released Francesco's hand.

"Go!" I called to him. "Go without me! Save yourself! We shall meet in Rome!" Marines poured past me but they didn't know where to go. By the light of their torches, they, and I, could see the choice of passages that led out of the back of the undercroft.

"Get after him!" cried the captain, staggering to his feet, but his men were baffled and hesitated. More marines now tumbled down the stairs and the captain called to them,

"Corporal! Take four men and get Miss Knight and Smith back to the boat. The rest of you follow me." And he too stumbled past me, following the torches into the catacombs.

I was bundled up the stairs and out into the blinding sunlight. For a moment, I could see nothing, but then I heard Smith say 'what happened?' and the corporal say 'close order' and his men hemmed us in and hustled us out to a street thronged with people. The Lazzaroni had multiplied. They filled the street and the marines had to jostle and push to force a way through them. It was bedlam. My mind was so full of Francesco – the warmth of his body, his kiss, his vanishing into the dark – I hardly knew what was happening. The Lazzaroni were chanting for the English and the king – which should have been some reassurance – but they pressed in so close and so hard that, as reality dawned, I grew frightened. Even the corporal was worried: he shouted and shoved to force a way through and cursed that he had so few men and so we proceeded, at a snail's pace, from the palazzo down to the dockyard and it was there, as we passed through the gates, that the crowd's mood changed.

"That's Caracciolo's bitch!" The gatekeeper jabbed an accusing finger at me and the Lazzaroni roared. I am conspicuous at the best of times but for that last hundred yards that we struggled along the quayside wall, I might have been standing in a tumbril and had the marine corporal not feared for his own life as much as my own, God knows what would have become of me. He fired off his musket with a tremendous crack and, instantly, he got silence.

"Fix bayonets!" he shouted and, in the time that it took for the nearest Lazzaroni to realise they had not been shot, the corporal had me and Mr Smith penned behind his men, retreating along the quayside wall. The marines were as frightened as I. Sweating inside their woollen uniforms and shakoes, they cursed their God and their mothers while Smith, at my elbow, recited his prayers. The launch's crew, seeing our danger, came out to meet us, brandishing their cutlasses and shouting foul oaths at the crowd and it was their midshipman who led me and Mr Smith down the steps to the boat. The oarsmen quickly followed us, and then the marines and then, with a parting musket shot, we cast off and the men pulled away.

I sat in the stern-sheets, shaking and sweating with fear. Oh Francesco! I prayed to God that he'd escaped. I could not lose him now. He said he knew the catacombs and I hoped he did. Hadn't they defied intruders for centuries? Now, they must again.

We pulled to the end of the mole and into the open bay. Smith, sitting opposite, was turned from me, staring out to sea. I wondered if he were ashamed of himself – of his unmanly behaviour – or perhaps he was ashamed of me, Caracciolo's bitch. I would have been mortified to hear any woman so abused but for that woman to be me ...

I took out my handkerchief and wiped the sweat from my face and chest then I put up my parasol. Francesco had looked exhausted. The last thing he needed was a hunt and him the quarry. We rounded the mole and came into view of the transport ships. So, I thought, beginning to regain myself, he had passports for Rome. I could enjoy Rome with Francesco – and so could Mother – Rome had been our home for longer than any other city and, under Francesco's protection, we would be safe there, with or without the French. We came abreast of the transport ships and they seemed to be on the move. There were fewer of them than before and I could see that two were under tow. Were they preparing to sail already? If so, Nelson had been quick to keep his word. I turned and looked back at Naples receding behind us and thought, why delude yourself Cornelia? Mother can't go to Rome. She hasn't the strength to leave the house let alone go to Rome. Was that then to be my choice? Mother and Palermo or Francesco and Rome?

I went straight to my cabin when we got back. There had been no one on deck to meet us – for which I was glad – but before I had chance even to change my robe, there was a knock at my door and Sir William came in. He was agitated.

"I'm glad you're back, Cornelia. Have you seen the transports?"

"The transports?"

"The ships with the Republicans in," his voice was thin and anxious, "have you seen what is happening?" He was casting about my tiny cabin like a caged stag.

"Won't you sit down?" I suggested, and he sat down on my sea-chest while I sat on the little camp chair beside my cot. "Now, tell me, what is the matter?"

"I am in despair of him." He looked up to the roof-beams, fighting back tears. "He has disgraced his country and disgraced me; my name in Naples is ruined." I leaned forward and put my hand on his knee.

"Who has disgraced you, Sir William? Tell me, calmly, what has happened?" He looked down into his hands to gather his thoughts.

"Nelson is towing out all the transport ships with the Republicans in them and mooring them alongside the English ships." I nodded that I had seen something of it. "He is going to leave them there, under his guns, until the king arrives. The Republicans are his prisoners. He has reneged entirely on the agreement that went out under my name less than forty-eight hours ago."

"But he cannot do that." Sir William gave a bitter laugh.

"He has the guns and the forts. Why does he need Cardinal Ruffo? Or Honour? Or diplomatic convention? Or the law? And now, he has the king's prisoners, for which, no doubt, he will be handsomely rewarded."

"So his *volte face* was a trick?"

"Evidently. And played in my name."

I had seen many sides of Nelson over the past nine months but I had never seen duplicity. I found it hard to believe what Sir William was telling me but then I remembered the smile on Captain Shand's face when he saw Francesco. Why had Nelson sent his senior marine officer? And with a double guard? A cold chill ran through me.

"I think we have both been tricked." Sir William looked puzzled.

"You have been tricked?" Then he remembered. "Oh, I'm so sorry. How did you get on this morning? Did you find Francesco?"

"I did, and my marine escort very nearly caught him. I think Nelson has used me as he has used you."

We heard a commotion outside – feet running across the deck, and men shouting. I opened the door and seamen were crowding the landward gunwale, cheering and waving over the side.

"What is it?" Sir William asked.

"I don't know." I went out and crossed the deck and looked out over the seamen's shoulders. They were cheering a longboat pulling in from the town. It was carrying a platoon of marines and, hemmed in between them, with his back to me, a man with dark curls and artisan's clothes.

I looked away. It could not be him. Francesco was too clever and too quick to be taken by English marines in the catacombs. It must have been one of the Republicans from the transport ships – a leader perhaps, being brought under guard to parley with Nelson. That, I told myself, would be it, that would make sense, such sound sense that I calmly looked back to confirm it, only, when I looked back, the man was offering his profile and, without doubt, it was Francesco.

I felt weak. It was still only mid-morning but the sun was blisteringly hot, beads of sweat smarted my eyes and my head swam. I stepped back and took hold of the newel post at the bottom of the poop deck steps. Perhaps Francesco was coming to parley. Just because he was in a boat with marines did not mean he was under arrest. Sir William would help him. But then I remembered it was Sir William who had told me that Francesco was beyond help, he had fired on Nelson's ships, making Nelson his enemy and now he was being brought in.

And I had done this. I had led the marines to him. Without my nattering Sir William to bring me to Naples, Nelson could not have laid his trap and Francesco would still be free. 'Leave Francesco to manage his own affairs' Mother had told me and she'd been right. He would have been in Rome by now and making arrangements for us to join him but instead he had stayed in Naples because I had interfered. I'd been a headstrong fool, a spoiled child with no more sense than the newel post I was clinging to. I had, like Judas, planted a kiss on the cheek of the one I loved and betrayed him. Francesco! I looked out again over the seamen's backs and the boat was nearing the side.

"What is all the shouting?" Sir William asked behind me.

"They have Francesco." More marines now flooded up from the lower decks to clear a path through the seamen who now leaped up the ratlines to get a clear view. One of them called down to the boat,

"Catched-yer-Catcherolo!" and two hundred voices took up the taunting chant. I pushed my way through to the marine cordon, as close as I could get to the gate, and looked over the side. Captain Shand was stepping onto the platform, leaving his men and Francesco in the boat. I cupped my hands and shouted down.

"Francesco!" He lifted his head and I saw that his wrists were bound behind him. It was hard for him to look up but he saw me and smiled. "Sir William is here," I shouted and Sir William, beside me, waved. "We shall soon have you freed." I had said that to reassure him but it was also my solemn pledge: if I had put Francesco in manacles then, somehow, I would get him out. Captain Shand was halfway up the steps.

"You have no right to detain Prince Caracciolo," I shouted down to him, "you have no authority in Naples, and England and Naples are not at war." At the top of the steps we came face-to-face: he, wearing a light smile and I, in earnest. He said,

"Excuse me."

"I am quite sure you understood me, Captain."

"I have no wish to banter with you, Miss Knight; I am simply asking you to let me pass."

"No!" I was not going to be brushed aside. "You owe me an explanation. You used me in your illegal abduction so justify yourself or release the prince." The captain feigned a sigh and looked to Sir William.

"Cornelia." Sir William put his hand to my arm. "Captain Shand will have his orders. These decisions are not his. You must let him pass."

"Orders!" I answered, getting angry. "Soldiers, sailors and orders – whatever happened to Honour?" I glared at the smug marine captain and he turned from me to Sir William.

"I am going to bring the prisoner up," he told him. "I do not want any trouble." Sir William, himself deeply affronted at the day's events, looked round the deck at the lines of marines.

"I'd say you were sufficiently prepared, Captain." The captain lost patience.

"Sir, I shall ask you plainly now: will you please escort Miss Knight to her cabin?" Sir William raised an eyebrow at me.

"Absolutely not!" I told him, and Sir William told the captain,

"We shall stay."

With no higher authority to call on, the captain had no choice. He signalled two marines to come and stand in front of us then he called down to the boat,

"Bring him up!"

More cheers rang out from the rigging.

"*Ça Ira!*" someone shouted and a new chant started taunting Francesco with the French 80 he had lost to Nelson off Genoa. I looked over the side. The marines were trudging up the steps with Francesco between them. With his hands tied, he could not raise his head to look up so I did not call out until he reached the top. His shirt was soiled, he was dishevelled and a bruise glowed on the side of his face.

"Francesco!" We were a yard apart, separated by the marines. "We shall soon have you freed. This is completely illegal." He looked at me. His eyes were hollow with fatigue and he was about to speak but then his guards pushed him on.

"Keep him moving," a corporal shouted, "and keep him bound. He's going in the bilboes."

"What?" Now Sir William exploded. "No, never, that is outrageous!" He pushed through the marine cordon and challenged Captain Shand. "You will not put Prince Caracciolo, the commander of the Neapolitan navy, in shackles." Sir William was puce with rage but the captain stood firm. With Francesco disappearing down the steps to the gun deck, he coolly told Sir William,

"I shall do what my admiral orders." He was so smug, the sly little man, I could have smacked him there and then but instead I took Sir William's arm:

"Come on!" I told him, and I marched him off to the great cabin.

Nelson was standing in front of the windows when we walked in, talking with one of his lieutenants, and Emma too was in the room, sitting at a writing desk.

"You have now completely exceeded yourself," I told Nelson, "I demand that you release Admiral Caracciolo." Slowly, Nelson turned from the lieutenant.

"You demand?" He looked at me doubtfully.

"The Law demands it," I extemporised, "Neapolitan law, international law. You," I jabbed a finger at him, "a foreigner, have no right to abduct a Neapolitan citizen from his own streets. King Ferdinand's Vicar-General – Cardinal Ruffo – has, as you well know, forbidden anyone," I repeated, "*anyone*, other than his own officers, from interfering with any Neapolitan citizen." My heart was thumping in my chest but I was determined to finish my piece. "*You* are without the law in this Nelson – it is abduction, kidnap – you have to release Admiral Caracciolo, either completely or into the hands of Cardinal Ruffo."

"Cardinal Ruffo?" Nelson moved down the cabin towards me. "I seem to recall that you were in this room with us, Miss Knight, only a day or two ago, when I read back to Cardinal Ruffo the letter sent to him by King Ferdinand, the letter in which the king made it as plain as words can that Admiral Caracciolo was the most dangerous of all his rebels." Nelson's brow darkened. "You and I both know – *don't we?* – that Cardinal Ruffo has had ample opportunity to detain Caracciolo and that he has chosen, for his own reasons, not to. I am merely doing his job for him." Sir William stepped up to my side.

"But in irons, Nelson," he pleaded, "For pity's sake. This is no Jack Tar you are dealing with, no common criminal. He is a prince, the commander of the Neapolitan navy – your own peer." Sir William dashed me a sideways glance. "If you feel you have to detain the admiral then let it be in a cabin, post a guard at the door if you must, but for God's sake don't leave him in irons – and untie his hands."

At the back of the cabin, Lady Emma rose from her desk with a letter in her hand.

"But Nelson cannot do that." She moved towards us with a patronising smile. "I received this letter from the queen only this morning, and I will not spare Miss Knight to tell you that Her Majesty considers Admiral Caracciolo to be ..." she lifted up the letter, "I shall read it, '... the most noxious of all the rebels. Such a pirate at large might imperil the sacred person of the king and therefore I should wish this traitor to be put beyond the power of doing harm.'" Emma lowered the letter and her patronising smile sank from sad to sickly. "He must be closely confined." I hated her: her arrogance, her artifice, her cheapness. I wanted to tear that lying smile from her face.

So," I said, "you speak for the queen and Nelson speaks for Ferdinand. Who, on this English ship, speaks for King George?" I looked to Sir William. "Where is English justice? Would any English king invite a foreign navy to abduct his First Sea Lord from a London street and clap him in their irons for him?" Again, I jabbed my finger at Nelson. "*You* are the outlaw here Nelson and when the Admiralty hears of it you will have to answer – which is something else that you and I both know!" Nelson looked stunned. I had wounded him and I was glad. "King Ferdinand's lackey!" I pressed on, "You should not even be here! You are supposed to be on King George's service, preparing to meet a French battle fleet five hundred miles to the south."

"That is enough!" Nelson's patience snapped. "I will listen to no more of your twisted prattle, Miss Knight. One might fairly ask where *your* loyalties lie. We all know that the only reason you are talking this nonsense is because you are blinded by a romantic attachment."

Oh," I answered, "well, you would know. You might hold up that mirror to yourself," and I glared with contempt at Lady Emma. Shocked, Emma twitched in confusion. Which Attitude would she choose? The insulted? The imperious? The insinuating, assertive, transgressive, suggestive – and every one of them false? I had torn off her mask and she was ugly.

"Get her out!" she hissed and I thought she was going to pounce on me – I wished she would – I was angry enough – but then Sir William laid a hand on my arm.

"Look here, Nelson," he said, attempting conciliation, "you really are on quite shaky ground with this you know – legally, I mean – there could be consequences." The younger man thought for a moment, absently fingering his medals.

"Very well then," he decided, "we shall follow the law. Let Caracciolo be tried by a Neapolitan naval court martial. Will that satisfy you, Sir William?" Sir William did not look at all satisfied but before he had chance to speak Nelson said, "Good," and he turned to the lieutenant who had been standing quietly at the back of the room. "Lieutenant Parkinson," he called to him, "ask the Master to clear a cabin in the wardroom and have the prisoner untied and installed in it with a marine guard." Then, as the lieutenant walked out, Nelson said to Sir William and me, "Now, if you will excuse me, I have a court martial to convene," and we too had no choice but to leave.

As soon as we were out on deck, I confronted Sir William.

"You must send for Cardinal Ruffo. He is the one man with the authority to save Francesco." Sir William raised his fingers to his forehead. I knew what that meant. "Sir William, you must!"

"Yes, yes, Cornelia. As the king's Vicar-General, the cardinal is the ultimate legal authority in the king's territories but on an English man-of-war?" He was stroking his forehead. "You see what I mean? I am not so sure about that."

"But Nelson is convening a Neapolitan court martial aboard an English man-of-war. If that is legal then the cardinal's intervention must be."

"Yes, well, that too. Is a foreign court martial legal aboard an English ship?" Sir William frowned and pursed his lips. "I really don't know."

"Well, can't you decide?" I was beginning to lose patience with him. "You are King George's ambassador and this is his ship. You are senior to Nelson as Ruffo is senior to the Neapolitan naval officers."

"Ah, yes. Now you have raised another question: that of authority ashore and authority on board ship and I am afraid that on board ship the admiral trumps the ambassador – and again – the court martial is not supposed to be an English matter, is it? Do you see what I mean? It is rather complicated."

"Sir William!" I made him look at me.

"Yes, Cornelia?"

"Francesco was illegally abducted from Naples. Write to Cardinal Ruffo – *now* – and tell him to come and claim him."

"Yes, Cornelia." He nodded vigorously. "You are right. I shall do that straight away." And he disappeared below to look for Smith.

I tried to see Francesco but was forbidden. He was to have no visitors, no representation and no witnesses were to be called in his defence. I had the chilling feeling that his court martial might be an even greater travesty than I suspected and then, when I heard who was to chair it, my worst fears were met. Four Neapolitan officers were scraped together from around Nelson's squadron to be presided over by Count Thurn. I was incensed. I went looking for Sir William but instead ran into Nelson. He was on the quarter deck with a clutch of junior officers.

"You said a court martial of Neapolitan officers," I called to him across the deck and he and his minions turned to me.

"Not now, Miss Knight," he snapped, annoyed, "there is a time and a place." I strode straight up to him.

"Count Thurn is not Neapolitan. He is Austrian. This is not legal." Anger flashed in Nelson's good eye but, aware of his audience, he supressed it.

"Commodore Count Thurn," he explained through his teeth, "is in King Ferdinand's service. He has been for many years."

"In the king's service?" I answered, struggling to control my own anger, "or in the queen's? Thurn is another of her Austrian lackeys – another Mack. Who has put you up to this?" I challenged him, "Lady Emma? Another instruction, was it, in that letter she received from the queen?" Nelson's eyes were cold as steel but he did not frighten me. "Thurn cannot preside," I told him. "You will have to replace him." Nelson took hold of my arm. He evidently thought his young audience had heard enough from this woman and he drew me aside.

"You, Miss Knight, need to remember your place. That is the second time you have tried to tell me what to do. You might consider what the consequences would be if you were a man." He pushed away my arm and turned as if to leave, but then he decided to add, "I shall tolerate you for only so long as you respect my rank."

"I do respect your rank," I told him, "more than you imagine. I just want you to live up to it."

Just as Sir William's letter to Ruffo was leaving in one boat, Thurn and the other officers of the court martial were arriving in another. They went straight to the great cabin to be briefed by Nelson and then, after less than five minutes, they went down to the wardroom to hold their court martial. I remained in my cabin, pacing like a caged cat, with my heart thumping with fear and my head spinning with images: of Francesco bound, of Nelson's cold eye and my own despicable guilt. For the first time in years, I got down on my knees and prayed – which was where Sir William found me, two minutes later. He looked down at me and shook his head.

"I could not object to Thurn. Since Francesco's defection, he has been Head of the Neapolitan Navy. He has the king's warrant. I cannot argue with his presidency."

"But it is happening so quickly." I rose to my feet. "Only this morning I was with Francesco in the cellars of the Palazzo Sessa. And now he is on trial for his life and it isn't even dinner time. It is a conspiracy, isn't it?" Sir William sighed and raised his eyebrows.

"God speed the cardinal," was all he could say, then he kissed me on the forehead and left.

I couldn't stay caged in my cabin on my own. I went out on deck to get some fresh air but the air was not fresh, it was midday on 29th June, the sun was at its zenith and swelteringly hot. I put up my parasol and paced the landward gunwale, looking for Cardinal Ruffo. What more could I do for Francesco? Sir William – poor, compromised Sir William – had his limits and we seemed to have reached them. Francesco had other friends, clever, loyal and influential friends, but weren't they all captives now, languishing in those prison ships? Francesco's mother was in Avellino, so who else was there? No one, only Ruffo, he was our only hope but, though I scanned every inch of the bay, there still was no sign of him.

Lieutenant Parkinson came up – the same that Nelson had sent to attend Francesco.

"Any news?" I asked him. He glanced over to the great cabin to make sure that no one was watching.

"They've reached a verdict."

"Already?"

"Already." I walked at his side towards the great cabin. "I am sorry, Miss Knight. Guilty of high treason. Excuse me." And he went in to Nelson.

I reeled back against the bulkhead. My legs went weak, I felt faint with the heat, and sweat was seeping down my temples. *Guilty of high treason*. Doesn't that always mean death? Sentenced to death? I turned my head to the bay, looking for Cardinal Ruffo but still there was no sign of him. The mate came into the wheel deck and rang the ship's bell – twice – one o'clock. All this, and the day not half gone! My head felt heavy as lead. I wanted to sleep, or faint – any oblivion would do – but then, at my side, the cabin door opened and Lieutenant Parkinson came out holding a note.

"What did he say?" I asked him.

"He didn't say anything. I gave him the verdict and he scribbled this note."

"What does it say?"

"I don't know. It's for the President of the Court."

"Is it about the sentence?"

"Please, Miss Knight, I am only the messenger, now if you will excuse me?" I put my hand on his arm.

"Could I see him now, do you think?"

"Nelson?"

"Francesco."

"I would have to go back and ask Nelson."

"If you would." The lieutenant sighed and turned back into the great cabin. I felt so grateful to him. A few moments later, he was back.

"You may see him." He gave me a kind smile. "I shall take you down to him."

Francesco was being held in a cabin just like my own and, strangely, immediately beneath mine in the stern of the gun deck. Two marines were on guard but, on Lieutenant Parkinson's approach, they parted and one of them opened the door for us. I entered behind the lieutenant, just as far as the threshold.

"I have taken the verdict to Nelson," the lieutenant told Francesco, who rose to his feet.

"What did he say?"

"Nothing to me. He just gave me a note for the President. Have *you* heard anything?"

"No, not yet." Then Francesco saw me. "Cornelia!"

"Yes," the lieutenant stood back, "I have brought you a visitor." He smiled at me. "I shall leave you alone for a few minutes." He squeezed between me and the bulkhead and then, with a touch of my arm, left us, closing the door behind him.

Francesco, standing in the corner – dirty, bruised and bearded – gave me a resigned smile. I went to him and we fell into each other's arms and stayed there for a long time. It had been only a few hours since we last embraced but, in that time, the earth beneath our feet had moved so far that we teetered on the edge of a precipice with only each other to cling to. I could have burst into tears but I told myself I must not. This crisis was of my making; Francesco was the victim and I the one who had to be strong. Francesco lifted my face and kissed me through his prickly beard.

"I'm sorry," he said.

"For the beard?" I had wanted to make him smile and he did.

"Well, yes, for the beard and the dirt on my shirt but, you know," he shrugged, "dragging you down to this."

"You didn't *drag* me. You told me to stay in Palermo if you remember. It was my own impetuosity that brought me here – and with two platoons of marines in tow – it was *I* who dragged *you* down to this."

There it was. I had said it. The brutal truth of my guilt was out. I felt sick with the enormity of it and, at its first test, my resolve to be strong failed me. I put my head in my hands and sank down onto the cot.

"No, no," Francesco sat beside me and put his arm round me, "don't say that, don't think it. The republic was a doomed mission. I think I knew that all along but it was a heroic doomed mission, a Romantic doomed mission, and I wasn't going to be left out." He gave me his schoolboy's smile. "If the marines hadn't found me in the catacombs, the Lazzaroni would have found me somewhere else. You probably saved my life."

"Saved your life?" I wiped the tears from my cheeks and looked at him. It was the most deluded speech I ever heard. Did he really expect me to believe it? Did he believe it himself?

"Francesco," I said, examining him, "you are in grave danger."

"The high treason you mean?" I shook my head and looked away. I was not going to play charades with him. "The court martial was a formality," he went on, "less than ten minutes. They had to convict me because it was true, I did fire on *Minerva,* but every officer on the panel is one of mine. I brought most of them up in the service."

"Thurn?"

"Yes, even Thurn. I think he's quite pleased to have taken over the Bourbon navy from me but he has no wish to hang me."

"Francesco, don't say that."

"Well, shoot me then. The navy doesn't hang its officers." He seemed so confident. I wondered if he already knew something.

"So," I made myself ask, "what will they do to you?" He removed his arm from my shoulder and took hold of my hands.

"They are not going to kill me." He saw, at last, that I needed him to be serious. "I am not going to die. The range of punishments available to the court does include death and imprisonment – God forbid that – but they also include fines, confiscation and exile, and my crime was not great."

"High treason?"

"In a military court. It was not a political trial. I didn't plot a coup d'état or leap at Ferdinand with a dagger; my crime was to fire on one of his ships and no one was killed. No, honestly, Cornelia, we can be sanguine." He was so calm. He believed what he was saying so, should I? For the first time that day, I dared hope.

"But exile? You love your country; Naples is the passion of your life."

"No, Cornelia, the passion of my life is not Naples." He closed his hands over mine. "Do you remember that stormy night when you got me out of bed at The Officers' Club?"

"Of course."

"When the Bourbons were abandoning Naples and I'd decided to stay?"

"Yes, I remember."

"And do you remember, when I saw you, the choice that I made?"

"You dropped everything."

"I did. I took Naples' most valuable ship and a crew and sailed off after the Bourbons, leaving Naples, as they had, but for you. And I could be in Rome now: the cardinal and Maria were both urging me to go, they offered me passage, but I said 'no', I would wait for *you* – because I love *you*. *You* are the passion of my life, Cornelia, for richer for poorer, in Naples or in exile – for ever." He took my face in his hands and kissed me, his eyes so full of hope.

"To Rome then!" I smiled.

"Rome, London, anywhere."

"London's too cold."

"Paris?"

"Too polemical. Montpellier," I suggested. "Good climate, intelligent society, not far from the sea." Francesco laughed.

"You don't suppose your mother will have a view?"

The cabin door opened. Lieutenant Parkinson looked past me to Francesco.

"The court is ready to pass sentence." The words dropped like a guillotine. We rose together, hand in hand, from the cot and I could feel Francesco was trembling. I took him in my arms and pulled him to me.

"It will be alright," I rubbed his back, "in five minutes time we shall know and it will be alright. Montpellier – Rome – Paris if we must." I could not bear to release him, but then the lieutenant said,

"The guard will escort you to the wardroom, Admiral. I shall take Miss Knight to her cabin."

"No," I told him, "I shall wait here."

"I'm afraid not. I have my orders. You should say goodbye now." *Goodbye!* I looked in alarm at Francesco. He gripped my hands.

"I love you," he said. His eyes were shot with fear. I hugged him and kissed him.

"I love you too." And then, in a thin voice, he said again, "I'm sorry."

Up on the quarter deck, we found Sir William looking out over the gunwale and Lieutenant Parkinson left me with him.

"Any sign of the cardinal?" I asked but he shook his head.

"No, not yet. I'm afraid there are more men than Francesco looking to him for salvation today," and he looked down the line of transports. My heart dropped into my stomach.

"You know they are passing sentence."

"Oh, my dear." Sir William's face fell. He opened his arms and I went to him. "Look at you," he held me tightly, "so pale. This is a terrible moment but the decision might be less awful than you fear. Confiscation and exile are handed down as often as anything worse."

"I know," I said, my face pressed to him, "that's what Francesco said."

"Then let us hold to that." He lifted me back from his shoulder. My cheeks were streaked with tears and when he brought out his handkerchief I took it. I was so grateful for Sir William: always steadfast, always kind, always right. "Let's get you out of the sun," he said, "there's nobody in the dining cabin. We can wait for news there."

We went in and sat beside the long dining table and Sir William ordered iced lemonade and then, as an afterthought, brandy. The cabin was cool and quiet although, beyond the panelling, we could hear the murmur of Nelson talking with another man. I hoped that they would continue talking, and stay on their side of the panelling because, in my fractured state, I did not want to have to face Nelson.

"Where is Lady Emma?" I asked Sir William; she being another I did not want to face.

"Resting against the heat."

The lemonade arrived and I took a long draught. It was cold and astringent but it did not cut through my mind's dull cycle of *imprisonment, exile, death* and, *how would I hear and from whom?* My hand was trembling on the glass so I carefully put it back down. Sir William sighed and crossed his legs. The waiting would be agony for him too because he loved Francesco and his position was horribly compromised. I wondered if he'd have preferred not to be there.

"Would you like to go through to Nelson?" I suggested. "He will get the news first."

"No, no," he waved the idea away, "I shall stay here with you," but then, on reflection, I added,

"I would rather you did go through. Then, when you get the news, you can bring it to me. Whatever it is, I would rather hear it from you than from Nelson."

"Yes." He nodded sagaciously and took a drink of his lemonade. Then he got to his feet and went through to Nelson.

Lieutenant Parkinson's face gave nothing away. He came in from the wheel deck, removing his hat and pushing his fingers through his hair, then he knocked on Nelson's door and went in. I remained where I was, on a chair by the table, and never felt so alone. The silence was profound. All I could hear was the beat of my heart – the blood pumping through it, through my throat, through my ears, through my head, I stood up, I needed to move. I paced up and down the cabin floor until, after a minute, the lieutenant came out and, without a glance, strode past me and out to the wheel deck.

Raised voices now penetrated the panelling. I could not tell what was being said but it sounded like Sir William's voice and then Nelson's as well. I went and put my ear to the panelling. I caught 'unprecedented' from Sir William and 'damnable' and then, violently, 'no, no, no!' Nelson's voice was less strident than Sir William's but I caught 'Caracciolo', definitely, 'Caracciolo' but it was impossible to hear more, the panelling was too thick. I walked to the end of the cabin and looked out of the window. A Neapolitan frigate, flying the king's colours, had been drawn up and moored about two hundred yards from *Foudroyant* but there was still no small boat that might have been carrying Ruffo. I turned and walked back down the cabin, wondering what I should do. At the glazed doors to Nelson's cabin I stopped and looked in. Sir William and Nelson were standing over a writing table, patently arguing with one another while, in the far corner, Campbell was quietly working at his desk. If Sir William and Nelson were disputing Francesco's fate, I could not stand by. I put my hands on the handles and pushed open the doors. Both men turned and when they saw me, Sir William cast his eyes to the floor and Nelson glared at me.

"No, Miss Knight. Not now." But I would not be put off.

"What is to happen to Francesco?" I demanded.

"No. I must ask you to leave …" but Sir William interrupted him. He lifted his eyes from the floor and glared at Nelson.

"Tell her," he said. "You say the decision is immutable, so for God's sake tell Cornelia and spare her the suspense."

"It is immutable," Nelson replied, ignoring me. "It is *their* judgement, fairly pronounced by officers of his own country. Neither you nor I have any power to intervene." They were bickering like schoolboys over Francesco's life.

"*What have they done?*" I screamed at them both. "*Tell me. What is the sentence?*" Sir William, leaning with one hand on the writing table and with the other on his hip, continued glaring at Nelson and Nelson hesitated. He glanced nervously at me and then stiffened.

"I am very sorry, Miss Knight, but the Neapolitan court martial has determined that, for his crime of high treason, Admiral Caracciolo must hang."

"But the decision must be disputed," Sir William shouted, standing up now from the table, "appealed against. It is unprecedented for an officer of Francesco's rank to be hanged and dropped in the sea."

"Dropped in the sea?" These words – *hang, drop, sea* – they exploded over me like mortars, stunning me deaf to their meaning. A sentence of death is a horror but … "What do you mean dropped in the sea?" Nelson shot Sir William an angry look, he had evidently said too much.

"The decision of the court is, Miss Knight, that the admiral be taken from here to a Neapolitan ship where he will be hanged from the foreyard until sunset. Then the rope will be cut and the body fall into the sea." Nelson's eyes, usually so steady, were flitting. "I am sorry," he concluded, "the decision of the court." I looked at those flitting eyes and I thought of Francesco's confidence in the court's leniency.

"I don't believe you," I told him. "What was in that note?" Nelson blenched.

"What note is that, Miss Knight?"

"The note that you sent to the President of the court martial after the verdict and before the sentence. This sentence is yours, isn't it?" Nelson shook his head and attempted an empty laugh.

"No-no-no-no-no," he tried to insist but the more he insisted the less I believed him.

"You could commute this sentence couldn't you, Nelson?" I told him and he said again,

"This is entirely a Neapolitan matter." But Sir William now had his doubts.

"Is this true, Nelson? Can you commute the sentence?"

"No, Sir William, I cannot."

"And what do you mean by 'sunset'?" I then asked, picking up on another word that had exploded over me. Again, Nelson blenched. He cleared his throat before he next said,

"The prisoner is to be hanged at five o'clock, and the body cut down at sunset."

"Today?" It could not be. "Not today!" and Sir William too exclaimed,

"This afternoon? You didn't mention this. Nelson, you cannot do this. Every condemned man has at the very least twenty-four hours to make his peace with God." Nelson lowered his eyes to the floor and pursed his lips. He said again,

"This is the decision of the Neapolitan court." The room went quiet. I could hear my heart in my chest and the breath funnelling through my nostrils. I looked at Nelson and his eyes were lowered, unable to look at me.

"Pilate!" I spat the name at him. "This is your doing and you know it." He raised his cold eyes to me and I thrust out an accusing finger. "Every time you wash your hands for the rest of your life you will see Francesco's blood. I shall tell you why he won't give him twenty-four hours, Sir William. Because he knows that Cardinal Ruffo will veto this grotesque sham. He wants Francesco dead before Ruffo gets here."

We heard men's voices shouting from the quarter deck and the cabin door opened. It was Hardy, Nelson's Flag Captain.

"Excuse me, my lord," he leaned in with his hand resting on the door handle, "the prisoner is being transferred." Nelson gave him a nod. I was not surprised that he could not speak.

"Oh, Cornelia," Sir William advanced to comfort me, "I am so sorry."

"Sorry!" I exclaimed, now desperate. "For me? Francesco was sorry too but this is not about *me*." I turned from Sir William and ran from the room. Out on deck and up in the rigging, the entire ship's company was shouting and jeering at the condemned man. I could see him over their heads. He was with Lieutenant Parkinson, moving towards the boarding steps between two lines of marines.

"Francesco!" I called out, but my voice was lost in the crescendo of noise. It could not end like this. He would not leave me like this. I pushed my way through the throng of seamen to get to the boarding gate only, when I got there, I was stopped by the cordon of marines – but I could see Francesco. His hands were tied at his back again and Lieutenant Parkinson was leading him to the gate. I called out again,

"Francesco!" and this time he heard me. He looked up and saw me waving at him from behind the cordon. "Wait!" I shouted, "Stop!" The lieutenant saw me too and when they got to the gate, they both halted in front of me. I pushed my face between the heads of two of the marines, "Lord Nelson has made a mistake!" I told them. "This is not legal!" The lieutenant came closer to catch my words. "You must stop!" I told him. "This is not legal!" My heart was pounding so hard I could hardly speak. I stared open-mouthed at the lieutenant. He was only young, about twenty-two, with an open, friendly face. He hesitated for a moment then, keeping a hand on Francesco's arm, he came up to me.

"What did you say?" We were face-to-face now between the heads of the marines. "Nelson says what?" I had his attention. That was all I wanted – to engage him, keep him, delay him.

"The trial was not legal," I said again, almost breathless. "The arrest was not legal – and Cardinal Ruffo – the king's regent – is coming for Francesco – to take him into his own custody – to make it legal." The lieutenant was listening intently, taking it all in. He looked round at Francesco. Poor Francesco! Everything about him proclaimed the condemned man: his shirt and breeches were stained, his feet were bare, his hair tousled and his bearded face frozen in shock. I called out to reassure him,

"Ruffo is coming!" I attempted a smile and nodded vigorously. "Just wait, wait." I looked back to the lieutenant. "He is on his way!" and, to confirm my claim, I pointed over the gunwale. The lieutenant came close to me again and frowned.

"Are you telling me, Miss Knight, that Nelson is staying the execution?"

"Yes, that's right," I nodded vigorously at him, "a stay. You've to stay on the ship." I hardly knew what I was saying.

I only knew that I must keep talking and keep the lieutenant talking for as long as I could. "Yes," I repeated, "stay on the ship. Don't leave the ship. Take Francesco back to his cabin until Cardinal Ruffo arrives." I was making progress with the lieutenant, in spite of his doubts, I could tell. He stood up straight and looked over to the great cabin; frowning, thinking, wondering what to do.

"I shall need confirmation," he said, and I couldn't answer. I had run out of words. Of course he would need confirmation. He wasn't going to take it from me. I caught Francesco's eye and jerked my head towards the central companionway, signalling that he might turn back. He looked behind him, not understanding what I had meant and then I noticed, over his shoulder, beyond the gunwale, a boat. It was a good-sized boat, a launch perhaps, and it was pulling towards us from the direction of the town. I couldn't believe it. Were my prayers to be miraculously answered? I whispered some thanks to God and called to the lieutenant.

"The cardinal's here!" I threw out my arm, jabbing at the boat. I looked at Francesco and shouted to him, "It's the cardinal!" and he and the lieutenant both looked out over the side just as a tricorn hat came bobbing up the boarding steps. It was Shand, the Captain of Marines. When he reached the top, he scowled at the lieutenant.

"What's going on?" he asked him. "My marines have been embarked for ten minutes and it's hot. What's the delay?" The lieutenant was phlegmatic.

"A stay apparently, until Cardinal Ruffo arrives. Some question of legality." The captain jerked in his chin, feigning shock.

"Oh? And who's told you that?" The lieutenant nodded at me. "What?" Shand jabbed a finger at me. "This? The accomplice?" He gave the lieutenant a contemptuous look. "You've been out in the sun too long, Mr Parkinson, you've gone soft."

"But the cardinal has been sighted." Now the lieutenant pointed over the side but the captain took no notice and stepped up to him.

"This has nothing to do with any cardinal," he said into his face. "She's trying to make a monkey of you. Now," he stepped back, "escort your prisoner to the boat."

"But the cardinal is here!" I yelled, and I threw out my arm again towards the boat but both officers ignored me.

"I think we should get confirmation," the lieutenant was saying.

"Confirmation? Of what?"

"Of the orders." A sneer curled the captain's lip.

"I was right. You have gone soft." He screwed his finger into the lieutenant's chest. "First law: obey orders. You don't question them, you don't *ask for confirmation* – you obey them." He stepped back onto the platform at the top of the steps. "Now, go on," he nodded to the steps, "carry out your orders; take him down to the boat." But still the lieutenant was unsure.

"I think we can wait. If that launch is the cardinal coming…" Captain Shand snorted with exasperation and turned to look at the approaching boat. Francesco looked pitiful. He had stood, all this time, bound and helpless under the savage taunts of six hundred seamen. It was alright for me: I could stamp and shout and throw out hares and red herrings to divert myself but Francesco was powerless; he could do nothing except stand and wait and dwell on what might be to come. Our eyes met. His were wide with fear and I could see now that he was trembling. I reached out my arms between the marines and the lieutenant saw me. He gave the marines the nod to let Francesco through and, when he came to me, I embraced him. He smelled, as always, of Francesco, of the man that I loved, only now more intensely since I feared how fleeting that essence might be. My lovely man. The nicest man I ever knew, the best friend I ever had. I wanted him to put his arms around me but, with his hands tied, he was helpless in my arms, helpless in the world. I stroked his hair and lifted his face and kissed him. He tried to kiss me but his lips were trembling and his eyes glistening with tears.

"I'm sorry," he whispered.

"Don't say that. Don't ever be sorry for loving me." I kissed him again and cradled his head. "You have given me my life and for that, I shall always love you." I held him tightly, trying to still his trembling, kissing his head and his hair. He had abandoned hope and such hope as I had was slowly slipping away.

"That's not a Neapolitan launch. It's one of ours," Captain Shand shouted to the lieutenant. "Look at it. You can see who's in it: Captain Foley and his senior officers. It's *Goliath's* launch. Nothing to do with Cardinal Ruffo." He put his hand on the lieutenant's chest and pushed him back. "Get a grip of yourself and get this over with." But the lieutenant was still not sure. He looked at me, his young conscience struggling in his eyes, then he looked at Francesco and back to Captain Shand.

"Cardinal Ruffo might yet come," he told Shand, "there is a man's life at stake here. I'm going for confirmation." He turned to go back to the great cabin only to see, standing five yards behind him, his commanding officer, Captain Hardy.

"Lieutenant Parkinson," Hardy called to him and six hundred men fell silent. "You will escort your prisoner to his place of execution or be taken under guard to your cabin." Francesco moaned. His head rolled back, showing his teeth and the whites of his eyes and Captain Shand pulled him from me.

"No …" I cried and Lieutenant Parkinson looked back at me. "Don't leave him," I begged him, "not with Shand," and, under the renewed roar of six hundred seamen, the lieutenant ran back to Francesco whom Shand was now pulling down the steps. I tried to follow him but could not, the marines were penning me in, I shoved at their backs and screamed against the deafening din but it was no use. Francesco was gone.

CHAPTER FIFTEEN

I should have been with him. I wanted, like Mary Magdalene, to share his suffering, to feel his pain and humiliation – his death was cruel enough without his dying alone. I ached for him and craved his body. Cold, tortured and in its filth, I did not care, it was my body, the body of the man I loved, I wanted to lay my face against him and plead his forgiveness because had I not brought him to that terrible end? Nelson, Shand, Emma, Thurn – they were small part players; if I had stayed in Palermo, as Francesco had asked, he would be in Rome by now and I making plans to join him. Mary Magdalene did at least have Christ's body and the sacred privilege of its care. Francesco's was cast into the oblivion of the deep; all I had to nurse was remorse.

The marines had put me back in my cabin where Sir William found me. He sat with me on the cot, cradling me in his arms while beyond the cabin's flimsy walls six hundred men bayed at the promise of a ritual death. At the appointed hour their noise rose to a roar: 'See him dance!' they cried, 'See how a real prince kicks a dance!' It was more than I could bear and my mind, unhinged by that single word, withdrew from present horror to the night of the Palermo ball. During those minutes that Francesco choked and wrestled to remain alive, I danced with him again, round and round that spacious floor, gliding past mirrors and stuccoed walls while the musicians smiled and then I must have slept. Cardinal

Ruffo did not come, injustice was done and, in the morning, I returned to Palermo.

I took the daily courier boat. Usually, this would be a cutter or a brig but, on that particular morning, it was the frigate *Thalia* and, as chance would have it, I knew her captain: Nelson's stepson, Josiah Nisbet. My broken heart sank. Nisbet was, without doubt, the most volatile naval officer I ever met and yet, on that awful morning, he could not have been more kind: he insisted that I have his great cabin and his steward; whatever I needed, I would have and my privacy he guaranteed. I would be cocooned and pampered all the way to Palermo.

It was a kind thought of Nisbet's but, with only memory and imagination for company, my isolation became oppressive and the cabin filled with ghosts: Captain Shand smiling on the cellar steps, Lady Emma purring over the queen's letter, Nelson's eyes flitting – and Francesco – the terror in his eyes when Shand dragged him away. And these were just my memories. The visions of Francesco's death that my imagination conjured cannot be described and after a day cocooned with my tortured self, I craved the company of another and asked Captain Nisbet to join me.

We had supper together – or rather – Nisbet had supper while I watched because I could not eat, my stomach was stitched with grief, but I drank some of his wine. It was Tuscan and excellent and, after a glass, my demons began to withdraw – although my host felt obliged to detain them.

"You have my condolences," he said, stripping the flesh from a bream, and instantly my tears welled. I couldn't help it. It had to be. I had wept in fits all day, as succeeding waves of grief engulfed me and now I was deluged again.

"Oh I'm sorry," Nisbet put down his fork and touched my arm, "would you rather I left?"

"No, no," I lifted my napkin to my eyes, "if you can put up with me, please, stay, I should like that." He returned to his bream.

"He was always good to me, your admiral."

"Thank you," I said, holding the napkin to my eyes, "at the Naples dinner, you mean?"

"Well, yes. He did stand up for me there, didn't he? Saved me from a Troubridge thrashing, but I was rather thinking of when I knew him in '95." I put down my napkin.

"You knew Francesco four years ago?"

"I was on *Agamemnon* with Nelson during the action off Genoa."

"When Nelson took Francesco's prize?"

"Close run thing though." Nisbet tore open a roll and mopped up his plate. "Nelson shouldn't have been there, he'd broken line, but Caracciolo's reputation nettled him and he saw the chance to take him on."

"What do you mean, his 'reputation'?"

"The finest sailor in the Mediterranean, they said. Nelson, being Nelson, took that as a challenge, which was why he cut Caracciolo for the French 80."

I remembered Francesco telling me. We had been sitting in Sir William's library before dinner; Francesco in his dress uniform with his legs stretched out, ankles crossed.

"There was a rivalry there," I told him.

"There was for Nelson. Couldn't speak for Caracciolo."
I could, I thought. I remembered Francesco's begrudging congratulations to Nelson after the Battle of the Nile, and his glee at the damage he sustained taking the royal family to Palermo, but I said nothing.

"Rivalry, jealously and ambition – that's about the sum of my step-father. May I?" He had finished his bream and was nodding towards mine that I had set aside. I passed it to him and he slid it onto his plate.

"I do wonder," I said, taking up my wine, "why you continue in Nelson's service. You obviously dislike him."

"Ah well, as soon as I see England again, I'll quit. I never wanted the navy." He was de-boning the second fish as expertly as the first. "I wanted to be a man of letters, a lawyer or something like that, only when my father died and my mother married Nelson, I was dragged off into the navy, no choice in the matter, and I hate it."

"I'm sorry to hear you say that," I told him, feeling steadier for the wine, "I have always regarded the navy as the noblest of the professions. I shall put your disaffection down to your circumstances."

"*Noble*?" He looked up from his fish with a scowl. "If you'd ever seen action, you wouldn't call it that."

"I can imagine it must be frightening."

"Do you think you can imagine it?" He put down his knife and fork and picked up his wine. "Taking cannon-fire? Ball, chain, grape? At close range? And sniper fire? Hour after hour? The din and the smoke, the flying shards of oak tearing into men's bodies while you force them to maintain their rate of fire when their hands are blistered on the barrels, their lungs choked with smoke and their feet skidding on their dead mates' guts? Noble, Miss Knight? Where is the nobility in that?" His face was flushed and his eyes dilated. This young man could not take his wine but I was not having him disparage the service.

"The nobility is in the stoicism and sacrifice you have just described," I told him. "Endured for the greater good."

"The greater good!" Now he sneered. "Greater glory you mean. Prize money, medals, titles, rank – that's what Nelson sacrifices his men for and it's not how I want to live."

"But not all naval commanders are like Nelson; there are plenty of honourable officers who also love letters. The two pursuits do not have to exclude one another."

"You are thinking of Admiral Caracciolo." I was, of course, and my heart heaved.

"Among others."

"But didn't Admiral Caracciolo already have titles, money and rank?" His words caught my breath and fresh tears started to well. I took up my napkin.

"Your point, Mr Nisbet!"

"Like I say, Nelson would have been jealous of him."

Jealousy. It was too small a motive for so great a crime. But what matter? Jealousy, justice, expediency, vengeance, or appeasement of the Harpies at Nelson's back, the cold fact was that I had led Francesco's enemies to him, the crime was mine and my sentence was to live with the knowledge. I have little memory of that slow beat south against African winds, I was still numb with disbelief. The leviathan of my grief stirred from time to time, gripping my heart, parching my throat and flooding the tears to my eyes but there were periods too when I thought of nothing at all. Captain Nisbet was kind in his young-man's ham-fisted way. His brutal candour was preferable, I suppose, to cloying sympathy and, anyway, it prepared me for my next ordeal: telling Mother.

I left the footman with the trunk and the cab and went straight up to her. She was not in our room which, for a moment, alarmed me but when I called down the corridor, Valentina appeared from the grand salon and told me that

Mother was in there. It was a room we had never used but, as Valentina whispered on the way in, Mother had wanted to look at the sea. She was sitting in a chair in front of open windows that looked out over the garden to the promenade and the bay beyond. I walked round in front of her so that she might see me.

"Hello, Mother." I had been gone for less than two weeks but Mother was changed: her skin was translucent and mottled and it sagged from her cheekbones in fine folds. I think she had been sleeping.

"Cornelia?"

"Yes. Hello, Mother." I went down on my haunches and took her hands.

"Where have you been?" She looked confused.

"I have been to Naples," my throat was tight with what I was about to tell her, "to find Francesco."

"But why? What is the matter?"

"You remember," I told her, "we had not heard from him and I went to find him."

"Well, he would be on his ship, wouldn't he? Did you look there?" Mother was still half dreaming. This was not the best time to impart my news but my heart was too full to stop now.

"Mother, listen to me." I took a grip of her hands and of myself. "I found Francesco in Naples and … he is dead." Now Mother awoke.

Dead?" She sat up. "But when? How? He was here only last evening with Mrs Cadogan. Valeria made up a four and we played *rouge et noire*."

"No, no," I shook my head in despair, "Francesco has been gone since February. Who was playing cards with you last evening?"

"Why, Admiral Gould. Of whom else do we speak?" It was too much for me. My heart was bursting to unload my awful news but Mother wouldn't let me. I got up and walked down the room and looked out over the bay. My head was spinning and my heart beating so hard it caught my breath but I managed not to succumb and, after a minute or two, I went back to Mother.

"Do – you – remember – Francesco?" I asked her, framing each word. "He is – he was – an admiral in the Neapolitan navy. This villa belongs to his family. You stayed with him at his palazzo in Naples when you injured your ankle. *I am engaged to be married to him!*"

"Yes, dear, yes," Mother waved me away, "I know all that, there is no need to shout." But then she looked doubtful. "I just didn't know that Admiral Gould's name was Francesco."

And then she wanted to know how Gould had died and I had to explain that he hadn't. It was awful. She seemed to have lost all memory of Francesco, every reference to him she attached to Captain Gould – and 'no', Gould had not been promoted in my absence! Mother thought I was engaged to him. I soon realised, of course, that her mind was confused and she was completely overlaying more distant memories of Francesco with recent ones of Captain Gould. I was longing to spill out my grief to Mother because she too had loved Francesco but now she had forgotten him. My heart was in despair, but the next day, when I had slept on it, I recognised that Mother would not now know how Francesco had died and from that I took comfort.

Captain Gould, it seemed, had called regularly in my absence. Mother had developed a bladder infection just after I'd sailed which left her confused and Captain Gould had taken it upon himself to watch over her. It was chivalrous of him and, when I saw him off the premises after his next visit, I told him so.

"Not at all, Miss Knight," he had answered. "I always enjoyed your mother's company. Plain-speaking English ladies are in short supply out here."

"Not so plain-speaking at the moment," I observed sadly, and the captain gave me a kindly smile. We were walking down the villa's carriage drive to the Marino.

"Never mind, I am sure she will soon be better and anyway, since I was stood down from Cape Maritimo, I have time on my hands."

"Stood down? I thought *Audacious* was looking out for the French fleet while the squadron is at Naples."

"We have a new Commander-in-Chief, Lord Keith, and he does not think the French ever were heading for Sicily but for our base in Minorca. He is ordering the squadron to sail there now with all speed."

"That must be a great relief to you," I suggested, "standing out there, waiting for a battle fleet with one ship and three frigates."

"Absolutely," he agreed, "and it will be to Nelson when he sees the orders. If the French *had* come while the squadron was five hundred miles off station, well …"

"A court martial?"

"Without a doubt, and with consequences." We had reached the villa's gates.

"So, now you will be leaving us for Minorca." I put up my hand against the lowering sun.

"Nelson won't have the orders yet. I only had it verbally myself from the dispatch officer when he passed through this morning. I expect I shall be in Palermo for a few more days."

"Well," I said, ready to return to the house, "thank you again. You have been very kind." He gave me a bow.

"Please accept again my sincere condolences, Miss Knight, and if there is anything that I can do to help your mother, or you, I am at your disposal."

King Ferdinand finally left Palermo for Naples that week, alone. Despite Cardinal Ruffo's and Nelson's separate assurances, he decided that his capital was still too dangerous for his family so he left them behind with the queen. It was a time, again, for waiting. The queen waited on her husband's reports, Captain Gould waited for new orders, Mrs Cadogan waited for the Hamiltons and Nelson to come back and refill the echoing Palazzo Palagonia and I waited … what did I wait for? I had waited for four months in the Villa Caracciolo for Francesco but now, since sailing to Naples to deliver him to his death, I waited for what? For Mother to get better? Certainly, and I hoped she soon would, but beyond that I stared into a void. I had my usual purpose: I looked after Mother, assiduously, watching out for her every need, and I made up the four when Mrs Cadogan and Captain Gould called in for a few hands of cards. It was the old routine of the spinster companion to her ageing mother, the routine I had followed all my adult life – till it was broken, briefly, by love. And I wept. Oh, how I silently wept in the night with my back turned to Mother. Those watches were anguished but more so my dreams. They were strange and agitated, full of worry and searching through unfamiliar settings of familiar places from Montpellier, my childhood or Rome and everything irritatingly wrong – a street of stairs too steep to climb, a fishpond for a parlour floor, endless curving corridors – I searched these places, anxiously, urgently, not knowing why and running, always, out of time until, rounding a corner or sitting waiting on a garden seat, there would be Francesco. He would smile and come to me and my anxieties would melt away. We would talk; his warm baritone thrilling the base of my spine, then his arms would enfold me, his cheek would brush mine and our lips would meet. Francesco's love, Francesco's warmth, Francesco's gifts of peace and the promise of a lifetime shared until, of course, I awoke when, in the suffocating darkness of my shared bed, the waves of grief would engulf me. There never will be closure. My loss will last for as long as I live.

I received a letter from Sir William in mid-July. It might have come from the Fields of Hades.

Dear Cornelia,

I write with news that will distress you but which I want you to hear from a witness rather than the garbled gossip that is bound to follow. Yesterday, Francesco's body surfaced off *Foudroyant's* starboard bow. It was upright, on account of weighting in the garments and, having viewed the body, I can tell you, without doubt, that it was Francesco's. You will understand how much it pains me to relate what it pained me to see so let me hasten to the nugget of good. The first to see the apparition was King Ferdinand himself, from the quarter deck. He recognised it at once and burst into feverish wailings, declaring it a portentous haunting but his chaplain, with great presence, suggested to him an alternative view; that Francesco was come to appeal for the king's pardon and a Christian burial. It was an account that Ferdinand was pleased to embrace and the upshot is that Francesco now lies in the little church of Santa Maria della Catena in the Borgo Santa Lucia. The brothers of the fraternity there solemnised the interment so, you see, our dear friend now lies in peace and a stone's throw from his family's home.

Cornelia, I am glad that you are not here to see what is happening in Naples. Nelson, as you know, has been holding the Republicans in the ships 'awaiting the king's mercy' and now that the king is here, the quality of his mercy is revealed to us. What can I say about this man I have known since he was a boy and who is so loved by the common people? I wish it were something good but in the days since he arrived he has shown himself still to be that spoilt little boy and, shocked at what he sees as the withdrawal of love, he is venting his wrath on the Republican prisoners. His first act, when he arrived, was to appoint a High Court of State, comprised of his cruellest judges, to try the civilians. Every day, I watch boatloads of these unfortunates being rowed ashore to be chained up in gaols less wholesome even than the sweltering ships – and as to the sentences passed down to them: some die by the axe and some by the halter while others will die slowly in prisons so foul that even the charitable Brothers of the Bianchi will not enter them. Already, I have lost friends: Giuliano Colonna, Gennaro Serra and our matchless poetess, Eleanora Pimentel, whom I know you met and admired – it is terrible – even the gentle Domenico Cirillo, physician and botanist and Fellow, with me, of the Royal Society in London – gruesomely executed in a packed market square. I plead with the king for individuals, and urge on him the wisdom for future stability of a general pardon but his heart is not for clemency and, in that, the queen stands with him.

I am reluctant to return to the fate of poor Francesco but, in the light of what is happening now, I would suggest to you that Nelson, in his hardness, might have saved Francesco from worse. He and the court martial were, after all, executing what they read as the king's command and they did it in swift naval fashion but, with Ferdinand now here and adhering to no rule but his own, we might, in these dark days, acknowledge that military justice is better than no justice at all.

Can such an acknowledgement assuage grief? I hope so because, in conclusion, I have my own sad news to impart. Besides the judicial murders being committed in the king's name, there are many scores more being committed in the streets and a victim of one of those also was a dear friend: my Head of Household, Vittorio Santino. I heard it from Jean-Carlo and went straight away to view the body at his family's home. He had been stabbed to death while walking home on his own. He had not been robbed and he never meddled in politics, it was, they said, in these troubled times, just one of those things. It could simply have been that he wore his hair longer than most. It suited his bone structure, and he was not one to change his style for the sake of fashion. That was probably all it was. To the fevered Lazzaroni, searching for prizes to deliver to their king, long hair is considered Jacobin and so Vittorio, still fit and well at fifty-one, was killed.

So, Cornelia, you and I are just two more who weep. I long to leave this ship. I feel weak with the heat and the burden of it all, and Nelson too is sick, confined to his cot with feverish pains in his head. Emma, thank God, stays strong and ministers to us both.

Keep well and remember me to your dear mother.

Sincerely yours,
William

It was, indeed, some comfort to know that Francesco was at peace, and it would be to his mother and everyone else who loved him, but as to Nelson and his compassionate swift justice… I shall never argue with Sir William, I understand his contending loyalties, but with Francesco's short walk to the gallows paved with so many illegalities, his death was no justice at all.

I passed on Sir William's good wishes to Mother, which she was pleased to receive (she remembered him at least) but as to the rest of the letter, I spared her that. What was the point in upsetting Mother with so much sad news? There was nothing in the letter that she needed to know and if she did not remember Francesco, I was sure she would not remember Vittorio or any other of Sir William's unfortunate friends. Mother's mind was going and her strength with it. By 19th July, the walk from our bedroom across the landing was more than her lungs would stand and Captain Gould persuaded her to let his ship's surgeon see her. The surgeon came and examined her but he was not sanguine. He said that Mother's shrunken lungs were being flooded by the high humidity and that she should be moved as quickly as possible to a drier climate. In the meantime, he applied leeches to her chest and ordered bed rest. Mother was philosophical.

"It is all working out nicely, isn't it, Cornelia?" she said, once Captain Gould and his surgeon had left. "We have looked after one another very well since my admiral passed on and, now that I am going, you have your own admiral to look after you." Again, my heart sank. Mother was confused, I knew, but I really could not talk about death and admirals. I wanted to leave her and walk over to the windows but her old, watery eyes were so placid, I did not want to confuse her further. I took hold of her hand.

"You are not going anywhere, Mother." I gave her a smile.

"Oh I am, dear." She returned my smile. "I know, and I don't mind, so don't you mind either. You have been a wonderful daughter to me. The best companion I could ever have wished for and if I was sometimes slow to show it, I was always very proud of you, you know." She squeezed my hand and a shiver ran through me. She sounded so sure. With everything else that had filled my mind these last days, I never thought that Mother might die. It was unthinkable. How could she? Without Mother, what was I? Then, as if she had been reading my thoughts, she said,

"He has an agricultural estate in Somerset, you know, and coal mines that bring him in rent, and all not too far from Bath." Then Mother extended her fingers along mine and, admiringly, touched my ring. It was too much. I jumped up and walked over to the window.

"I am not engaged to Captain Gould."

"*Admiral* Gould dear." Did I have to submit to this? After a lifetime of ups and downs with Mother, through tussles and sulks, whatever else we ever were to one another we were always, both of us, honest. If she were dying, was that a time to start lying to her? I turned back from the window.

"My admiral is also dead, Mother. Admiral the Prince Francesco Caracciolo, Duke of Brienza and Head of the Neapolitan Navy. He gave me this ring on our engagement to be married and he also is dead."

"Duke of Brienza?" She looked baffled. "An Italian?" She shook her head. "I don't think that would be suitable, dear."

She did not change. Even in her senile confusion, Mother was the mother she had always been and I was glad that, to the last, we remained honest with one another. She died that night, peacefully, in her sleep. It was her stillness that woke me. Soft light was presaging dawn and I turned and put my hand to her cheek. It was cold.

"Mother?" I sat up and took her face in my hands. It was crumpled and yellow in the pre-dawn gloom and there was no doubt that the life had gone out of it. I looked at that face, more familiar to me than my own, and I examined it, carefully, etching into my memory every fading detail because, once I left it, I knew, I should never see Mother again.

I stayed with her, through the rising light, until the two Vs arrived when I passed her into their care. Should I have stayed to help? I had never lost a mother before so I did not know the protocol but, even on that mournful morning, I was haunted by more ghosts than Mother's. I left Valeria and Valentina and descended the stairs to the small parlour.

The table on which we had taken our meals had been folded down and stowed against the wall but otherwise the room was unchanged. Our couch was still there, against the back wall, and the chest where I kept my cloak. I lifted it out. I put its rich fabric to my cheek and wrapped it around me, then I lay down on the couch and gave myself up to my grief.

* * *

'What will you do?' It was the question that everyone asked: the naval chaplain who conducted the service in Palermo's Anglican chapel, the Camerons of Droitwich and every other member of the English community. 'It is too soon to decide' had been my stock reply, which satisfied most people's need to have shown concern but it did not Mrs Cadogan's. When the last of the mourners had left the Palazzo Palagonia, she came and sat with me.

"You cannot stay at the Villa Caracciolo on your own." Like Mother, she came straight to her point. "The solitude. The ghosts." She took my hand and frowned. "You would not stand it." We were sitting beside an open French window in the vast painted drawing room where Mrs Cadogan had provided the wake.

"But they are the ghosts of those I love." I was thinking of Francesco. The Villa Caracciolo bore his name and his essence suffused every room. After my ring and my cloak, it was all that I had of him.

"You should not be alone at a time like this," she went on, "believe me, Cornelia, those you have lost will haunt you enough without your seeking them out." She leaned forward to catch my eye. "Does the villa belong to Francesco?"

"The villa?" I'd been only half-listening. "Er, no. A cousin I think, or a half-cousin. Why?"

"It's a large house and must be expensive to run. I just wondered who was supporting you there." I hadn't given it a thought. I had no idea who owned the house and paid the bills but Mrs Cadogan was right: I was living alone in a very grand house at someone else's expense – a complete stranger's expense.

"You're right. I can't stay there, can I?" She took both my hands into hers.

"Why don't you come and live here with me?"

"Oh no, no," I shook my head, "you're very kind but I couldn't possibly." It was the conventional reply.

"But I have fifty rooms," she flung out an arm, "and with Emma and Sir William gone, and all the naval people, I'm lost here." She smiled in appeal with her big, oval eyes. "Please say 'yes', Cornelia. I'm sure your mother would want it, and you would be doing me a great favour."

And so, with a heavy heart, I left the Villa Caracciolo and moved in with Mrs Cadogan. Her welcome could not have been kinder – so much so that, at first, I was embarrassed by her attention – but then I realised that she too was grieving and caring for me was her way of honouring her friend. During the time that we were together at the Palazzo Palagonia, Mrs Cadogan was a more attentive mother to me than my own had ever been and I shall always thank Providence for her. We shared an embarrassment of space: fifty rooms, vibrant with frescoes; an army of servants with little to do and equipages waiting for somewhere to go – all for the two of us. We took walks together round the gardens and along the Marino, or sometimes, in the mornings, before it was too hot, we would go into town. Mrs Cadogan was not a talkative woman, I never did learn much about her, but she had that generous capacity to coax and listen and I had not been with her for more than a few days before she knew all about Francesco. She was good for me; the right woman in the right place at the right time, and I was blessed with another good friend: Captain Gould.

"Now then, Miss Knight, have you decided yet what you will do?" Again, that question.

"No," I told him, "and I probably never will. I have lived all my life as a wanderer so I expect that is how I'll continue." He looked across the tea table at me with a look of deep concern. Mrs Cadogan had left us to find the housekeeper and the captain and I were finishing our afternoon tea.

"But alone?" he asked. "Surely you will not travel alone? It would not be safe."

"As a woman, you mean?"

"As anyone without a proper entourage." I put down my cup and saucer.

"I don't know," I told him honestly, and I looked out of the French windows to the manicured gardens beyond.

Captain Gould had been a rock in the two weeks since Mother died. He had arranged the Anglican funeral and interment, made contact with the owner of the Villa Caracciolo and eased my departure from there; he had proved, in short, to be as solid a friend to me as he had been to Mother and I was glad of him.

"Perhaps I shall go back to Rome." It was all I could think of to say.

"Rome? Alone?" He leaned forward and took the last almond roll. "I am not familiar with Roman ways, but is it possible in that city for a woman to remain respectable alone? Unaccompanied? Unprotected?" He popped the small pastry into his mouth. He was right of course. I had not seriously been thinking of Rome, I just wanted to move the conversation along, but he was right. Mother and I, wherever we had lived, had always managed to find a protector: Le Comte de Périgord in Montpellier, the Prince of Palestrina during our first stay in Rome and Cardinal de Bernis, during our second – and in Naples, of course, we had had Sir William. Could I secure the protection of a grandee anywhere now, on my own? Palestrina and Bernis were both dead, I no longer had an assertive mother to force the introductions – and would it be safe for a woman of my age to try? I turned back from the garden to answer Captain Gould. I could only repeat,

"I don't know."

A letter arrived for me that afternoon. It had come down on the courier boat from Naples but its seal was not Sir William's; it was the lion rampant in a sun burst, the badge of the Caracciolo, and a cold chill shot through me. I turned the letter over in my hands, examining it like a jewel, then I took it through to the library where I would not be disturbed. I sat down at a desk and broke the seal. It was from Francesco's mother.

My dear Cornelia,

Yesterday, I received the awful news of the death of your mother. Lady Knight was a strong, spirited woman and I know that you two were close; after the martyrdom of Francesco, I wonder how you can bear it, and also, if I can help.

You may remember that, on your engagement, I invited you and Lady Knight to live with us here. At the time, you thought it inappropriate – for reasons I understood – but that invitation still stands and if, after this second tragedy, you feel the need of a home, I want you to know that you have one here, now, and for as long as you wish.

I will not add the burden of my grief to that you already bear but I have been wanting to write to you and now, after this latest tragedy, I feel that I can. I am, as you know, blessed with other children besides Francesco and you might expect that their support would temper my grief but it does not. Do not misunderstand me: each one of my children has his and her qualities and I love them all but, with my first born, I had an exceptional bond. The rest of the family understood that, it was part of the family lore but, as none of the others could share that bond, so none now can share my grief and I find myself thinking of you.

Your bond with Francesco was exceptional too, I saw that. Francesco always had admirers from being a boy, and there were girls and women who amused him over the years but none ever fathomed his true depths – until you. Francesco was so proud of you, and it was clear how much you loved him. I had looked forward to our becoming friends through Francesco, because you and I share many interests, and I wonder if, even without him, we still might. I hope so, because we did both fathom him didn't we – his sense of honour, his innocence, his philosophical rigour, his creative flair – and if his true memorial is to survive then surely it must be through we two.

I hope you can accept my offer. After the shock of your mother's death, it will take time for you to re-focus your life, I am sure, but, as the woman whom Francesco loved, you would be, for me, his greatest memorial – far greater than anything we might raise over his remains – and, of course, you would be near him, living in his home, a member of his family.

Providence, in her wisdom, has made you an independent woman now Cornelia and what you do with the rest of your life is entirely your own affair but that bond that I had with Francesco, I feel now extended to you, and my hope is that you too will find comfort in that connection. I look forward to hearing from you, but only once your thoughts have settled.

God bless you.
MC

I set the letter down on the desk and looked out of the window. I felt for her. There is no greater loss, they say, than that of a child and for that child to be so deeply loved and then, in her own word, martyred … yes … I felt for her. I thought about her offer. The dowager princess was an interesting, intelligent woman; in many ways a woman after my own heart and no doubt easier to live with than

Mother. But did I want to stand in permanent vigil with her over Francesco's memory? To dwell in the past in a city whose present was in turmoil? But I would be secure with her, socially and financially, and my life would be my own. I decided I would heed the princess's advice and take my time.

The long listless days of July elided into August. The heat and humidity were insufferable and with my mind as lethargic as my body I spent most of my time indoors. The library was my usual refuge, and when I felt like stretching my legs I would wander off through the endless enfilades of frescoed halls, idly deciphering the allegories on the ceilings and the wars on the walls and whatever route my wanderings took always brought me back to the ballroom. I might have pretended I was there for the air – with six open windows, it was the coolest room in the palazzo – but, if that were my pretence it was a weak one; the force that drew me was stronger than air. I would stand in the corner where the musicians had played and watch us: Francesco in his dress uniform and I, complementary, in cream and blue, dancing together, round and round the floor while the lawn curtains lifted on the breeze and I missed him. I missed him so much that my heart would heave, flooding my eyes with convulsions of tears that left me gasping for breath and I wanted that: I wanted to feel the pain of my loss – and intensely – because the greater the pain the stronger Francesco's presence became and I craved that much more than solace. It was my observance, my daily kindling of the flame of remembrance, but if I thought I could keep that room as my shrine, I was soon disabused when, on 8th August, *Foudroyant* and most of the rest of the English squadron sailed back into Palermo Bay.

It is absurd, I know, but since Francesco's and Mother's deaths, I had looked no further than a day at a time and, thanks to Mrs Cadogan, I had faced no demands that I should. That the Palazzo Palagonia was the embassy and the naval headquarters, to which Nelson and Emma would one day return, had not occurred to me but now, with them back, my sanctuary would be invaded. I could not live under the same roof as Francesco's murderers, I would have to leave, to move on, and I went to tell Mrs Cadogan.

I found her, after a long search, in the second floor linen room, sorting through piles of sheets with the housekeeper.

"Mrs Cadogan," I told her, "I think it is time that I left."

"Left, Cornelia?" She looked shocked. "Are you sure you are ready?" I did not feel remotely ready: not to leave and not to stay.

"Yes," I lied, "I think this would be a good time. With so many people arriving and so much for you to do, I am sure you could do without me." Mrs Cadogan frowned darkly and, taking my arm, led me out onto the landing.

"Well, no, Cornelia," she said, once we were out of the housekeeper's hearing, "I don't think we can do without you. Where would you go?"

"Not far," I extemporised, because I had not given it any thought. "In the town. I shall not be far away." Mrs Cadogan was watching me. I could see that she did not believe me. She let go my arm and looked away down the landing, then, still looking away, she said,

"You know that Emma writes to me?"

"I imagine so." She looked back to me.

"Emma is worried about Sir William. These seven weeks away have taken their toll on him. What with the heat and being cooped up with the king … then Francesco and Vittorio," she took my hand into both of hers, "Sir William loved them both, you know, and all those other poor people … it has been too much for him and it has made him ill." She gave me a sad smile. "I know that you and Emma do not get on particularly well but she does her best for Sir William. She, too, is under great strain from the queen, and she has Nelson to look after – he too is unwell." Her hands closed tighter round mine. "I just thought, Cornelia – I just hoped – that, as his friend, you would be here for Sir William, and for us all."

I walked out of the house. I would not be seduced by Mrs Cadogan. I could not remain at the Palazzo Palagonia, it was time I looked after myself. I strode to the end of the carriage drive and turned left towards the harbour. I had to find my own place – that, I told myself, was the immediate priority and I must do it myself because, was that not to be my new life? To do things for myself?

The sun was fiercely hot, glinting steel shards off the sea and, even in my light lawn, sweat was beading my brow. The promenade was busy with everyone going in the same direction. Flags and lanterns were hung in the trees and, as I drew nearer the harbour, stalls were set up handing out sweetmeats and ices, courtesy of the king, and on the buildings, banners were proclaiming the names of Ferdinand, Nelson, Emma and Sir William Hamilton. So, this was what was drawing the crowds: Ferdinand's landfall. Another vulgar show of real or bought affection for the pantomime king and his English impresarios. That Sir William should be associated with it! When the adventure had cost him so much! I hoped he'd be allowed to slip away and leave Emma and Nelson to endure the queen's kisses alone.

Bands were playing ahead and the thickening crowd burst into spontaneous song. This was not why I had left the Palazzo Palagonia so I turned off the waterfront into a side street that would take me south, deeper into the town. It was immediately cooler and quieter there with just the odd family hurrying past, and then, at the end of the street, I found myself in a small square of terraces that included a small hotel. Its board proclaimed it the Hotel Rosalia and it occupied two houses on the north-facing side of the square. I stopped and looked at it and, seeing nothing obviously amiss, I walked round the square and went in. The owners were a couple in their fifties, they were respectable and welcoming and they showed me to a first floor room that they said was available. It was clean and nicely furnished, over-looking the square and, at fifty-five ducats a week – with meals – it was within my budget. They gave me a few minutes alone in the room while I made up my mind. I sat on the bed and it was comfortable, and in the upholstered wing chair, then I stood at the window and looked out. The square was well-kept, tidy and quiet – very quiet – a place, I thought, to be lonely. Could I live like that, I wondered? I had never known loneliness in my life but just then, looking down onto that square, I felt it stealing in.

Fireworks crackled, shattering the quiet of the square. That would be Ferdinand coming ashore to his hero's welcome. No doubt Nelson and Emma would be with him, imbibing their share of the popular acclaim, and Sir William? I hoped he had managed to escape it. He had suffered too much from the Bourbon's vengeance to share their stage. He too had lost Francesco, and other long-standing friends – Colonna, Serra, Cirillo, Pimentel – all murdered by the Bourbon's friends –

and, of course, Vittorio, who had been so much more than a friend. I felt for Sir William. He had lost so much more than his palazzo and his treasures; he had lost much more than I. I turned back from the window and looked round the room. We do not need to live in a cell to be lonely. Today, Sir William would return to a Palazzo Palagonia bustling with staff, servants and naval personnel and he would be lonely. Vittorio gone to God, Emma to Nelson, and now me. I could see his face when he learned I was gone; he would be desolate. Mrs Cadogan had been right. If Sir William could survive Nelson and Emma cooped up on *Foudroyant*, then I could survive them in a fifty roomed palazzo.

I declined the room and walked back. I felt better for my decision. I had looked down into the abyss of loneliness and Mrs Cadogan's appeal had dragged me back. I needed to find Sir William. I had not seen him since that dreadful night when he had held me in his arms. We had shared so much.

A landau was drawn up under the carriage porch when I got back and when I walked in I asked straight away for Sir William. He, Lady Emma and Nelson, I was told, had just arrived and gone up to their rooms. I took to the stairs, striding them two by two, and when I got to the first floor landing, there he was, talking to the housekeeper.

"Cornelia!" He was in the buckles and braids of his full court dress and holding his plumed hat. He was terribly thin and looked, I thought, like a turtle emerging from a highly-polished shell. He abandoned the housekeeper and came to me. "Oh my poor dear!" He put out his arms and embraced me. It was a needy embrace, an embrace that demands the warmth of the other and I was glad to share mine with him. "How are you?" he asked, and I had to tell him,

"Not good." He stepped back and examined me, then he pointed his hat down the corridor.

"Shall we go to my room? It's just along here." I followed him down the corridor, away from the state apartments, towards the principal bedrooms in the east wing. Sir William's room was large and airy with windows to the east, overlooking the pleasure gardens, and to the north, overlooking the bay. He put down his hat on a side table and undid the top button of his coat. Among the decorations on his chest, I noticed, there was a large jewelled brooch that I had not seen before, bearing the image of King Ferdinand. He noticed me looking at it.

"Oh, don't look at that," he said, embarrassed, and he unclasped it and set it aside.

"Why? What is it?"

"Oh, you know," he cast, absently, about the room, alighting on two armchairs between the windows. "Shall we sit down?" I followed him to the chairs and we sat. He took out a handkerchief and dabbed at his eyes. "The wages of sin."

"The wages of sin?"

"You know what monarchs are," he wafted his hand with the handkerchief, "a jewelled brooch for me, diamonds and gowns for Emma and Nelson gets his dukedom." I lowered my eyes to my lap. Wages of sin indeed, I thought; laurels for merely being there while Ruffo regained the kingdom – that, and murdering the prisoners. Sir William saw what I was thinking. I did not want to embarrass him.

"I was sorry to hear about Vittorio." He raised his sad eyes to me. His hand was on the chair arm and I laid mine over it.

"Thank you," he said, "are we not a desolate pair?" He attempted a smile. "And then your poor mother ..."

"Well," I reset myself in my chair, determined not to succumb, "her end was peaceful, and you know that she had been poorly since Christmas."

"I know," he agreed, "but when it is your mother ..."

"She was ready to go. She said as much, only the day before. She knew that her time had come and she was reconciled. Believe me," involuntary tears welled in my eyes, "she had a good end; she was a good age." He passed me his handkerchief and I dabbed at my eyes. This talk of loved ones' deaths had to be got through but I was not ready to talk about Francesco.

"Tell me about Vittorio. Had he been with you long?"

"All my life – all my life in Naples at least – Catherine and I took him in as a page soon after we arrived and he never left us. Thirty-five years."

"Catherine, your first wife?"

"Yes. She loved him as much as I." Sir William managed a smile. "It was his beauty, you see. I am sorry you never met Catherine; I am sure you would have understood – beauty – aesthetics – they were the foundation of our marriage, our sensibilities were wonderfully attuned and Vittorio's beauty enchanted us both." I smiled that I understood and Sir William went on. "He used to sit for us and then, when he asked to draw himself, Catherine taught him the rudiments of watercolour and he became quite adept. Likewise, with music. He would sneak into the music room in the evenings to listen to us play – whether he were on duty or not – and when he asked to learn the viol, I gave him his first lessons and then, as he improved, we played trios." Sir William was brightening. "Don't you find the young irresistible?" he asked, "Their openness? Their eagerness to learn? Their unspoiled beauty?" I had to agree that Vittorio was a handsome man. I had seen him at Posillipo, and also the drawings of him as a younger man at Portici.

"Didn't I see studies of Vittorio on the walls at Portici? Would they have been by Catherine?"

"No, no, not those." Sir William's eyes twinkled. "Those were some studies that I made at Posillipo. Vittorio and I used to slip away down there in summer, when Naples was too hot, to bathe and talk and relax, as men will."

"And what did the ambassador and his man talk about?"

"Oh, you know: life, art, the ways of the ancients."

"And of love?"

"Ah," Sir William's smile broadened, "what is there to say about love? The passion inexpressible?"

There was a loud rap at the door and, with theatrical timing, Lady Emma burst in like a dame from the opera. She was wearing one of the queen's passed-down gowns: fern green with heavy gold borders and a gold sash. She had a matching turban on her head while, suspended round her neck from a gold chain, she sported a diamond encrusted miniature of the queen wearing the same dress. Emma had put on more weight and looked ridiculous.

"Pliny!" She blinked her long lashes at us both. "What are you doing here?" She looked down at our locked hands. "We have to be at the cathedral for the service of thanksgiving. We should have left by now and you are hiding here." She picked up the plumed hat from the table and Sir William rose. "Don't look so grumpy. She'll still be here when you get back, won't you, Miss Knight?"

The celebrations over the next three days were grotesque. After the *Te Deum* in the cathedral there were masques and concerts and an elaborate state banquet, bells rang and cannons boomed and everywhere, swathed in flags and lanterns, shone out the names of Hamilton and Nelson, the latter now augmented with 'Duke of Bronte'. Who could have thought other than that Nelson had reclaimed Naples for the king and Hamilton was his gallant lieutenant but none of it was true; the whole expensive charade was a fantasy and when Sir William finally got away he took to his bed. To heap upon physical and emotional exhaustion, the torment, to a noble mind, of having to stand by ignoble deeds, was too much and he was forced to rest.

I sat with him in his room for just as long as he wanted; visits that, as the days passed, grew longer. All he wanted was to rest – as he told me, 'to enjoy the present because the past was all loss and the future bleak' – and how true was that for me? Mother, the companion of my past, was gone, and Francesco, the promise of my future, gone too. Sir William understood that and he quietly shared my loss; sometimes with a word or, more often, in silence because 'what is there to say about love?' That room became my haven during those weeks of late summer and Sir William my solace. Mrs Cadogan had been a godsend when Mother had died but, with her own daughter back and demanding her attention, she was lost again to me. I should have been thinking about the Dowager Princess's offer but, somehow, I found it hard; it was, I supposed, still too soon.

And so I leaned on Sir William and Sir William leaned on me because his wife was no help; she was too busy resuming her life of debauch. Every night, as before, saw a banquet or a ball followed by faro played long into the night when Nelson would retire and the indefatigable Emma play on. I did not understand why Nelson was still with us. I had expected that as soon as he had landed the king, he would be off with his squadron to Minorca. It was, after all, more than a month since Captain Gould had told me that Nelson was ordered there 'with all speed' and yet, even with Naples subdued, he and his squadron still languished in Palermo. When Captain Gould paid one of his bi-weekly visits, I asked him if the orders had changed. He had laughed.

"Yes, the orders have changed. Orders do change don't they?" Mrs Cadogan had furnished me with a small parlour since I had agreed to stay. It was immediately across the landing from my bedroom and Captain Gould had called on me there.

"Nelson was ordered to hold the squadron off Cape Maritimo, if you remember, when the French fleet had been expected, but he didn't, he took it to Naples and, luckily for him, the French didn't come. Then, the French fleet was expected to attack Minorca and Nelson was ordered there. Again, he did not go and, luckily again, nor did the French, so he got away with that too and now the French have left the Mediterranean for the Atlantic. He has been extraordinarily lucky but don't think that his superiors like it. They do not. Nelson is in bad odour and Lord Keith will expect him to answer."

"But why is he so reckless? This is a valuable squadron and he does not have the right. If any officer of his disobeyed him he would be merciless." Captain Gould raised his eyebrows.

"Perhaps there is something in the Kingdom of Naples that eclipses his sense of duty."

We were taking afternoon tea. It had been Captain Gould's preferred time to call on Mother and he continued the habit with me. I did not mind. He was easy company: one year my junior, a naval officer, and with a weakness for strong-minded ladies. I did sense however that, behind his bachelor's reticence, there might linger deeper feelings but such was my confidence in his sense of propriety that I did not expect him to declare them so, when he did, he surprised me.

"Miss Knight." Having finished the cakes and drunk his tea, he re-settled himself in his chair. He hesitated. "I have received new orders." I nodded. "You will remember that two French ships managed to escape from Aboukir Bay and Nelson likes to blame me for it." Again, I nodded. "Well, one of them, the *Guillaume Tell*, is blockaded inside Valetta harbour and they think she is preparing to run for it. Nelson wants *Audacious* to stiffen the blockade and be ready for her."

"Congratulations," I said, "that would be a great prize."

"Yes, yes, it would." He leaned forward, frowning, and locked his big hands over his knees. "The thing is though," he shot me a glance, "I don't know how long I shall be away and …" now his eyes levelled with mine, "I worry about you."

"You worry about me?"

"Yes, I do." He sat up straight now, filling his chair. "I know that this is not an appropriate time, so soon after your terrible loss, and I would not have broached the subject if I had not been going away but," he opened his palms in appeal, "you have said it yourself: you do not know what you are going to do. Your mother …" he spread his arms wider, "and the terrible tragedy of Admiral Caracciolo … and now

Sir William being offered passage ... there will be no one here – and you cannot travel – as you yourself explained to me – not on your own through a Europe riven by war, so, yes, why should I not worry about you?" He looked so earnest, and his eyes were so full of kindness, I appreciated his concern, but I could not answer him.

"But you see how settled I am," I attempted, indicating my parlour.

"But Sir William will go home," he repeated. "He and Lady Emma and Mrs Cadogan, they will all leave and this house will be let go." Suddenly, I felt exposed, as if the walls and floor had fallen away.

"You should not assume, Captain ..." I began, but then I had to stop, I could think of nothing to say because he was right: if Sir William sailed, I would be left completely alone. I felt the colour rising in my cheeks.

"Miss Knight," he continued, "I am going away, and I do not know when I shall see you again so I want to leave something with you." He leaned forward again, clasping his hands together. "It is an offer. I have, quite apart from my naval career, an inherited estate in Somerset, not far from Bridgwater. It provides a small competency and it includes at least three good houses, any one of which would make a comfortable residence for a retired naval officer and his lady with all offices, gardens etcetera ..."

"Captain Gould!" I protested but he held up his hand.

"You could write your books there," he pressed on, "at your leisure. I have also inherited a good part of Henry Fielding's library, which would be yours; you would be an hour from Taunton and a day from Bath, the hub of naval and literary society ..."

"Captain Gould!" I protested again, and this time I would finish. "Are you proposing marriage?"

"No, no," he shook his head, "nothing could be more distasteful after your recent loss – no – I would never do that, it is only that circumstances force me ..." he looked at me in desolate appeal. He felt dishonoured. I understood that. I appreciated his sense of honour, and his offer.

"I understand," I told him, regaining my command. "As you are going away, you are leaving me with the offer of proposing to me at some future date." He sat back into his chair.

"Am I?" He scratched his head. "Yes, that's it." And, at last, he smiled. "Thank you."

I appreciated Captain Gould's offer but I could not take it seriously – I could not take anything seriously, my mind was too numb. I passed my days, sitting, like the old maid I was, in my second floor grace and favour apartment, reading my books, or gazing out the window at the lovers in the pleasure gardens: she, in her abundant silks, like a galleon in full sail and he, in his navy coat, like a patched–up coracle. There was no doubting their happiness – those two who had robbed me of mine. I tried not to dwell on it. I did not want to become the sour old spinster but it was hard: I was, for the first time in my life, alone, and the only other being for whom I felt any affection was himself in low spirits.

We did have the occasional stimulating visitor that autumn though; most notably, Lord Elgin and his young bride. Elgin was on his way to Constantinople to take up the post as British Ambassador there. He was, like Sir William, an antiquarian and he was looking forward to exploring Turkey's treasures and perhaps collecting and cataloguing some of them as Sir William had in Naples. Elgin was, also like Sir William, an urbane and elegant scion of the Scottish aristocracy and, at thirty-three, sailing out on his career just as Sir William was about to sail back. We had a pleasant few days with the Elgins, although I felt the poignancy of youth displacing age, and the talk of ancient treasures raised again the enormity of Sir William's loss.

At Christmas, I received a letter from Captain Gould. It was a nice, seasonal letter, written in light-hearted vein. He wished me the compliments of the season and happiness in the New Year – the New Century – 1800! He did not labour his 'fore-notice of proposal', as he risibly described it. I was glad he could see the funny side of his blundering performance but he also gently confirmed the sincerity of his offer which, though I still could not consider it, was touching. His letter went on to relate, again in humorous terms, such news as sailors have on blockade: the exaggerated significance, through boredom, of trifling events such as his favourite cheese disappearing and re-appearing on a gun-deck mess. That would have meant the cat on some ships but Captain Gould settled it with scrubbing out the heads and the withdrawal of rum. He was a lenient officer and I liked him for that. He never mentioned the *Guillaume Tell.*

In the New Year, Sir William finally got the news for which he had been waiting: official confirmation that, at last, his replacement had been appointed and could be expected by the spring. He was Arthur Paget, a younger son of the Earl of Uxbridge who, though only twenty-nine, had already distinguished himself at the courts of Berlin and Regensburg. I congratulated Sir William. Now, definitely, he would be going home.

"Thank you, yes, although I don't know about *congratulations*. For most of my life I have regarded Naples as my home and I had rather hoped I should quietly slip into my dotage there."

I had joined him at the breakfast table. I'd found a timeslot between Nelson quitting the breakfast room and Lady Emma's later arrival and, now that he was up and about, Sir William seemed to choose that time too. He was sitting in the middle of the long table, as close as he could to the fire, and I joined him there with my sardines and rolls.

"You must be looking forward though, to getting back to England?"

"My creditors are looking forward to it. Plenty to look forward to there." He was toying with a plate of scrambled eggs and ham and the footman poured us our coffees.

"Couldn't Lady Emma help you?" I suggested, flicking out my napkin. "She seems to have a bottomless purse."

"That's the Bourbon's bottomless purse – she's a kept woman – but don't you worry about me, Cornelia. Who knows? The engraver's plates may yet turn up for my third volume of *Vases*, and there is my wife's Pembrokeshire estate."

"Emma has a Pembrokeshire estate?" Sir William choked on his coffee.

"Oh dear!" he laughed, "I'm sorry." He wiped his mouth with his napkin. "My first wife, Catherine, she had a Pembrokeshire estate. I have promised it to my nephew, but, perhaps he can help." I opened a warm roll and spread it with butter. The sardines had been grilled in a piquant tomato sauce and were delicious.

"It will be a great wrench for Lady Emma," I suggested, "when she has to leave."

"I'm afraid it will, yes. She really has done remarkably well here. Extraordinary when you think about it: a queen's favourite; getting the royal family out of Naples, and that terrible voyage. If you had known that girl when she was first abandoned to me ..." he shook his head, smiling with pride. "The stuff of fairy- tales."

"I was thinking more of the wrench from Lord Nelson."

"Ah well, now," Sir William took up his coffee again, "Nelson has just been telling me: he has half a mind to go with us. Lord Keith has asked for a meeting with him and I don't think he's looking forward to it. He told me, ten minutes ago, he is thinking of asking for leave." Sir William pushed back the breakfast that he had hardly touched. "He can always cite his headaches. The world knows he is a martyr to them."

I thought about the Hamiltons and Nelson, sailing home together *en famille*, and I thought of Captain Nisbet.

"But Nelson has a wife at home. If you all go home together, Lady Nelson will not be as forgiving as you are. She will make Nelson choose and it might not be Emma." Sir William sighed,

"I know. Poor Nelson." He gave me a doleful look. "I'm sorry you don't get on with him better. He has a kind heart you know, and he is terribly generous." Sometimes, Sir William's detachment was breath-taking. I set down my knife and fork.

"So, that's it now is it?" I told him, "it's poor adulterous Nelson and let's forget Francesco."

"Oh no, Cornelia, please don't punish me with that." He reached out to me. "How could you say I would forget Francesco? I loved him, from being a boy, and do you think

I shall ever forget his death? I was there. I had to watch it. It is seared into my mind, so, please, let neither of us play light with our remembrance of Francesco but … tolerance …" He dropped his eyes as if he were overcome, but then looked up at me. "Tolerance," he repeated, "sometimes demands the effort to assume another's shoes. Do you think that Nelson was oblivious to your feelings that afternoon? Or to mine?" I didn't answer. "Nelson's chosen profession is war, Cornelia, as was Francesco's and your father's. These men receive and give orders, and when the order comes and the visor goes down, they cannot question or qualify, they must obey. It is perhaps harder for a woman than a man to comprehend but these warriors lead stern lives and if we do not always love them for it, we do when we need them." He reached out again, this time taking my hand. "I am sorry that I suggested you get on with Nelson, that was crass, but I do not apologise for asking you to understand his position and, one day, perhaps, sympathising with it."

I felt desperately sad. Sir William's logic could have tinkled out of an automaton for all the impression it made on me. I did not believe that Nelson had been obeying another's order; I blamed him for Francesco's death. Sir William was watching me, expecting an answer.

"Sympathy for the man who robbed me of my chance of happiness?"

"Your *best* chance of happiness."

"Yes," I agreed, "my best chance of happiness." Sir William pushed back from the table to the side of the hearth and looked down into the fire.

"Shall I tell you, Cornelia, what is the single most important thing that the years have taught me?" I waited.

"That the world is and always was in perpetual flux. That the only constant is change and though we cling to past memories we cannot know what awaits us in the future." He raised his eyes to me. "I'm afraid you probably have lost your *best* chance of happiness, but please don't disdain all others."

It was a pretty speech and no doubt sound philosophy but it carried no meaning for me. I decided to change the subject.

"Francesco's mother has asked me to go and live with her." He looked surprised.

"Permanently?"

"Yes, I think so." He put his long fingers to his chin.

"And do you think you will?"

"She is an interesting woman, I like her, and she was very kind to Mother. I think we would get on." Sir William looked sceptical.

"Very generous of her."

"Oh, her invitation is not entirely selfless. I think she sees me as a living memorial to Francesco. Taking care of me would be something she could do for him."

"A little morbid, don't you think?" He picked up his cup. "I don't like to think of you as a memorial." He sipped at his coffee and pulled a face. "This is cold. Shall we have some fresh?" My coffee, too, had gone cold and I let Sir William order some more. I pushed my chair back from the table and sat across the hearth from him. He smiled at me and crossed his long legs.

"I saw in the post box that you had a letter from *Audacious*." He was trying, I supposed, to lighten the talk.

"Yes."

"How is Captain Gould? Any movement from the *Guillaume Tell*?"

"He never even mentioned her."

"Still bottled up then." The coffee arrived with fresh cups, and while one footman poured, another removed our used cups. Once we were alone again, Sir William continued, "so, all is well with him?" I looked across the hearth at Sir William, his long face was drawn and tired but there was a twinkle in his eye. I could see what he was thinking. He had seen plenty of Captain Gould in my company over the past few months and, as I had no strong attachment to the captain, I saw no reason to be evasive.

"He is offering to marry me."

"What! More offers?" He put down his cup. "Captain Gould has proposed?" I laughed.

"No, not exactly, but he has assured me quite firmly that should I ever wish him to propose, he would oblige." Now Sir William laughed.

"How very Bath!"

"Funny you should say that. He has offered me roses round the door and genteel retirement a day's journey from Bath." Sir William gave me a comical look.

"And if the good captain granted you your wish for him to propose, would you accept him?" The conversation was descending into whimsy and at the captain's expense.

"I think the point of the captain's convolution is that, though he is being gallant, the matter is only hypothetical."

"Why hypothetical?"

"Because why would we marry? Captain Gould is a kind man who has been close enough to me these past weeks to see what I have suffered and he wants to help. It is generous of him and gallant but marriage is not the remedy."

"Why?"

"Because I do not love him. I don't think I ever could."

"But, in the past minute, you have told me he is kind, gallant and generous. He is a reader, he is evidently forbearing, and if you do not think that you can love him, he is obviously in love with you." Sir William set me a level look. "Catherine and I were married for twenty-four years, Cornelia, and we were happy."

Nelson left in *Foudroyant* a few days later for his meeting with Lord Keith at Leghorn. It was the first time in sixteen months that Emma and Nelson had been parted and I might have expected Emma to be listless but she was not. Evidently reconciled now to having to leave with Sir William, she was dashing about the palazzo ordering the packing of this and the selling of that as excitedly as a child before Christmas. Emma never lost her talent to surprise and she surprised me further when, for the first and only time during my stay at the palazzo, she came up to my parlour to see me. When I answered her knock with 'come in', she put her head round the door and scanned the room.

"Not started packing yet?" It was midday and she was still in her dressing robe. It was not easy to know when Emma was being serious and when she was teasing. I decided not to answer and remained in my chair with my book. "You should at least make a start. Have you decided where you will go?" She was not teasing.

"Mr Paget has not even arrived yet," I pointed out, "it is a little early for packing."

"Lord Nelson has gone to tell Lord Keith that he is going home with us." She slid into the room and leaned against the wall. "Something has come up." She put a hand on her belly.

"Something is *coming* up." She fixed me with an insinuating smirk, daring me to guess at her meaning.

"You mean something unexpected?"

"No," she replied, as if I should try again, but then she could resist no longer. "I think it is the very first thing the world expects of a man who has been honoured with hereditary titles: a barony, a dukedom." She slid her hand lower and, without loosening her watch of me, her smirk shifted from insinuation to triumph. I closed my book and set it aside.

"Are you telling me that you are carrying Nelson's child?" She raised her palm in a military salute.

"Doing my duty." She pushed closed the door and came over to warm herself at my fire. "Aren't you going to congratulate me?" I resented her closeness, her visit and her news.

"A child has to be legitimate to be an heir," I reminded her.

"One more reason to hurry home. Nelson has arrangements to make."

"Arrangements to make? Are you telling me that he is going to divorce Lady Nelson?" Emma was Delphic.

"I have done what he expected of me. Now he must do what I expect of him." She sounded so cold and her logic so ruthless.

"And you always do what is expected of you, do you? Whatever the consequences?"

"I try to." She looked down at me in my chair. "Don't we all?" She was standing over me, monopolising my fire in my parlour and she did not look like leaving.

"Won't you sit down?" I nodded to the armchair behind her and she sat. "And what about your own marriage?" I asked her. "Are arrangements to be made for that too?"

"Well, one thing follows another, doesn't it? We have to move on." She gave me a smile, which I did not return. "Oh, don't keep looking at me like that," she chided, "if you were less judgemental about me you might recognise that loyalty is my golden rule." I think I might have raised an eyebrow, which nettled her. "You are free to think what you like but I was loyal to Sir William when he was not loyal to me." She shifted in her chair. "For all those years when he was playing Pygmalion, I did everything he expected of me, everything – I was dutiful, and loyal – only this Pygmalion didn't fall in love with his Galatea, did he?" She dashed me a bitter look. "Over all those years when I had every prince in Europe at my feet, he never loved me. He married me, yes, but he never loved me, and now when he expects nothing of me, I say, it's time to move on." She patted her belly. "This little fellow will expect everything of me, especially love."

"And for that, you would abandon Sir William? When he has lost everything?"

"No. He'll come with us. We'll look after him. Anyway, look at yourself. How different are you? You've spent your entire life doing what someone else expected of you. You might ask yourself who expects anything of you now?"

Who expects anything of me now? She might have said that to hurt me but it was a fair question. We do not make our own way through life. Clearly, Emma Hamilton understood that very well and she was right about me and Mother. I had clung, since her death, to Sir William because we both needed each other but, if he were to leave now, what then? I could not stay in Palermo, where my memories were so sad, and try as I might to be positive about Naples – surely, all that the dowager and I really shared was loss and so all would be sadness there too. Perhaps it was time I took Captain Gould seriously? Any disinterested observer would call it an attractive offer: a well-set house with all offices and gardens, surrounded by Henry Fielding's and my own books, and the captain, though rustic, was a gentle soul who sought only domestic retirement. I went to my parlour window and looked out over the gardens to the bay. Sir William thought I should marry Gould – what responsible father wouldn't? And Mother had always liked him – she would be delighted. And Francesco: what about you?

Arthur Paget arrived to relieve Sir William and, soon afterwards, Nelson returned on *Foudroyant* so all seemed set for Sir William to finally go home – until Emma sprung her surprise.

"The queen is taking me to Vienna!" She had burst into the library where Sir William and I were reading. "She has made up her mind. She is taking all her daughters to stay with the Empress. She wants to secure their marriages and I'm to go with them." I looked across at Sir William. He put his silk into his book and his fingers to his forehead.

"Vienna my dear? But we are going home. It has been planned for months. Nelson is recalled, I have to meet my creditors – and what about you? You are with child. You cannot go gadding off to Vienna on your own."

"Oh I agree, and I won't." She was standing in the middle of the floor, commanding centre stage in her voluminous Court gown and ostrich feather. "The queen and I have discussed it. We can *all* go to Vienna. It will be wonderful. We will be guests of the Emperor, fêted and paraded as the heroes of the Nile."

"I am sorry, Emma," Sir William held up a hand to check her, "but has Nelson agreed to this?"

"I haven't seen him yet. I've only just come back from the palace, but the queen has agreed, in fact, it is her idea, she is inviting you and Nelson to join us." Sir William shook his head and put aside his book.

"No, no, no, no, no," he told her emphatically, "we cannot. My business in London, and Nelson's, are too pressing to be put off. I am no longer ambassador to the Neapolitan Court and under no obligation to the queen. You must decline her invitation."

"But can't we make it on our way home?" she persisted. "We could go overland. Isn't Vienna on the way to England?" Now Sir William laughed.

"Everywhere is on the way to everywhere else by some route or another but as most of Europe is occupied by the French, ours would be circuitous indeed – and remember your unborn child, the months on rough roads, and the organisation of it all. No, Emma. You speak to Nelson and I am sure he will be as adamant as I that we sail."

Nelson was not as adamant as Sir William, or, if he had been at first, Emma managed to change his mind. Sir William was mortified.

"It will probably kill me." I had gone to find him later that day. We were sitting in his bedroom in the chairs between the windows.

"It is an insane idea."

"Yes it is."

"I am amazed at Nelson. He abhors coach travel – he's afraid of horses."

"I think it was the promise of a triumphal progress through the Courts of Germany and the Low Countries that tipped it. Nelson's vanity is as susceptible as Emma's." Sir William looked so frail. His shoulders were down and I put my hand on his on his chair arm.

"Does Emma not fear for her unborn child though? Banging about in a carriage for hundreds of miles? She might lose it before she got home."

"You know Emma." He raised an eyebrow. "She thinks herself immortal."

"And what about you? This journey worries you, doesn't it?" He threw back his head and looked up at the coving.

"It does, to be frank. It will be brutal, and I really haven't the strength, but do I have any choice? Without Nelson, I can't get a ship."

"And what about Mrs Cadogan? What does she think?" Now he smiled.

"Grandmama you mean? She is so thrilled with the baby, she'll follow Emma anywhere."

I thought about Mrs Cadogan and her pregnant daughter, sitting together in a closed carriage with Nelson, the proud father, while the bond between them grew with the developing child. And sitting with this new family in the closed carriage there would be Sir William; detached, dispossessed and dependent – the cuckold, the outsider, trapped with them in their rattling box for months on end.

"I shall come with you."

"What?"

"I want to come with you on this brutal journey."

"But you can't. It will be awful."

"Brutal?"

"Yes." He reset himself in his chair and looked at me. "But it isn't just the journey. We are travelling to London.

You always told me you hated the place – and you won't know anyone there."

"I shall know you." Our eyes met.

"You would do this for me? A wrung-out old man?"

"Tending to the old and wrung-out seems to be my forte." He shook his head.

"No, Cornelia, you've not thought this through. You would be confined for months inside a carriage with Emma and Nelson." He frowned at me. "The memories. It would be more than you could bear."

"But together we could bear it, and besides, where else would I go? There is nothing for me here."

"There's Captain Gould, and Francesco's mother's offer."

"Both of which I have considered. I have written to the princess declining her offer and I shall do the same to Captain Gould."

"Oh, Cornelia." He shook his head again. "I am glad you're not going to the princess but Captain Gould – he is such a good man. He can offer you everything."

"Except love."

"Love."

"Yes. You remember what that is?"

"Remember it? I'm haunted by it."

"And so am I." I gripped his hand and smiled at him. "You and I have such a bond. Together, we shall be proof against any Emma and Nelson." He gave me a long, fond look.

"You don't have to do this for me you know."

"Oh, I think it is what the world would expect."

POSTSCRIPT

Cornelia travelled with Nelson, the Hamiltons and Mrs Cadogan by overland coach back to England. They drove with Maria-Carolina's entourage to Vienna and then on, with just their secretaries and servants, to Prague, Dresden, Magdeburg and Hamburg, being fêted at every stop. They arrived in London at the beginning of November where, after three years' absence, Nelson was greeted by his wife. For a few weeks, he stayed with Frances but he made no secret of his devotion to Emma Hamilton and, after returning to sea in the New Year, he never went back to his wife but lodged, when ashore, with the Hamiltons in Piccadilly. Sir William was content with the ménage but there was no place in it for Cornelia and she withdrew to old London connections.

On 29th January 1801, Emma gave birth to a daughter, Horatia. Being over-weight and favouring loose-fitting robes, Emma had kept her pregnancy secret and so she did the birth. Nelson was overjoyed but unable to share it as his daughter was quietly passed into the care of a foster mother. He sailed north, as Second-in-Command of the Baltic Fleet, and, in April, won the Battle of Copenhagen for which he was promoted to C-in-C Baltic and Viscount. In March 1802, he bought a small Surrey estate, Merton Place, where he and Emma could spend time with Horatia, now officially styled as Nelson's – but not Emma's – adopted daughter. Sir William remained at 23 Piccadilly, where he died, twelve months later, with Emma and Nelson at his bedside. The following month, May 1803, Nelson sailed south as C-in-C of the Mediterranean Fleet and he remained almost permanently at sea until August 1805 when he spent a month at Merton before re-embarking for Cadiz and the Battle of Trafalgar.

Nelson's death devastated Emma and left her in financial straits. She owned Merton Place but had always lived beyond her means and was in debt. In a final codicil to his will, Nelson had entrusted Emma and Horatia to a grateful nation but, despite Emma's vigorous lobbying, no state pension was granted and her debts grew. In April 1809, she had to sell Merton Place and when, nine months later, her mother died, she began a tragic descent.

Refusing to moderate her lifestyle, Emma moved from house to apartment to lodgings, begging and borrowing from a shrinking circle of friends until, in 1813, she was taken to the King's Bench Prison for debtors. She was not confined within the prison's walls but 'Within the Rules'– forced to live in a prescribed 'spunging-house' close by.

In July 1814, after eighteen months 'Within the Rules', Emma took fourteen-year-old Horatia and slipped away to Calais where, the following January, she died of liver failure in a cheap rented room. Horatia was brought back to England to join the household of one of Nelson's sisters. When she was twenty-one, she married a Norfolk clergyman, they had nine children and she lived on until 1881 when she died at the age of eighty.

Josiah Nisbet returned to England in *Thalia* in 1800 and resigned his commission. After a period living in London, he moved, with Lady Nelson, to Exmouth in Devon. He established himself as a dealer in government bonds on both sides of the Channel, sailing back and forth in his own thirty foot yacht. He was successful in business and continued to look after his mother. In 1819, he married Frances Evans, a goddaughter of Lady Nelson's, who bore him five children. Nisbet died in Paris of pleurisy in 1830 at the age of fifty. His mother died the following year, at the age of seventy-three, and they are buried together, along with four of Nisbet's children, in the churchyard of St Margaret and St Andrew, Littleham-cum-Exmouth.

Cornelia took private lodgings in London but she was not short of invitations from her naval and Court connections and, in March 1805, she was invited by Queen Charlotte to be companion to her five unmarried daughters at Windsor. A grace and favour house went with the position with a maid and £300 per annum and Cornelia accepted. It was during that summer of 1805 that Cornelia published her magnum opus, *Latium*. It is an historical travelogue of the Campagna illustrated with twenty of her own etchings. The work is written with verve, Cornelia recognising that the idyllic eighteenth century landscapes that she had known were rapidly disappearing. Her book remains an important document.

Cornelia wrote three more books while at Windsor, principally for the use of the princesses: A *Chronological Abridgement of the History of Spain*, ditto *of France* and a translation of German prayers and hymns. She also contributed to an anthology, *Miscellaneous Poems* (1812), that included works by W R Spencer and Samuel Rogers. All four of these books were printed privately at Frogmore.

The Windsor household was known, even to its members, as The Nunnery and Cornelia found it 'dull, uninteresting and monotonous' but she stayed until 1813 when she moved to Warwick House off Pall Mall to be companion to the Prince Regent's seventeen-year-old heir, Princess Charlotte. That situation only lasted a year however because, when Princess Charlotte refused to marry the Prince of Orange, her father dismissed her entire household.

Cornelia returned to her London lodgings but, alone again with no one to look after, she left England in May 1816 and, at the age of fifty-eight, returned to travelling. Over the next twenty years, she moved from one princely house to another, accepting invitations from the royal and noble contacts she had made in the Courts of Europe. With her polyglot erudition and deep stock of anecdotes, 'the far-famed Cornelia Knight' was welcomed from Paris to Naples, Rome to Würtemberg and back sometimes also to Frogmore and the ageing unmarried princesses. It was while visiting England, in 1833, that her last book was published. *Sir Guy de Lusignan* is an historical novel in the style of Walter Scott and, to the modern reader, her best read. Cornelia died in her Paris apartment, after a brief illness, on 17th December 1837, and is buried in a corner of the Cimetière du Nord.

Also by S. R. Whitehead from Ashmount Press

He was Mr Brontë's right hand man and Charlotte's husband. He fell in love with two sisters and revered a third while, to the troubled brother, he tried to be a friend. Arthur Bell Nicholls was the intimate witness to all the triumphs and tragedies of the Brontës' adult lives and *The Last Brontë* is his testament.

★★★★★ 5 star reviews on Amazon and Goodreads

'This book is outstanding: a story for the heart, the mind and the soul.'
Dr Jodie Archer, co-author of The Bestseller Code

'A wonderful imagining of Charlotte Brontë's enigmatic husband. A must for all intrigued by Britain's most celebrated literary family.'
Rebecca Fraser, biographer of Charlotte Brontë

'I am in awe: what Whitehead has achieved is remarkable and so worthwhile.'
Prof Brian Wilks, biographer of the Brontë family

e-book £3-99   paperback £8-99   from Amazon & bookshops